ENTER THE WORLD OF THE DRAGON'S HARP

ARTHURIAN HISTORICAL FANTASY FOR THE 21st CENTURY

"From the first page I was drawn deep into Pruitt's beautifully-realized Celtic realm, so vivid I felt as if I'd stepped right into the tale... With shades of The Mists of Avalon, the story is a magical blend of Welsh and Arthurian myth,

"All the characters are so vividly rendered they soon lay siege to your heart, and you find yourself loving them, rooting for them, terrified for them, and utterly captivated by them..."

— Jules Watson, bestselling author of *The White Mare Trilogy,* *The Swan Maiden,* and *The Raven Queen*

IN AN ERA OF DRAGONS A YOUNG GIRL COMES OF AGE

Before Gwenhwyfar became Queen—before Arthur met Merlin—a tribal Welsh princess met a young Heatherlands Mage.

Together, they will create a legend.

PRAISE FOR THE DRAGON'S HARP

"Rachael Pruitt is a gifted storyteller, able to create vivid, three-dimensional characters in prose that is, by turns, lyrical and powerful. Readers who enjoyed the novels of Parke Godwin, Persia Woolley, Rosemary Sutcliff, and Marion Zimmer Bradley will love The Dragon's Harp, in which Gwenhwyfar comes of age; best of all there are four more books to come..."

— **Sharon K. Penman, New York Times Bestselling author of *Lionheart, Here Be Dragons,* & *Time and Chance***

Inside a mist of beauty and brutality waits the Arthurian legend as you've never heard it before. Enter the world of *The Dragon's Harp*, a realm of blood lust and vengeance, of spellbinding magic from the beginning of time. The realm of Princess Gwenhwyfar: a young girl torn between magic and desire, born with magical powers she can either wield to save her people from destruction—or deny to save her soul.

"Rachael Pruitt is a natural story teller, and her love of the Guinevere character shines through every page of The Dragon's Harp. It's a pleasure to discover her take on this very old story."

— **Persia Woolley, author of *The Guinevere Trilogy***

ERA OF DRAGONS:
THE LOST TALES OF GWENHWYFAR

BOOK ONE

First in a five book series of historical fantasy, Rachael Pruitt's unique take on a beloved legend reintroduces the mythic characters of Gwenhwyfar, Merlin, and Vortigern against the gritty backdrop of sixth century Wales, where scenes of shape-shifting and heartbreaking romance vie with torture, murder, and battle in a dragon-haunted land.

WHAT READERS SAY ABOUT THE DRAGON'S HARP

"From the first page I was drawn deep into Pruitt's beautifully-realized Celtic realm, so vivid I felt as if I'd stepped right into the tale and could not only see but smell, taste, and touch her creation. With shades of <u>The Mists of Avalon</u>, the story is a magical blend of Welsh and Arthurian myth, thrilling adventure, romance, and otherworldly enchantments—while also managing to be funny, earthy and believable. All the characters are so vividly rendered they soon lay siege to your heart, and you find yourself loving them, rooting for them, terrified for them, and utterly captivated by them.

"The child Gwenhwyfar is brave and spirited, sensitive to the mysterious otherworld of goddess rituals, druids and dragons that lie just beyond the more brutal reality of her father's warriors and their bloody swords. The story leaves her as a teen coming into her powers—and under the spell of first love. I can't wait to see the woman she will become in future books. Bravo!"

— **Jules Watson, bestselling author of** *The White Mare Trilogy,* *The Swan Maiden,* **and** *The Raven Queen*

"The Goddess is most definitely afoot in this engrossing novel by author Rachael Pruitt. The Dragon's Harp courageously depicts the roles of mothers, daughters, queens, and priestesses in a time when men fought battles while women abided by a far more ancient law. The tale is woven with lyrical language that resounds with the hills, trees and rocks of a land where the mist between worlds falls easily away—one small step beyond a fairy stone.

"Ms. Pruitt masterfully guides her reader through not only a mystical retelling of the Arthurian legend, but educates us with her historical expertise of the time. Her attention to detail drowns our senses into this world where kings rule the land, but the land and all who live on her ultimately answer only to the Goddess. I cannot recommend this novel highly enough. Ms. Pruitt is a gifted storyteller with a powerful story to tell."

— **Molly Padulo, writer and shamanic healer**

THE DRAGON'S HARP
Era of Dragons: The Lost Tales of Gwenhwyfar
Copyright © 2012 by Rachael Pruitt
Cover painting, "Guinevere—The Queen" © 2012 by Jo Jayson
Cover design © 2012 by Marilyn Hager Adelman

Editing by Tara Fort
Formatting by Signe Nichols

Published in the United States by Dragon Harp Productions:
http://www.dragonharpproductions.com

Direct any queries relating to this book or author via this website:
http://www.dragonharpproductions.com

Print ISBN: 978-0-9850588-1-4
eBook ISBN: 978-0-9850588-0-7

1) Arthurian legends—fiction
2) Historical fantasy—fiction
3) Celtic women before 1100 CE—fiction
4) Druids—fiction
5) Welsh mythology—fiction
6) Dragon mythology—fiction
7) Merlin—fiction
8) Ancient Celtic Kings and Queens—fiction
9) Queen Gwenhwyfar and King Arthur—fiction

The Dragon's Harp

Rachael Pruitt

Era of Dragons:

The Lost Tales of Gwenhwyfar

Book One

AUTHOR'S ACKNOWLEDGEMENTS

This book is a labor of love and effort that has been graced with the assistance of a cast of characters only marginally smaller than the borough of Manhattan. Given the impossibility of naming everyone, I will focus here on naming a very precious few.

First and foremost, I would like to thank my writing goddesses: Sharon Kay Penman, Jules Watson, and Persia Woolley. Not only did these gifted authors write novels that inspired me to find my own creative voice, but they were gracious enough to take time from their own busy careers to offer feedback, moral support, sage advice, and practical suggestions. They were there at every turn to share humor, inspiration, and the warmth and comradry of friendship with this fledgling in their midst. Ladies, Gwenhwyfar and I both thank you from the bottom of our hearts!

Equally as dynamic an inspiration is Dr. Pam Kimsey. Her invaluable suggestions at a critical juncture in the eight year process of writing *Dragon's Harp* made a key difference in the overall quality of the book you now hold in your hands. My eternal gratitude next dances to my beloved friend, Molly Padulo, who cheered and drummed *Harp* and its weary author onward as only a true shaman could. The seasoned editorial wisdom and encouragement of Bob Mecoy also helped my manuscript immensely. The three of you will be forever in my personal Writer's Hall of Fame.

Seton Hill's MFA Program in "Writing Popular Fiction" located in Greensburg, Pennsylvania not only provided me with an academic framework to complete the original draft of *Harp*, but a lifelong writing community of a caliber most authors only dream about. If any one of you is looking for a truly unique, genre-based, refreshingly down-to-earth graduate writing program, I highly recommend Seton Hill. This real-world Hogwarts features haunted hallways, paleolithic elevators, and some of the finest writing instructors in the world. I offer special thanks and appreciation to my own spectacular writing mentors, romance author Barbara Miller and Asimov-award-winning poet Timons Esaias.

My life has also been greatly enriched by the professional talent, cutting-edge insights, and encouragement of Seton Hill's Dr. Michael Arnzen (proud owner of the most maniacal giggle this side of Dante's Hell), Dr. Lee McClain, Dr. Albert Wendland, Diane Turnshek, and the incomparable Larry Connolly—to name just a few. Kudos and thanks to my wonderful peers and writing colleagues, especially my dear friends Ceres Wright and Heidi Ruby Miller. Thank you both for your friendship, support, and inspiration. You were there at the darkest of times and I thank you. Mary SanGiovanni, Rhonda Mason, Chris (CPC) Carey, Kim and Russ Howe, the terrifying Dark Lord—Dave Corwell, Mike Mehalek, Lainey Ervin, Venessa Giunta, Jason Jack Miller, Chun Lee, Sharon Gunn, Ron Edison, Ron Shannon, Jen Brooks, Diana Bosford, Maria Snyder, and the awesome Sally Bosco—thank you all for lessons learned and dreams shared! It is an honor to have "broken bread" with such wonderful creative spirits.

For those interested in more information about the Arthurian and Celtic mythology and ancient Welsh history reflected in *The Dragon's Harp*, I have included some additional references in my Author's Notes at the end of the novel. I will also be writing several blogs on my website on this subject. Here, however, I wish to acknowledge three authors whose environmental and spiritual wisdom is not only imbedded within the pages of *Harp*, but whose works have greatly enriched my own life. David Abram's landmark *Spell of the Sensuous* is both joyous and unforgettable. Frank MacEowen's books eloquently explore Celtic mysticism. For anyone interested in exploring this fascinating subject, I recommend *The Spiral of Memory and Belonging: A Celtic Path of Soul and Kinship*. The poet Martin Prechtel has created a profound and elegant body of work beginning with *Secrets of the Talking Jaguar*, based on his journey to Guatemala. Martin knows the way to the true heart of magic. I am blessed to have worked with him on two separate occasions that will forever dance in my memory. Honey in the Heart, gentlemen. Thirteen thank yous, Martin!

The brilliant mythologist Dr. Joseph Campbell has been a lifelong inspiration for me. Hopefully, I have done at least some justice to his memory within these pages.

I am also enormously grateful to Jen Delyth, a gifted Welsh artist whose wonderful book *Celtic Folk Soul: Art, Myth, and Symbol*, sits proudly on my coffee table, tempting me to thumb through its pages instead of writing my own myth! Ms. Delyth's book and website are a mother lode for anyone interested in learning more about Welsh mythology, ancient gods and goddesses, and the symbolism behind Jen's own beautiful artwork (www.kelticdesigns.com). Likewise, I am indebted to Celtic author and visionary Mara Freeman, whose book *Kindling the Celtic Spirit* has been an invaluable resource. Mara runs an Avalon Mystery School which I long to attend. In the meantime, I keep myself happy exploring her website at www.chalicecentre.net.

Heartfelt blessings also go out to the gloriously talented Jo Jayson (www.jojayson.com) whose painting of "Guinevere—the Queen" graces the cover of *Dragon's Harp*. Marilyn Hager Adelman's wonderful cover design makes me want to sing whenever I look at it—which can be a little embarrassing if I am in my neighborhood bookstore.

When I began this process, I never dreamed I would be fortunate enough to find a team of experts to guide me through every step of the editing, publishing, and marketing process with the finesse of savvy angels. I would like to thank Tara Fort, editor extraordinaire (any remaining bloopers are mine alone!) and Signe Nichols, whose formatting assistance is not only spot-on, but whose graciousness, efficiency, and humor continue to be a balm to my oft-challenged spirit. I would especially like to thank Amy Bruno of "Historical Fiction Virtual Book Tours" for her enthusiasm and support of "our" book and her brilliance in promoting it on a blog tour—piecing this complex mechanism together with the same ease my former mother-in-law possessed as she whipped up enough spaghetti to feed the entire neighborhood in the time it took us to cross the street.

Thanks also to the kind Welsh readers who helped organize the phonetic Welsh-name pronunciation guide that follows these acknowledgements. Any remaining mistakes in spelling or cultural wrong-headedness are my responsibility entirely—and I apologize if they exist. My intention here is to honor Welsh culture (it is my ancestry as well!), not degrade it in any way, however unintentional any oversight might be.

Lynn Serafinn, author of *Seven Graces of Marketing* and my newest role model, thank you for your keen eye, your vision and your analysis of what is needed—and your willingness to provide it—immediately! You are truly awesome, Lynn. I thank the Internet Goddess daily for introducing us!

In closing, I would like to thank the Dykstra clan—whom I have been blessed to reconnect with after many decades apart. Special thanks to Arjen for an early reading of my manuscript and to Frieda, Mick, Colin, Kari, Ella, Evey, Tanya, Rayme, and Tasha. Eternal thanks for your comradry, for your outrageously excellent food, and for your plethora of liquids ranging from seriously great coffee to killer gin and tonics. Most importantly, thank you all for welcoming me back to your boisterous, creative, free-spirited hearths. I'm a very lucky woman to be invited into your family. Mick and Frieda, you could teach a nation about love. I only wish you would be given the opportunity to try.

To Michelina Saunders, "heart mother", whose inspiration and kindness is a gift beyond words. To Grandmother Lulu, and to all my mothers, Edna, Freida, Louise, and Mickie: women who taught me love in all its incarnations, shadow as well as light. Women who covered me in Indian bedspreads, read me stories by candlelight, taught me to surf the mysteries of the ocean, the night sky, my own soul. Most of all, thank you for teaching me the importance of service to our planet and to never give up on myself no matter what mess comes my way; to meet the tests of life with courage, faith, and resilience as you have done. Namaste, my Mothers. I live in gratitude for your wisdom, your examples, your strength, and your love.

To my dear new friend Lisa, thank you for Sebastian. To treasured friends, Penny Kavan, Lynn Hallanan, Mark Wallek, Ted Buschek, Daryl Hlavsa-Clements, Kate and Bob McGeary, Andrea Dombecki, Cecily MacArthur, and Dave and Sheila Kenyon—my life is so much richer, so much more joyous because of your friendship. Bless you all!

Special acknowledgement goes to John Dickerson, colleague and friend, for continual encouragement whenever we met in the halls of the public school where we taught. The book is really, truly, actually here, John. You can *finally* stop asking about it!

Last, first, and always, my heart and gratitude goes to my beloved daughter, Elena, and her wonderful husband, Riley. You both continue to inspire me with your grace, love, and talent. I smile every day just because I know you. I am divinely blessed to have you in my life.

Thank you all from the bottom of my heart!

phonetic welsh pronunciations

People

Gwenhwyfar	Gwenwhivar (with a rolled "r" and aspirated "h")
Ceridwen	as spelt, with a hard "c" as in "car"
Rhiannon	as written – with the "h" aspirated.
Cadwallon	Welsh "ll"– position tongue to pronounce "l" then emit . . . breath without using voice.
Cynan	Cunan . . . "u" pronounced short as in "fun"
Iorwerth	Yorwerth with both "r"s rolled
Iolo	Yolo
Cunedda	Cinedda – "i" pronounced as French or German "u" without . . . rounding lips.
Hwyrch	Hwirch – heavily aspirated "h" and "ch" as in Scottish "loch"
Vortigern	as spelt – not a Welsh name
Chalan	gutteral "ch" as in Scottish "loch"
Maelgwyn	Mailgwin – "i" short as in "is" ai as dipthong as "mail"
Sari	Sarie – "a" long as in "arm"
Lleu	Llay-Welsh "ll" eu dipthong "e" as in "get"+ "u"as in Cunedda.
Lugh	Not Welsh – Irish would say Lug (as in Luke) with "h" . . . aspirated.
Epona	Gallic/Roman horse Goddess – adopted during Roman times
Emrys	Emris – "i" short as in "is"
Medraut	Medrite – "i" as "a+u" "u" as in Cunedda
Brea	Breya- as in Freya
Godraith	Godrith – "i" as in "file", soft "th" as in thrush
Mica	Meeka – with a short "a"

Tribal Names (possible Welsh-Roman linguistic combination)

Ordovices	Ordovichez
Deceangli	Deke-anglee
Votadini	Votadeenee
Seaxon	Saeson "ae" as "a" in "name"

Other words

Dinas Emrys	Deenas (town or city) of Emrys (as above)
Annwn	Annoon
Tylwyth Teg	"Fair and Terrible Ones" Tulwith (soft "th") "e" long as ai" in . . . Fair.

AUTHOR'S PREFACE

Fascination for the Arthurian legend appears to be eternal. Medieval British chronicler Geoffrey of Monmouth is credited with popularizing the Arthurian story in the early twelfth century, but, in reality, versions of the tale were told around soldiers' campfires and peasants' hearths centuries before Geoffrey turned them into one of the first popular bestsellers of early Europe. Almost one thousand years since Geoffrey walked the earth, the epic remains magnetic to our 21st century culture, spawning popular television series, films, and influencing countless fantasy writers from C.S. Lewis to J.K. Rowlings.

Much ink has been spent on just why Arthur, Gwenhwyfar, Merlin, Lancelot, Medraut, and their exalted band of friends and followers have captured the imagination and loyalty of millions across time and place. Perhaps it is simply the well-told dynamic of passionate love and loss, honor, self-sacrifice, and courage against overwhelming odds, framed within a shimmering veil of magic. I've always thought that it's much more than that, however. It is the Arthurian characters, their flaws as well as their heroism, that make the realm of Camelot come alive. No matter that our battles are now fought with explosives instead of lances, Arthur's mysterious Hall seems to shine just on the horizon of what could be—if we only knew where to look.

Dragon's Harp is my own visit to this haunting realm. Weaving mythic fantasy into what little is known about the history of the time, *Dragon's Harp* opens with Gwenhwyfar's coming of age in early northern Wales soon after the Romans left Britain. *Era of Dragons: The Lost Tales of Gwenhywfar,* will continue this 5 book series, following the life of perhaps the most famous legendary Queen of all.

Like most readers, I dislike novels that do not offer a satisfying conclusion, and I assure all of you kind enough to gather around my "storytelling hearth" that you will not be disappointed here. Although it is clear "Gwen's" story will continue, *Dragon's Harp* comes to a dramatic conclusion within these pages. For those of you who want to follow

Gwenhwyfar into the second volume of her life, its sequel, *The Dragon's Breath*, will continue the tale as soon as its author can complete it without losing too much sleep!

In the Author's Notes which follow the novel, I have included several reference sources for anyone interested in more details about early Welsh history & mythology, ancient Celtic culture & religion, and the Arthurian legends themselves—including the fact that it is likely that Cunedda, Maelgwyn, Vortigern, and Merlin may well have been historical figures (although their characters and relationships within these pages are entirely my own invention.). More source material is also available on my website at http://www.rachaelpruitt.com. My Author's Notes, also include Welsh language information and an apology to Welsh readers for a few liberties I took with northern Welsh geography and mythology. Most notable is that the Welsh name of the sun god is "Lleu", not "Lugh". (However, since Lleu is a major character, I thought perhaps he would not mind sharing his sun-godship with his cheeky Irish equivalent!)

Dragon's Harp takes place in a violent and frightening time, historically as well as mythically. The kingdom Gwenhwyfar is born into in the fifth century C.E. is being ravaged by the Scotti (Irish) raiders. While her people are fighting the Irish in the West, they are also vulnerable to invasion from the south, east, and north. The Romans have left the country, the Druids have returned (My theory is they never really left.), and the new Christian influence is being felt. And then there are the dragons...

The dragons of Dinas Emrys, whom you will meet within these pages, have their roots in Welsh folklore, as does the existence of Merlin himself. Eulogies offered by Gwenhwyfar's grieving kinsmen are taken from authentic Welsh sources—originally they would have been spoken at the burial of ancient kings over a thousand years ago.

Although the Welsh names of my characters may seem unusual at first, I could not have told the story differently. They are the names that a Welsh Gwenhwyfar would have known and loved, as flowing as river water, yet as strong as the northern mountains of Wales where she was born.

Readers, thank you for coming to my storytelling hearth. May you find wonder and joy and inspiration within these pages—and may your own life be made full of magic in this wonderful world that we all share.

Blessings to you. Shall we turn the page and begin?

To my beloved Elena; daughter of sunlight, grace, and savvy

To my beloved Sebastian; furry Sage of the sweet-wild
　　who taught me that Light has a scent
　　　　that rainbows grow beneath our fingertips when we're not looking
　　　　and to open my heart to love—
　　　　　　it is the only thing that we keep forever

To the Land and People of Wales: *Diolch yn Fawr!*

And to those beloved souls who raised me and who now live beyond
the stars. Thank you, all of you...

FIRE IN WATER

I have been told,
"The sun on deep waves is beautiful."
And have dreamed on those words.
I will dive down to the edge of darkness,
to see where fire is drowned
in understanding.

— Sr. Fionntulach of the Céile Dé Order

Arm not after the evening meal. Be not sad of heart.
Keen is the wind. Bitter is poison. . .
The thrill in my heart tells me
That we are of the same blood.
Long hast thou delayed thy coming!

— 14th century, Welsh

"Love is the child that breathes our breath
Love is the child that scatters death."

— William Blake

THE DRAGON'S HARP

A NOVEL

BY

RACHAEL PRUITT

PROLOGUE

Gwenhwyfar

510 CE

Men have called me beautiful. But the gods men worship now have cursed beauty.

My name is Gwenhwyfar, born daughter to Cadwallen, Ordovician King of Dinas Emrys in the North. As a young woman, I married Arthur, High King of all the tribes of Albion. I am no stranger to the ways of sovereignty. I know much of pride and stature. Yet I am old now. I see my past and shudder.

I stand, barefoot, on my favorite beach at dawn, a bit dizzy with the joy of escaping my small cottage before Mica can rise, dress my hair properly, and insist I behave like the queen I once was.

Strange, how the sand of this small, forgotten island feels like the grit of home beneath these old toes. For it was in the hills and not beside the sea that I first tumbled out of bed and saw the stars.

Many times I have sought to send my spirit back to the fog-shrouded hills of my birth. There, in some lost valley of Gwynedd, I would choose my life again. This time I would become a child of sheep-herders. As I grew, my hands would become calloused by chores. Possessed of no ambition beyond preparing the next meal, I would be a wrinkled crone now, my breasts and belly sagging from bearing many children quickly. Old, toothless, filled with harsh stories, I would sit, surrounded by grandchildren in a dark and smoky hut.

There are other, worse fates.

Listen, seagulls call. Like lonely souls ascending from the battlefield, they swoop around me and fly towards the pounding sea, into the cloud-covered sky.

And my hair, this hair that was once the envy of hundreds, seeks to follow them. It blows, white and desperate, across my face, whipped by the north-seeking wind as it speeds its way home towards the ice.

I stand here—rooted in sand—letting this small tempest of wind, sea, and flight buffet me. Grateful for the small things. For in these heartbeats, I remember the wild girl I once was. More comfortable in bare feet and homespun than linen and sea pearls. Happier to feel the touch of my lover's hand than to sit in the king's treasury and count all the gold in the realm.

Arthur, my husband, my lord and my king, is dead, murdered by a pirate's battle-axe. Yet Arthur has a nation to mourn him. The finest bards in the kingdom share his eulogy with the world, as Seaxon invaders overrun our land, killing our children, setting fire to our crops and homes.

Medraut, my love, Brea and Godraith, my children, have only myself to remember them. And I will vanish from this earth soon enough.

A gull lands and drops a broken mussel shell at my feet, staring at me with its small dark eye as if it has given me a great gift. I bend and touch sand shimmering from the outgoing tide. The shell lies, sharp and welcome, against my palm.

The gull watches, then flies away, hidden immediately within the dawn's mist.

The child, Mica, is coming, pounding through the wet sand on the shoreline as if she flees a dragon, hurrying to reach me before I catch the chill. Her feet pelt the air like tiny war drums; the weight of the cloak she brings is almost more than she can carry. Yet she smiles as she runs, letting the wind tease her hair, blowing it back and behind her like the kites my children used to fly at Camlann long ago.

Clucking like an old woman, she stands on tiptoe to arrange the cloak around my shoulders. "My lady, you must not be in this wind without a wrap! Come inside. Your broth is ready."

"A heartbeat more…" I turn back to the sea.

Clouds cover the rising sun, yet it is still strong enough to outline them in gold and shadow like the illuminations in the fine fat book Father Pendragon was writing when disaster befell us all.

I lift the mussel shell the gull gave me, letting my cloak slide to the sand, and ignore Mica's fuss. With all my might I fling the shell into the air.

It makes a high arch and lands with a small splash beyond the second wave of foam.

"Farewell." A fresh waves crashes and I see the faces of my two children on the day before they died. See again the face of my beloved as he leaps on his horse for the last time, turning to look down at me. Fury, love, and pain blend in his eyes as he sets his face to the west where the worst of the battle rages.

Mica tugs at my arm.

"Yes, yes. I am coming…"

"Will you tell me a story as we spin today, Lady?" So hopeful. She looks up at me, her voice as light as a wren's, a dark-eyed ten-sunturns-old survivor of last summer's Seaxon raids.

"Perhaps. *If* you finish your chores without complaint." She starts to skip, masters herself, and walks sedately beside me carrying the rejected cloak. "And this time, do not attempt to tell me that the goat ate all the yarn."

Mica's grin splits her tiny, dark-skinned face like a sudden jewel brought to light. Hard indeed to believe that only nine moontides ago I found her sitting, dazed and witless, beside the blood-drenched body of her mother, crooning a lullaby to the endlessly open eyes as if it would make them sparkle back to life again.

But she walks safe beside me now. And for her, if for no living other, I will tell my story. For her soul, for her smile, I will line my words up in rows like obedient Roman soldiers marching through a glen. Perhaps the wind will hear it, and let my children live again, if only for a little while. Beside the peat fire of this simple cottage hearth. Far away from where it all began.

Ah, but how does one begin such a tale?

Mica scampers ahead of me, pushing through the doorway of our small fisher's croft as if she is a wolf cub scenting milk. I pause before I stoop to enter, my hand pressed against the northern runes Seawyn of the fisher-folk has carved into the lintel of the doorpost.

"Lady, come inside."

I turn back towards the sea.

Perhaps I should begin with my first sight of Arthur's golden dragon, hung in woven majesty behind the High Seat of the new young King.

Or in the hills of my birth when I first beheld the Tylwyth Teg, the fairy folk of southern bedside tales.

Perhaps the bright midsummer day when I met Merlin?

Or on the night Medraut, Raven Lord of the Orkneys, strode into our lives, polishing his chipped and bloodied sword by the light of stable torches, so fresh from the Northern Isles, his eyes still gleamed with their ice.

No, for that was nearly at our end. And Mica is yet a child. No, this tale began long before Medraut arrived at Camlann, long before the Northern wars began.

Perhaps I should start in my own father's fortress as I slept, safe and warm, in the straw of the stables curled close to my favorite hound. Having escaped my nurses yet again.

A raven caws, its voice as bitter as a gull's.

"Lady, please..."

I take a final breath of salt air and enter the darkness of our home.

The raven caws again, lands with a flurry of feathers on the strand behind me.

It cries a third time and flies into the orange, pink, and lavender of the rising sun.

It has left a feather.

I pick it up. It shimmers with water and dawn.

Leaning against the doorpost, I turn the feather around. Hearing his laughter again for the first time in many weary scores of seasons. For long before Medraut the Raven Lord came into my heart, there had been another, much younger lad who ran with my brother Cynan and me when we were yearling foxes alive and hunting adventure in the northern lands of my birth.

I take a stool beside the fire and smile at Mica as she hands me a chipped bowl of broth. "All right, little one, I will tell you the story. It began when I was only a little girl, even younger than you, running wild in the mountains..."

PART 1

NORTHERN WALES: 460-468 CE

CHAPTER 1

As a child, I believed my father was made of magic. Even now, if I close my eyes, I see his great long moustaches and the blue-etched dragon tattooed into the skin of his right arm. When I grew older, I learned that he limed his moustaches so that they would keep their shape in even the fiercest mountain wind. But, as a child, I thought they stood out straight by magic of the strongest kind.

My father's comings and goings were also great mysteries. He would appear when I least expected him and vanish when I most wanted him to stay. Evenings at a feasting, if his mood was kind, he would let me sit upon his lap and nibble from his joint of venison. There I first noticed the blue-woad dragon. It began at his wrist and snaked up his forearm, ending beneath the burnished gold of the warrior's band clasped over the bulging muscles of his upper arm.

When I asked about it, Father grunted, eyes fixed on something far away. "It was a gift, girl." He would say no more, no matter how many times I asked, no matter how hard I wheedled.

The dragon began to haunt my dreams. Soon it would seek me out as well; had I known, I would have feared it.

But in this spring of my eighth sunturn, dragons were just another mystery. It was a time when I still heard the voices of horses and hound puppies talked back to me when I petted them. War surrounded us, but since it was the only life I knew, I thought it normal for Mother and her women to spend as much time stitching warrior flesh as they did carding wool.

It was also this season that I found the small stone nook behind Mother's favorite woven hanging, the morning I first saw Father angry.

It was early in the season, the leaves of the old oaks beyond the western watchtower just beginning to uncurl. The rain and fog had lifted early and rare morning sunlight poured through the unshuttered windows of the Hall, lighting dust motes that danced in the air like tiny fairies.

The Hall itself was emptied of all but a few servants busy clearing the remnants of the morning meal, but the clattering of wooden platters and familiar chatter did little to ease my discontent. I had no one to play with. Restless, I kicked at the fresh rushes on the floor, releasing the scent of sweet meadow herbs and wildflowers. Even my brother Cynan had deserted me.

I turned to exploring.

The nook was a wonderful find, a tiny stone space just barely wide enough for me to sit in if I curled up my legs. It was near the High Table and I was hidden from sight by the dusty dark curtain of Mother's prized Byzantine wall hanging, yet from my position I could peek out carefully at will.

I was deep in a daydream, waving a wand filled with magic in the middle of a sunlit cave when Father slammed into the Hall. He pushed gruffly past the guard, bounded up the steps of the King's dais, and threw himself into the High Seat.

Fresh from battle, blood and filth still stained the scarred leather breast of his armor. Too angry to sit, he rose with a curse and began to pace the Hall.

"Cerid—"

Mother appeared out of nowhere and offered him a mead horn.

If my father was made of magic, Mother was bright light and rippling water. Now she sat down near my hiding place, waiting, as still as a night star.

I curled close to the edge of my nook, aware something important was about to happen.

Careful, even in fury, to spill the dregs on the ground for the gods, Father wiped his moustaches with an impatient flick of his wrist and threw the horn against the stones of the central hearth. Its clatter echoed, scattering the sleeping hounds.

He strode across the flagstones separating them and sank to his knees beside Mother. "Lugh's balls, woman! They want me to be Battle Lord! Battle Lord—not King. Never yet a King!"

Mother stroked the filthy brown length of Father's hair as if it were fine linen. "Hush, love, your father yet lives. Would you hasten his death with your rage?"

"He lies as one dead!" Father threw off her hand and stormed across the empty Hall. Nearing the King's dais, he slammed his fist against the wall—so close to my hiding place his arm raised a draft.

Frightened, I curled up as tightly as I could, making myself as small as possible. I had never seen him rage like this, certainly not at Mother.

"His wits wander like the birds of autumn, Ceri! He has lain like this for two sunturns now. And the land lies cursed around him. He would hate it if he knew— Cunedda Iron Hand, of all men, would seek an eagle's death!"

Mother rose from her bench and crossed the Hall to join him.

They stood together without words. Then she led him away from the dais, so small beside him that the top of her head could nestle beneath his chin. "Let his end be in the hands of the gods," she said as they passed my hiding place. "Do not seek to hasten it—that is the old way of our fathers. It will bring you no peace."

Father reined in his stride to accommodate Mother's smaller steps. They paced the length of the Hall in silence.

I knelt, craning my neck to track them, and almost lost my balance as I pulled too hard on the wall hanging. They were coming back. Mother placed her hand on Father's arm. "You love your father more than the very air you breathe," her lilting voice was breathless. "To take the sacrificial dagger to his heart would kill you as well."

Father stopped walking.

Mother touched his cheek. "You are Battle Lord now—be worthy of it. It is you, not the King, who must lift the curse our land is under."

Father reached out his arms, enfolding her.

She stood on tiptoe to kiss his forehead. "Make Cunedda proud, love." She kissed him again, this time on the mouth.

He groaned and drew her closer.

They spoke no more, but as they stopped kissing, Father's hand came to rest on Mother's hair. His dark eyes smoldered, then sparked, as she smiled up at him, her long tumbling black curls giving her features the softness of a dove at dawn.

As they walked past my hiding place for the second time, I curled farther back against the stones and held my breath.

I need not have worried.

They had eyes for no one but each other as they disappeared

from the Hall, heading towards the inner room that held their private chambers.

I waited but a heartbeat before jumping down from the nook. Stopping to shake the pains from my cramping legs, I left the Hall, slipped across the muddy inner courtyard, and entered the high watchtower of the Northern Keep. Of the three standing towers of Dinas Emrys, the northern tower was the tallest — and the most dreaded. I was on my way to visit my father's father, the bloody Cunedda.

I had always been afraid of him. Servants whispered that he was a warlock. One night last winter, while pretending to sleep, I listened as Nurse whispered the bloody story of Cunedda to mother's maid Marudd: how, as a lad, he had celebrated victory by tearing out the hearts of his enemy and eating them, how as a new-made Battle Lord, he had toasted his warriors with their enemy's blood—blood which he drank from the dead warrior's own skull.

But this morning I determined to see the old man for myself. I waited until I was sure no one was watching, then slipped over the threshold of the tower and began to climb the ancient curved stairway.

I tiptoed, even though there was no one to hear me, only the oppressive stillness of damp watching stone, its grey gloom penetrated by a faint haze of light from arrow slits rock-cut at each outward turning of the stairs. The worn steps felt like carved bowls beneath my summer-bare feet.

Breathless, I followed the twisting stairs, clutching at the clammy uneven stones, refusing to give in to the panic that grew stronger with every forward step.

Just when I felt I could climb no farther, I reached a small landing and knew the room beyond was Cunedda's. Quivering with excitement, I wiped my sweating palms against the rough homespun of my tunic, made the sign of the goddess, and pushed against the thick oak door.

It swung back to reveal a small room with two narrow windows just wide enough to let bowmen shoot their arrows and to let in a small portion of the grey light of day.

The smell of chamber pots and vomit was thick enough to touch.

An old man lay asleep in a narrow carved bed, his right arm resting above the furs, his fingers curled up like a badger's claws. A dozing attendant slumped on a stool between the windows, his bearded face snoring against the stone wall.

A chest lay open near the door. I tripped over it, the pain in my toes quickly overwhelmed by my horror at the noise I had made.

The old man's right eye snapped open, blazing with fury beneath uncombed white hair. Cords of muscle stood out on his neck as he tried to reach for a sword that wasn't there, with an arm that would not move.

His clawed hand trembled. I backed up, terrified, measuring the distance I had to run to make it safely down the stairs.

With a curse, the servant woke and started towards me, but the man on the bed calmed when he saw it was only I who had disturbed him. The old King snarled a command through his frozen mouth. The servant sat down again.

Cunedda's good eye did not leave my face.

The servant spat on the floor, glaring at me as if I had intruded on a private ritual.

"C-ome here, girrrl." Only the right side of Cunedda's mouth moved, the rest of his face was as still as a midwinter mask despite the anger that remained in his clouded blue eye.

Frightened as I was, I straightened my shoulders and walked into the room, keeping my eyes fixed upon the strange old man's face—my own grandfather—although I had never seen him this close before.

The servant used his foot to push an empty stool in front of me, letting it scrape across the floor.

"Sit. S-stop jumping about like a witless rabbit!" The right side of Grandfather's mouth worked without ceasing. Cursing again, this time low enough that only I could hear him, the attendant removed a dirt-smeared rag from a fold in his tunic and dabbed at the spittle falling down the contours of the sick man's chin.

Ignoring him, I leaned closer to the bed, tilting my head like Nurse had taught me, trying to catch as much sound as possible. Grandfather's words were still hard to understand, but I began to make sense of them.

"I will not harm you, child." His right eye moved restlessly over my body. His left eye was frozen, half-shut, staring endlessly at the ceiling.

I tried not to flinch, thinking of the many children he must have eaten. I would be brave.

"Which one are you?"

"G-g-gwenhwyfar."

"What—Gwenhwyfar? That makes you Ceridwen's youngest."

Growling the hovering servant away, Grandfather's clawed right hand plucked helplessly at the bearskin fur that covered him despite the summer heat and the fire blazing in the hearth. He regarded me as if I were a pony he was thinking of buying.

"You have the look of your grandmother about you. She gave you those eyes."

Since my mother's mother, the Lady Rhiannon, had eyes as dark as mountain shadows, I knew he must be talking about his own wife, Lady Malcora, my father's mother. This grandmother I had never met. All that I had ever heard of her was that she was long dead and buried in the Eastern mountains of northern Alba.

"Ah yes, you have her eyes..." Grandfather looked away from me, his right eye turning to the window, the left still staring at the ceiling.

I already knew my eyes caused whispering among the servants. They were not the eyes of others. I, myself, had only seen them in the wavy reflection of my mother's bronze mirror or in the forest pools where Cynan and I played. They were deep sea green and my mother had once told me that they offered violet shadows like hers when I grew excited or angry. Yet they held golden sparkles all their own.

"They are the eyes of the Old Ones, Granddaughter." The old man's eye returned to me. Holding both ferocity and pain, it seized on my face with such strength I felt as if I was held within a hawk's talons. "The eyes of a *truth-teller*." He struggled to move, gave it up with a groan, and glared. "Do you always tell the truth?"

"Y-yes."

"See that you do so always. Lies are the mark of a coward." Spittle ran unchecked from the corner of his mouth. I bent closer, brushing a lock of stringy grey-white hair away from his ravaged face and wiped his spit away with my own hand.

The old king's mouth twisted as I did so. For a heartbeat there was warmth within the depths of his good eye.

The sullen servant roused and joined me, easing a pillow beneath the old man's head. "Your grandfather is tired. Let him rest."

I stuck out my tongue. A child again. Now that I was here, I had a hundred questions. Who were the Old Ones? What had my Alban grandmother been like—she who had given me her eyes?

But I had already received one beating for rudeness that week and my backside was not eager for another. I looked at Grandfather to see if he would save me from being dismissed, but the warmth was gone. He was no longer looking at me. His right eye had returned to the narrow window, as if he were straining to see something. I was forgotten.

I did not want to be forgotten.

"Grandfather?"

Nothing.

His clawed hand began to twist. Gobbling sounds came from the overworked side of his mouth.

Suddenly, I was afraid.

His right side arched towards the ceiling, dragging the rest of his body across the bed.

"Grandfather!"

His good eye snapped back to me so quickly I almost screamed. What he had seen beyond the window must have been the stuff of nightmares, for the frightening old king's eye was so clouded with terror that I felt myself spinning, drowning within it.

"Go!" He shouted in a young man's voice, spittle flying from his mouth. His frozen left eye filled with blood. "Go! Before the darkness comes..."

His frozen body arched even higher from the bed, as if it fled the night itself.

"Run—before it finds you..."

I ran, pelting down the twisting stairs with no thought of falling, stopping only after I gained the safety of my parents' Hall.

Late that night, I snuggled into the cozy warmth of my mother's lap while Nurse waited to lead me to bed. In her accustomed seat beside the hearth of Mother's chamber, Nurse Hwyrch's ever-busy hands spun freshly carded wool, her sharp bird-like eyes content as she watched Mother unbraid my hair.

I looked up at Mother, unwilling to go to bed yet. "What is wrong with Grandfather Cunedda? Why doesn't he ever come to the Hall?"

Her fingers paused above the last braid. "You've been to see him, haven't you?"

I ignored the question. "Somebody could carry him down the stairs so he could visit us."

She pursed full lips and was silent, smoothing a tangled strand of hair back from my face. "Grandfather Cunedda is lost in his memories,

Gwen," she spoke at last. "His mind is wandering in another time."

"You mean he is like old Livia?" Once Cook Maeve's helper, Livia was now too feeble to work; she sat beside the baking ovens happy to cut leeks as the life of the kitchens went on around her. I loved to listen to her, murmuring of fairies as she stirred meat stews and lugged heavy kettles from the well.

Mother glanced at Hwyrch and smiled. "Yes, he is a bit like Livia. But you must always remember that once your father's father was a great man—a mighty King. You must never mock him."

Remembering the old man's sharp eye on me, I shivered. "I won't, Mother. He scares me."

"He doesn't mean to, Gwen. It is just that his soul is in its winter and he knows no other way."

"But, what does—"

"That's enough. Let your mother be." Hwyrch rose and held out her hand for me to come to bed.

"No!" I burrowed against Mother.

"That will be quite enough, Gwen!" Mother rose, fixing me with the dark look I dreaded. "Hwyrch, she is to go to bed right away without even one story."

Nurse nodded, her many chins bobbing like pigeons. "Yes, indeed! We'll have no more of that temper of yours tonight, young lady!"

I knew enough to be quiet then and meekly kissed my mother's cheek, letting myself be led away by the hand.

As soon as I was tucked in and Nurse and I were alone, I turned towards her and forced my eyes wide open. "Just one story, Hwyrch? A little one? I'll be good, I promise!"

Nurse sighed and sat down on the rough stool beside my cot, just as I had hoped she would. "Just one—and only if you promise to stop giving your poor mother fits!"

I nodded happily and sank back, snuggling against my favorite wolfskin, closing my eyes to hear the story better.

"Once, long ago, when giants still lived in the mountains and the Tylwyth Teg danced beneath the bright light of the sun…"

But it was not the comforting patter of Nurse's voice that followed me into sleep; it was the fear-rasped voice of my grandfather that came back as I closed my eyes.

"Run! Before the darkness finds you…"

I pretended to be asleep. Nurse tucked the deerskin covers around me and blew out my bedside rush-light. Long after she went to her own pallet in the far corner of my room, I stayed awake, clutching my wolfskin to my face. Breathing its beloved wild scent, I tried not to think about the black night that filled the chamber now—a night that was no longer friendly.

A darkness that had eyes.

chapter 2

I had grown up with rumors of an evil that stalked Dinas Emrys, slithering beneath the surface of our fortress like an adder darting into the weeds of a river. Now, all the servant's tales I'd overheard linked with Grandfather's fierce warning...Mother's sudden intakes of breath when entering a dark room...Grandmother Rhiannon's refusal to enter the crumbling stones of the ruined South Tower.

As spring faded into a glorious high summer, I felt icy hands reach for me when I was alone.

Enough, I told myself. I was a Battle Chief's daughter after all, not to be bested by shadows. That late summer morning I stood beside Mother, my hair tossed within the dawn breeze, hopping on one foot, then the other in a fury of impatience to greet Father's war band, riding victoriously up the western hill track. They reached us at last, a colorful dirty procession of familiar faces, their jokes and laughter competing with the jangle of weapons and bridles and the snorting of tired ponies smelling home.

Father's bloodshot eyes twinkled as he caught sight of Mother taking quick steps through the morning fog to welcome him with a victor's horn of mead. Suddenly shy, I ducked behind her skirts.

I heard her gasp and peeked out to see why.

Suspended from Father's battle lance were two shriveled bloody heads, their eyes empty but for the whiteness of the dead, blood and gristle still leaking to the ground.

Fascinated, I let go of the soft linen of Mother's overdress and reached up to Father's lowered lance, touching the matted, filthy hair on the nearest head. "Who were they, Father?"

"Gwen!" Mother's voice cut into the sudden silence like an oar through pond water. Only fiercer, fiercer than I had ever heard her. "Get back here now!"

She did not need to speak twice. I jumped like a squirrel back to her side. She gripped my hand tightly enough to hurt but I knew enough not to whimper. "And why, beloved lord, do you bring things of pagan evil to our Hall?" Her soft voice was deep, husky with rage. "Have we not had enough of blood within these walls?"

The warmth in Father's eyes died. He raised one eyebrow and regarded her in silence, only the whitened knuckles around his lance betrayed his tension. "Lest you forget your place, my lady, this is my father's Hall. And I bring whatever I choose inside."

Mother bit her lip hard enough to draw blood, but she nodded curtly and offered him the mead in silence, her hands trembling hard enough to shake the gold-encrusted bone of the ritual horn.

He drank in matching silence. Men and horses shifted uneasily behind him, my mother's bitterness a pall cast upon warriors who had been boasting and joyous only heartbeats before.

Father turned and raised his hands to them. His weary brown eyes sought me out. "Gwen, we bring you the spoils of Eire! Long Tooth here will no longer despoil our lands." He drew his sword and cut one of the heads loose from the lance, catching it neatly by its hair as it fell. Tossing the bloody thing to his Shield Brother Hwyll, he slashed up again and the second head fell like rotten fruit into his grasp.

"And Gormach, he of the Northern Longboats, will no longer slay our youth, no longer steal our women, no longer burn our homes. My own sword has cast him into the darkest pit of Anwnn, where he will stay like the twisted worm he was until the gods themselves draw final breath!"

With a great roar he held Gormach's head up, high above us, so that all his men could see. Their answering cheer set the dogs to barking and brought the last of the sleepy-headed servants racing from the Hall and outlying huts.

I twisted free of Mother's hand and ran to clasp Father. I could only reach his knees, but, giving his lance to a nearby warrior, he scooped me up one-handed and held me against his chest, the pirate's head dangling an arm's length away. The cheers surrounding us increased. Men kneed their ponies closer, slapping my father on the back, wishing us both good cheer.

"Never forget, my girl, you are the daughter of a Battle Lord. And Battle Lords do not lie cowering in their Halls like women!"

"I don't either, Papa," I said fiercely, trying to ignore the laughter that followed. "I won't ever cower like a woman!" To prove my point, I swallowed my disgust and reached out my hand to touch the shrunken cheek of Gormach's decaying head.

From far away, I heard Mother's soft cry; from the corner of my eye I saw her raise a jeweled hand and cover her mouth.

Quickly, I turned back to Father, but not quick enough to ignore the rustle of her skirts as she spun around and I knew that she entered the empty Hall alone and furious.

Father shrugged to see her go; only his darkening eyes let me know he was pained.

My fingers stroked Gormach's cold, flaccid skin in wonder that it did not come alive at my touch. As if spelled, my fingers wandered across the pirate leader's face, sensing the bumps of an oft-broken nose, the liver of thin, bitter lips, the eerie sharpness of stubble on a beard still growing on a now-dead face.

The circle of blood-stained warriors drew closer.

"Enough." Father removed my hand from the grisly head and kissed the top of my hair. I reached for the head again. "Enough, Gwen."

He clasped my still-moving fingers, massaging them between his own. In the distance, a pony whinnied, anxious for its oats.

Father folded my fingers into a fist, holding it within his own. "You are warrior's get, indeed."

The soft mist that clung to our summer hilltop like an old woman's shawl parted. Sunlight sparkled on the bright gold of the warriors' bounty, dancing across the armbands and jewels they had taken from the Scotti invaders whose settlements dotted our coast like vipers' nests.

Tossing Gormach's head to a grinning stable boy, Father dismounted, carrying me with him. "Men, you have brought honor to the barrows of our ancestors this night! Rest, rise, and seek me in the Hall." He cast a lopsided, wry smile towards his band and shrugged his shoulders towards the Hall, whose carved oak doors seemed to ring with Mother's rage. "It appears I must be brave once more and soften my graceful lady's heart so that we may feast in joy tonight!"

The men laughed at even this weak of a jest. Mother was well-liked and I sensed that her anger had unnerved them, although, as warriors, they would never have spoken such a thing aloud.

A warrior called out, "There's but one way to gentle a woman that angry! Take care with yourself, lord, or you may be too weary to join us at the feast board!"

I looked over Father's shoulder and saw it was Cruan who had spoken. The old man with his face full of scars was a favorite of mine, so I smiled happily at him, not caring that the meaning of his speech made no sense to me.

The men began to drift away, leading ponies to the stable. The freemen who traveled on foot simply headed towards the huts they shared with other folk who lived inside the inner battlements or wandered, tiredly, back down the dirt track that led to the village beyond the lower palisades at the foot of our great hill. All seemed in better spirits now, and jokes and bright laughter were once more flung like Roman coins across the courtyard as men rubbed down their mounts and held their womenfolk close once again.

Whatever magic my father performed, Mother accompanied him into the Hall that night and even served his warrior band with her own hands. The next day, when Father had the dreadful heads mounted on poles lifted high in front of the entrance to the Hall, she merely watched in silence. Only her thinning lips gave her away to me.

I tried not to pay attention to her and turned to Father. "Why are you sticking those ugly heads up on poles outside our home, Papa?"

He ruffled my hair. Although it was only early morning, it had already begun to escape the braids Hwyrch had been at pains to create. "The Old Ones of this land believe that if you mount the heads of your greatest enemies near your own Hall, they will have to protect you for eternity with all the strength they once used to fight you."

I eyed Gormach's bloody eye sockets doubtfully. "Are you sure that it works? If I were in those heads, I would want to destroy my enemies any way I could!"

Father laughed. Seeing Mother turn and walk across the courtyard, he started after her, giving me a brisk pat on the bottom. "Go find that scamp, Cynan, and get something to eat."

I perked up at the mention of food and scampered off to find my brother.

I should have known that Mother was only biding her time.

She waited until Father left with his war host the following day to patrol the mountain borders of our Otter clan. The next sunrise, before anyone knew what she planned, Mother ran down the hill and through the village, to the edge of the great forest where the White Christ hermit lived.

I was abroad early as usual and crept out to investigate. By the time I discovered them, the old man Mother fetched was already climbing one of the carved poles outside the Hall, his filthy grey robe belted up about his mud-encrusted shins. Horrified, I watched as he freed Gormach's head from its high perch and tied it grimly to the rope around his waist.

Mother waited below.

Once he reached the ground, the hermit handed it to her. Wordless, she wrapped the foul thing in a grimy rag and watched as he climbed again to retrieve the second rotting head. Mother wrapped this one as well; her quick, efficient movements still not quick enough to disguise the raven's work from me.

Gormach's ally, Long Tooth, had already lost his eyes and half of his right cheek. Gormach, himself, had fared little better. His eyes, too, had fed the birds. His forehead had been savaged, and bits of flesh still clung to it like threads of bright cloth upon a loom.

"Mother—"

She startled, spinning around to where I crouched behind a corner of the Hall.

"Get inside! Now!"

Not waiting to see if she was obeyed, Mother turned back to the hermit standing beside her. Tall and gaunt, he ignored me utterly and wiped his bloody hands on the front of his stained robe.

"What now, Lady? Do we burn these abominations?"

She picked the grisly bundles up and gestured him to follow. Together they stalked around the Hall. I waited the space of three breaths, then crept out from behind the wooden barrel where I had hidden and followed.

Mother led. They strode past the smithy, the kitchens and granaries, and the weaving shed. Keeping the stables to their left, they circled the small huts where the freemen of the fortress lived. I kept to the shadows of the Warriors' Hall on my right, ready to jump back against the high wooden walls if either of them chanced to look around. Neither of them bothered. It was still very early, not even the servants were astir and Mother and the White Christ priest seemed well content to be alone.

Skirting the twin springs, whose water flowed past storage huts, down the hill in culverts of Grandfather's design, Mother and the priest passed the grim stones of the North Tower and came, at last, to the middens that lay along the northwestern palisade wall, near the little-used northern gate, as far as possible from our dwellings. Their reek was already powerful, despite the early hour. By midday, their summer stench would be unbearable.

Sheltering behind an abandoned tanning shed, I watched, fascinated, as Mother wound her arm and tossed one of the heads into the midden pit, as if it were a hunting stone hurled at a squirrel.

The old priest took up the second head and launched it likewise into the air. His throw was weaker then Mother's and the ragged wrappings fell away in mid-air, leaving Long Tooth's dead, decaying face exposed as it sank into a bog of garbage and shit.

I shrank back against the rotting wall of my hiding place, suddenly terrified. Surely the souls of the dead men would claim vengeance for this insult.

Backing up, I stepped on someone's boot.

Mother's mother, the Lady Rhiannon, glared down at me.

Before I could make a sound, Grandmother's hand clamped over my mouth. "If you value your hide, say nothing! Your lady mother will answer to me for this outrage."

She let go of my arm and pushed me towards the Hall. Shocked into tears, I ran, not caring if Mother heard me, only afraid of what I had seen in Grandmother's face. For I loved her well, and although I had often seen her fury turned on others, I had never felt its force turned on me before.

I ran fast, sobbing, half-blinded with tears. In the Hall, I dodged past a nodding sentry, slid through the grumbling commotion of servants setting up trestles for the morning meal and escaped down the corridor to my room.

A hound lying on the sheepskin at the entrance to my sleeping chamber stretched and rose to greet me. Ignoring even him, I crept past my sleeping nurse and leapt beneath the covers of my cot.

Pulling my ragged wolfskin against my face, I let the tears take me, muffled by the sweet grey pelt that had been mine from earliest memory.

My world was on fire. I loved Grandmother Rhiannon in the same way that I loved the feel of the crisp north wind pounding against my face when I ran down the hill beyond the inner palisades. She was all that was fierce and wild and loving.

And I loved Mother as I loved my wolf pelt, soft and comforting even against the fears of deepest night.

And Father? I loved my father as I loved the brightest dragon tales. Courageous, brave, filled with wonder and fire was my father.

They were mine, these three. Beloved beyond words.

Now those filthy heads had come and there were tears and there was pain.

I made my decision.

Instead of waiting for Hwyrch to rise, rub her eyes, and smile at me—her nearly toothless mouth a comfort, even as she advanced on me with her dreaded comb and water bowl—I would spy out what was to happen next. No matter how painful it would prove.

To do this, I would have to find a hiding place in the Great Hall that offered me a better vantage point than the stone nook.

I crept out of my chamber, careful not to disturb the still-snoring Hwyrch, and entered the kitchens, managing to smile at our Scotti cook Maeve and the bustling activity around the ovens and fire-spit. I was everybody's pet, and impatiently endured great handfuls of time being cosseted and fussed over before I escaped down the corridor that led into the Hall.

No one from my family was sitting at table yet, not even my two oldest brothers, Tegid and Iorwerth, who usually fled Dinas at the first light of dawn in pursuit of hunting, fishing, fighting, or women, depending on their moods.

The only people in the Hall were warriors gathered around the central hearth breaking their fast with steaming bowls of porridge and baskets of bannocks, smoked fish, and cold venison. To them I was invisible: a small girl child, no matter my right to a ruler's torc. Grateful for this, I slid past their circle and found the large clothes chest I remembered shoved up beneath a line of pegs designed to hold cloaks.

I flung it open. It was filled with winter woolens and furs, as I had hoped. Under cover of a burst of laughter from the men, I shoved the chest against the wall and hid its top beneath a hanging black cloak. With a final glance at the warriors, whose attention was now taken up by a contest between two snarling hounds, I jumped into the chest and curled up beneath a winter cape, settling down to wait.

I must have dozed, for the next thing I heard was Grandmother's strident voice.

I sprang up. The smell of wool and cured furs reminded me of where I was. Whatever instinct had encouraged me to seek answers in the Hall proved to be right, for when I peered out from my hiding place, I saw Mother sitting on the dais in the Queen's Seat presiding over a nearly empty Hall. What few folk still lingered, scattered quickly as Grandmother stormed to the foot of the dais, her back as tall and straight as an ash tree. Thick silver hair hung loose to her knees, interspersed with the small braids of a priestess.

Mother did not move. She sipped from her goblet, watching Grandmother's advance until the older woman halted beneath her.

"Daughter!" Despite her great age, Grandmother's Druid training resonated in the rich timbre of her voice, a voice pitched to carry its message across the Great Hall and beyond.

"Mother?" Mother's own voice held the same tired tone she used when she had to explain things more than once.

"You have cursed us all!"

Mother placed her goblet with exaggerated care upon the well-used oak trestle board, rose, walked behind Father's High Seat, and let her tiny hand come to rest on the white wolf pelt that covered it. Her slender fingers grazed the thick fur as if by accident "I have done no such thing. I merely placed those foul things in the garbage where they belonged."

Grandmother stood, as still and silent as a hunting cat. But in her silence, she loosed hungry shadows that prowled the Hall like beasts.

Mother flung her head back, loosening her silver coif so that it jangled against the narrow queen's torc around her neck. "It will take more than maggoty heads to remove the curse our land is under!"

"Fool!" Grandmother spat into the rushes beneath the high table. "It was a dark day when I sent you South, child. It is a sickness of the soul you received from those chanting Dumnoni monks. Cristos, indeed!"

"It is not Cristos who cursed this land. And well you know it!" Mother turned on her heel, stepped down from the dais, and left, heading for her chambers.

"Only the mad followers of the tree god are stupid enough to pray in the face of battle axes!" But Grandmother was speaking to the shadows.

When she realized Mother had left her, Grandmother's posture relaxed. Exhaling a breath I could hear as far as my hiding place, she mounted the dais and sank into Mother's chair.

For a long span of time, Grandmother scanned the Hall as if looking for something she had forgotten. At length she put her head in her hands and slid wearily forward. "Come here, Granddaughter!"

I jumped.

"Come here, girl," Grandmother repeated impatiently, her voice still muffled by her hands. "Or do you still think to pretend I can't see you?"

Caught, I climbed out of the fur chest and began reluctantly to walk the length of the Hall, miserable at the thought of the beating I would receive for spying.

When I reached the dais, Grandmother lifted her face from her hands. I was awed to see tears streaking the high craggy cheekbones of her face.

She stood, holding out her hands to me. "Walk with me, little one."

I did so.

We left the Hall and walked past the now-empty stakes where the pirates' heads had watched our comings and goings. If any of the freemen or slaves of Dinas gave their loss more than a passing thought, I did not see it. Occasional worried glances, a few signs to avert the evil eye, even a few Cristos followers making the sign of the tree god—these I saw as Grandmother and I crossed the main courtyard of the hillfort, heading down the steep eastern pathway to the grove of the ancients. But I saw no anger, no fury such as Grandmother had expressed.

"I am growing old, Granddaughter." She lowered herself to her favorite boulder, sparing a glance at the quiet shadows of Anu's pool as she waited for me to find my perch beside her.

The grove was my favorite place in the world. Halfway down the hill of our fortress of Dinas Emrys, nestled in a natural hollow, the grove was well within the second palisades of the fort, safe to visit even if it was too dangerous to venture into the great forest beyond the third, final palisades of our protection.

The oak, hazel, willow, and rowan trees surrounding the Goddess' pool were older than anyone could remember; their trunks and branches gnarled and bent into wonderful shapes. Grandmother said they had been alive long before the red-cloaks came to our mountains and that they would exist as long as people lived who would honor them. They were also wonderful to climb.

Although the Goddess' pool beneath them was always still and quiet, half-covered with leaves in summer and autumn, it was never boring at all. It was quiet like a cat was quiet, always watching, hiding things that it would like to share if you could only see them. Grandmother called it a place of mystery, a sacred place where you were not supposed to yell. I only knew I liked it because it was friendly, like my wolfskin. It smiled at me sometimes as if I was learning to see the things it wanted to show me.

"Why do you care about those ugly heads, Grandmother?"

She brushed a thick strand of hair away from her face and looked into the still surface of the pool without speaking for a long time.

I knew better than to move.

Still looking into the pool she began to speak. "Because the taking of such battle trophies is a part of who we are."

She swept her hand to the east. "Long before the Romans came, your ancestors walked free in these forests and mountains. They honored this land and its spirits. Men and women both, they lived to fight bravely, to die singing in battle."

"But what does that have to do with us now?"

She snorted like my pony, Shadlock. "Because it is dangerous to forget the Old Ways. Our land lies cursed because we have done so."

I reached out to pull a small twig from the shimmering mass of her hair. She turned to me with a smile that lit up the harsh lines of her face. Bringing my hand to her mouth, she kissed it.

"It is only by remembering the land—the ancient rituals the Druids have tried to keep alive—that we will stop the destruction of all that matters and halt our murder as a people."

"But—"

"Hush. Listen to the world around us."

Obediently, I closed my eyes. But although I listened very hard, all I heard were sparrows quarreling and squirrels scrambling in the branches of the hazel tree behind me. I smelled nothing but the deep sweet moisture of the pool and the crushed grass beneath my fingers.

I opened my eyes. Grandmother's eyes were closed, her head resting against the trunk of a rowan tree I was tempted to shake her to see if she was still awake, but knew that would lead to disaster.

I turned to the pool again and saw something flicker at the very edge of my sight. Startled, I squinted my eyes to see more clearly. There, at the far edge of the pool, a flash of red suddenly turned orange, like a tall candle flame, then disappeared. A trickle of laughter followed, hanging in the air like the final chord of a harper's song.

It was probably a trick of the breeze.

I decided to risk her temper. "Grandmother?"

Her eyes opened slowly. They were as black as rocks beneath a waterfall. Capable of great sweetness or icy fury, they were my favorite of her features—next to her beautiful hair and its mysterious braids.

Now they looked like they were coming back from a great distance. "Did you see something?"

I shook my head, deciding it was much easier to pretend that the flash of orange, the other-realm laughter had been really nothing at all.

Besides, I was still angry with her for shouting at Mother.

If she was disappointed, she hid it well. "It is much harder to find true magic now than it was when I was young." She rose and held out her hand to me. "Still, it is there—and it alone can save us."

"Save us from what, Grandmother?"

She did not answer. In silence she touched the bark of the rowan tree against which she had rested, murmuring to it as if it, not I, had spoken to her.

I knew enough not to ask again. One of the first things I had learned from Grandmother was that she alone would choose what secrets she would reveal—and when and how she would reveal them.

We started back to the Hall and left the grove behind before she broke the silence. "You are my blood, my only living granddaughter. Now that your mother has turned from the path of her ancestors, it will be up to you to fulfill the responsibilities of the Sage Singer of the Ordovice."

Much as I loved Grandmother, she made me uneasy when she talked this way. I skipped ahead, concentrating on the narrow track that lead from the grove to the inner ramparts on top of Dinas.

"Don't worry, child," she called after me. "There is one who is coming to teach you. His name is Emrys the Hawk, although his nickname suits him better."

Curious despite myself, I let go of the wildflower stalk that I was picking. "What is his nickname?"

"Merlin. He is my son, although he lives in the north and I have not seen him for far too many seasons. He is coming to teach you magic, child. The magic of your ancestors that your mother denies."

chapter 3

So now I knew I had an uncle no one had bothered to tell me about. This annoyed me less than that this newly discovered relative was expected to teach me something. A new taskmaster—when I already had one tutor I hated!

In this I was in perfect agreement with my nine-sunturn-old brother Cynan, who almost broke my head the next morning pelting rocks through my window.

"Ass-wipe! That hurt!" Grabbing the stone that had grazed my cheek, I took aim at my prancing brother and lobbed it back. He needed to be punished.

A direct hit. Ha!

"Stop! You'll wake the whole Hall. Here, catch!"

The stone he threw was covered by ragged parchment tied with yarn cribbed from Hwyrch's basket. On it, Cynan—who could never find enough surfaces for drawing—had sketched a picture of two standing stones beside a hill barrow.

King's Rock.

Haunted and wonderful. A rare place to explore.

"When?"

"Today."

Hwyrch snored on her pallet behind me. I lowered my voice. "What about Celius?"

"What about him? He was drunker than Iorwerth last night. He'll barely notice if we leave him. Now get out here and help me."

Throwing on yesterday's tunic and trews, I grabbed my sandals and slipped past Hwyrch for the second morning in a row. She would not worry, knowing I was expected at lessons in the West Tower, where Celius, our Latin tutor, would pace, whining like a droning fly in a voice that could put warrior stallions to sleep. Our only hope was that, since Celius usually started his mornings drunk, he was easy to befuddle and escape.

I leapt down the stairs and joined Cynan, now idly pitching pebbles at the drooping dragon banner flying over the Warriors' Hall.

"Can Tali come?"

My brother looked solemn for a heartbeat. He started to speak.

I interrupted. "Useth's been beating him again!"

Cynan nodded and threw a rock as hard as he could, taking a twig off from the old oak beside the stables. Tali was Cynan's best friend next to me, a stable slave beaten far too often by the bullying stable master.

"Let's visit him tonight and tell him everything we saw."

"All right." Cynan still looked pained. "But listen, you've got to help. Ask Maeve for some food."

"Why me?" We were walking towards the West Tower by now, dread slowing our steps as we neared it.

Cynan rolled his eyes. "Because she likes you, midge-brain."

"Well, it's not my fault you stole her prize chicken."

"That was moontides ago—and she still hates me." We reached the bottom of the tower where the Latin master had his rooms.

"Now," Cynan shoved me. "Go to the kitchens, filch what you can. Ask Maeve, if she's in a good mood. Hide the food in the South Tower—"

"The South Tower? We're taking the tunnels?" A delicious shiver of nerves ran down my back. The tunnels were terrifying, at the center of the darkness that had been eating at me since my visit to Cunedda's chamber.

"Of course. Gwern has guard duty this fortnight. The tunnels are our only way out."

Cynan ran fingers through his shaggy brown curls, imitating our older brother Iorwerth planning a cattle raid. I wasn't fooled; he was as worried about the tunnels as I was. But Gwern was the only guard captain we had not managed to wheedle into our way of looking at things. If he caught us it would be a disaster: Celius would throw a fit, Mother would back him up, and Cynan and I would be conjugating Latin for the rest of our lives.

The tunnels it was.

"By the time you get up there, I'll have already started on Celius.

Just follow my lead and we'll be in the hills before the sun tops the pines!"

We clasped hands with a grin and went on our separate missions.

Kerinne, Maeve's oldest daughter, was in the kitchens. Her mother was nowhere to be seen—a good omen for our plans.

"And just where do you think you're going with that?" she asked as I loaded bits of fish and yesterday's venison into a sack that I'd already stuffed with fresh hot bannocks and a round of cheese.

"Just making a snack for later."

"Don't play me for a fool, girl. Here," she said, wiping the sweat from her forehead and handing me a delicious bit of honey cake. "Take this while you're at it. And say hello to the outside world for me!"

I stood on tiptoes to kiss her.

"Off with you!" She swatted my bottom, turning me to the open archway leading to the stables. "And don't get caught this time!"

I needed no second urging. As soon as Kerinne turned back to her bread-making, I skirted the courtyard, and made my way cautiously along the side of the Hall, heading to the ruins of the South Tower.

The presence of my dying Grandfather in the Northern Keep filled folks' souls with dread of the place. But fear of the ruined South Tower was much older and went much deeper. It lurked like a bad dream beneath the ramparts, in dark contrast to its view of the pleasant southern river meadow and the ancient copper mountain beyond.

No one went near it if they didn't have to. Even Cynan and I avoided it, until the need to escape overcame us.

As it had today.

Rotting air swooped down on me as soon as I entered the ruins.

Its roof had fallen long ago, leaving only jagged remnants of its existence behind. Taking a deep breath, I avoided looking up at the roof's sinister silhouette, concentrating on clambering over the pile of rubble in the doorway.

Inside, mist and shadows danced within the tall circle of remaining stones, spilling in through lichen-covered rock.

Something was watching.

Stones, rubble, and mysterious filth covered the once lovely multi-colored mosaic floor. Willing myself not to give in to panic—I was not an infant, after all, and had no business letting my imagination run away with me—I ignored the heavy, too-quiet hush of the place, walking carefully over the broken stones until I saw a rotting wooden beam that would do nicely, strong enough to support our food sack and keep it safe from rats until Cynan and I could claim it.

Something was behind me.

Nonsense.

Icy prickles ran up and down my spine. I bit my lip and climbed a mound of rubble to hang our food sack from the sagging beam.

Yes. There it was again. Rustling, soft and stealthy, behind me.

I cat-walked towards the entrance as quickly as I could without breaking into an undignified run. The rustling was louder now, ending in a noise that sounded like stones skittering down a pile. A sound that would happen only if something big was underneath.

I fought a scream and jumped over the jumbled stones that blocked the entrance.

Outside, taking in great gulps of wet morning air, I looked back. Shadows danced within mist and light. Nothing out of the ordinary. It had probably been only a loose stone tumbling from a pile of others. Or rats.

Nothing more.

I ran across the courtyard, dodging yawning warriors and freemen on their way to share food and gossip in the Hall. Iron pots and weapons clanged, ponies neighed, familiar voices and laughter barked through misty air. All the smells and sounds of the early morning world of Dinas came alive around me. Still, I ran as if pursued by the hounds of Anwnn.

My friend, the silent blacksmith Huw, scratched his nose wart at me in greeting, but even his molten-magic forge could not tempt me now and I pretended not to see fat Andelis struggling to carry her overflowing laundry basket. Any other morning, I would have stopped to help her, but fear and excitement pushed me on.

Were the stories about South Tower true? Some of the ghosts who moaned within its stones were rumored to be children. Folk even whispered that Grandmother knew more about them than she would say.

Why hadn't it been repaired? Why hadn't the Druids been summoned if evil spirits dwelt there?

Yet it was the West Tower—its high ramparts in good repair—that loomed above me now. *It,* not the South Tower, was the tower that waited for me. No fear of ghosts or slithering, foul-breathed evil here, no fanged soul-stealers were allowed. Only tedious lectures and the pain of fingers cramping after clutching a metal stylus for far too long.

I shook myself like a dog emerging from a lake. *Not today!* I threw my shoulders back and ran up the narrow inside stairs.

Celius and Cynan were well into a lesson, Cynan already etching crooked lines across a much-used wax tablet with the miserable concentration he reserved for collecting horse dung.

Celius stopped pacing to raise disapproving grey-watered eyes at me.

"Since you have already missed our discussion of the Second Punic War, Lady Gwenhwyfar," he accented every syllable of my name as if it were a foreign conjugation he despised, "you will begin by copying Livy's interpretation of Roman moral virtues and the sad lack of them amidst non-Roman races."

His high-pitched voice fell like owl screeches into the thick dusty air of what could have been a cozy room. With Celius living in it, however, the empty dressed-stone walls and the cold Roman death masks he'd hung on them made the room resemble a burial chamber.

I reached for my stylus with a sigh. He thrust a terrifyingly long scroll at me as if it was a throwing spear.

Cynan looked up from his own drudgery and winked. I revived. Escape was coming. Obediently, I began to etch the first characters of yet another dead Roman's words into wax.

The Gaels are factious and headstrong, and lack staying power; while the Greeks are better at talking than fighting, and immoderate in their emotional reactions...

My brother's first groans were so low, I barely heard them. His kick to my shins roused me and I looked up, squinting from the horrid yellow parchment.

Long ago, Cynan had perfected the trick of turning his face so pale that the freckles across his nose stood out like drops of black ink on white linen. He was making it happen now.

His groan this time was loud enough to bring the old crow to his side. "Cynan?"

"Magister Celius, I'm sorry, I—" Cynan's voice trailed off piteously.

"What is it, boy?" Celius' voice rose.

"It's my—my stomach, sir. I think I'm going to be—" without giving the old man a chance to stop him, Cynan doubled over and ran out the door. His rushing footsteps echoed, taking the spiraling stairs two at a time. Jealous, I turned back to Celius, plotting my own timing.

The crow wiped his dripping nose with a corner of his threadbare toga. "Continue with your studies, girl. When your tablet is complete, we will begin our discussion of the founding of the Roman Senate."

"But, Master Celius, what about Cynan? He looked very sick."

Celius raised his bleary eyes to the ceiling. "Your brother often suffers from a nervous stomach as I am sure you have already noticed, Mistress Gwenhwyfar. Best not pay too much attention to these attacks of his, lest through your misguided sympathy, he weaken even further."

I bit my lip and looked down at my tablet demurely. Celius was still talking, pacing the floor in small, dizzying circles as was his habit when he got excited or was roused to reprimand us for some reason. Cynan and I made him pace quite often.

"I despair at how soft you young people are becoming, Mistress Gwenhwyfar. Why, when I was a boy, far to the south of this barbarian muddle, we were not allowed to display any weakness. The least whimper, Mistress, and we were beaten within a hairsbreadth of our lives. The Roman way it was. The reason we conquered the world. No weakness should be tolerated in the young, no indeed. Why when I think—"

Lugh's balls, not this again. He'll never be quiet now.

I rose, pretending to shake. "Forgive me, Magister, but I must use the privy." It was a weak excuse and would buy us only a little time. But I could stand no more.

Without looking back, I too ran down the stairs. Celius' irritated shouting fell away behind me.

He would, I knew, do one of two things when he discovered we were not coming back. If he was angry enough, he would run to Mother and complain. We would then be beaten and lectured, but freedom was well worth it. Yet—if Cynan and I were very lucky—there was always the chance Celius would grumble to himself for a bit, then dig for the wine skin he kept hidden at the bottom of his clothes chest. After a few sips he would forget about us entirely, caught up in the dim world of his memories.

Celius had done this many times before, frequently enough that it was only Mother's pleas that kept Father from selling him to pirates. Father himself said that even pirates deserved better.

I jumped down the last three steps of the tower. Free! Taking a delicious breath of breezy smoke-filled air, I vaulted over a fox fur staked out to dry, skirted the twin springs that were crowded with women at this time of the morning, and edged my way past the smithy and the stables. I had started to creep along the sturdy whitewashed stones of the Hall, my goal, the ruined South Tower, in sight, when our friend Tali waved a pitchfork at me.

"Gwen!" He was just starting to muck over the churned mud and straw beyond the stables but his bare feet and oft-patched tunic were already filthy.

I made our secret sign for "Silence."

Obediently, Tali shut his mouth and smiled, a smile so wistful, it made me sad. How I wished we could take him with us!

Everything was always more fun with Tali along. Ever since Cynan and I had met him, a runaway infant like us, eating mud in the courtyard, the three of us had become fast friends. Only a sunturn older than Cynan, Tali could tell stories like no one else I'd ever heard, filled with gruesome battle descriptions or funny details that made me giggle all day. He could also play the harp well enough to attract the attention of my bard-souled brother Bran, the only one of my four older brothers who cared more for the singing of sagas than for the fighting of them.

If only he were not a slave, free to make his own way at Dinas! But Tali wasn't free; he had been captured by slavers as a baby and brought from a Dumnoni village to Dinas, where Father had bought him and his tiny hill-born mother, Bela.

Hwyrch said that unless the gods themselves intervened, Tali would most likely die without an honor price.

Not if Cynan and I had anything to say about it!

"Get over here now, boy—unless you want to feel my strap again!"

That rancid lump of lard, Useth, stood, leaning on an oak staff, in his usual spot by the stable doors, surveying Dinas as if he were king instead of stable master.

I sidled closer to Tali. Even if I could do nothing to protect him, at least I could remind him he had a friend.

"Didn't you hear me, boy!" Useth roared, taking a threatening step forward, his oak staff raised.

Tali rolled his eyes at me, picked up his pitchfork, and started back inside the stables. When Useth turned away and only I was looking, Tali pretended to throw it like a spear at the stable master.

"Bastard!" he muttered, speaking in the special language he, Cynan, and I had made up.

"Shitass," I agreed. "We'll meet you tonight in the grove."

Saluting in answer, Tali disappeared into the stables, his tall gangly form moving with more grace than Useth would ever dream of.

"Hurry!" Cynan hissed from behind the piled stones at the entrance of the South Tower.

I followed him inside, blinking as my eyes adjusted to the darkness.
"Did you bring flint?" he asked.

"What do you take me for? You're the one who always forgets it."

I had already dug my fire kit out of its pouch. As I worked to make fire, Cynan began to shove rubble away from the shadowed corner where it masked the tunnel's entrance.

We weren't supposed to know the tunnel existed, of course. Nor would we have, had it not been for our older brother, Iorwerth, who remembered well what it was like to be trapped inside Dinas at lessons when there were rabbits to hunt and worlds to explore. He had shown us the entrance on a dreary afternoon last winter when freezing sleet and short tempers had made Dinas more prison than home.

"Just remember to be careful," Iolo had said, rubbing his hands as he prepared to scare us to death.

"Never go down here alone. If you fall or hurt yourself no one will find you until after you are torn to pieces and eaten by the blood-sucking demons that lurk down here, waiting for stupid children. All that will be left of you will be bones. No more honey cake, no more racing down the hills, no more putting spiders in old Livia's porridge. You'll be just another ghost the old women will gossip about."

"Stop it, Iolo!" I giggled nervously. Then, as now, I looked into the heavy blackness that opened beneath us with a terror I was too proud to show.

"Ready?"

I nodded, not trusting my voice. I held the torch I'd lit with my flints over the hole and watched Cynan descend, our food sack tied over his shoulder. He used the stout rope we had fastened last moontide to the ancient iron hoop in what remained of a once massive trap door.

A heavy thump: he had landed. I slanted the torch down the hole, as far as I could. He reached up and grabbed it from me.

"Your turn."

Even the magic of King's Rock paled as I looked into the blackness.

The torch, in Cynan's hands now, flickered in an underground draft, a draft I couldn't feel. Torch-fire cast my brother's face in light. The rest of the tunnel just looked blacker.

"Hurry up!" Cynan looked into the darkness ahead of us and licked his lips.

I grabbed the rope, put my legs over the edge of the hole, and pushed off.

Underground air sucked at me: rank, heavy, frightening.

I slid down too fast, the rope burning my hands, and fell hard.

"Balls!" My knees were bleeding, the warm trickle almost comforting in the gloating darkness.

A sound like a sigh echoed down the tunnel.

"Come on!" Cynan's voice was higher than usual.

I followed closely, not wanting to be outside the tiny oval of torchlight.

Cynan reached back for my hand. "I don't want us to be separated. You'd get lost and than I'd get in trouble."

"Liar. You're as scared as I am!"

He made a sound that could have been a nervous giggle. "We turn here."

We turned. I screamed.

A skeleton leaned drunkenly against the earthen wall, strands of flesh and hair still hanging from its face. The back of its skull was shattered, the bones of both arms broken in two, its left hand missing altogether. Spiders scampered busily up and down its rib cage and up to its eye sockets, decorating it with huge, sticky webs.

"This wasn't here before!" My words echoed in the narrow tunnel. Too late, I dropped my voice to a whisper. "What shall we do?"

Cynan's hand began to shake so badly the torchlight danced in mad circles. I grabbed for it. He mastered himself and the torch steadied, illuminating a spot where dank uneven stones gave way to complete darkness.

"We're almost there. Let's go."

I jumped over the bones, not daring to look down. Who was it? How had they died?

We had almost reached the final turning leading up to the hillside cave and freedom when Cynan stopped.

This was the hardest part of the tunnel to get through. Not only was the passage very narrow but the rock ceiling, already unpleasantly close to our heads, dropped even lower, so that we were forced to crawl on our hands and knees. Under ordinary circumstances, we would have taken turns balancing the torch. But these were not ordinary circumstances.

Ever since we had entered the tunnel, I had been aware of a smell much worse than the usual dank underground, as if something ancient and dangerous were rotting. The level of moisture was much greater than it should have been. We had been down here often enough to know that the walls, floors, and ceilings of the tunnels were always damp, dripping with rock sweat and decay, and smelling of things best not dwelt on. But this moisture was something fouler than I had ever known.

It was thicker than water beneath our hands as we touched the stone walls that surrounded us and as slimy as pond scum beneath our sandals.

Pushing down my fear, I crouched, preparing to crawl on my hands and knees. The viscous liquid beneath me glistened in the torchlight. Its stench grew stronger, great enough to set me coughing.

"What is it?" I whispered.

My brother said nothing.

Wind whistled down the tunnel, coming from beyond the bend, from the turn we would need to take to reach the cave and its promise of safety. The sudden draft of foul air stirred the surface of the liquid in front of us, causing it to ripple in a way that made it seem to come alive.

Evil was stalking us. Great evil. I knew it in every fiber of my being.

I backed away, pulling on Cynan's arm. "We've got to get out of here!"

Cynan did not move. Guttering torchlight cast his face in shadow.

"Come on!" I tugged desperately at his arm.

He looked at me at last, his eyes stranger than I had ever seen them. "I think there's something—"

"No, there isn't!" To hear my deepest fears expressed was more than I could stand. "There's nothing down here! *Nothing!* We come here all the time!"

A new darkness danced into his eyes; he looked at me as if he had never seen me before.

Terrified, I threw myself into the muck on hands and knees, ignoring the horrible sucking sounds beneath me—the sense that one wrong move would see me gone forever beneath the greedy, death-scented ooze.

I crawled forward. It was hard—terribly hard—to move. "Hurry!"

I looked back.

He stood as still as a Roman statue. Drafts of tunnel air played with his curls as if they were amused.

The torch was almost out.

I heard a sound, coming from the turning just beyond us. It could have been the shifting of rocks or a draft of stale air whistling out of the many hidden pockets and caves.

But it was louder than either of these. Louder and lower. As if the wind had grown claws and was coming down the tunnel towards us.

"Get back!"

I flung myself up. Despite his shout, Cynan hadn't moved. Staggering, half walking, half crawling back the way I had come, I pulled myself out, one step at a time, from the mud.

When I had gained the relatively dry patch beside my brother, I grabbed his shoulders and screamed into his face. "Run!"

He shook himself like a dog reaching the shore.

"Take the torch!" he cried. "Come on!"

With one look to make sure he was himself again, I grabbed the dying torch from his hand and led us back, away from the mud, back in the direction from where we had come. He followed me in silence.

A great howling filled the tunnel behind us. I bit my lip savagely; if I gave way to panic now it would be the end of me.

"This way." Cynan's hand on my shoulder was as calm as his voice. There was a narrow cleft in the wall beside us.

"We'll be trapped!"

"Would you rather be killed out here?" It was really Cynan again. The eerie frozen stranger was gone.

Behind him, a rank fog was developing, gaining in thickness as I watched. It filled the tunnel, moving forward in waves, so overpowering in its stench that I couldn't breathe. Within it, something howled in hunger.

"Now!" Cynan pushed me through the tiny cleft. I made it, barely, and sank to the ground, coughing and crying.

His right arm and leg followed. "Pull!"

I yanked as hard as I could on his arm, ignoring his curses of pain as he tried to ease past the unyielding rock. Frantic, I braced myself and pulled his arm even harder.

Nothing.

Icy fingers gripped mine, adding their strength. Too terrified to do anything else, I pulled again.

With a cry, he tumbled through, landing against me so suddenly, I almost lost my footing.

I pulled him as far as I could from the opening. "Are you all right?"

"No, you idiot!"

The torch was lost. Whatever phantom had helped me free my

brother was gone.

It was too dark to see, but as I hugged him, I felt the deep rent in his tunic and the stickiness of blood across his belly where he had scraped it on the rock.

I pushed him. He toppled over. We laughed hysterically in the darkness, rolling on the filthy uneven earth.

Beyond our sanctuary, a great roar shook the tunnel. Its echoes died, but scraping sounds filled the silence, pacing. They stopped right outside the cleft, followed by short panting breaths like the sniffing of a giant hound. The scent was of something great and terrible, long dead, now risen.

Flames flickered across the small opening of the rock. Whatever horror lurked on the other side, it possessed fire.

Silent now with terror, Cynan and I slowly backed away.

What I had thought was only a tiny cave opened up beneath my groping fingers. Warm air brushed past us. Cynan's hand closed over mine.

"We're in another tunnel."

It was, indeed, a tunnel, and since we were stumbling in pitch-blackness, it was only a shift in air currents that warned me of its sharp descent.

Without any light to guide us, the feel of my brother's hand was the one thing that held me to earth, hoping we might find a way out of this terror. Clumsy as a babe in clouts, I followed him.

The air of this place carried the scent of living water, of hidden things that watched but were not evil—merely curious.

There was no more stench of death; the darkness was no longer frightening.

"Wait!" I called.

In our flight, I had forgotten I still carried my fire pouch. "Let's stop here. I can make a fire."

"What good is that without a torch? Wait—"

He stepped away from the tunnel wall.

"There's another cave ahead. A big one!"

He took my hand. We left the tunnel, stepping out into an open space. My senses agreed with him; wet rushing air, a lightening of pressure, the echo of something that sounded like lapping water all indicated that we had just entered a large cave.

"Hello!" I called.

Echoes danced back as if they were laughing.

A very large cave.

"I'll make a fire now."

Cynan said nothing, although I could hear him exploring. Picking up rocks, mumbling to himself. Useless!

"Did you bring *your* fire bag?"

He ignored me. Which meant he hadn't.

Luckily, he had me along. By feel I extracted my well-worn fire pouch, the flints and tinder would be enough to start a small fire. I tried not to think of how we would ever get enough fuel to feed whatever small blaze I produced. Beyond that fear was the greater one—how were we ever to leave this place alive?

It took a long time for me to start a blaze. Moody air currents and my own shaking hands worked against me, but finally a tiny flame kindled. I fed it what little fuel I had, sat back on my haunches, and looked around.

"Anu's Mist! Look at this!"

Our feeble light exposed a deeply shadowed cavern, with rows of stone pillars marching away into the blackness. The fire reflected on a lake, a lake so large that I could not see the end of it.

But that was not the greatest wonder.

"Trees!"

A grove of ancient oaks stood like sentinels in a semi-circle directly in front of us. Stunted in their upward growth, they had thickened into fantastic shapes, their roots coiled like dragon's claws ripping into the earth.

Beyond them, the waters of the underground lake lapped merrily at the pebbles along the shore.

I walked over to the closest tree, touched its bark in amazement. Then I laughed. "Look! A torch!"

For beneath its gnarled trunk lay a fallen branch, a branch both thick and straight when all its other limbs twisted like fisherman's knots.

I touched the oak's trunk again and chanted the ritual words of thanks, then raced with the branch to my dying fire.

At least, for the handful of time it took the branch to burn, we would have light.

My makeshift torch was quick to catch, but once alight it did not burn as quickly as I had feared it would. Instead, it burned even slower than the torches at Dinas, providing us with a steady glowing light that brought comfort as well as vision.

In wonder I looked at the grove of twisted oaks.

"Thank you," I whispered.

The branch flamed up higher, yet its light remained as steadfast as a candle.

I touched the nearest tree. It vibrated beneath me, with an old man's chuckle.

Cynan and I made our way through the grove, heading towards the lake. Around us on either side were the stone pillars I had noticed before, bordering the lake and extending beyond it in all directions like an army of warriors. Now I could see that each one of them was carved with runes in circular designs that ran up and down their length. Each pillar bore different markings, many were wildly beautiful, covered with designs of animals, plants, and trees. Yet I could not decipher any of them and felt a great yearning within me to know what they spoke of.

"Look—over here."

Cynan dragged me by the arm to the wall of the cavern. He stopped, speechless.

All around us were paintings of great and wondrous animals, drawn so large and so well it was as if they yet lived. There was a bird in flight, its feathers so clearly etched I could feel the soft breeze its wings would make as it flew past me. There crouched a grey wolf. There jumped a red deer. Beyond them were animals that I had never seen before, those great creatures that I had only heard of in stories or seen in dreams.

Cynan took the torch from my hands and wandered from picture to picture, raising the torch at each one to examine it more closely.

"What is this place?" I asked. The torch flickered, making the wolf's eyes glow and the deer begin to spring.

"I don't know, but it's wonderful, isn't it! Hold the torch, will you?"

He stopped at a picture of a great hulking beast with curved horns and a pelt shaggy enough to provide wool for our entire clan. Cynan began to trace the lines of the creature's body with reverent fingers.

"Whoever made these had great magic. Ah, Shadow, to draw like this—"

He gave off tracing and began to spin around and around in mad circles. "Oh, to draw like this. To draw like this. I would give anything—*anything!*"

I sat down, still holding the torch, and began to laugh with him. So near to the lake, the earth floor was damp and gritty with pebbles.

Soon we had both collapsed on it, the nightmare of the tunnels all but forgotten.

Something splashed, deep within the dark waters of the lake.

We jumped up, backing away from the water as quickly as we could, bumping into pillars in our panic until we felt the rough stone of the animal wall against our backs.

Everything was quiet.

"Let's go back and look." Surprised at my own courage, I picked up the torch we had lodged in the damp earth and ventured back through the rows of decorated pillars. Their runes were now glowing with soft fire.

I reached the lake. Cynan followed close behind me, muttering under his breath about idiots.

Whatever made the splash had disappeared by the time we got to the water, but the rippling rings of waves it left behind were great enough to disturb the entire surface of the lake.

"Could it have been a fish?" I asked.

"No fish I can think of would make waves that big."

We looked at each other in horror.

"Let's go around the water. There's got to be a way out of here," Cynan said.

We crept back through the pillars to the relative safety of the animal wall.

Before I could follow my brother, a desire to see the water one more time rose within me, as compelling as the smell of oatcakes baking in Maeve's ovens on a winter morning.

I turned back to the lake.

Cynan grabbed my arm. "Are you mad?" The torch shook. Shadows danced around us. "What's the matter with you?"

I shook his hand off, deep in the grip of something I didn't understand.

"It wants us to come closer," I told him.

The pillar's carved runes were now incised with fire. I walked between the rows. They burned as I passed, yet the stones of their columns were still cool beneath my touch. Like the trees, it seemed they were filled with a night sky's worth of stories, forever silent in the lost blackness of the cavern.

Small pebbles slid away from my feet and made tiny splashes as they entered the water. I crouched beside the surface of the lake.

The air grew too heavy to breathe.

"Shit! Get away from there!"

I shook my head and strained my eyes into the distance where the lake disappeared into the shadows of the cave.

"It wants to tell us something."

"It wants to kill us, you mean! Let's go!"

He grabbed my arm, trying to pull me away from the lake shore. I fought to break free of him. Before either of us could move further, ripples rose to the surface again, coming fast across the lake in our direction.

The ripples turned to waves great enough to crash over the lake's bank. Cynan jumped back with a shout. Our torch flickered weakly, went out, then flared up again, burning as loyally as ever.

A great fish surfaced, so close to where I sat, I could see my reflection in its scales.

I reached out to touch it in wonder.

"What seek ye here?"

The fish's language was not words, but thoughts that floated by so quickly they needed to be caught like summer fireflies before they could disappear.

Cynan crept closer. "Did you hear that?"

"Of course I heard it, midge-brain. Be quiet!"

The fish moved closer.

"I asked what ye seek." The thought-speech slowed and grew deeper, as if it were getting annoyed.

"W-we seek safe passage home."

Cynan shoved me.

The fish reared higher, until its top half was out of the water. With a sound like a sigh it landed its head on my knees, drenching me in water that was as warm as my own blood. Amazed, I stroked its silver scales. A salmon, larger than I'd ever imagined a salmon to be.

It flashed its mouth open in what looked to be a laugh. But fish did not even know how to smile.

Still, thought-peals of laughter echoed in my head.

"You small ones are fortunate that you have such powerful friends! Otherwise you would be going home in pieces!"

"What are you talking about?" The fish's weight was suddenly very heavy on my lap. "What friends do you mean?"

The fish said nothing; it just raised its great head to look at me, regarding me with one of its small black eyes, an eye that managed to convey amusement, sorrow, and wisdom within its depths.

In silence, it returned to the water, diving deep beneath the surface. A huge wake rose behind it.

"It wants us to follow it."

Cynan was still rooted on his knees, staring open-mouthed at the spot where the fish had disappeared.

"Come on, before it disappears again!"

Cynan still didn't move.

I left him, following the fish's wake. Rounding the curve of the lake, I looked back to see my brother rising at last.

"Hurry!"

As if shaking off a spell, Cynan took wing, running past me without a word.

The fish emerged from the water, a stone's throw ahead of him.

I picked up speed and caught up. "Together! Don't leave me in this cave alone!"

He nodded, breathless. This time when the fish disappeared, we both pelted along the shore of the lake as if whatever had chased us in the tunnels was still close behind us and gaining fast.

At the far end of the lake, the fish rose a final time.

"Through that opening, children. And remember to be careful where ye trespass. Next time might come a different end altogether..."

"Thank you." I turned to take one last look. But the carved stone pillars and expansive lake water had retreated into shadow, beyond the range of our fast-dying oak torch.

With a loud splash, came a thought-speak. "Go in safety, little one. Do not tarry."

The dark behind me deepened; its shadows no longer friendly. Rustling began from the invisible ceiling, gaining in strength as I hesitated. Wings?

The dead of the Rock await ye. Go!

The fish's thought-speak roared across the cavern, shaking the ground beneath us. A large rock crashed down, missing me by a hairsbreadth.

I bit down on a scream and ran to catch up with Cynan.

chapter 4

Fast on Cynan's heels, I tumbled out of the cave and into a forest of brambles. Terrified, we fought our way through, not caring that thorns snagged our clothes and cut our hands and feet.

When the thorns became impassable, I dropped to my knees and found passage beneath a low thicket. Crawling on my elbows for what seemed like a lifetime, I won free at last.

Cynan appeared a heartbeat later, his forehead and right cheek bleeding from deep thorn scratches. He leaned over, panting, and turned back in the direction we had come. "Look!"

A rock wall loomed above the chest-high thicket behind us. There was no sign of the cave we had just escaped. Lichen, grasses, even a few buttercups sprouted on the rock's surface, like stubble on a warrior's chin—as solid as my pony despite the fact that we had tumbled free from it only a hand's span of time ago.

A burial barrow. We had escaped from a burial barrow!

The grasses began to sway in a wind I did not feel anywhere on my body.

Gloomy even in sunlight, this barrow was not for the human dead. It was a resting place for the Tylwyth Teg. An entrance to the underworld.

A place from which no mortal emerged alive.

The wind came for us, pushing through the thorn thicket as if its deadly brambles were a field of barley.

I pulled at Cynan and tried to run. No use. My legs were no longer a part of me.

"*Move!*" Cynan yanked me on. My body resisted, still watching the wind with the same fascination that had taken me in the cavern.

"Move!" This time Cynan's shout broke through whatever spell I was under. I ran as fast as I could, running until I was breathless, neck and neck with Cynan.

We raced across the meadow, diving into the forest as if it were a welcome pool of water. After what seemed like days of dodging tree roots, holes, and branches, I stopped, too exhausted to continue, and dared to look back.

The wind had stopped; the summer woods were peaceful, heavy with afternoon sunlight. Whatever trap the wind had set, we had outrun it.

"Where are we?" I crouched, panting, beside a fallen alder, cursing the panic that had caused us to abandon our food in the caves.

My brother frowned at the slanting sun, dappling the tops of the willows on the opposite bank. "I think we're close to Ruag's hut—King's Rock is just beyond."

We found a stream and followed it. Trudging wearily behind Cynan, I was still pulled, despite my exhaustion, by a force I had no name for.

Just as the sun touched the tops of the western-facing trees, we came to all that was left of Ruag's hut. The once cozy wattle-and-daub cottage was sinking into the earth now that its maker, Grandmother's old friend Ruag, was no longer alive to protect it, although the old wise woman's magic still haunted the clearing, dancing in the play of a dragonfly above tall grasses, a whispered blessing beneath the breeze.

We stopped to rest, bringing fist to heart and forehead, then making the secret signs we'd been taught to make within a place of spirits.

A doe cautiously emerged from the ruined walls of the dwelling. Its large round eyes regarded me solemnly before it leapt into the shelter of the forest.

I smiled at the leaves that quivered with its passing. *Ruag,* I whispered and ran to catch up with Cynan.

The wind picked up as we reached the bottom of King's Rock and began to climb. It stirred the long grasses of the hillside and whistled past the great grey stones that guarded the king's barrow on the summit.

Shading my eyes, I looked up the gentle slope to where the two great rocks stood, as tall and proud and silent as death itself. What had they seen in the countless seasons of their lives? What did they know?

They gazed back at me in grandeur and challenge. Who was I but a little girl to them, these great stones who had seen the birth and death of dynasties beyond counting, the births and murders of great kings and queens, the execution of foul villains?

We reached the top. I drew close to Cynan, wind whipping at my hair.

We had come to our destination at last—this silent haunted tomb of kings.

The burial place of our ancestors.

We walked to our favorite spot, a great lichen-covered rock, half submerged in the earth to the right of the long barrow and the two giant stones that guarded it. The hill fell away beyond us and the forests and valleys of our clan lay, quiet and inviting, beneath the late-slanting sun.

Yet, even as we watched, clouds raced across the sky, casting shadows across the land, causing us to shiver in our summer tunics.

Something in the air ignited, waiting like the summer sky before a lightning bolt.

"Can we go now?" The question sounded foolish, even to my own ears. A silly, babyish question born out of exhaustion and the nerve-tingling fear that this day was not yet finished with us.

"It's a long way back. Let's rest awhile." Cynan did not laugh at me; a rude comment or a push would have made me feel much better.

I eyed the western-facing barrow as it caught the light of the descending sun. The long-finger shadows cast across it looked as if they were playing the harp—a harp I did not want to hear.

Clouds now covered the entire sky, plunging the hilltop into grey. The wind gained strength, shimmering the tall grasses as if they were the skirts of a high-born lady.

Tendrils of mist appeared, circling around us.

The great stone that covered the burial mound, shielding the dead from our eyes, rolled away without a sound. Like the breath of a giant, a plume of fog escaped from the opened mouth of the barrow.

Cynan and I clasped hands. In silence, we began to descend the hill, walking fast. At the least sign from the other, I knew we would give way to panic and break out in a run.

It was already too late.

A foul gust of wind rushed past us. Blinded by the chilling fog, I tripped over a stone. My battered knees began to bleed again.

The mist was now so thick I could not even see my brother.

I got to my feet, coughing, sightless, reaching my arms out— *"Cynan!"*

Hands emerged like ghosts through the fog. They gripped my arms. I sagged with relief at the warmth of my brother's fingers.

The fog retreated enough to form a tunnel of vision between us and the barrow. As we watched, too terrified to move, a twisting column of stinking air and hurling leaf ushered from its mouth.

The spiraling pillar of mist, dead leaf, and rock whirled, grew taller, gigantic, grabbing up mist as it danced up into the clouds.

A roar shook the hilltop, echoing death across the valley. Bits of leaf turned to gold-crimson scales. Spewing fire, a dragon lunged from the cloud, its eyes as dark as holes in the night sky, regarding us without mercy.

Air strong enough to push me to the ground whipped past, rising into the sky where the dragon hovered. Breath was wrenched from my own lungs, as if it, too, raced to feed the monster.

"Down, quickly!"

I was already kneeling, Cynan pushed me flat. Struggling to breathe, I held on to anything I could...to grassy clumps of soil...to flying rocks...to the lichen-covered half-buried stones that groaned as the wind tried to whip them free—anything to fight the up-rushing tempest that threatened to send me sailing like a bird into the hungry sky.

Grasses stood like spears in the vortex, the sky above us thundered with rage.

Cynan's shout fought the wind. "Look!"

Shielding my eyes against flailing debris, I looked. The great dragon poised above us grew smaller, its golden scales flying in all directions.

Falling to the earth, its fire mouth danced madly in front of me— no longer attached to its face.

The dragon's fangs melted like ice beneath the sun growing smaller...thicker...sharper; the fire behind them split into two balls, which writhed and spat like angry wildcats not more than a spear's length from where I lay, facing my last heartbeats alive.

The fireballs glowed like the coals of Huw's forge. The column of debris descended on them. With a breathless whoosh of air, raising a stench worse than any midden I had ever smelled, it arranged itself like a cloak around them and changed—teeth, fire, and all—into a great wolf that sprang towards Cynan and me with a hungry snarl.

I rose, screaming. Forgetting everything Grandmother and my brothers had taught me about predators, I raced like a blind puppy for home.

Cynan tackled me, then rose to face the wolf, hurling a warrior's curse into the nightmare wind.

I lay, frozen, already feeling the wolf's crushing weight on my back, his rank breath coming for my throat. But, instead of blood-chilling snarls and screams of anguish, I heard Cynan's voice calling out in wonder.

The wind died to a murmur, fog tendrils drifted past my still prone face like a caress.

I looked up and scrambled to my feet, amazed.

The wolf's red eyes had melted into the molten gold of sunset, its slavering jaws into soft white fur and twitching whiskers. A giant hare sat, regarding us with amused golden eyes.

Before I could take another breath, the hare's back began to shimmer, wings unfurling from its fur like spring buds.

"Get down!" I pulled Cynan behind the first shelter I could see, an ancient boulder weighted with lichen, moss, and stories.

"Why hide now? A hare cannot harm us!"

"It's not a hare!"

He looked back. The gentle muzzle of the hare was shifting. Before our eyes it grew longer, curved into the cruel, tearing beak of a hawk, a hawk that rose from the ground to hover above our hiding place, growing so large its wings were great enough to blot out our view of the sky.

With the triumphant cry of a hunter, it swooped for us, its gigantic talons reaching out for our flesh.

A blur of silver flashed. Cynan threw our only weapon, his meat dagger.

The hawk shrieked and tilted to one side, our dagger lodged in its wing. Mist rose to hide the creature from our eyes.

For many heartbeats the hill was silent, with only the newly thickened mist to remind us that nothing here was ordinary.

"I'm going to look for the dagger."

"Don't!"

But he had already left the shelter of the rock.

Screech! The hawk appeared again, diving towards Cynan. I raced across the wind-flattened grass, screaming in fury myself, grabbing clumps of rock and stone as I ran, lobbing them wildly at the wounded bird.

The bird circled away, landing beneath the tallest of the guardian rocks in front of the burial barrow.

Mist and wind deepened, circling around the bird. The hawk itself seemed to be watching us, its head tilted with interest.

Its shape changed again. Wings and feathers disappeared, its talons shrank, became human legs…a human back.

The hawk's sharp beak became a slender nose, a wide human mouth twitching in amusement, despite the blood running down its right arm.

I crept closer, too fascinated to be frightened. Grass rustled beside me. Cynan was coming too.

We were now close enough to see the hawk's golden eyes take on the color of new spring leaves, as green as the shadows of a fairy pool. Clothes materialized, covering his nakedness.

It was a man, a man even taller than my father who towered over all the men of Dinas. But a man nevertheless, dressed in clothing and jewels that caught the light of the westering sun, wearing the neck torc of a prince and the golden head circlet common to the lords of the North.

The man stepped from beneath the shadow of King's Rock, directly in front of the open mouth of the burial barrow. Waving one dark flowing sleeve into the air, he banished the mist from the hillside around us. With a second sweep of his hand, the entrance stone rumbled back into place, sinking into the great groove in the grass fronting the barrow with what sounded like a grunt of relief.

The stranger then turned to us.

"Hello."

Goosebumps rippled my skin at the sound of his voice. It was a beautiful voice, filled with the resonance of bard-song and the mysteries of trees at twilight. Yet within it was a thread of loneliness, the haunted cry of a gull lost at the sea. Despite its beauty and the wonders I had just seen, I turned to flee.

"Wait! I'm sorry if I frightened you. I did not know anyone was here when I began to practice."

Practice? I did not dare to turn around, knowing that once I did, my life would change forever.

"Gwen! Come here!"

I ignored Cynan, concentrated on not tripping over the mess of rocks and leaves the wind had strewn across the path home.

"Farewell then," the stranger called. "It appears I must make my own dressing for the wound you children gave me."

At this, I stopped and grudgingly turned around.

The man-being had taken a seat on our favorite lichen-covered rock. Cynan was already walking to join him, loping across the hilltop as if he were just setting out for a morning of fun, rather than landing in the midst of an adventure beyond our greatest imaginings.

I, on the other hand, was exhausted and not afraid to show it. Filled with misgivings and the sense of my whole life changing as surely as the wild wind had almost swept me up into the sky not long ago, I slowly retraced my steps and sank down in the tall grass beside Cynan. We looked up at the tall richly-clad stranger as if we were nothing so much as two babes wanting to hear a bedtime tale.

"I'm sorry about your arm," Cynan was saying, "but you frightened us. Who—what—are you?"

Busy tearing a strip of cloth from my filthy tunic to bind the stranger's wound, I glanced up to watch his face as he answered.

"I am called Emrys, Prince of the Votadini, a heatherlands tribe far to the north and east of here." Prince Emrys took the dirty length of cloth I had torn free and inclined his head in a small bow, holding it as if I had offered something worthy. With a flick of his wrist and a murmured incantation, he removed the dirt, tying it deftly around his own forearm.

"Thank you," he said solemnly. The wafting smell of healing burdock and boiled comfrey suddenly rose in the late afternoon air, although no such plants were near us. Producing a pack from somewhere, he pulled out a wine skin and took a long draught, passing it to Cynan with a wink.

My brother eagerly quaffed the unwatered wine, a forbidden treat that Mother only allowed on feast days.

Emrys took the wine skin and offered it to me. Puzzling over the stranger's name, I was reminded of something I could not place. I shook my head, too proud to admit I was parched.

He shrugged at my refusal and wrung the last of it into his open mouth. "That's thirsty work you just saw and my throat's been sore for the past fortnight as it is."

"How did you *do* all that?" Cynan's excitement was becoming irritating. Some strange tide within me would not allow this man to know I was amazed by his magic.

As if he sensed my confusion, Emrys smiled at Cynan, but addressed his words to me. "I'm afraid I cannot tell you that—not yet—and certainly not before I know who you are. The magic you unexpectedly stumbled upon is very old—not mine to give away at all."

"I'm sorry. You gave us your name; we forgot to give you ours. My name is Cynan, son of Cadwallon Long Brow, grandson of Cunedda Iron Hand."

"I am Gwenhwyfar," I added, still sullen. "Daughter of Ceridwen the Sweet-Voiced, granddaughter of Rhiannon Singer of the Otter Clan, Sage Singer of the Mountain Ordovice."

"You are Rhiannon's granddaughter?" Emrys' ringing voice rose in surprise. I had not yet noticed any clan marks or northern tattoos on any part of his face, but now he leaned forward, raising the long black hair that glistened like sealskin beneath the slender band of gold on his head. Three crescent moon shapes were incised above his temple in an arrowed pattern—the greatest honor to which a healer, Mage, or clan singer could aspire. Emrys was a Moon Singer, keeper of the oldest mysteries of all the tribes of Albion.

I could not resist. I raised my hand and touched the sacred tattoos in awe. Emrys smiled, a smile that lit up his face, making him look as young as my brother Iorwerth, who at seventeen sunturns still thought he could tell me what to do.

"I was given these by the Druid Helios in the northern highlands before I answered the summons to come here."

"Who summoned you?" All my earlier reserve had melted away. Now it was I, not Cynan, who jumped up beside Emrys on the rock, preparing to pelt him with questions.

"Why, your own Grandmother, the Lady Rhiannon. She said she had need of me." Emrys shifted his weight on the rock. The long scabbard he wore at his hip clanged against the stone, echoing across the sunset stillness of the hills.

"She gave a quiver filled with reasons," he added. "But the one I felt most important was that she is my mother—a mother I was torn from as a child."

So this was my uncle! The uncle whose coming I had dreaded.

Emrys leaned forward earnestly, staring into our faces as if taking our measure as warriors, not children.

"The second is that our land of Albion is now entering a time of great danger and unless we honor the old ways of our people, we will be lost forever—clan, tribe, and soul."

Emrys paused, looking out over the hills. When he spoke again, his voice was pitched lower, its cadence a spell of far-seeing. "The red-cloaks are gone, the Sea Wolves and pirates tear at us from all sides. We must remember who we are and unite as a people beneath the great dragon that roars to be unleashed—or we will perish."

As if exhausted by his own speech-making, the prince rose, locked his fingers and stretched his long slender arms to the sky, breathing a sigh of relief as his back cracked in response. Dusting the front of his fine linen tunic, he headed back down the trail to Dinas as if he knew the way already.

"Rhiannon wants me to teach her granddaughter the ancient mysteries that already flow within her blood like fire."

He rumpled my hair as he walked past me, then turned to Cynan. "And to teach her grandson Cynan the secrets of the warriors who first roused the war-dragon long before the red-cloaks set eyes on Albion."

"You are our uncle!" I ran after him. "Should we call you 'Emrys'?"

He turned back to me. The skin between his eyebrows reddened, a new crescent shape appeared, glowing with fire, disappearing as quickly as it had come.

"My friends call me Merlin, after the hawk I once found and nursed back to life as a boy."

"Merlin," I repeated.

Cynan skipped past us, leaping down the trail. "Come on! It will be dark soon."

Merlin and I stood for a heartbeat longer, looking into each other's eyes. In his I saw hawk, dragon, wolf, and hare flit across their depths, leaving behind the quiet darker greens of the mysterious forest, the place of my most secret dreams.

I could not look away.

It was as if the rocks and wind and trees had melted together and I was standing beside a god.

CHAPTER 5

"Prince Emrys, if you will follow me," Cynan gestured grandly across the short stretch of meadow that separated the forest edge from the great earthworks that formed Dinas's first line of defense. Sunset's gold turned black as it touched the sloping grass banks and glinted on the spear tips of two sentries.

"Cynan, Gwenhwyfar, who is this man?"

I closed my eyes in frustration. It was Gwern, no doubt inspecting the defenses as he did far too many times, not trusting anyone else capable. Sometimes I wondered if even Father managed to earn his respect.

"Your Lady Ceridwen's kinsman," Merlin replied, pushing ahead of us, "Prince Emrys ap Cerinneth of the Heatherlands Votadini."

Gwern stepped to meet him, spear at the ready. Our new friend casually brushed his hair behind the gold circlet on his head, exposing the crescent tattoos on his temples. Even in the half-light of day's end, they seemed to glisten with fire.

Gwern backed away. "Of-of course, my Lord. Enter in peace." Gruff old Gwern bowed low, bringing fist to forehead in the old sign given to the Hidden Ones.

As Merlin passed through the gates, Gwern shifted his attention to us. "Your grandfather Cunedda Iron Hand has gone into the shadows, children."

He looked us up and down sternly as if we were fledgling recruits for whom he was responsible. "Your mother has been seeking you both. She is not happy."

Cynan and I sidled past, not giving the old soldier the satisfaction of a reply.

It was not until we were well within the earthworks and approaching the wooden watchtowers of the second ring of defense, that I heard the wailing. Rising in pitch like winter wind against weak shutters, the mourners' cries filled the evening sky with anguish.

I drew closer to Cynan. Merlin let us approach the second ramparts ahead of him. Our friend Nudd stood guard in front of the high wooden wall which was reinforced with a spear's length of stone and earth and protected the bottom of our hill, encircling most of the small village that had sprung up beneath our fortress.

"You picked a poor time to go adventuring, rascals. Your grandfather has died and your mother's been scouring the breadth of the fortress for you."

Nudd nodded politely at Merlin. If the night were not so heavy with death, Nudd would no doubt have greeted him with his usual lack-toothed smile.

"It would seem you have fetched us a visitor. May I ask your name, my lord?"

High keening wails split the air, a frightening end to an unimaginable day. I ran up the hill, not waiting for Merlin's reply.

Night torches had been lit on top of the stockade surrounding the final gate high above me, seeming to dance in company with the ritual cries that echoed across the valley. Racing ahead, I wound my way through the haphazard huts and livestock pens that dotted the hillside, ignoring the curious crowd gathering to mourn Grandfather's death. The unexpected presence of a highborn stranger who looked like Merlin would have been cause for curiosity at any time. On a death-night such as this, it was cause for superstitious fear.

"There you are!" Mother ran halfway down the hill and burst into the crowd, towing Cynan and I roughly away. When she had dragged us far enough from the villagers to have some semblance of privacy, she let go of our arms.

"If you dare to move I will skin you both like a prize deer. Where have you been? Is it not enough that you decide to desert poor Celius? Must you also terrify Hwyrch, and waste the time of three servants sent to look for you instead of tending to their own jobs for the better part of the day?"

"But—"

She interrupted me with a furious slash of her hand. "No, of course it isn't. You had to pick this very day—the day your own Grandfather, the great Cunedda Iron Hand passes into the shadows—to go gallivanting. And where are you? Up to your usual mischief with no thought of anything in your heads but foolishness! Never mind that these forests are filled with pirates, never mind that you could have just as easily been captured by slavers as be standing here safe within Dinas' walls!"

"But Mother—"

"Don't try to talk your way out of punishment this time, Gwenhwyfar. You will be beaten. That is final."

"But Mother, we met someone. A kinsman! Your own lost brother! And he does magic and can turn into a—"

"Stop this nonsense immediately, Gwenhwyfar!"

"My Lady, the child speaks true. In this at least." Merlin stepped forward, eyeing me in a manner that silenced me quickly. "I am called Emrys, the name given to this very fortress. In the lands of my birth, I am called 'Hawk'. My father is Cerinneth, Lord of the Votadini, second husband to the Lady Rhiannon—your mother and mine."

He paused to gesture towards the eastern mountains and the towering peak of Yr Wyddfa.

"They were hand-fasted in the sunturn that she journeyed far beyond these mountains of her birth. It was a season of great grief for her, but my father remembers her with joy and has long wished that we be reunited, mother and son."

This speech seemed to render Merlin exhausted, for although he bowed politely and gave Mother the ancient sign of homage, fist to heart and forehead, I saw him sway as he waited for her response. I ran to support his arm. Only then did I see the effect his story was having on Mother.

Her back had stiffened as he spoke, as if she were a red deer scenting danger. She stood in absolute silence. Her deep violet eyes ranged up and down his lanky frame, her lips parted in shock.

In the lingering twilight, I saw the crescent tattoo rise between Merlin's eyebrows just as it had done when he first offered me his true name on the summit of King's Rock. His brow lit up with fire, as if an invisible artist labored beneath the surface of his skin.

Uncle reached for Mother's hand. She gave it. He grasped it tightly. The fire-light on his forehead vanished as quickly as it had appeared, as if it had received an answer.

A breeze danced between them, scented with Mother's imported

Roman lavender, although no flower was near.

"I am called Merlin by my friends, Lady."

Uncle's strained face broke into a radiant smile. He still held Mother's hand.

"It is an honor to meet you face to face. I grew up on tales of your family. Even in the Druid fastness of the Northern Crags, tales of Rhiannon, Sage Singer of the Ordovice, and Cunedda Iron Hand, scourge of the Scotti and conqueror of Gwynedd, are sung with honor in these dark times."

Mother reached out her free arm and clasped Merlin's wrist in the greeting of a kinswoman, her voice soft with wonder.

"And I had heard nothing of your existence until this night. Welcome Lord Merlin, to the lands of the Ordovice. Welcome brother, to this fortress that bears your name, Dinas Emrys. May your stay bring you peace and comfort."

"I thank you, Lady. Although it would appear I have come at a time of sorrow."

Mother shook her head as if dispelling cobwebs. "The oak branch has already gone out to the clans. My Lord's father, the same Cunedda Iron Hand you spoke of now seeks the Hall of his Fathers. His Death Song will be sung tomorrow when my husband returns with his war band."

Memories of the wild-eyed old man who had both frightened and fascinated me three moontides ago sent cool fingers of ice down my spine. I looked nervously behind us. Full dark had fallen, turning the looming palisades behind me into a fearful presence, ready to pounce. The last of the villagers had climbed the hill long ago.

We were alone on the hillside.

As if she too felt the strangeness, Mother briskly took Merlin's arm, guiding him back to the path.

Cunedda's death wails floated over the battlements, louder now that the ritual mourners had been joined by village folk paying homage to a man who had saved their families from slavery and death.

"Your children do you credit, sister." Merlin glanced back at us with a smile as we scrambled tiredly to keep up. "They offered me a most royal welcome when we met this afternoon."

"Be that as it may be, it was not their place to be dawdling about forest paths." Mother's tone regained its previous frustration. "Not when they should have been applying themselves to Latin scrolls."

Cynan opened his mouth. I elbowed him fiercely. Silence, I was learning, was sometimes the best response.

"I do understand your complaint, Lady—it yet seems strange to call you 'sister', does it not? But, I confess that, as a boy, I too showed a regrettable tendency to wander out of doors instead of applying myself to the theorems of Euclid or the mapping of the planets. Perhaps this wanderlust runs in the blood of our family?"

We had reached the torchlight of the inner ramparts. Merlin met Mother's skeptical eyes with his own of sparkling green.

Knowing she was being charmed, Mother gave in with good grace.

"As you say, Lord Merlin. Perhaps it does run in the blood. However," she eyed us as a cat does an insect it has decided to release, "that does not excuse either of you from the work you missed today."

A piercing wail split the night. Mother winced and sighed. "After Lord Cunedda's funeral, you must work doubly hard on your lessons. I will order Celius to make sure of it."

She ran her eyes over us—a cat still undecided if the bug should go free. "And I still think a few blows with a leather strap might help you remember that your most important responsibilities lie in the library—not the wild."

"Yes, m'am," Cynan and I murmured. We hung our heads, feigning repentance, careful not to let her see the joyous gleam in our eyes. If luck stayed with us, she might forgo the beating altogether. We just had to be very careful not to do anything else to make her angry tonight.

We began to creep towards the gate and the comforts of the Hall.

"Stay!"

We froze.

Mother turned back to Merlin. "Where are your companions, brother?"

"I came alone, Lady."

"Surely an unusual choice for a prince?" Her eyes narrowed with the same expression I had seen so often, when she did not believe a word I was saying.

"It is, Lady." Merlin inclined his head. "I ask your tolerance in this. Strange things are in the wind these days. I was told to come along pathways I am not yet free to share even with a new-made Queen."

Mother straightened her spine and opened her mouth to speak. Of a sudden, I saw the resemblance between them. Although she was exceedingly tiny and he exceedingly tall, both not only shared thick raven-hair but mouths full and rich for speaking and laughter and high-cheekboned faces suffused with a passion for life, song, and argument.

Perhaps Merlin, too, saw the resemblance, for he took her hand and bent to kiss it, killing whatever words Mother intended to say.

"I come as kin, and as a friend, Lady Ceridwen. I beg you accept my homage."

Mother nodded. "I will not press you—though I am filled to overflowing with questions." She gave a little laugh and removed her hand. "I believe you speak the truth. But I warn you, brother, if you think to betray this trust, the Ordovice are not mocked."

"Nor are the Votadini, Lady. Blood calls to blood in this unhappy age. We stand together."

Mother smiled and took his arm, leading us all within the final ramparts of the fortress. "You must be thirsty, Prince. There's mead to be had in the Hall. My mother—our mother—and her women are dressing the body of Iron Hand. They will soon join us and I daresay she will be overwhelmed to see you."

Mother looked Emrys up and down, appeared on the verge of speaking further, but thought better of it, adding merely, "Will you come with me and wait for her?"

Merlin's smile beneath the torchlight caught at my heart with its beauty. We were inside the fortress now and although folk politely gave way for us, neither the villagers nor the freemen and women of Dinas took their eyes from Merlin, whose circlet proclaimed him Prince and whose tattoos proclaimed him Druid. I knew gossip had already started.

Merlin inclined his head to us. "I thank you for your assistance, Lady Gwenhwyfar, Lord Cynan. We will see each other soon, I have no doubt."

Taking this excuse to leave, we slipped quickly away, heading into the crowded courtyard where folk huddled, speaking in whispers, waiting for Grandmother and her women to bring the body of Lord Cunedda Iron Hand, Snow Eagle of Gwynedd into the Hall.

Mother's voice found us before we had gone more than three paces. "Cynan, your brothers await you in the Warriors' Hall. Gwen, go to Hwyrch. She will prepare you for your part in your grandfather's passage to Anwnn."

Knowing it was useless to argue, we parted.

Frightened by the intensity of the mourners, worn to a cinder by the events of the day, I ran up the lonely stairs of the East Tower where Hwyrch and I shared a room every summer.

It was a large rounded chamber near the top of the tower that gave out on a lovely view of the mountains. But tonight the stone stairs were haunted with spirits and I forgot all dignity, running until I reached our room, diving wildly at Hwyrch, forgetting in my fear that I wasn't a small child anymore.

"Hsst! Little one, be still. You are safe now!" She rocked me for a long time. When, at last, I raised my head, she took a linen washcloth to my face.

"You are as filthy as a mud lark, child. Whatever demon possesses you to run wild in times like these?"

As always, I ignored her fussing. "Hwyrch, why do they wail so?"

She dropped the washcloth in its basin and gathered me into her arms, gazing out the unshuttered window into the ghostly night. "They mourn the passing of a great man, child. Your own grandfather, Cunedda."

"Why was he so great?" I made short work of the cold venison she had saved for me and snuggled against her lap, letting the wonder and terrors of the day fall from me as if they were but a cloak I could take off at will. I knew the story well but never tired of hearing it.

"Long ago, when your own mother was yet a little girl like you, dark times came to Dinas. Your grandmother, Lady Rhiannon lost all that she loved and left the Queen's Seat empty. She traveled far, and where she went is still a mystery, hers to share with you one day if she so chooses.

"She left behind a people racked with fear, beset by savages. Killers and pirates stalked these lands, enslaving our children, murdering our old ones, smashing the heads of babies against the stone walls of their parents' huts."

I always shivered at this part, and now I reached for Hwyrch's hand. She did not respond as she usually did, with a squeeze and a comforting smile.

I raised my head from the soft slope of her breasts. She did not see me. Her eyes were elsewhere looking into the darkness of the opened window.

"Hwyrch?"

She came back to me, but her eyes were wet with whatever she'd seen in the night.

"Aye, child. Those were harsh days indeed. So harsh that the clansmen cried out to the warlords of the South, to those who had set themselves up as kings after the red-cloaks left our shores. The Vortigerns, they called themselves, High Kings of all the isle of Albion— as if there could ever be such a thing—as if such cowardly filth could aspire to rule more than a dung heap."

She brushed the matted hair from my face, tut-tutting only a little at its condition. "Your grandfather, Cunedda Iron Hand of the Votadini, was the Vortigerns' kinsman, but he was a warrior true-blooded and the Druids asked him to stay to drive the raiders from our lands. The price was your Grandmother Rhiannon's throne."

"But where was Mother?" I was getting drowsy, snuggling into the fat curves of Nurse, smelling the familiar scent of her: night sweat, rosemary, and milk-stained wool.

"Ah, your Mother was safe in southern Dumnoni lands, in a fortress on the rocks of the western sea. She was not much older than you then, child."

I tried to imagine my regal mother as a disheveled little girl filled with schemes. I gave it up and went back to Hwyrch's tale.

"So it was that your grandfather, Cunedda Iron Hand came to Dinas, bringing his two youngest sons, Cadwallon and Maelgwyn. He left his oldest son, Urien, in the North to inherit the Votadini throne, for Cerinneth, Cunedda's older brother, was childless and loved Cunedda's Urien as his own."

Nurse shifted her bulk on the chair, adding as if the thought had just occurred to her, "No doubt, it pleased Cunedda to have two kingdoms beneath his hand."

I sat up in her lap with excitement. "But Cerinneth did have a son! He has just come to Dinas. His name is Prince Emrys, but his real name is Merlin, he was raised by the Druids—"

"Hsst, girl. If this is so, the boy was born after Cunedda came to the lands of the Ordovice, and has no part in this night's tale."

I subsided with a wiggle. Hwyrch carried me to bed and tucked my wolfskin beside me. She settled in beneath the covers and blew out my bedside candle, leaving only the small hearth fire and the night stars to light our chamber for tonight she would share my bed as she had done when I was a very little girl afraid of the dark.

Ever since I could remember, Hwyrch had driven my night terrors away. Her voice, with its song-like rising and falling and the mountain twang of her Decleangli accent, was the best medicine I could ever wish for against the poisons of my imagination and the monsters that lurked in the dark.

She raised her arm in invitation. I burrowed like a puppy against her body. "When Cunedda came, the clans despised him. He knew he must unite us or perish. Taking his sons with him, he set out to travel the length and breadth of our forests and valleys, going as far as the snows of Yr Wyddfa and beyond, as far east as the Wolf Lords of the Decleangli, as far north as the Albion Brigantes, as far south as the Silures of the flower-strewn sea cliffs. Wherever he went he fought every clan leader who challenged him in the old way—single combat before all their people.

"One by one, he defeated them," Hwyrch's voice dropped as it always did when she spoke of this impossible triumph.

"First the Otter then the Gull, then the Fox and Bear and Lynx acclaimed him as their Battle Lord and united to drive the Scotti pirates back to the sea."

Hwyrch shifted her giant bulk in the bed with a satisfied sigh. "He won every battle he fought in, save one. And that was with the skulking leaders of my own birth-clan, the Decleangli. Wolf Lords they call themselves, ha! Carrion-eaters would suit them better, for they know no way of fighting but to ambush and retreat. Cunedda never could bring them to heel, but he won all his other battles—and the hearts of our people, as well. Never forget, little one—before illness took him, Cunedda was a Battle Lord to rival the ancient tales."

"And his son, the Lord Cadwallon, is my father," I murmured, drifting into sleep despite the noise that wafted through the open shutters. The wailing mourners had quieted at last, but the night was still punctuated by shrieks and sudden bursts of laughter. Drinking had begun.

"And your mother, Ceridwen, is the daughter of Dinas' true Queen, the Lady Rhiannon, in whom the blood of the ancient Ordovice flows."

"Hwyrch, why do Grandmother and Mother fight so much?"

She did not answer. It was a trick of hers, pretending not to hear me, but I was too tired to nag her.

As the cozy silence between us deepened, I snuggled against her. She did not seem to notice. She patted me absently, but her eyes were far away.

Stroking my wolfskin, I remembered Mother's tale of Hwyrch's arrival at Dinas, four sunturns before I was born. I had learned of it only eight moontides ago on an unpleasant winter morning. We were in the Hall and Hwyrch tried to make me eat more porridge than I wanted. I was seven sunturns old then—far too big to be told what to eat. I shoved her away and called her fat and mean.

Overhearing, Mother boxed my ears, took me by the hand, and sat me on a stool in her chamber. She looked me fiercely in the eye and told me that Hwyrch had lost all three of her children to raiders, two killed before her eyes, the third taken south as a slave. After the raid, my nurse had climbed the hill of Dinas half-mad with grief searching for her beloved husband, only to discover that he had been killed a fortnight before in battle with the same Scotti who had murdered their children.

Mother's hands clasped the silver handle of her prized Roman hairbrush, looking as if she was about to use it on me. Suddenly, she dropped it and knelt before me, meeting my eyes in the way she did when she had something very important to say. I was never—under any circumstances—to disrespect Hwyrch again. Her husband had given his life to defend us and she had no one but us left to honor his memory and to protect her from starvation. Worse, after losing her own children, any insult Nurse endured from me would hurt even more than pouring salt into an open sore.

"Hwyrch?" I murmured.

She took some time to answer and when she did, her voice was sleep-mazed, "Yes?"

"I'm sorry about your children."

She was silent for a long time. "It does not bear to speak of."

The fire crackled. The night was quiet at last. I took her hand in mine. She whispered in a voice pitched so low I knew I was not meant to hear her.

"You are my family now. May Anu protect you from that which waits…"

cbApter 6

Grandfather's burial at twilight on King's Rock was the first highborn funeral I ever saw.

I was to be Grandmother's assistant and stood nervously beside the very barrow where Cynan and I had first encountered Merlin's magic. With both hands I clutched the ceremonial bowl of blue woad paste with which I had been entrusted, so awed and excited by the coming ritual that, at first, I felt no true sorrow at the death of the strange and terrifying old man who had somehow won my heart.

The funeral procession climbed up the hill beneath us, the litter bearers circling the spirals of the burial path instead of the straight hill track that ordinary folk followed. For when men carried the dead, their walk became a ceremonial turning and twisting, the same pattern that marked our dancing steps at the Beltane rites of spring. Life and death, Grandmother explained, were simply partners in the same labyrinth of life.

I risked a glance at her face now. She stood close to the open mouth of the barrow beside me. The wind whipped the folds of her white priestess gown and her hair danced within it, her braids woven with white gull feathers, her face as unyielding as the great rock behind us. She was no longer my grandmother, but the Goddess of Death come to take Cunedda's soul to the sky.

The wind rose, flattening the torches that the mourners carried, bringing with it a gust of dank air from the waiting grave behind us. Shivering, I shifted my grip on the bowl of woad.

"Hsst!" Grandmother grabbed my arm, the jeweled serpents of her armbands clinking as she touched me. My fingers tightened so much on the wooden bowl that they turned white.

"Easy." Mother's hands gripped my shoulders. She stood with us tonight out of respect for Cunedda, although her Cristos faith disapproved of what we did. The bitterness she felt towards Grandmother was apparent only in her insistence on standing as far from her as possible.

Merlin stood beside Mother, his presence a great comfort in the haunted twilight. He had been at Dinas only two days but I felt as if I had known and loved him all my life.

Holding on to the bowl with rigid fingers now, I looked impatiently down the hill, frightened by the wails and chants, willing the king's litter to hurry. Inside myself I remembered the old King's fierce eyes, the wonder I felt as he glared at me. He was gone now, forever beyond my reach. Taking a deep breath, I distracted myself with a study of the folk who held the torches to light the litter bearers' way along the labyrinth.

Their torch-fire illuminated unfamiliar cheekbones and strangely braided hair. Summoned from distant steadings, caves, and mountaintops, they had come down from the hills before the oak branch symbolizing Cunedda's death could possibly have reached them; as if his death song had traveled in the air itself and people had answered in the old ways, gathering weapons and offerings, hurrying down ancient mountain trails and forest tracks to honor a warlord who had saved their lives.

"Come," said Grandmother and led me to face Grandfather's body as the litter bearers lowered it to the wooden platform that waited for it in front of the barrow. They were grizzled warriors, survivors of Grandfather's old wars, save for my own two brothers, Iorwerth and Tegid and Father himself—the new King of Dinas—who walked five paces behind Cunedda's litter, his face set and pale.

"Look!" A warrior cried into the heavy silence.

Squinting into the darkening sky, I saw a lone eagle flying towards us, its harsh cry echoing as folk murmured in excitement. It circled the barrow where Grandfather would lie and rose again until it became a smudge of winged shadow disappearing beyond the eastern crest of Yr Wyddfa.

A spirit come to lead Grandfather, the Snow Eagle of Gwynedd, home.

Grandmother coughed, breaking the stillness that followed the eagle's passing. Her eyes were distant, her mouth set in the way it did when she faced a distasteful task. I watched her raise her arms in blessing over Cunedda's body and thought about Hwyrch's story, wondering how

Grandmother must feel to see a man she resented, a foreigner from the eastern heatherlands put to rest beside the High Kings and Queens of her native clan.

I looked from Father's grim face to Mother's thoughtful gaze behind me. Perhaps it was destiny or perhaps merely the luck of the Goddess that Cunedda's son, Cadwallon, and Grandmother's daughter, Ceridwen, had met one morning in the forest. Father had been hunting, Mother herb-gathering. They had loved and married, uniting Cunedda and Grandmother's lineage.

But Grandmother had neither forgotten nor forgiven Cunedda's seizure of her throne. So, it was with ice not normal to the rich tones of her priestess' voice that she recited the ritual words of our people, blessing the spirit of the dead, asking our ancestors to grant Cunedda safe passage to the ghost halls of Anwnn. Her fingers were firm on his brow, however, and her voice rose in pitch as she nodded for me to come forward with the woad.

I held it high for her. She dipped her long calloused fingers into the sacred paste and marked the dead king's sunken cheeks and forehead with the ceremonial swirls that would gain him admittance to Anwnn.

The brief summer night had fallen completely—an eerie dark moon night. The dancing spiral of torches beneath us provided the only light besides the stars that shone like sparks of fire in the open sky.

A chant rose, a sad soft drone, like a lover's goodbye.

One of the bearers stepped apart from the group and knelt beside the corpse. Surprised, I recognized the ill-tempered servant who had chased me from Grandfather's side earlier in the season.

The small brown-bearded man stepped back two paces, rent his tunic from neck to chest, and reached for the dagger in his belt. Without bothering to watch where his blade fell, he cried out in misery, and stabbed at his own chest and arms.

Blood ran in small streams down his body. His voice rose in a great wail, ululating like a wolf's, echoing across the valley. When the last of it died, he placed one hand upon Grandfather's brow and addressed us all; recounting the deeds Hwyrch had told me. When the great tale of Cunedda was finished, the singer slashed his chest deeply, pitched his voice higher, and lifted his cupped hands to the stars, filling the final stanzas with his own heart's cry:

It is the death of Cunedda that I mourn and shall mourn
Between the brine and the high slope and the fresh stream water,

As the sighing of the wind over the ash wood,
He who was brave, unyielding, fierce,
He who granted me cattle in midsummer; he who granted me
horses in winter
Is now cut off by the Lord of Death.
Grief wakes me, holds me beneath dark wine
The sleep of the ancestors is destroyed.
Lord Cunedda,
The sleep of the ancestors is destroyed.

Absolute silence followed the end of Grandfather's death song. The call had been made. Grandfather's ancestors now knew that he was dead and would be on their way to greet him so he could enter the realms of the dead a hero as great as he had once been on earth.

The strange man with the beautiful voice bowed to the body of his lord and slipped away into the night. I never saw him again, but for ever after, I carried his song in my heart.

The sleep of the ancestors is destroyed, I whispered, watching the litter bearers carry Grandfather into the barrow. The voices of the people were raised in song again, a melody I recognized as the parting of the waters, a chant designed to send the dead peacefully away from the living, so they would not return to haunt our forests and dwellings.

Father followed Grandfather's body into the very mouth of the barrow. He too had ritually cut his arms and chest, so that flowing blood partially masked the dragon on his arm. I could still see it though, flashing beneath the running blood. Torchlight flickered for the last time on the thick gold torc on Cunedda's neck and on the hilt of the great sword that rested upon his breast. Then his body disappeared into the yawning barrow—the old King's new Hall beyond the worlds.

Impressed by the solemnity of the occasion, sorrowing for the Grandfather I would never meet again, I sought my brother Cynan and found him across from me surrounded by the warriors of our older brother Iorwerth's war band. Seeing him in this enviable company, I raised my nose into the air and turned back to take Mother and Merlin's hands.

They let me lead them down the hill, following the people's descending torches as we began the long walk back to Dinas where a great feast had been prepared and the mourners could revel the night away.

Indeed it seemed as if the reveling had already begun, for as soon as the old King was placed within the barrow and the great stone rolled to block the entrance again, folk began to call out to each other in such joyous tones that I knew I was not the only one to be relieved that we could now leave the dead behind us, brooding on their eternal hill.

Midway along the forest trail, I turned back to look for Grandmother. I heard her call me without words, for when I found her she was standing still, staring into the blackness of the trees, oblivious of the passing tribesmen. "What is it?"

She shook her head. "Ssshh! Will you never learn to be quiet?"

I bit my tongue before I could tell her that the folk around us were making far more noise than me. I knew it would be useless to remind her of such a thing. Where I was concerned, Grandmother was unlikely to be fair.

I waited until the last of the crowd had gone beyond us, hurrying towards the delicious meal and exciting stories that awaited them in the Hall.

"There is something I must do tonight," she said.

"What?"

"Nothing that is of concern to you."

Then why didn't you tell me to leave you alone? I thought, rebellious.

"I had hoped you might have sensed them too, but I guess it is too early to expect such things," she sighed, gripping my hand more tightly than necessary as she started to walk towards Dinas.

"What things?"

"Must you sound like a magpie? What? Who? Where? Why?"

I was grateful the blackness of the night hid me from her eyes. Her words were bad enough. Yet perhaps a new spirit had entered me at Grandfather's tomb, for I spoke before I could stop myself.

"Grandmother, why are you so unfair? You say you want to teach me things, but you don't like to answer any of my questions. I'm just supposed to puzzle things out by myself. And I can't. Most of the time, I just can't."

She dropped my hand. I heard a muffled grunt that sounded like laughter.

"Are you all right?"

It was laughter. "Of course, I'm all right."

Her cold hard fingers reached for my hand again. "Just surprised. You are right, Gwenhwyfar, of course you are. I am becoming a foolish old woman, as arrogant as that usurper Cunedda before the gods froze his limbs."

"Grandmother!"

"Don't be shocked, child. I but speak the truth. Now, as for this other matter, I had hoped you heard the forest ones calling. But it is too early to expect such ability on your part. You must forgive me, I am rushing you again."

I stumbled on a stone. She helped me right myself. I could sense her thinking, hesitating. She spoke at last just as we reached the earthworks of the outer palisades.

"Daughter of my daughter, you must understand the forces that are gathering against us—from this earth realm and from beyond the mists themselves. Our time together grows short—and there is much to teach—"

"Then teach me. What was I supposed to hear?"

She shook her head. "To describe it is to lessen its power. The forest ones speak in the voice of the wind, in the rustling of grass, in the screech of an owl. Do you not hear them?"

The yearning in her voice was so raw, I tried even harder to hear something more than the night. But there was nothing.

"They are your kin," she added so softly, I could barely hear her, "the *estethra*..."

"The *estethra*?"

"Shh! They will not come if they hear you speak their name. It is given only to those whom they permit to see them."

Before I could ask any of the questions bubbling like cauldron water inside me, she shook her head, gripped my hand tightly, and added in a voice that permitted no further discussion, "Quickly now, or we will be late for the feast."

Later, as Father claimed the High Seat for the first time and raised his mead horn, a new-made king, in honor of Cunedda, I was not surprised to see that Grandmother had left the Hall.

I crept away to look for her, but even as I climbed the eastern ramparts and strained my eyes against the night, I knew that I would never find her in the endless shadows of trees and mountains that stretched beyond the fortress. I balanced on a block of stone, standing on tiptoes at the top of the highest palisades of Dinas, searching the eastern horizon for Grandmother. Beyond the sentries on the ramparts, on hilltops that ringed the lake of Dinas, great watch-fires burned high and fierce to light Cunedda's path beyond the stars. But no matter how hard I squinted into the brisk night wind, I saw no sign of Grandmother, the Priestess Rhiannon.

Nor did she return for a full handful of days after Father took unto himself the power of the land and was crowned King of Dinas Emrys, Lord of the Mountain Ordovice, head of the clan of the Otter and, by right of Cunedda's treaty, overlord of the Fox and Gull clans.

Yet, when, at last, Grandmother did return from the forest, she, too, had changed. She had grown softer, less bitter. Hesitantly, she and Mother seemed to reach an understanding. The shouting between them stopped and laughter filled our Hall once more.

I was greatly glad of it—for I loved Mother and Grandmother as I loved both sun and moon. But a new word had entered my heart, and, just like Grandfather's death song, it was never to leave again. I whispered it softly as I explored the forest with Merlin and Cynan, and as my tall handsome uncle explained the wonders to be conjured from simple stones and trees. I muttered it in boredom during the rare visits of Mother's Cristos hermit to our Hall. I played with its syllables as if they were an incantation as I drifted to sleep at night, "*Estethra…estethra…*". Careful never to speak it aloud.

What it was, what it meant, I did not know. Only that the sound of it brought magic to my heart, as if everything I ever dreamed was possible.

I determined that, no matter who or what tried to stop me, I would discover what the *estethra* were and what I had to do to find them.

Meanwhile, the phantoms that lay between Mother and Grandmother were rising again, like nightshade in a winter stew.

chapter 7

No sooner had Cunedda been sent to the gods then Scotti pirates launched renewed attacks along our coasts. On the same windswept morning Father and Iolo left to fight them, Father sent the rowan branch of treaty to our eastern neighbors, calling for a gathering of allies during the approaching harvest festival of Lughnasa.

Amidst the bustle of a fortress readying for both feasting and war, I slipped out to follow Grandmother Rhiannon as she gathered herbs beside the river. Fidgeting with impatience, I watched as she waded into the reeds, healer's knife at the ready, homespun skirt belted above her knees.

At last she rested beside me on the riverbank.

"Grandmother, tell me of the *estethra*." I asked, careful to keep any trace of pleading from my voice.

For the space of a breath, her ancient face reflected the pain of a trapped bird who knew not what direction to fly. There was terror, I was sure of it. Then, quickly, her eyes took on the opaque blackness of a priestess: her look the scathing glare I dreaded. "Were you meant to know of them, they would have come to you."

Risking her temper, I asked again. Furious, she dropped the root bulbs she'd been sorting. "Speak no more, girl! Unless you seek the hiding of your life!"

I ran then, up the hill, angry, but determined to uncover the mystery that seemed yet one more bloody sinew of what stalked the Halls of Dinas. Instinct pushed me past the door of Mother's chamber where she stood, weaving at her loom, humming softly as woad-dyed blue yarn danced beneath her fingers. The old Cristos hermit sat, crouched beside her on a stool, his guttural speech falling like drumbeats in the sunlit air.

"Mother, do you know of the *estethra*?" She stilled her hands. Several heartbeats passed in silence before she spun around, her normally placid face as treacherous as a frozen river, surging with deadly currents beneath. "Do not speak of such things, Gwen. They are pagan madness."

"But, *what* are they?"

Before she could answer, Grandmother pushed through the door, followed by two of Father's hounds.

Seeing her, the hermit rose stiffly, "It is time I returned to the forest, Lady, where I can worship Our Maker in peace."

"By all means, seek the forest, you lice-ridden madman." Grandmother watched stonily as the hermit laid his dirt-encrusted fingers on Mother's head, murmuring a blessing in sonorous Latin.

Grandmother lifted her skirts to avoid contamination as he stalked past her, then sank to the bed and began to braid my hair.

But her words were not for me. "Have you indeed forgotten all that matters, daughter?"

Mother spoke to her loom. "I want no part of your lies. It is your old ways that have doomed us."

"You cannot—"

"Leave!" Mother spun to face us, her eyes flashing fire. Seeing Grandmother's hand on my head, her voice broke. "Leave me, both of you."

Grandmother pushed me before her, deserting me quickly on a bench in the Hall. She stopped my protest with one upstretched hand. "This is what comes of asking for what is not yours to know. Do not speak of it again."

She stalked out of the Hall, leaving me to the mercies of the servants.

Daughter of the ruling house or not, I was soon fetching and carrying in the hurry to ready Dinas for the harvest celebration. Knowing further speech was useless, I found solace in the tasks they asked of me. Yet my unquenched heart ached. As I helped grind barley in the kitchen and carry water from the spring, I vowed to get to the heart of the mystery. It was *mine* to know too, no matter what Grandmother said.

Father's war band was victorious and a fortnight later, he and my brother, Iorwerth, galloped back to Dinas in high spirits. They left my oldest brother, Tegid, on the coast to finish off what was left of Gormach's surviving brother, Nestor Lack-Tongue's, forces.

We had already heard from all the clans Father had invited, save for the Decleangli Wolves. All were coming to Dinas; there was a new stirring in our northern mountains. All wanted to meet with the new-made King, while the memory of great Cunedda's Death Song was still fresh in their spirits.

Father and Iolo rode into the courtyard, their laughter ringing out across the bustling fortress. Cruach, Father's messenger to Chalan, Lord of the Decleangli Wolves, had been waiting for them and raced past Tali and I as we mucked outside the stables.

Breathing with the trained breath of a runner, Cruach knelt in front of Father, speaking carefully memorized words:

"Chalan Grey Sword, Lord of the Decleangli Wolf Clan sends this message to Cadwallon Long Brow, Lord of the Ordovice Otter Clan, would-be Lord of Albion: Greetings. I thank you for your invitation, yet as Lord of the Eastern Passes, I have duties more pressing than to feed a new king's vanity." Cruath paused nervously as Father's face lost all traces of joy and Iorwerth began to curse in a low threatening monotone,

"I am sorry, Lord," Cruath added.

Father dismounted and led his war pony into the stables, flinging his reins to Tali and giving me the arched eyebrow that meant he knew I should be elsewhere—studying with Celius or weaving with the women.

"You serve me best by speaking true," he said to Cruath, then gestured to Iolo, who had just thrown a spear at a nearby tree. "What else did our lord of the dung heap have to say for himself?"

Cruath jumped up from his kneeling position, pushed tangled hair back from his face, took a deep breath, and continued. "His court laughed into their drinking horns, Lord, and Chalan spoke again, 'I fear indeed that I have caught a summer cold that has weakened me so greatly I must spend Lughnasa in bed nursing it with possets.'"

"Anything else?"

Cruath shook his head, the wild curls he had inherited from his father Nudd bouncing like babes at play.

"You have done well," Father continued in the deceptively soft voice he used just before he exploded into one of his rare rages. "Now go, seek your ease in the kitchens. I believe Maeve has just made some venison-pasties."

Cruath's earnest face lightened at the thought of Cook's famous cakes.

As Nudd's son bowed and disappeared through the wide stable doors, Father pulled free the spear Iolo had embedded in the tree, hefted it for balance, and tossed it back to my brother.

"Son, I know the loss of your red cattle rankles still."

Iolo caught the spear one-handed and clasped Father's forearm in glee. "Chalan's herds feast this very heartbeat on the tall sweet grass of their summer pasture near Giant's Leap."

Smiling at Tali, and winking at me, he followed Father to the stable door where the afternoon sunlight greeted them.

Father turned in the stable doorway and gripped Iolo's shoulder.

"It would appear you've kept a hawk's eye on these Decleangli cows."

I sidled closer, pretending to muck out my pony's spotlessly clean stall.

Iolo's smile flashed and was gone. "Chalan's herds are rarely far from my thoughts. I only seek the opportunity to relocate them to our pen."

Many folk still saw my brother Iolo as a prankster filled with mischief and fun. This indeed he was and had been since he was a boy. But it was just one face he liked to wear—a Beltane mask that disguised him well. He was more than that, much more, and as he plotted the cattle raid with Father, his good-humored voice dropped, taking on the bite of a sudden bitter wind. When Iolo hated, he did not forget.

And he hated Chalan. For the Decleangli Wolf Lord had made it a habit to raid our cattle every few moontides, growing increasingly bold as Cunedda's poor health crippled our defenses, leaving Father's war band unable to fight the Scotti and raid the Decleangli as well.

Quick as Iolo was to mock others, my brother's pride was legendary. His manhood could not laugh at the insult that Chalan offered.

"Here." Father picked up stable master Useth's abandoned oak staff and began to sketch into the dirt at the stable door. Iolo squatted beside him, adding pathways with his fingers.

I worked my way closer. Finishing with Father's pony, Tali picked up his rake and joined me. Father saw us from the corner of his eye, but said nothing.

"You think the gorge beneath Giant's Leap?" he asked.

"Aye, it's perfect." Iolo's voice took on a leveled tone, although both a chuckle and bitterness were just beneath the surface. "We can hide in the tree grove when they lead the cows through and take them after they enter."

Iolo drew two lines in the dirt. "We'll attack from both sides. They won't be expecting us at all—it will be like taking honey from dead bees."

Father sank back on his haunches with a satisfied grunt.

"The taste of such honey will be welcome. Chalan has had it his way for too long. The Decleangli won't think we'd dare!"

Iolo rose and stretched like a cat, kicking the stable mud so that their hastily-sketched map disappeared.

"We'll leave tonight, Father. I just wish I could see the bastard's face!"

"Eating his cattle will do just as well." Father gripped my brother's arm in farewell.

"Take my blessing upon your head, son. My shield upon your arm. Ride swiftly. Fight well. Return in triumph."

Iolo grinned, the lopsided smile that made women rush to serve him in the Hall. He remembered his manners long enough to bow and then ran to gather his warriors, skipping across the courtyard like a boy.

Father paced the battlements while Iolo was gone, restlessly looking to the east where the Giant's Leap lay. Meanwhile, the kitchens were in a frenzy, with Cook Maeve and her daughter, Kerinne, running about like determined boars chasing the last acorns of fall. Even I did not dare Cook's displeasure, and spent my days with Cynan, or trailing after Merlin and Grandmother on the mornings Cynan was summoned to train with the warriors. We ignored Celius entirely, and Mother was too busy with her preparations to threaten us with more lessons.

Cynan and I never spoke of the nightmare day when we had first met Merlin. Yet I was haunted by it and I knew, by the troubled new glint in his eye, that my brother was as well.

On a night soon after Iolo had gone, I dreamed of burning runes marching across a night sky as giant fish danced down the hillsides of Dinas on spider-thin legs. Grandmother appeared, covered with blood, screaming as she carved into her own breast with a knife.

I woke, frightened, to a morning of cold wind and hard rain, as if winter wanted to send us a message it would be here all too soon. I ran downstairs before Hwyrch could catch me and was wiping crumbs of bannock bread from my mouth when Iorwerth's Shield Brother, Eiddwen, ran into the Hall and bowed to Father. He was dripping wet and grinning.

"My Lord, your son returns. Although he makes slow progress due to a large and unfamiliar herd of cows!"

"Ha!" Father jumped up from the High Seat and slapped Eiddwen heartily on the back. "Good news at last! Take yourself to the kitchens, lad, and tell Maeve to give you of her best! Gwen, come with me!"

Father took my hand and together we ran up the steep winding stairs of the East Tower, passing the door that led to my summer quarters without a glance. We reached the top, pushed against the heavy door leading to the battlements, and were immediately deluged with wind and rain. Father bundled me in his cloak and held me close, letting me sit on top of the tower ramparts, safe within his warrior-muscled arms.

The wind attacked us both, whipping my hair free from its braids. Although the wind beat just as hard against Father, it was powerless to move the long brown moustaches he kept so carefully limed. It did toss his long, free-flowing hair about his face where it mingled with my own, creating a soggy cloud of brown and red-gold.

In the distance, emerging from the thick trees beyond the earthworks, Iorwerth appeared. He and his war band rode out from the dark forest track, driving a herd of shaggy red-brown cattle single-file along the muddy trail. We watched them come on across the meadow in front of the outer ring of our defenses, the cattle lowing in confusion as Iolo's warriors rode, cursing, up and down the line. The hooting sentries at the guard post waved, cheering them inside.

The rain increased in spate as Iolo's men drove the Wolf Lord's cattle into the livestock pens midway up the slope beneath Father and me. Fierce wind and dagger-sharp rain brought on another chorus of cursing as men fought to drive the frightened cows inside the high fences of their new home. From where I sat, perched almost directly above them, the milling cattle looked like a drenched patchwork cape of red, brown, black, and white, mooing in distress at this miserable disruption of their lives.

My brother broke free of the cattle pens and rode up the track beneath us. Rain lashed his thick red hair into wet ropes across his face. He saluted Father and then broke into a laugh, pumping his muddy fist wildly in the air.

"Great Lord Cadwallon of the Long Arm and Balding Brow, I bring you a king's ransom in flea-bitten cows!"

"I thank you, son." Father's attempt at regal dignity failed. "Get up here, boy! I knew those rapscallion tricks of yours would pay out sooner or later! Now go—and tell your mother to broach the Old One's mead this night! The whole steading is welcome at our board!"

Still laughing, Father spun me around in a circle, backing away from the edge of the ramparts. "So Chalan thought he'd have my balls for porridge, did he?" He spun me again. "God, but it's good to be King!"

I giggled and couldn't stop giggling as he spun me higher and danced across the battlements. He threw me up and I spread out my arms. The world became a twirling mass of green muddy earth beneath and dark rain-pelting sky above, my vision a dizzy view of rain, black sky, high green hills, and trees.

At last he stopped and I rested against him, my nostrils filled with the wet wool smell of his workaday tunic, looking happily past his shoulder at the comforting stones of the inner wall of my home. He kissed the top of my head and let me sit upon the rampart again, dangling my bare feet over the edge of the great tower in a position that would have set Hwyrch to screeching. Queen of all that my eyes could see, I was still glad of Father's firm hold on my waist.

I had just enough time to imagine the wind into a dragon and I poised upon its back, ready to fly across the world, when Father swung me up again. He set me on his shoulders and carried me inside. We started down the steps, I still dizzy with rain and power and joy. We walked more slowly this time, in dark, descending circles that never seemed to end, our way lit only by torches set in brackets on small landings here and there. The gloomy inside walls of the tower seemed to close in on us and I played my old game of trying to touch both sides of the wall and still stay balanced on Father's back.

I was just reaching out for a peculiarly shaped stone that protruded from its smooth neighbors like a vulture's beak, when Mother rounded the stairs and saw me, arms outstretched, wet and dirty as ever.

"Gwen! Get down from there this heartbeat!"

I could feel Father's amused shrug as he reached up to deliver me to Mother.

"Do not be too harsh with her, Ceri. It was my fault as well—this time at least."

"It is you I seek." Nevertheless, Mother grabbed a handful of my tunic when I tried to slip by her. "And don't *you* move!"

"What is it? Have you seen Iolo? He just lifted four winters' worth of cows."

Mother's mouth thinned. "As if he had no better activity to occupy himself—and he a prince. He is no less a thief than Chalan!"

Father laughed, trying to slide past us. Mother stood her ground, blocking the stairs. He sighed, his face just short of angry.

"What is it now, Ceri?"

"Our son is not the only one to return today. Your brother Maelgwyn has been sighted a half day's journey away. He is coming from the South, husband—although you sent him to treaty with the Scotti of Eire."

At the mention of Uncle Maelgwyn, Father's face lost all trace of play.

"He is no doubt up to his usual double-dealings. It explains why he did not return for Father's burial rites."

"He is a coward and a murderer, husband. A bastard from the realms of hell." I looked up at Mother in shock. She never cursed, her Cristos faith forbade it. "Treat him as you would a viper."

"Worry not." Father released her hand from my tunic, warning me with a lifted eyebrow what would happen if I ran away. He kissed the hand he had freed and pulled Mother against him.

"I am King now. He can do nothing."

"That is exactly why I worry. Maelgwyn's hatred will be masked as ever behind the honey of his words. But it is power that he seeks and what you have earned, he will try to take."

"Sshh, beloved. He is my brother."

"So said Abel of Cain." Mother muttered.

"Enough of your useless Cristos tales! Come, wife, let us see that our daughter's appearance no longer offends your Roman sensibilities and join our thieving son in the Hall. Time enough to worry about my scheming little brother when he ascends the hill path—and I can ignore his existence no longer!"

chapter 8

Iorwerth's warriors sprawled drunkenly about the Hall looking more like Hwyrch's rag dolls than Ordovician cattle raiders. Mother had suddenly remembered Celius' lessons, but the old man was already into his third wineskin and it only took a quick lie to escape him. Cynan and I crept into the Hall to see the excitement.

"Ho, you two," Iolo waved his drinking horn in a dizzy half-circle, moving over so we could join him on the bench. "Don't tell me you've wearied of conjugating Latin already!"

Eiddwen the Shield Bearer handed us a mead horn.

"Let's begin at the beginning," he said and started to tell the tale, contradicted by roars and shouts every time he took a breath.

Tales of the raid grew wilder as the afternoon wore on, but we listened to them all in great excitement. Father strode in and out of the Hall, deep in conversation with his Shield Brother, Hwyll, honoring us with a proud, if distracted, smile.

All was well until Mother came in from the kitchens where she had been helping Maeve. Smudges of cooking ash decorated her face like warrior tattoos.

"Out!" she cried, pushing the nearest of Iolo's band off the bench where he'd been snoring.

"To the Warriors' Hall, the lot of you!"

Grumbling, singing, the warriors left, staggering on each other's arms.

Iolo was the last to go. "A little more gratitude, if you please, Mother." He swept her an extremely clumsy bow that almost cost him his balance.

"Out, you fool! We need to ready the Hall for your uncle!"

"M-Merlin-n?" Io staggered, looking confused. "Why would he care if we're here?"

I began to giggle.

Mother stomped her foot. "Not Merlin, you idiot. Maelgwyn!"

Iolo swayed, trying to pull himself together.

"And just what do you think that pr-prancing c-catamount will do if he runs into my warriors? Try to f-fuck them? Ha! They'd cut off his balls and throw them to the hounds."

Cynan and I fell off the bench, laughing. Iorwerth winked in our direction, did a mock dance step, and had to hold on to a pillar to stop from crashing to the floor.

Mother was not amused.

"Out! All of you!"

Cynan and I ran out into the rain, jumping across the worst of the puddles in the courtyard until we reached the relative comfort of the stables.

Tali was by himself. The three of us curled up in the dry straw together and began to share the news of the day, huddling together for warmth.

We were not to have time to talk however for Useth returned, cursing to himself as usual. "Filthy parasites won't let a man rest! Oh no, it's Useth this…Useth that…Useth you wouldn't mind walking out on this god-cursed day and taking care of yet another spoiled lord's fucking horse. Oh no, Useth, wouldn't mind sir. Not at all, sir! Kiss your fucking ass, sir. Useth wouldn't mind a bit. A knife in the gullet is what they deserve. A knife in the gullet—"

"Useth!" It was Father.

"Make sure there's plenty of fodder ready. The gods alone know how many horses he'll be bringing. We'll just have to make do. See to it, will you?"

Father left. We stayed hidden in the straw torn between giggles and fear at what we were overhearing.

"See to it, will you?" Useth's voice became a nasty falsetto.

We heard a soft thud, a yowl of pain. He'd kicked old Maex, the stable hound.

Outraged, I started to rise. Cynan yanked my arm, warning me still.

"Where's that fucking boy?" Useth kicked a stall door, ignored the pony's answering snort, and went out in search of Tali.

"Let's go," Cynan whispered.

Tali shook his head sadly. "I can't. He'll beat me worse if he can't find me."

"We'll find a way to free you one day." I gave Tali a kiss and crept outside with Cynan, sparing a heartbeat to pet poor old Maex.

The rain had not slackened at all, but we saw Father waiting beside the guards of the inner palisades and ran to join him.

"Aren't you two supposed to be at lessons?" We were all drenched. Even Father's moustaches drooped.

"We're finished," lied Cynan.

Father laughed, a warm booming sound in the miserable downpour.

"You are hopeless, the both of you. Come, stand beside me. Maelgwyn is already past the earthworks. You can greet him with me."

We watched as Maelgwyn and his riders stopped at the second palisades and struggled up to the top of the hill where we awaited them. They looked even more miserable than we did. Maelgwyn himself was covered with journey muck, his once fine hooded wolfskin cloak wet beyond recognition. But no rain could disguise the beauty of his horse, nor the woman riding behind it. Maelgwyn's horse was an arch-necked black stallion, far larger and sleeker than even the finest of Father's shaggy war ponies. The woman behind him rode another elegant horse, this one silver with black spots and tail, but she herself shivered in thin garments that looked to be merely a collection of wet veils clinging scandalously tight to her lovely body. Her face itself was all but covered in veils; only her large black eyes could be seen. They peered fearfully around her, as if she had reason to believe we would attack her.

Despite the chill, hard-falling rain, Uncle made no move to cover her with one of the colorful woven blankets I saw protruding from the basket behind his saddle. He reined his proud stallion to stop before us, but instead of removing the wolf cloak's hood from his head as was expected of a guest, Maelgwyn cleared his throat and spat on the ground near Father's feet, just far enough away to not give insult. Without speaking, he swept one jewel-heavy hand towards the long line of pack mules and the stuffed wicker baskets they carried, arrayed like a small army behind him.

"Brother," he motioned the woman forward and put a possessive hand on her scantily-clad knee, "I bring you gifts from Vortigern, Southern overlord of the Demetae and the Silures, conqueror of the

Atrebates, the Belgae, and the Dobunni."

"I know who he is, Maelgwyn. But I fail to see how a man who prides himself on his sense of direction can mistake south for west."

Maelgwyn's warrior band had come up the hill and was fanning out in protective formation around the mules. Father raised the same eyebrow he used to warn me when I had gone too far. "It would seem your honor guard is reluctant to part with these fine gifts you describe."

Maelgwyn flung back the hood of his sodden cloak at last, exposing a handsome clean-shaven face. The rain had begun to slacken, allowing me to see his cold black eyes, the high cheekbones he shared with Father, and the sensual pouting mouth that Iolo said he used to lure both women and men to his bed.

"Old habits, brother. They have guarded it for many leagues and are reluctant to stop until its rightful owner takes possession."

It had been more than a sunturn since I'd last seen Maelgwyn but I had not forgotten how his speech twisted and turned like the labyrinth path at King's Rock. Handsome, elegant, and vicious. Hwyrch said the only way Uncle knew how to rule men was through bribery and fear.

Father pushed us behind him and stepped forward, speaking in a voice that carried to the warriors posted furthest away.

"Our messengers could not find you, Maelgwyn. Though they tried, they did not think to look for you in the South. One, Turach of the Crooked Arm, even gave his life to reach you. He has vanished into the mists of Eire, set upon by Gormach's kin, no doubt—savages who pretended not to see the rowan branch of a messenger that he bore."

Maelgwyn said nothing. Father pitched his voice even louder.

"Our father Cunedda has joined the ancestors. He is dead. As his eldest son, I am King of Dinas now."

Maelgwyn's eyes narrowed in shock, then darkened in fury. In a heartbeat, he changed his expression to polite disinterest. Shifting in his saddle, he covered a yawn.

"So, Brother," Father continued, "I am the rightful owner of this tribute. And since your warriors are both cold and hungry, let us not make them wait to deliver these goods any longer."

Useth appeared at Father's elbow, mumbling under his breath.

"See to the horses, stable master, and show these men to the kitchens."

Sullen as ever, Useth reached for the bridle of the nearest horse. Its rider quickly dismounted, heading with a group of his fellows towards the fragrant smoke of the kitchens.

The horse, misliking Useth's rough hands upon his bridle, shied from the stable master. Useth swore. Maelgwyn's own black stallion snorted and it was only Uncle's quick hands on the reins that stopped him from rearing. A sudden crash of thunder over the eastern mountains frightened the uneasy horses even more.

"Take the men inside, Useth," Father ordered grimly. Ignoring the ill-omen, he himself went among Maelgwyn's horses soothing the restive ponies in the soft loving undertone he used to work his horse-magic and, at last, order was restored. Maelgwyn's men followed squat grumpy Useth through the gates.

As Maelgwyn's guard dispersed, Father turned back to Uncle, nodding to the bedraggled woman beside him.

"Come into the Hall and acquaint me with your travels. I am curious why you chose to disobey me."

I saw Uncle's mouth tighten, then a spate of hard rain followed on the heels of pealing thunder. His face blurred into the storm.

The Hall, emptied of Iolo's raiders, was now spotless. A feast of cold venison, smoked fish, fresh mutton, cheeses, bannocks, and berries had been placed on the King's board, with a pitcher of Mother's prized heather mead set beside two fine drinking horns.

Cynan and I crept in to listen. Father allowed us to do so, as long as we remained silent. He, like Grandmother, believed children should learn early as much as they could of the adult world. For me, it was a relief—this sunlit anger of men—after the undertow of ghosts and shadows that colored my dealings with Grandmother and Mother.

"It is useless to parley with the filthy Scotti! You know it well, Brother King," Maelgwyn's deep voice was bitter.

"After a fortnight spent wandering through bog and black forest expecting an arrow in our backs at every turn, I felt it best to head south, where one can at least expect the trappings of civilization."

Cynan and I slid onto a bench near the dais and pretended to be absorbed in a game of chance, listening as intently as we could.

Father put his mead horn carefully on the table and paced across the Hall.

"It was not for your comfort that I sent you to Eire. Gormach's brother, Nestor, may be greedy, but he has intelligence. Had you offered alliance he might well have grasped at the chance to exchange our copper and brooches for his wolfhounds and peace between our peoples."

Father stopped walking, his back to Maelgwyn, sheathing his anger-flushed face into a stern king's mask. When it was as cold as a Roman god's, he faced Uncle again.

"Hard man he may be, but Nestor Lack-Tongue has been battling the southern clans of Eire since I was a stripling boy. Even he might relish a chance to fight only one foe for a season—yet you did not even try to approach him!"

Father picked up his mead horn with studied calm and waited, watching Maelgwyn as a hound prepares for a feint from a hare.

Uncle shrugged his shoulders, reaching for a bannock. "I thought it better to make a pact with those who could do us more good. And I was right—look at all the pledge gifts the new Vortigern has sent us."

The mysterious veiled lady chose this moment to enter the Hall. She had changed her clothing and her new veils flowed around her like the gossamer of a fairy queen.

"Ah, let me present the Lady Sari." Maelgwyn's chuckled. "Here, girl, warm my lap."

The lovely woman had been making her way to the hearth fire, no doubt still chilled from her miserable ride. She looked to be little older then Bran, my fourteen- sunturn harp-spelled brother. At the sound of Uncle's voice, she froze. Like Father, she pushed all the animation out of her eyes and turned to obey, walking as slowly to the dais as if she was going to Celius' Latin lessons.

Stiffly, she climbed into my uncle's lap.

"One of the Vortigern's most thoughtful presents." Maelgwyn's rings flashed, his hands groped her small breasts.

"A slave from beyond the eastern seas, a faraway kingdom of moon-crescent swords. The very lands we once dreamed of conquering as boys, 'Wallon." Maelgwyn lowered one hand and caressed her lap, pushing roughly into the graceful folds of the flowing material.

The girl sat, motionless, staring at nothing.

Uncle pinched her bottom.

She wiggled away.

Maelgwyn smiled, pinching harder.

She stood up.

Maelgwyn pulled her roughly down, pinching her nipple hard.

"Though very young, she pleases me—but she has much to learn. Best remember who your master is, child."

He kissed her, open-mouthed and angry.

She recoiled.

He slapped her. "Remember and you will not suffer."

"Enough!" Father intercepted Maelgwyn's arm before he could hit her again.

Sari stumbled on the step of the dais and sprawled on the rushes, her fey-looking veils askew so that I caught a glimpse of a full-lipped mouth, a regal nose, and the red mark of Maelgwyn's hand.

I ran to help her. At my touch she flinched, then regarded me solemnly, as if she were a captive doe resigned to expecting her death blow.

Maelgwyn gripped her arm and pushed her behind him. "Back to the kitchens, girl."

Turning to Father, he added, "If you are too uncouth to thank me for the trouble I have taken on your behalf, perhaps it is best if I retire to my lands."

A short bark of laughter from Father. "It is not that easy, brother. You do not yet seem to have grasped that I am your King, a King who does not play with traitors even if they share my blood."

His voice dropped to a whisper, "Especially if they share my blood and have been known since boyhood to cheat at tawlbwrdd."

"Do not play the dragon warrior with me, 'Wallon." Maelgwyn slammed his dagger into the trestle board, spilling his mead horn, scattering bannocks to the floor.

"But a single sunturn of life made you the eldest. Under the laws of our adopted land—this very earth you so cherish—I could challenge you for a share of the kingship."

Father reached the dais in two long strides and grabbed Maelgwyn's wrist, all pretense of politeness gone. "Challenge if you dare, little brother."

Maelgwyn's handsome black eyes regarded Father steadily, although Father's grip must have hurt. After a long heartbeat, he gave another of his casual shrugs.

"Unlike you, I do not lust to lay claim to this miserable backwater of rock-shit. Nor do I seek to rule the sullen superstitious fools crazed enough to live here. I would as soon sell myself to slavers.

"But, brother, beware," he yanked his arm from Father's clasp, "you do not make me more of an enemy than you already have. Well you know, I do not easily forget a slight."

He pulled his dagger free, glared at Father, and began to toss it slowly from hand to hand.

Father drew back, reclaiming his poised calm.

"And well you know, I am not fool enough to turn my back on you."

Maelgwyn clasped his heart, mocking. "This is thanks indeed for the news I bear."

Father said nothing. He mounted the dais and sank heavily into the King's Seat, stroking the sacred white wolfskin that covered it as he reached for the still upright pitcher of mead and poured them both a horn.

"Ah yes, the news from the South. By all means, share it. What tale do you carry from your unauthorized sojourn with the Roman-remnant lords?"

"Roman-remnant, no more." Maelgwyn took a sip from his horn and glanced down the length of the Hall, noting Cynan and I as if for the first time.

"I see you still let babes play at being courtiers." He mocked us with a mead toast. Cynan kicked me hard beneath the trestle and we pretended not to notice him, concentrating on casting the bones.

When he saw that it was useless to torment us, Maelgwyn spoke again. "This new Vortigern—the third cursed fool to bear the title—is all for going back to the old ways: wicker cages, human sacrifices, all that muddled Druid shit. The people fear him, but they follow—and their fear has fed his coffers."

Maelgwyn looked about our Hall. I had always thought it beautiful with its majestically-carved pillars, lush wall hangings, decorated wall scions, and graceful hanging lamps. But my uncle curled his lip with disgust.

"Perhaps you should take a bite from his loaf, brother. This soot-filled disaster of a Hall does your sovereignty little credit."

Father ignored this. "And just what message does this rogue overlord have to offer us at Dinas?"

"Ah that!" Maelgwyn clapped his hands. It was so quiet in the Hall I could hear the heavy jewels on his rings click together.

"He offers the new King of Dinas Emrys a treaty of alliance. These gifts are but a foretaste of the bounty he extends to his allies. He is eager to meet with the King of Dinas." Uncle's voice dropped.

"And it appears that would be you, dear brother."

Maelgwyn fished in the inner pouch of his tunic and brandished a roll of parchment. "Lord Vortigern the Third sends invitation to attend him after the Lughnasa harvest festival at his seat in Caerleon."

Father took the message from him and read it in silence. I tried very hard to concentrate on our game, but even Morag, my favorite hound had grown bored watching our play and left to investigate the rushes beneath the dais.

Cynan sneaked a glance and pinched my arm. "It's something important, Father's biting his lip."

Indeed, beneath the shelter of his still damp moustaches, Father's teeth were grinding at his lower lip. "This is more than an invitation. But I have no doubt you already know that."

Maelgwyn shrugged modestly.

"This very fortnight Vortigern plans to travel with his warriors to secure his northern boundaries."

Father put the parchment down, smoothing it carefully as if to make sure he was reading it correctly. "And since he heads in our direction, the man thinks to invite himself to Dinas itself—for Lughnasa!"

Father laughed and sailed the parchment in the air. It landed in the rushes near us, but Cynan stopped me before I could jump and grab it.

"The man's got more balls than sense! He thinks to bring a war band into my lands without an invitation?"

Maelgwyn chewed on a piece of venison, swallowing carefully before he answered. "I daresay he thinks yonder parchment is all the invitation he needs. Did I not tell you, he is more than a bit mad?"

"You told me he sought to bring back the old ways. That alone does not make him mad. Here at Dinas, we have never left them. Those Druids who yet survive in the mountains remain our teachers—as you well know, brother."

Uncle had been cutting a slice of venison with his dagger. His hand froze in midair. His lip raised in a sneer, as if he were a dog backed into a corner.

I remembered the rumors.

Long ago, Hwyrch said, Maelgwyn had fallen in love with a young Ordovice girl, a girl promised to the Druids as a seer who could never know the touch of a man or her sacred visions would be defiled. Yet Maelgwyn had pursued her day and night, haunting her mother's round-hut in the forest, following her as she collected herbs and flowers, trying to speak with her as she feed her mother's goats and took her washing to the river.

Always the girl ignored him, for to acknowledge him would be to open the door to the destruction of her vows. It mattered not that Maelgwyn was the son of Lord Cunedda. The Druids had ruled the forests long before Father's family came to Ordovice lands and their word was sacred.

On the morning that the girl reached her fourteenth sunturn and made ready to depart for the Druid's school on the isle of Mona, she went down to the river to wash. She was never seen alive again, although many days and nights were spent searching for her and her mother wailed like a mad wolf beneath the moon.

Six days passed before a fisherman trudged sadly up the hillside of Dinas, carrying a bloated corpse that stank so badly people turned their heads away. It was, indeed, the girl, her face no longer lovely, drowned and battered by the river rocks, swelling with water and decay. But that was not what caused Grandmother and the women who attended her to draw away in horror, for the girl's body bore a vicious pattern of knife wounds incised in stabbing swirls across her torso.

Nest the midwife cried out in shock when she bent over the body, for not only had she been the poor girl's mother's sister but, as a healer pledged to honor birth, she recognized the blood knife pattern as a mockery of the Druid's most sacred spirals of life, desecrating the body of a girl who should have lived to see her prophecies grace the hard lives of her people.

Furiously Grandmother raged, accusing Cunedda of letting his youngest son Maelgwyn murder without blood-debt. But Maelgwyn had left Dinas soon after the girl had disappeared, nor did he reappear until many summers had passed; summers filled with enough misery and battle that the sad fate of a young girl who had not lived to claim her seer's power had lost some of the outrage it once caused.

Yet memories were long in the hills and forests of the Ordovice and Uncle did not often venture out alone.

The girl's murder had happened many sunturns before my birth, yet Father's hint of it was still enough to shake Uncle's calm.

"Mock me not," he snarled. "Even your filthy Ordovice have given up putting captives in wicker cages and setting them on fire instead of merely mumbling their prayers like nice little Romans."

It was Father who shrugged this time. "You say he likes to instill fear. What better way than this? Nor does the man understand what he does. Even in ancient times such sacrifices were rare."

Father's knowledge of the old ways no longer surprised me. Although he still preferred a sword or lance to talk of gods or spirits, Merlin had explained that Father's dragon tattoo was the highest honor a warrior could receive and was granted only by the Druids of Mona after many painful moontides of ordeals.

Maelgwyn, who possessed no such honor, threw a piece of fish to Morag, starting a ruckus with the other hounds.

"Why do you care about such sacrifices? The Vortigern rules his own people. Remember, he invites us to join him at Caerleon after harvest."

Uncle yawned loudly, watching the hounds snarl over the fish. I stole another look at him. Any time Maelgwyn acted bored, he was up to something.

"He is merely coming for a convenient visit while he is near our borders—a new ally come to call."

Father laughed and jumped up from the High Seat, whistling for Caselt and Magog, his own favorite hounds. "Do you truly think me simple?"

Maelgwyn did not bother to reply, concentrating on picking lint from his damp tunic.

Caselt nudged Father, eager to get on with it. Calming the hound, Father explained for our benefit, "He comes to spy us out to see if we are worth his bother. The man is a warlord, you said it yourself. He does not make alliances; he *conquers*—unless one is strong enough to resist him." Father winked at us, pausing by our trestle long enough to throw the bones. They came up doubles, a good omen.

"Oh, and, brother," he turned the full force of his smile on Maelgwyn, "I would appreciate a full report next time. This Vortigern of yours has also invited an entire fellowship of Sea Wolves to help him keep order in these lands where people tremble in such fear of him. Odd, don't you think?"

Uncle's full red lips tightened. "Take care," he shouted, goaded beyond restraint, "Vortigern is not to be trifled with!"

"Neither am I, brother—neither am I!" Father called not looking back.

Just before he reached the door, Merlin pushed it open.

"My Lord." Our other uncle inclined his head as Father strode past.

"Emrys! Well met—I have been meaning to ask you about spells of disappearance—"

The heavy door slammed shut on their words. Cynan and I hurriedly gathered up our bones and crept out of the Hall before our fuming uncle could take note of us again.

How could we have known that the fates were listening closely to what transpired in our Hall—gathering strength to spin our world like a single, falling leaf in an autumn gale?

CHAPTER 9

Lord Vortigern's uninvited appearance at Lughnasa forced Father to welcome our new allies in secret, three days before the festival, rather than inflame the southern king's suspicion of a new power rising at Dinas. As we prepared to welcome the northern clans, my oldest brother, Tegid, and his war band watched the coast for Vortigern's ships, with orders to escort the Southern troops to Dinas and keep them out of mischief along the way.

Cautious as ever, Father also sent mountain scouts south through the midland valleys to keep a warrior's eye on Vortigern's Romanized fortress of Caerleon, sorting the truth from Maelgwyn's lies.

At Dinas itself, amidst the cheerful busyness of baking and the whitewashing of the inner stone walls of our Hall, warriors kept watch on our defenses, expecting an angry visit from Chalan Grey Wolf of the Decleangli to revenge Iolo's raid. Yet all remained quiet in the Decleangli forests.

Merlin replaced Celius as our teacher to Cynan and my delight. Lessons became a joy. Most were held outdoors for, under Merlin's tutelage, the rocks and trees had voices and we learned their language along with the much duller syllables of Greek and Latin.

Mother's friendship with her newly-discovered younger brother blossomed, lightening her step and softening her sternness. Although Merlin was as deep in thrall as Grandmother to the old ways of our people, she accepted his influence on us much more graciously than she had ever tolerated Grandmother's attempts at teaching us the forest ways.

In the meantime, unknown to Mother, the forest Druids welcomed

Merlin as a long-lost leader. Following after him like hound pups, Cynan and I learned much of the whispered ways of their all but forgotten religion.

Indeed, I would have enjoyed these final days of summer and been as happily carefree as a meadowlark, had it been possible for me to forget the mystery of the *estethra*. As it was, even with Merlin and Grandmother, I found myself restless, yearning for something of which I could not speak.

For his part, Uncle Maelgwyn unpacked his wicker baskets of loot in the finest guest chamber in the Hall and set about making himself as annoying as a cloud of horse flies. He seemed to be underfoot everywhere, asking needless questions of busy servants.

He made an unlikely friend of fat Useth and I often saw them together, chatting by the livestock pens, my elegantly-clad uncle perched upon a railing like a slender bird of prey listening to Useth's bile as if the stable master uttered the wisdom of gods.

His warriors were no better, forever nosing about the stables and courtyards as if they were looking for a lost treasure hoard. Tali even caught one kicking at a rotting post near the storage shed that hid Grandfather Cunedda's secret tunnel into the forest. Although the tunnel had fallen in long ago and never been repaired, the underground cave at its entrance still served as an underground hiding place, large enough to conceal a small village of women and children.

"Your uncle is either a mad fool," said Tali. "Or up to something. And we all know he's no fool."

Instead of answering, I kicked the leather ball we were using for our game, careful not to look at Tali's face, which bore the black marks of Useth's latest beating. Tali returned the ball with a hard kick across the courtyard, running as gracefully as ever, but wincing as he put weight on his right side. I swore beneath my breath, knowing Tali would not thank me if I made a fuss.

Since Maelgwyn's arrival, Useth's cruelties towards Tali had grown even worse. The care of Maelgwyn's horses had fallen on Tali's shoulders despite Father's orders that two village lads be hired to help with stable chores.

Tiring of our ball game, Tali flung himself up into the branches of the old oak by the stables and began to sing an old riddling song in a voice to rival the birds.

"Get over here, boy!" Useth snapped from the stable doorway, glaring at us both.

"Farewell, Shadow." Tali jumped from the tree, landing with a whoosh of air as if descending from another realm.

Knowing it was useless to argue, I raced back to the Hall and soon found myself watching for Dinas' other prisoner, the mysterious lady Sari, as she flickered about the fortress like a lost spirit. Forced to live in Maelgwyn's chamber, she left each morning as soon as she could and took herself to the kitchens where, through a combination of hand gestures and ability, she had made a friend of Cook's daughter, Kerinne, for they were close in age despite a world's realm of differences.

When my chores were done, I was free to seek out the comforting glow of the smithy. Busy as we were from dawn to dusk, only Huw, the blacksmith, seemed to stay the same. He worked in his usual silence, always sparing a smile for me. I watched him lift red-hot new swords and spearheads from his coals with the same tongs he used to pick up horseshoes, meat daggers, and griddle cake irons. I found myself visiting him more and more frequently as the fortress grew busier around me, not much caring that he was making far more weapons than usual, simply finding solace in the red heat of his forge, the transformation of everyday objects into glowing mysteries, and the shy gentleness of his smile.

At last Lughnasa was upon us.

Father's face glowed when he came upon me the afternoon of the great feast, as I was practicing my needlework under Hwyrch's unforgiving eye in Mother's small herb garden behind the kitchens. All about us the day was heartbreakingly beautiful, the kind of late summer day filled with the smell of earth and sunshine and a wafting breeze that came all the way from the river to tease me into following it. But, there I sat, stuck with bloody fingers, more knots than thread in my embroidery, and an ill-tempered Nurse.

"We've done it, Gwen!" Father picked me up, scattering needle and thread. Like a hero of old, he ignored Hwyrch's protests, set me on his shoulders, and carried me beyond the low stone fence that separated Mother's plants from the muck of the courtyard. "The Bear clan family of the Ordovice—the Fox and Gull—the Venedotae of the coast—even the Badger and Hawk of the Decleangli have all marked blood upon the treaty! Whether the next attack comes from the Scotti or the South, we face battle as a united people. Not since the early days of my father have this many clans united!"

I clamored to be let down. When he obliged, I jumped up and down and hugged him tightly, breathing in his afternoon scent of stables and hard sweat.

"I want to fight too!" I cried, dancing like a warrior in circles around him.

He stopped me, suddenly serious. "Not this time, girl. Not ever if I can help it. We fight now so that you and Cynan can grow up in a world in which battles need not be fought every season, where bard song is heard more often than death cries."

I made a face. "That's boring, Tad!"

He laughed. "Then you can hate me for it! Now get out of here, Scamp and—"

A scout was ushered through the gates.

The young man clasped one arm to his side, gasping for breath as he bowed to Father. The gull feathers marking him as Tegid's warrior were stark white against the loose black fall of his hair.

"They are coming, Lord. The Vortigern and a force of four score warriors, accompanied by Tegid and his band." The scout's flushed face broke into a grin. "A nasty bunch—more Sea Wolves among them then Southerners—and pissed as starving boars at being kept on the path instead of rampaging across our crofts."

Father clapped his hand on the scout's shoulder. "Get food and rest. Do you think we can manage if it comes to battle?"

The tired messenger's grin widened. "In a heartbeat, Lord! Let us have at them!"

As ever, Father's laughter shoved up his moustaches and warmed his forest-trained eyes. It was a laugh that won even the hardest warrior to his side. "Eat hearty, lad. And be ready if it comes to that!"

The man loped to the kitchens and Father turned to me. I was surprised, for suddenly he knelt in the dirt of the courtyard to look into my face. The laughter that danced in his eyes faded quickly.

"Go see your mother. Tell her the Vortigern will be arriving soon."

I stuck my lip out in a pout, reluctant to end our time together.

"Go!"

I knew better to argue with that tone of voice, but he caught me up and spun me in his arms, laughing once again. "Better yet, I'll carry you to her myself." He stuck his face against my belly and blew, making me giggle like a little girl half my age.

"I love you, Scamp." He swung me up on his shoulders.

"I love you too, Tad!" I shouted, looking with delight as all the familiar bustle of the hillfort went on beneath my new height. Late afternoon sun was fast giving way to a lingering summer twilight that suffused the forests and hills beyond our palisades with a mixture of soft lavender and heart-lovely blue, interspersed with a sad, soft gold—a shade so lonely that it seemed as if the world were saying its own secret good-bye to the sun.

We ducked our heads and went into the Hall to find Mother, but I turned around for one last look at the sky and kept watching it until we were too far into the Hall to see it any more. Why should the sky suddenly make me so sad?

We found Mother in her room surrounded by her usual colorful chaos. Hwyrch was standing behind her stool, combing the black tumbling curls that were long enough to sweep the floor. Behind them, bright skeins of yarn tumbled out of innumerable baskets, gowns and overdresses were thrown across the great carved bed Mother shared with Father like wild fairy rainbows in lands far across the sea. Two vases overflowing with wildflowers filled the room with light sweet smells. Mother's own ever-present attar of roses and the fresh lavender she grew in her small Romanized garden added a deeper, richer scent to the comfortable stone chamber.

At our entrance, Mother turned with a smile. "My wild ones, come sit with me."

Surprised at Mother's good mood, given the mind-numbing responsibilities of the coming feast, I looked in confusion at Hwyrch. Nurse's mouth was filled with hairpins, but she winked at me cheerfully, her pique at my lack of interest in embroidery forgotten.

No longer questioning my good fortune, I stripped quickly and draped the fancy Roman gown Mother had selected around me, smoothing it down my body, even though I hated the feel of it. The wearing of it was inevitable, better to get it on before Nurse could begin her fussing and tucking.

Father nodded in approval, pinning the soft blue folds at my shoulders himself, then he took the brush from Hwyrch, and began to slide it through Mother's hair.

"Mmm..." Mother closed her eyes dreamily and leaned back against his chest. He looked down at her with the expression he reserved for her alone, a look both fierce and tender.

I sat on a stool beside her chair and closed my eyes, content to smell the sweetness of flowers and the sunshine from Mother's freshly washed linen sheets. A breeze wafted in the open window. I pretended to follow it on its journey through pine forests, above the snow-crest of Yr Wyddfa, into the clouds...

"Beloved, the Southerners will be arriving before moonset," Father said.

I opened my eyes. Hwyrch was gone.

Mother's eyes tightened with the news, but she placed her hand over Father's as he continued to brush the rippling black waves of her hair.

"So be it, my love. We are ready," she murmured in the soft voice she used when she did not want to be disturbed.

"I must speak with Hwyll and Iolo. Take care to prepare Gwen." He kissed the top of her hair, lingering to smell the sun-kissed rose-scented depths of it, the same way I did when Mother kissed me good night.

She smiled. Her eyes sparked in the light of the expensive beeswax candles she allowed herself to use at twilight before she reluctantly blew them out and lit the rush lamps.

"All will be well, my Lord. Fear not."

"I do not fear, Lady." He bent to kiss her. "I will see you at High Table—and after."

She turned her face. Their mouths met in the way of grown-ups. Father whispered something that made her laugh. "Out!" she giggled, sounding not much older than me.

He kissed her again, harder this time. They were at it so long, I coughed to remind them I was there and deserved some of their attention.

Reluctantly, they broke apart.

"Tonight, my lady." Father whispered, a strained note in his voice.

He ruffled my hair on his way out. "See you at table, girl. And for the gods' own sakes, stay out of trouble for once."

Mother snorted, a very unladylike sound. I turned to her, offended, but she only smiled.

"I think we will do your hair in little braids, the way you like it."

She reached for something in her small chest of jewels.

"Here. This belonged to my Grandmother's Grandmother. You are old enough to wear it now."

It was a golden neck torc, more beautiful than any I had ever seen. It was red-gold, braided, with the spirals of life incised in patterns that seemed to swirl beneath my eyes. The ends that would frame my throat were formed by twin she-wolves with opened mouths. Inside each open mouth sat a small bird, looking curiously up at the beholder.

"This is for me?" I asked in wonder, not daring to touch it, thinking there must be a mistake.

"For you, dear heart." Mother smiled, adding briskly, "Put it on."

I slipped the magical torc around my neck. It fell heavily into place as if it had always been there, always belonged to me.

Mother held up the polished bronze mirror Father had brought her from the South.

"It's beautiful," I whispered, too awed to speak out loud.

She nodded, pleased. "It does look rather nice."

"Nice? It's wonderful!"

"Indeed…" She tickled me until I giggled, "Stop!"

She backed away, smiling.

I sat up straight, adjusting my dignity.

Mother replaced the mirror on its wall hook and we looked at each other in its reflection.

"Would you like to hear a story?" she asked.

Mother was the best storyteller of Dinas, better by far than old Cadfael, Father's bard. I wiggled to get comfortable. But suddenly my desire to hear a familiar tale of giants, wolves, or fairy queens gave way to my deepest wish.

"Mother, please tell me about the *estethra*."

She had been tsking at the condition of my hair, beginning to comb through its many snarls. Her hand now froze on the comb. "Has she dared speak to you of this again?"

I whipped my hair free and turned to meet her eyes. "Why do you hate each other?"

Mother bit down on her lip and started to braid my hair, concentrating on separating it into small strands.

"Tell me!" I shrieked into the silence.

"Be silent!" Despite the finality of her words, Mother gentled my shaking body with kneading fingers.

"Hush now, daughter. It brings ill luck to dwell on darkness."

I shuddered with frustration and yearning.

"Perhaps you would like to hear the Scotti tale of the butterfly princess?" She continued to plait my hair, humming a lullaby of the mountains.

But I sought no lullaby. I watched in the mirror as she turned the tumbling waterfall of my hair into delicate braids interwoven with jewels and clan feathers. "I want the truth, not a child's tale."

Instead of getting angry, Mother sighed. "Would a true tale of love suffice?"

I was silent. Mother finished braiding the first section of my hair. Avoiding my eyes, she drew the braids up, away from my face, and reached into her jewel chest, removing the slender gold circlet she had worn as a girl. She chose five jeweled chains and threaded them through the holes designed for them, then placed the headpiece on my hair and began another plait, this time taking care to weave a jeweled chain within it.

Despite my anger at her, I could not look away from the transformation she was creating.

"You are beginning to look like a princess." She smiled into the mirror.and tweaked a second braid, letting it fall into place with an elegant clink. It was immediately lost in the rampaging red-gold of my hair, but I knew it would resurface when I tossed my head or walked beneath a hanging lamp.

I closed my eyes. Felt her hands caress my scalp. Why would she not speak of what most mattered to me?

She had begun the tale before I even heard her voice. "I spent most of my girlhood in the South among our Dumnoni kin. This you know. What you do not yet know is that, after the plague killed my father, sisters, and brothers and swept across our lands, your Grandmother sent word that I was to stay there, safe in our cousin's fortress by the sea. She herself disappeared for three sunturns. I was but six and knew not how to bear the loss."

Mother's voice broke. I looked away from the mirror, trying to meet her eyes, surprised out of my own misery. Mother had had brothers and sisters besides Merlin?

She spoke on, concentrating on weaving jewels into my hair. The cadence of her voice became the far away lilt of a storyteller, as if this tale was not of her own life.

"My cousin Rislyn comforted me. She and her mother took me to a Cristos priest who lived in a simple hut by the sea. He spoke to me of a love that would not die, of a faith that did not count the seasons.

He taught me prayers that made the nightmares disappear. Oh yes," she nodded at me in the mirror, "I had evil dreams that season. Dark sacrifices…torrents of blood…the rotting bodies of kinsmen." She kissed the top of my head. "Those same dreams you have come to suffer."

"But—" I said no more. Moved by this image of Mother in a time I had not known, I bit back my questions and reached for her hand.

She squeezed my fingers and spoke again, in a determinedly cheerful voice. "Enough of those times. I promised a tale of love."

She sank down on a stool beside me, rummaging through a second chest of jewels.

"I did not return to Dinas until my seventeenth sunturn. By that time Cunedda and his sons had claimed our throne and your Grandmother had returned to live simply in the forest, returning to Dinas only when she had to. My arrival forced her back to the Hall to introduce me as the only surviving daughter of the old ruling house.

"Cunedda was kind and my herb craft was welcome. But my heart yearned for the South. The morning I met your father in the forest was the same morning I had determined to leave Dinas forever and return to the lands of the Dumnoni."

With a soft cry of triumph, Mother fished out strands of rare amethyst and sea pearls dangling free from a band of gold-woven net. They had been brought from the far Southern Seas long ago—a wedding gift for my great-grandmother, Angarad, from her bard-touched husband, Lord Rhodri, whose flowing red-gold hair I had inherited.

I had never been allowed to wear them before. As she placed them on my head, their lustrous purple and full moon shimmer whispered far away secrets of oceans and lost gardens. And of my mother, long ago.

"I had no room in my spirit for the spring beauty of the forest," she continued, "only anger at a mother who had left me to grow up far from home and my little girl memories of playing with long dead sisters and brothers.

"I stopped to pick a wildflower—one with no healing value at all—when an arrow thudded into the old oak above me, barely a handsbreadth from where my head had been.

"I dived behind a hazel thicket, thinking some pirate sought to capture me, hiding just in time to see a handsome young man step into the clearing. He reached up, whistling, to retrieve the arrow that almost killed me, scowling at the chittering squirrel that had clearly been his target.

"I might have stayed hidden and never met him at all, save for his hound who sniffed me out of my hiding place with a baying so overpowering you would have thought I was a wild boar.

"The young man looked shocked at my appearance, as well he should have," Mother's smile grew rich with memory, "for I was covered with mud, the skirt of my gown torn by brambles, and I was cursing his dog in language no Southern-bred lady should ever use."

"'Lady, I beg pardon,' he said, graciously enough, ordering his hound away. 'Did you fall?'"

I began to giggle. Mother laughed herself, her lilting chuckle as musical as birdsong. "You fool!" I answered. "You almost killed me!"

"He took my hand then, kissed it, and brought it to rest on his heart. 'I only meant to kill a squirrel. I did not seek to capture a goddess.'

"And that, my dear, is how I met your father— dread Lord of the Ordovice!" Still laughing, Mother kissed the top of my head. "I want you to wear this tonight."

With a mysterious smile, she turned to her jewel chest again and removed a delicate mesh veil of the finest silver, studded with eastern amber. Her most prized possession, her bridal gift from Father.

She arranged the veil carefully over my jeweled braids, where it floated like a breath from the fairy realms, translucent as a dream. Mother put a finger beneath my chin, tilting my face up, high and proud. We looked again into the mirror. Even with the distortion of candlelight and shadow, I looked as regal as I could ever have imagined in my wildest fancies.

Gently, Mother massaged my shoulders. I stared, rapt, at my reflection.

"You carry the love of generations on your head this night, my heart."

Her smile, though wide and lovely, was tinged somehow with sadness. Her eyes far away in whatever kingdom she saw before her.

It made me somehow afraid. "Mother?"

She shook herself briskly and bid me rise. "You will be a beauty, daughter. I wish you joy of it."

Frowning, she adjusted my dress. "Now, enough of stories. Let us join your father's feasting in the Hall."

A battle-horn of noise reached us, as we walked down the short passage from her chamber to the Hall, a shout followed by a roar of laughter and the pounding of fists and feet upon wood and hearth.

Mother's hand squeezed my own. I looked up at her. A dimple flared as she smiled down at me, her own bejeweled hair falling like sparkling black rivers down the front of her favorite crimson gown. "Ready, daughter?"

"Ready." I squeezed her hand in return, reaching up to touch her hair. "You look beautiful."

"Thank you, beloved. Now let us show these barbarians a thing or two, shall we?"

chapter 10

We walked straight into a Hall so crowded with revelry, I barely recognized it as my own home. Scurrying servants balancing great platters of boar and venison sidestepped hungry growling hounds. The Ordovice clans of the Gull, Bear, and Fox, the coastal Venedotae, the Badger and Hawk clans of the Decleangli, newly allied with Father, had stayed for the Lughnasa feast, their chieftains crowding the dais with their finery and boasts.

Never had the Hall looked so beautiful, so richly decorated for the sun harvest god Lugh. Below the thatch, each roof beam and every one of the twenty sculpted pillars of rowan wood and oak were hung with sheaves of grain, interwoven with berry branches and late summer wildflowers. Mother's hanging lamps were polished so deeply they shone like lake water in sunlight, reflecting the brilliance of the Hall in row after dizzying row of glittering bronze and firelight. Even better, Mother had filled them with her precious southern oil. My nostrils flared, eager to catch its elusive scent beneath the more familiar smells of smoke and roasting meat, of hounds and human sweat. For Mother's oil whispered of lands I had never seen, of lands that knew no winter, where children swam in oceans that stayed warm throughout all seasons, where mermaids came to smile…

And yet there was more. Mother's wondrous southern tapestries had been brought out to replace our everyday weavings and as I gazed at them, enraptured, I saw the magical beasts of Merlin and Grandmother's tales come prancing out to meet my eager heart: white-horned and winged horses, great red dragons, mysterious spirits of tree and earth and fire vied to take me into their world.

Placed carefully between them, the swords and shields of our ancestors were mounted proudly at intervals up and down the length of the Hall. The greatest of them all, the Dragon Shield of the Ordovice hung as always behind Father's High Seat on the dais.

Mother squeezed my hand and led me up that very dais, letting me sit beside her on the King's Bench instead of taking my usual place beside Hwyrch at one of the lower trestle tables.

Cynan was already seated and snorted at my appearance. With a regal toss of my head—careful not to dislodge my veil—I pointedly ignored him and reached for the horn of ale Mother had watered for me, concentrating on the play of lamplight and torches on the great carved pillars of the Hall as it danced against the carved runes and animal designs that decorated them.

In the heat of this late summer night, only two of the three central fires had been lit, flaming in welcome to our native folk and the many guests crowded at the trestle tables that rayed out on both sides of the fires.

A third fire blazed beside the harpers' bench to the left of the dais, allowing the bards of Dinas and any visiting harpers a modicum of privacy, some time to share and practice together before they were called upon to perform. Behind the fire's rising sparks, I caught a glimpse of my brother Bran leaning forward as old Cadfael tuned his harp, my brother's thoughtful eyes missing none of the aging bard's secrets.

Between the harpers' circle and the great hearth, other trestle boards were set and the freemen and women of the fort and village good-naturedly jostled for what little space remained. Dressed in simple grey homespun or forest greens and browns, the folk looked fit and fine, laughing as Breth, the laundress' son, somersaulted across the broad boards of a heavily-laden table, managing to avoid mead flagons and meat platters more by luck than skill as the good folk in his path quickly plucked potential hazards out of his way.

Nest the midwife blew me a kiss and then turned back to speak to the village girl beside her, resting her expert hand on the girl's vast belly.

Mother poured me a goblet of southern wine, a special treat, although, as usual, she watered it far too much. I sipped obediently, trying not to blush as she kissed the top of my head; an unwelcome reminder that she still thought me a child.

I shook my head, annoyed, and continued to look around the Hall.

Despite all the finery of our new allies and guests, it was the warriors who took pride of place, seated at their own table on Father's right. My brother Iorwerth was their star. As the war bands of the visiting chieftains tried to out-drink and out-shout our men, Iolo jumped up on the table and soon had everyone laughing as he performed a dizzying series of handsprings, on and off the table. I laughed too, but, as the visiting warriors—and ogling women—applauded, I saw again how, Iolo used his gift for laughter to herd others to his side. As always with my brother, the laughter he brought served a deeper cause.

Father sat on his High Seat, aloof. He appeared leagues removed from the crowd, his eyes overflowing with thoughts and plans, sipping his mead without speaking—no matter that Uncle Maelgwyn on his left tried time after time to engage him in conversation. Father froze him out, gazing around the Hall like a great eagle surveying his domain, regal power sitting as naturally on his shoulders as it did upon the mountains he now ruled.

Suddenly, folk rushed to throng the still-open Hall door, shouting praise at a late-comer to the feast. The blonde head of the newcomer bobbed like a small sun above them, laughing as the hillfolk parted.

"Tegid!" I shouted, but Mother was already standing beside Father, clapping her hands as she waited for my oldest brother to reach us.

Father's attention returned from whatever vision had possessed it. Throwing off his otter-trimmed mantle, he stepped from behind our table board, meeting Tegid as he mounted the first step of the dais. They pummeled each other, laughing, in an embrace tight enough to squeeze the breath from each other's lungs.

"Don't worry, Father. The Vortigern still swaggers towards us, flanked by all his bully boys. They'll be here before midnight comes. Selyf rides with them, watching as close as a nursemaid. I left Bledri in charge of the coastal fires."

Tegid's head topped even Father as they broke apart, still laughing with the joy of seeing each other.

"Worry not, we have the Scotti well in hand, licking the wounds we gave them last fortnight!"

He blew a kiss to Mother and winked at me. "But my soul could stand its loneliness no longer—I have come to celebrate Lughnasa in the bosom of my clan!"

I flung myself at him, forgetting all about the royal ransom in jewels I wore on my head. Tegid picked me up and swung me around, hard enough to knock my headdress askew. "Is that really little Shadow beneath all those gewgaws?"

My oldest brother was almost a giant, born to a village girl in Father's youth, long before he met Mother. Although not of her blood, Mother loved him as fiercely as the rest of us—even though she scowled at him now, struggling to tidy my headdress. I perched, grinning, in the crock of his arm, ignoring her.

"Ho, brother mine!" Iolo bounded up to the dais and swept Tegid a mocking bow. "You have come, of course, to honor me."

Tegid put me down, knocking my headdress to one side again. "I did hear something about a few lost cows that followed you home. 'Tis a shame you did not take me with you, brother, for I would have shown you the right way to pull off a cattle raid!"

The warriors hooted—Iolo's band as well as Tegid's honor guard.

"Truly?" Iolo inclined his head. "Perhaps since you missed your chance to teach me, you would consent to demonstrate how to wrestle instead?"

Amidst the cheers that followed, Father nodded his assent. Space was cleared before the dais. Warriors laid wagers. Dogs were lead away. My brothers stripped off their tunics and flung their boots aside. Arrayed in places of honor along the High Table, the visiting clan leaders leaned forward in excitement.

I settled myself on the bench beside Mother, pinching Cynan to move over, and watched Iolo and Tegid prepare. It was indeed well that my brothers loved each other, for far too many of our clans had been torn apart by fighting from within. Certainly, there was little brotherly love wasted between Uncle Maelgwyn and Father.

Perhaps what saved Iolo and Tegid from a similar fate was the pleasure they took in each other's company. Nor had Father or Mother raised them as adversaries. Tegid was as joy-filled and warm as the sun itself, so generous in nature that even moody Iolo adored him, although the two had little in common save loyalty and a strong battle arm.

As they stripped down for the wrestling match, my eyes went back and forth from Tegid's muscled godlike frame to Iolo's slender wiry menace. How unalike my brothers were, for just as their bodies were as different as the sun and moon, their spirits danced to vastly different rhythms.

Listening to the growing ferocity of the warriors' taunts, I leaned forward. Tegid's prowess as a warrior drew all men to him, but it was his easy charm of manner that caused them to stay and compete to be one of his chosen band. As night follows day, Iolo possessed great charm of his own, but his friendship was as elusive as the forest mysteries, for although Iolo combined a warrior's courage with a Druid's wit and skill at riddling, his pride and temper were famous and there was that in his personality that hinted at things best left alone.

It began.

"Come to your doom, sweet brother!" Iolo crooned like a nursemaid, crouched in the time-honored wrestler's position.

"Eat shit, sapling." Tegid adjusted his loin cloth, the only garment he wore, deliberately scratching his balls as he did so. In the press of the crowd behind him, I saw a freewoman attempt to push forward. Parting her lips like a dog after a rabbit, she jostled as close as she could to my brothers.

"Shit is it, braggart? I'll throw you in the middens myself." Iolo sprang. Tegid sidestepped and missed his first hold, swaying as he gained his balance back. Diving, Iolo kicked his calf. Tegid turned with a growl.

The crowd closed in, shouting. The wagers were almost even, with Tegid the favorite by one or two cows. But those who knew Iolo, knew enough to understand that what my older brother lacked in brawn, he made up for with grace and guile.

Soon both of my brothers were bruised and grunting. They circled, sweat glistening beneath the torchlight, eyeing each other with wary, drunken respect.

At a signal heard only by themselves, they ran at each other, howling like wolves, first one, then the other gaining an advantage.

Horns of mead passed from hand to hand amidst the shouting watchers, many of whom jumped up on the trestles to cheer on their chosen warrior.

I took a quick sip of unwatered mead while Mother's attention was distracted and looked over the heads of the shouting crowd, watching Nudd and his fellow sentry ritually close the open doors of the Hall now that all the invited guests were safe within.

Waving at Nudd, I squinted hard against the hearth smoke into the feast-heavy air, taking a deep breath of the familiar reek of sweat and stable and heather, the rich scents of laughter, mead, and excitement.

The barley crop was high and ready for harvest, the cattle and sheep fattened, ready to return from their high summer pastures, new alliances had been forged. Best of all, Father's men had burned Gormach's pirates out of their fledgling settlements along our shores, forcing them back to their own misty coasts for at least another sunturn. We of Dinas had good reason to celebrate this harvest!

Tegid used one of his Roman foot moves to flip Iolo on his back. I sneaked another sip of unwatered mead then looked over the heads of my brothers' shouting audience to study the quieter folk gathered at the harpers' bench.

I smiled, nudging Cynan. Tali had managed to slip away from the stables and was there beside our brother Bran, tuning Bran's own harp as my brother showed him the correct placement of his fingers. Old Cadfael, chief harper at Dinas, sat near, ignoring them both, speaking instead to a tall, suspiciously-hooded man.

Alert to danger—for it was rude for anyone to cover their face at a feast—I stared closely at the mysterious man who stood amidst the practicing harpers with the look of one who belonged. It was not until he raised a hand and threw back his cloaked disguise that I recognized Uncle Merlin. As if he'd known I was watching, Merlin inclined his head to me, sketching a wave into the air.

Bran noted the gesture and nodded in my direction, punching Tali who waved to us as well. Cynan and I put our hands on the mead horn I had been sampling and drank together, toasting Tali and Bran. Taking far too great a swallow, I coughed, letting Cynan have the horn.

Mother grabbed it away from us both. Trying not to choke as the mead fired down my throat and my eyes filled up with tears, I cheered at the sight of Tali's long black braids bent over Bran's harp, hoping that this might be a new alliance—an alliance strong enough to last even after Bran began his apprenticeship with the great harpers of Yr Ydrass in their secret mountain school. Perhaps Bran could even help to free Tali from Useth's clutches...

Leaving his harp with Tali, Bran reached for his hazelwood crutch and made his way to the dais. Degwel, the visiting chieftain of the Gull clan, raised an eyebrow and scowled in mockery as Bran limped past him, heading towards Cynan and me. With the grace of long practice, Bran dodged our flailing older brothers and the cheering crowd that surrounded them, taking no notice of the Gull chief's unfriendly eyes.

But Father overlooked nothing when it came to his children and as Degwel turned to say something to his neighbor—a black-toothed Fox chieftain—Father leaned across the table, gesturing for Bran to come closer.

Bran obeyed, resignedly blowing silver-blonde hair from its

cascade across his eyes.

Father reached out his arm for Bran's ritual clasp. "It is good to see you, son."

Sinking back against his wolf-skinned High Seat, Father arrowed a grim smile in Degwel's direction. "I hope you will favor us with a battle song later. It will be one of the last times your Mother and I will hear you before you journey to Yr Ydrass."

Bran ducked his head in assent and found a seat on the dais between Cynan and the Gull's chieftain.

A roar went up from the crowd as Iolo briefly pinned Tegid to the ground. But Degwel watched Bran instead. When my brother was seated, the chieftain turned to him politely. "You are young to seek a place among the bards."

Before Bran could even clear his mouth to speak, Father leaned over us proudly. "My son's gift has been recognized from the day he first picked up a harp to call the spring. The Chief Bard of the Mountains, Emlyn himself, has invited Bran to study with the hidden sages at Yr Ydrass."

Degwel placed his fist on his chest. "I would be honored to hear such a talented youth." All mockery gone from his voice, he poured Bran a cup of mead with his own hands.

Bran took it with the same shy smile that had gifted him with more girls than he knew what to do with—although, at fourteen sunturns, he was learning quickly. In this, as with the quickness of his mind, he was much like our brother Iolo. It helped that in the Hall of Dinas Emrys, a handsome young bard of a ruling house—even if lame—was well-worth a woman's favors. Nor did the whispers that Bran's strange silver hair was a gift from the fairy realms of the Tylwyth Teg hurt his popularity with the giggling young women of Dinas. If anything, it increased their fascination for my shyly-gifted brother, a boy who might easily have been exposed to the wolves at birth had it not been for the love our parents bore him.

Shouts rang out. This time it was Tegid who pinned Iolo to the floor. Iolo struggled, then lay still so long the warriors began to collect their wagers.

Tegid's body shone, slick with sweat, beneath the torches. "Give up, baby brother?"

Iolo didn't answer. Tegid pressed down on Iolo's arms, panting. "Never, you oaf!" Iolo spat in Tegid's eyes.

Swearing, Tegid loosened his grip for the heartbeat Iolo needed to pry back his fingers and wiggle out from under him.

Moving with a quickness that surprised even me, Iolo flipped his larger brother's body back and down.

Straddling Tegid, red-faced, triumphant, Iolo cried, "A boon to the winner—a boon!"

With one final, valiant effort, Tegid puffed his chest up and bucked like an angry stallion.

Taken by surprise, Iolo slid to the ground.

Tegid jumped on top of him, dramatically pinning Iolo's arms, careful to keep his face as far from Iolo as possible. Warriors laughed and Iolo swore a long string of curses, so imaginative that Mother tried to cover my ears.

"Dear brother, I believe the old wives say it is unwise to count one's chickens when the eggs have not yet cracked. I am the winner here—and it is my boon to claim!"

Tegid leapt up, pulling a still-cursing Iolo with him. Looking out across the laughing crowd, Iolo bowed mockingly to Tegid, conceding defeat.

"It is lucky that our clan continues to honor brawn as well as brains, dear brother, or you would be cast out on your ass!" Iolo flashed the chipped-tooth smile that lured women to his bed like ducklings.

Ignoring the laughter and back-slapping, Tegid clapped Iolo on the shoulder. "I've my eye on a few of those skinny Decleangli cattle you appropriated."

"How many?" Iolo's expression shifted from jesting to wary.

Tegid chucked him beneath the chin as if Iolo were still a boy, waving one giant paw in front of Io's eyes.

"This many, upstart." One by one, Tegid raised all five fingers.

Iolo looked relieved. "Done, you swaggering dimwit. Now, show me how you executed that last ill-begotten move."

As Iolo and Tegid moved to the far right hearth, beyond the warriors' bench to practice, trailed by their warrior bands and the young fighters of the visiting clans, Father stood and raised his mead horn.

Silence fell quickly as he began to speak, his voice carrying throughout the great, smoke-filled Hall with the ease of winter wind over sea waves. "Good folk, we are gathered here to celebrate the coming together of the clans. Welcome to the Otter, the Gull, the Bear, the Fox of the Ordovice, welcome to the Badger and the Hawk clans of the

Decleangli! Welcome to the proud Venedotae! May your stay be one of peace and plenty, of sweet mead and meat, and of good company. May our new unity prosper!

"Now, let us hear the songs of our bards and listen well to our people's tales of courage. Let us be reminded of the battle-honor of our forefathers. For there comes tonight, an evil wind, a southern overlord who thinks to lay claim to our lands, who seeks to part us from our sacred pledge with honeyed words, yet who would dagger us in our sleep if once we make treaty with his mercenaries."

Shouts broke out from the warriors gathered with Iolo and Tegid. Defiant cries and raised fists were echoed and then overwhelmed as villagers and freeman began to stomp their feet in ritual challenge on the rush-covered stone flags of the floor; a menacing wave of sound that threatened to raise the rafters of the Hall.

Father raised his arms for silence. My face grew warm with pride as I looked at the gathered throng across the crowded Hall and saw their eyes shining with the same clan-pride and warrior-lust that fired my own stomach.

"Let us be ready for this Vortigern. Let us be watchful of his men. Let none of us speak to them of anything we know. For though they come in peace, they plan for war. Be not fooled, my friends, they seek to take our homes and families from us if we let them. Will we let them?"

Furious shouts of "No!" rose high, past the fire-blackened beams above us into the very thatch of the roof. Hounds barked in excitement and even the central fire seemed to flare in response. At last, when the noise had begun to fade into echoes, Father nodded in satisfaction and raised his arms again.

"So be it, friends." He inclined his head towards the visiting chieftains.

"Now let us rest easy, knowing that our arms are linked. The night is young, there is much mead, wine, and song yet to come."

Father nodded to Cadfael. Our ancient bard had already risen and stood awaiting his cue. Now he approached the harper's stool in front of the High Table with the polish of a seasoned showman and strummed the chords of the great harp that waited there for him. Tali accompanied him as far as the central hearth and then sank to the rushes of the floor, happy to sit with the hounds in order to gain the best possible view of the performance.

I glanced over Cynan's head to Bran, sitting placidly beside Degwel of the Gulls. My brother grinned when he saw me and sent a wink in the Gull chieftain's direction, for big-bellied, drunken Degwel was rambling on about how he had once fancied himself a bard, and been told by his mother that he had talent pure enough to lure the very Tylwyth Teg themselves from the hidden lands beyond the mist.

Bran rolled his eyes and I laughed, unable to imagine the harsh-voiced Gull warrior as being capable of luring so much as a tone-deaf hound to his meat. Unfortunately, my laughter brought Mother's attention down on me. As she clucked at the disarray of my beautiful headdress, adjusting it, despite my embarrassment, I remembered my pride enough to sit tall and not fuss. Casting about for something to distract me, I chanced to look beyond Father to where Uncle Maelgwyn sat, clasping his Roman wine goblet so tightly his fingers had turned white; his face set in an expression so pleasant I knew it to be false.

Black and cold as Brigantian jet, his eyes roamed the crowd as if looking for someone. Lighting at last on Iolo and Tegid tussling amidst their warriors, his gaze rested on their naked backs with an expression that sent winter ice up my spine.

As if following my thoughts, Father turned to Maelgwyn.

"You must forgive me, if I advise our folk to be cautious about this visit from the South." A grim smile flickered across Father's face. "Judging from the gifts he sent with you, he means us to think him harmless. Wealthy but harmless."

Uncle sighed as if he was bored, but his hand was still white around the stem of the jeweled Roman goblet he preferred to our drinking horns. "It does not matter one way or the other to me. This Vortigern breaks promises as often as he breaks wind—disgustingly often, I assure you."

Uncle's lips curled as he delicately cut into his mutton, using a meat dagger with an intricate carving of a boar on its hilt. I had not seen its like before. He wore a silver ring that matched it on his smallest finger. The ring caught the torchlight and reflected it strongly, despite its humble size.

"I sought only to make you a useful alliance with the South. The Vortigern might use mercenaries to fight—but they are fearsome warriors for all that."

Father said nothing, pretending to concentrate on Cadfael's harping. Beneath the cover of his moustaches, he chewed his lower lip. He was puzzling something out and did not want Maelgwyn to know it.

After waiting a few heartbeats, Maelgwyn continued in a voice drenched with honey. "I'd be careful of your womenfolk when Vortigern arrives." Uncle nodded in my direction. "Young as she is, even little Gwen could be in danger from some of those animals he has playing at bodyguards."

Beside me, Mother stiffened. Father finished his mead and turned to face Maelgwyn. "What are you getting at?"

It was Maelgwyn's turn to let silence grow. When he spoke, he smiled brightly at Mother. "Only that you are surrounded by loveliness— and this is a warlord who lusts after beauty—no matter how young the child who possesses it."

Mother tossed her head, the jeweled clink of her headdress lost beneath the iron of her voice. "I will remind you, husband's brother, that you are a guest in this Hall."

Father put his hand on her arm. "My Ceridwen speaks true. I will not have my wife and child threatened within their own Hall by a brother whose every word is poisoned. After this night, I think it best you return to your own steading—and count yourself fortunate that I let you go free at all."

Maelgwyn took a heartbeat to lower his gaze and pick at a cuticle on one of his carefully manicured fingers. After the silence had stretched longer than a full stanza of Cadfael's harping, Maelgwyn raised his eyes and stared at Father with wounded innocence.

"How have I offended? I but speak to warn you of the nature of the man who now approaches—"

"A man you invited!" Father snarled, then stood as Cadfael finished harping. Amidst the applause that followed, Father flung an arm bracelet to the bowing performer.

Cadfael caught the ornament gracefully, bowed to Father, and began to play again, a softer sadder air that quieted the Hall.

As if they had been discussing nothing of greater import than what weather might appear tomorrow, Maelgwyn leaned back and stretched, "Speaking of beauty—come here, girl."

Sari, seated at a trestle near the back of the Hall, saw Uncle gesture for her and reluctantly detached herself from the gaggle of gossiping servants who had befriended her. Although she still wore a veil to cover the lower part of her face and a mantle to cover her hair, tonight Sari had dressed in the simple homespun gown of the hillfolk instead of the flowing fairy garb she had arrived in.

One of the kitchen maids clasped Sari's shoulder in sympathy. The girl shrugged her away and did not look back as she left the trestle bench and slowly made her way across the crowded Hall to the dais.

I was surprised when she looked at me, for a warm flicker of recognition passed over her face as she stopped beneath me. Then she masked her eyes and mounted the dais stairs.

As soon as she neared him, Uncle Maelgwyn pulled her into his lap.

Disgusted, I turned away. Cynan pulled on my arm. Eyes shining with joy, he whispered, "Gwen isn't it wonderful! We could go to war!"

"We're not going to war. Don't you know anything?" For all his nine sunturns, Cynan was still a fool. "Father's just going to impress that southern lord with how strong we are—and then he'll go away."

Cynan raised one of his eyebrows in an annoying impression of Father. "And what would you know about it—girl brat!"

Honor offended, I kicked him, forgetting I was wearing flimsy Roman sandals instead of my stout leather boots—with those I could hold my own.

Now, Cynan just looked down at my feet and laughed. "Oh, but aren't we the fine Roman lady!"

"Cynan! That will be quite enough!" Mother leaned over me and slapped Cynan's hand, forcing him to drop the honey cake he was just about to swallow. An alert hound gulped it down before Cynan could react and he glared at me, revenge chasing all thoughts of adult war from his eyes.

"Gwen looks lovely tonight," Mother continued, to my shame. "She is becoming an elegant lady and you should be very proud of her." I rolled my eyes and looked glumly down at my platter of boar meat and bannock. Cynan kicked me hard in my Roman-clad calf. Trust Mother to make it worse. Now, as soon as her back was turned, I would have to hear his high-pitched, mincing voice tell me how "elegant" I was and how proud he was of me.

I slid one of my sandals off and stabbed him in the ribs with it as hard as I could. It wasn't my best blow, but at least he grunted.

Cynan waited until Mother turned to whisper something to Father then pulled one of my painstakingly-arranged braids down from its placement on top of my head. I splattered him with boar gravy. We stood to wrestle. I was seized from behind by Iorwerth.

"What ho, little warrior! Queen of the meat sauce!"

Cynan began to laugh. Iolo let me go and grabbed him. To my

delight, he flipped Cynan over, twirling the annoying brat upside down. Jumping up on the bench beside our horrified mother, Iolo held Cynan by his ankles over the High Table, letting Cynan's dress tunic fall over my brother's face, its embroidered borders trailing in a large pot of leek stew. Taking happy advantage of the brat's position, I freed a raven feather from my braids and tickled his exposed stomach.

"Gwen!" Despite the anger in Mother's voice, I heard an echo of laughter beneath it. Cynan was cursing and giggling at the same time. "Iolo, stop that! Put him down immediately! One would think we were nothing but a family of barbarians!"

"Well, aren't we?" But Iolo was already standing a red-faced Cynan right side-up on the table. "Shall we play at hurdles, little brother?"

Cynan's face shone. Iolo was his hero and had already been forgiven.

"I'll come back for you later, oh beautiful Roman warrior!" Iolo buried his face in my belly with a mock growl, until I too could barely breathe for laughing.

Iolo picked Cynan up and set him firmly on his shoulders. But instead of taking him to the far hearth where the gaming was, Iorwerth froze. He looked beyond Mother and Father, to where Maelgwyn sat, fondling Sari's breasts as casually as if he were a freewoman choosing apples.

"Who is that?" He asked beneath his breath.

"Some slave Uncle brought from the South. Can we go play now?" Cynan urged.

But our older brother looked as if he had forgotten all about the game he had promised. "She is beautiful—like a full moon on water." Iolo whispered.

"She is Maelgwyn's and he's cruel to her," I said.

Iolo tore his gaze from Sari's bitterly downcast face. "She belongs to that bastard?"

I nodded.

"No longer." I had never seen Iolo's face so pale. It was so white that the last vestiges of his childhood freckles stood out like the ink blots I once made on Celius' prized papyrus scroll. "I swear by Anu, by the very hounds of Anwnn, no longer."

The front door of the Hall crashed open, revealing a deep night sky. Beuno, the eldest of the rampart sentries stood alone in the entrance, breathless. Silhouetted between Hall torches and black night, he looked to be a messenger from other realms.

All was silent for a heartbeat, then Nudd and our other Hall guard ran to flank him. Folk began to push and shout out questions.

"Silence!" roared Father. "Beuno, what news?"

Beuno pushed through the crowd to the king's dais. Behind him ranged five of the guards who had been posted along the inner ramparts.

Making the ancient signs of homage, Beuno bowed to Father but turned quickly back to the open door now filled with what looked to be a host of white-robed beings waiting beyond the threshold of the Hall.

Bowing so low, his head almost touched the ground, Beuno made the ritual sign of welcome to the Hidden Ones.

"Lord Cadwallon, King of the Ordovice—the High-Druid of Yr Wyddfra and his followers have come to speak with you."

chapter 11

I had only seen four or five Druids before, and then only as lonely forest-dwelling men. Never had I seen so many—never had I even known so many Druids still existed, for they had been tortured close to extinction by the red-cloaks.

Now the Hidden Ones marched into Dinas in all their glory and I rose from my seat. Nor was I the only one, for all the folk around me stood, awed to the very core of our beings to see row after row of the ancient priests and priestesses whose words had once brought rain or sun, death or healing to our ancestors.

Hooded beneath white robes, they walked in a measured rhythm, looking neither right nor left; the eldest of them beating a cadence with stout hazelwood staves. Folk moved back to make room for them, jumping up on trestles in order to see above the heads of the crowd. Male priests streamed to the right, women to the left; two score and eight of them arrayed themselves between the feasting tables and the central hearth. A humming began, as they took their places, faint at first, growing louder, filling the Hall as the night wind gains strength beneath the stars.

Cadfael stood, placed his harp carefully in its place beside the harper's stool, and bowed. As if this were a signal, all the priests and priestesses threw back their hoods revealing wreaths of late summer Lughnasa flowers set upon hair that ranged from white to grizzled grey to youthful blacks and golds and browns. The first of the row of men in front of me could not have been much older than Cynan, an acolyte whose chin still spouted fuzz. But when he felt my gaze and raised his face to look at me, his grey eyes burned into mine, as deep and watchful as an ancestor's spirit.

Father had risen with the rest of us, the gold of his torc gleaming beneath the light of the torches behind him. Slowly, he drew back the loose sleeve of his tunic, exposing the great dragon tattooed in a spiral around his arm.

"Hidden Ones of the Mountains, Old Ones of the Mist, we are honored. You are welcome in this Hall."

The humming rose again, louder and higher than before until it reached the pitch of bees loosed from a hive.

"You have come for a reason?" Father's dry voice was steady, his eyes clear, as they roamed the line of priests searching for a leader.

"And you would be right, Cadwallon Long Brow." The speaker stepped into view from behind the tall priest shielding him. People near him gasped in horror.

"Well you know, we do not bother to stir ourselves unless it is for events of great consequence."

I craned my neck as the man stepped forward. Short and squat as he was, he covered the ground between himself and the dais with strides designed to eat up long leagues of land quickly. The other priests moved back to let him pass, following him with their eyes as young wolves regard their leader.

One of his eyes was covered with the white film of age. What caused the folk to gasp was not the red, blood-filled lines that ran across the blind white socket, although that was rare and chilling enough. It was his other eye—the eye that wasn't there. In place of the priest's right eye was a shadowed pit. Tattooed blue lines radiated out from its puckered emptiness, patterned like the wing of a hawk. Indeed the horrible-looking man had hawk feathers strung throughout the small braids of his greasy grey hair. Perched upon his forehead, he wore a wreath of bones and human teeth. Mounted on the back of his headpiece was a hawk's skull, that now gazed out at our Hall with the empty bone eyes of a guardian of the underworld.

He stopped beneath the dais and turned his face up to Father as if he could see him despite the hideous blindness of his eyes. He did not bow nor did he offer Father any sign of homage.

"I am Haran ap Rhydian of the Mountain Ordovice, those you call the Keepers of the Caves." Cynan kicked me in excitement, all of our feuding forgotten. The Hall was filled with stirs and whispers. Folk tried to back away into the shadows. This was a dread visitor indeed.

Mother gripped my elbow, forcing me to stay standing.

The Druid's empty eyes swept the Hall, seeming to pause as they drifted over Cynan and me. I did not breathe. At last the terrible gaze moved on, coming to rest on Father who stood, proudly, patiently waiting.

With a mocking bow, Haran ap Rhydian continued. "I am known in the mountains as Blind Hawk, as many here have cause to know."

I grabbed Cynan's arm. "Blind Hawk?" Shivers of delight and fear lanced up my back. "I thought he was just a story!"

Blind Hawk was one of Hwyrch's favorite tales, one she used to terrify me when I had made her especially angry. Blind Hawk had first been called Mountain Hawk, an outlawed Druid captured and tortured by Roman soldiers at Segontium, the fort they'd built along the coast of the Venedotae's ancestral lands.

It had been in the time of Grandmother's youth when the red-cloaks were leaving our lands at last, setting sail for their southern homes. It had been only the very worst of luck that the young Druid, Mountain Hawk, chose that fortnight to explore the coast for oracles. Even worse that the red-cloaks who captured him were some of the most malicious vipers in their legion, so corrupt that even their fellows had left them deliberately behind.

They held the Hawk for two days. Young as he was, with one eye torn out and the other destroyed, even then his magic had been strong enough to curse them all. He had escaped at last and they had not bothered to pursue him. Yet every one of the soldiers who had tortured him met a bitter death—long before they managed to find their wine-sotted way across the Narrow Sea to the olive trees and palaces of their own ancestral lands. Indeed, all their bodies had been found within a league of the now-deserted fortress, staked to the earth, their cursed Roman entrails scattered in an oracle to the gods.

Ignoring the whispers, Father sat calmly and regarded the priest, although a twitch ran almost unnoticed up his jaw. "It is well you came to me, Haran, Blind Hawk. What do you ask of Cadwallon Long Brow ap Cunedda Iron Hand, King of Dinas Emrys, ruler of the Otter clan, Lord of the Ordovice?"

Blind Hawk stamped his hazel staff against the stone flags of the floor, waiting until the echoes of the resounding thud died before he spoke.

"I ask that this senseless raiding between you and the Decleangli

Wolf Clan be at an end. That you unite and face your common enemies—those raiders that come to our shores from the West—from the North—from the East. From those envious overlords in soft southern lands who, even now, cast greedy eyes to the river-tin and copper of our mountains, to the riches we have earned in trade, to the very cattle we war over among ourselves!"

Our own folk looked from Father to the Druids and back, wondering at the strangeness of Blind Hawk's words. Were the Druids so blinded by the wealth of the Wolf clan that they dared to insult our warriors for stealing their cattle—a war the Decleangli themselves had begun?

Father opened his mouth to reply, but what he intended to say was lost in the murmurs coming from the back of the Hall.

Grandmother Rhiannon strode out from the shadows near the door. Dressed in forest finery, she walked beside the priestesses' row, coming to a stop in front of the High Table. Her jaunty grin at Father was answered by an icy stare. Mother's eyes darkened; she too was furious.

Grandmother's dragon-belted tunic boasted our tribal colors of bright blue and yellow and soft green. Her skirt was travel-stained with mud although her prized plaid cloak hung gracefully from the Otter clan brooch that fastened it. Her long silver hair fell loose to her knees, adorned by a wreath of rowan berries and oak leaves, signaling she was among us as a priestess of the old ways, a harvest goddess come to protect us as best she could from the approaching winter.

"Cadwallon Long Brow," she addressed Father formally. "Give ear to the words of Haran, High Priest of Yr Wyddfa, Keeper of the Caves. He speaks wisdom in this season."

"No doubt he does, Lady Rhiannon, Sage Singer of the Mountain Ordovice, Mother of my wife. However," Father's leaned forward in barely controlled fury, "if I am to listen to the white robes, I would prefer to harken to the Arch-Druid of Mona and not merely to the words of a mystic, no matter how well intentioned."

Grandmother glared. Father ignored her as he ignored the shocked whispers that filled the Hall and the angry ritual humming that rose from the ranks of the visiting Druids.

Father stood, raising his arms as a king, inclining his head to include Blind Hawk in his speech.

"With respect, Lord of the Night, I find it hard to find the justice in what you speak this evening. Where were your white-robes when the Wolf Clan took cows beyond counting from the crofts of my people in the dark days when my father, Cunedda Iron Hand's spirit lingered between Anu's earth and Anwnn's Underworld Hall? Where were your priests when the Wolf Clan began this business long sunturns before our fathers drew breath? Yet you come this night—as my brave clan celebrates the victory of the Otter's sons!"

Father's words were like oil poured on dried rushes and set aflame. Throughout the Hall, folk shouted and stomped in agreement. Warriors made their way through the crowd and stood flanking the High Table as Tegid and Iorwerth leapt to stand beside Father.

"Hear our King, brave warriors!" Iolo shouted, picking me up in his arms. Cheers rang out all around me and I could feel my face flushing with joy as I raised my fist and screamed battle cries with the rest of my people.

Blind Hawk and Grandmother watched in silence. When the shouts at last grew ragged and the noise began to fade, Blind Hawk raised his arms high for silence. "You are right, Cadwallon."

Mild as his voice was, people quieted immediately. "I should have intervened long before this night. But—" Hawk fell silent, turning his face slowly from side to side as an animal does when testing the wind.

"Perhaps," he continued, "you know the hard path a man must follow if he is to bring up a son full of honor. I am afraid I have made the mistake of not curbing my own cub sooner."

He turned from us and faced the Druids. A tall priest with thick, grey-black hair stepped forward and walked towards the Hawk. When he stood beside the old man, the stranger shrugged off his robes and exposed the battered leather breast plate of a warrior. Pulling back his hair, he revealed tattoos high upon his cheek bones. I squinted and saw three straight lines and a narrow circle beside them—the clan marks of our enemy, the Wolf clan of the Decleangli!

The man bowed gracefully, "Lord Cadwallon, at last we meet face to face. I am Chalan Grey Sword, Lord of the Wolf clan, son of the Decleangli—and former owner of the plump red cattle who now bide in the pen beneath us!"

Amid the yells and shouts that followed Chalan's words, I chanced to see the young Druid boy whom I had noticed earlier, standing at the forefront of the priest's line. He was glancing wildly about him, no doubt thinking of how fine it would be to grip a spear as some small protection against the fury in our Hall.

"Hold, good people!" Chalan walked towards my father's High Table as easily as if he were pacing the floors of his own keep. Despite the angry shouts and threats that swirled around him like dust, he smiled at Father, his dark eyes alight with a twinkle that made me think of a weary fox returning to its den.

Before anyone could move to stop him, the Decleangli lord vaulted up the two steps of the dais and reached across the meat-laden trestle board to clasp Father's arm in friendship. "It is an honor, Lord Cadwallon, to meet you at last."

Father looked surprised for a heartbeat. Then, grinning, he gripped Chalan's arm with his own.

"Scoundrel! I bide you welcome to my Hall!" In the shocked silence that followed, Father began to laugh. "I could use an ally with balls of brass!"

He clasped Chalan's arm higher, faced the crowd and roared, "Now, my friends we shall see just what these Wolves are made of!"

Our warriors rose from their benches, pounding their fists on the tables in challenge. It was indeed fortunate for Chalan that clan laws of hospitality forced all warriors to keep their weapons outside the Hall.

Yet the Wolf Lord's smile whipped across his narrow face like lightning. "My Lord we are well met." As if the massing warriors were already bosom friends, he spread out his arms to embrace the Hall.

"Brave people of the Otter! Your ambush of our cattle was a plan we ourselves could envy. Tonight this is all I ask. That we put aside our old rivalries and let the future see us fighting side by side. Let us clear our mountains and coast of these foreign pirates—just as our ancestors fought as Sword Brothers to rid our lands of the red-cloak dogs many sunturns ago!"

Up and down the length of the Hall, people who raged, grew silent, considering. The standing ranks of Druid priests swayed in ceremonial rhythm, as tall trees will do when crossed by a strong wind.

"Wait!" Iorwerth's shout rang across the Hall. "And just who will we expect to find at our backs once we let you help us drive the Scotti away?"

Iolo jumped down from the dais where he had been standing beside me, scattering platters of boar and venison to the floor.

As soon as he was certain of the Hall's attention, Iolo leapt back up to stand in front of Chalan, careful to angle himself in such a manner that those in the Hall could see his face and hear what he said.

"You Wolves are not famous for keeping your paws only on what belongs to you by right. I, Iorwerth, son of Cadwallon Long Brow, say this—let hostages be taken to encourage Chalan Grey Sword to keep his word!"

Chalan's dark eyes flashed in fury for a heartbeat before he shuttered their depths with a fixed smile and an easy shrug. It was a look much like Maelgwyn's, a look that put the lie to his friendly smile, a look that I would not forget. Yet as the Decleangli chief stepped forward, he bowed so graciously to my brother, I almost doubted I had seen his malice.

"But of course, youngling. Hostages shall be exchanged. Though, I must say," he paused to regard my father, a questioning tilt to his heavily-bearded face, "I am surprised that Good Lord Cadwallon allows newly-weaned cubs to speak his council for him."

An angry uproar broke out. Before it could gather strength, Father rose to his feet, gesturing Iolo to attend him. No fool, Iorwerth strode to Father's side where he stood, quivering as if he was a hound on a tight leash, fierce with the scent of deer in his nostrils.

Father put his arm on Iolo's shoulder, careful to let the loose sleeve of his tunic fall back, exposing the woad dragon to the Hall. "In this, my whelp and I speak as one. For in the dawn of any clan's alliance, there must be offerings made to please the rising sun. So let it be doubly true for clans whose grandsires have played each other false."

Father stopped for a sip of mead, watching the Wolf Lord's eyes narrow as the words sank in. Clearly the Wolf Lord was not used to being denied something he lusted for. I studied him closely, noticing for the first time the yellowed human teeth strung beneath the crow feathers of his braids. An Eater of the Dead then. I had heard they still existed in the eastern mountains, but had thought it just another of Hwyrch's tales.

I shuddered, glancing over at Maelgwyn who sat casually on the dais, regarding Chalan as if the Wolf Lord was an unexpected gaming piece, one he had not yet decided how to move. This I could see, but for those who did not know Uncle, he appeared politely bored.

Father's and Chalan's eyes locked.

Neither spoke. The silence grew dangerous.

At last Father poured a horn of mead and passed it to the Decleangli Lord.

"Yet, you are welcome in my Hall this eve, son of the Wolf and you show great courage in the coming. Of this adventure, bright songs will soon be made, I have no doubt."

He glanced wryly across the central fire to where Tali had joined Cadfael and the other visiting harpers on the musicians' bench. Cadfael inclined his head. Father smiled and sat down. Running his fingers along the thick wolfskin that covered the arms of his throne, he addressed Chalan again.

"Drink my mead in peace, Chalan Grey Sword. I would be loathe to miss the chance to turn an enemy of mettle into an ally and a friend."

Standing, body taut and straining, Chalan's shoulders eased. Father met his eyes and nodded slowly, "If your words be true, we think alike, Chalan Grey Sword and an exchange of hostages will but make firm the terms."

Ignoring my furious brother Iolo, Chalan clasped my father's lower arms in both his own, his fingers supple and sure as they circled above my father's golden warrior bands.

"Then we are agreed, Cadwallon Long Brow. And much pleasure do I take in this alliance! As for a hostage, I offer my own son. Lleu, come forth!"

The boy, whom I had noticed amidst the Druids, looked about himself in dismay, casting grey-storm eyes across the width of the Great Hall. They met my own and held them in a gaze that crackled with sudden defiant fire. With a deep breath, he stepped out from the ranks of the white-robed priests and walked forward towards the dais where he joined his father, Chalan Grey Sword. Father and son turned to face my father, the boy squaring his narrow shoulders with a shrug.

"My son, Lleu, Dream Singer, grandson of Mountain Hawk, Guardian of Yr Wyddfra and the Caves of Arfon." Chalan placed one calloused warrior's hand upon his young son's shoulder and stepped sideways so that he faced Father and the crowded Hall at the same time.

"I ask that you care for him as if he were of your own clan. For he is beloved of the Wolf."

Father joined them, placing his right hand upon Lleu's other shoulder. "He stands strong, this son of the Wolf, with the far-seeing eyes of the mountains. We will treat him well, fear not. Does he follow the Druid's path, or merely disguise himself in their robes as does his father?"

Chalan's teeth flashed. "It is said he shows promise in the forest ways. Are there any who can walk with him along the ancient roads of our people? He will have need of further training."

"I, Rhiannon of the Mountain Ordovice, will see that he receives it.

We are not yet so tied to red-cloaks and nailed southern gods as we may seem at first sight." With a disdainful glance at Mother's Cristos hermit who sat with the villagers but refused to eat, Grandmother advanced towards the High Table. Ignoring Mother's angry intake of breath, she put her own hand upon Lleu's shoulder and raised her eyes to face Chalan. "Who would you ask of us?"

Before Chalan or Father could reply, a soft voice sang out, "I will go with the Wolf clan's leader in exchange for Lleu, his son."

All turned to the bench beside me where my brother Bran now stood, somehow managing to make his hazelwood crutch look like a post he casually leaned upon, instead of an implement he needed merely to walk across the floor.

"What madness is this, I forbid it! Husband," Mother rose, turning frantic eyes to Father, "Tell him no!"

Father ignored her, motioning Bran to stand beneath the dais beside Chalan and his son. My brother obeyed, managing the two short steps with the ease of long practice. Standing beside Chalan, he raised his eyes, fixing them not on Father but on the dragon shield that hung behind Father's throne. I could feel him, willing his twisted leg to straighten as he waited.

"Cadwallon, no!" Mother's cry echoed, the only sound in the breathless Hall.

Father turned to Chalan. "My son shall never become a warrior, never taste the blood mead of the initiate's Hall. Yet he is marked for greatness of another kind."

Chalan inclined his head. "Even our mountains know of the youngest bard of the Ordovice. Your praises run on the wind, boy."

He clamped his hand on Bran's shoulder. "But are you not expected at Yr Ydrass? Why do you seek to leave your own people?"

"The world is a wide and wondrous place, Wolf Lord." Bran answered with the same lopsided grin he always trained on me when I asked a foolish question. "As a harper, it is my right to see as much of it as I can. Even if it takes me far from those I love."

He spun round on his crutch and faced Mother.

"The Masters of Yr Ydrass know this well. I will go to their mountains later, when I have more of life to offer our people's songs. Mother, you know my need."

Mother drew herself up to full height and glared at Bran in silence, her front teeth visible as she bit deeply down into the fullness of her lower lip. She spared no further glances towards our father, or Chalan Grey Sword who was regarding her with a sympathetic expression in his cunning fox eyes.

Her own eyes ranged to the shadows near the back of the Hall. Grandmother stepped from behind a rune-etched pillar of smoke-blackened oak, her long white hair, a reminder of winter beneath the bright orange-red leaves of her Druid crown. Merlin stood beside her, appearing like a wraith from the far reaches of the harpers' bench.

"He speaks high words for a youth, daughter. Let them ease your heart, as he leaves our lands. For leave them he must. As surely as smoke rises to the gods, Bran must go forth from this Hall."

Merlin bowed his head in agreement.

Mother flinched and sank down into her chair, gesturing wordlessly for Bran to approach. Her face was whiter then I had ever seen it, a small drop of blood peeled upwards from her lower lip as she removed her teeth to speak.

"Son of my heart," her voice was barely a whisper. She coughed to clear her throat. In front of the High Table, Bran lowered himself to his knees, keeping hold of his crutch so that it stood tall beside his kneeling form.

"Son of my heart," Mother repeated. This time her voice was strong enough to fill the listening Hall. "Since the winter morn you drew first breath and defied those sages of doom who prophesied that you would not live beyond the coming sunset, you have brought enchantment to the world-weary corners of this Hall. You sing of the Land of Apples, of the Silver Realms beneath the sea. Your harp knows the whisper of angels, your voice the power of shrieking armies, of battle fury, of honor, and of blood. You give us dreams, my son. And still, you are but a boy."

She turned to Chalan, her violet eyes hooded with night. "Treat him well, my Lord. He is our greatest treasure."

Chalan clasped Bran's slender shoulder in a reassuring grip. Meeting Mother's bruised shadowed eyes, he solemnly took the hand she held out to him and lowered himself to kiss it.

"Lady, I will honor him as my own son. And fear not, there are things we too can teach him. We Decleangli may not have had as much traffic with the red-cloaks as your clan, but we are not shy of harping! He will learn from our finest, Mentone of the Silver Leaf, son of the River people."... Mother's smile was gracious, yet terribly sad. "I have heard of this singer, Chalan Grey Sword. He is indeed a fine bard. Able to sing the deer from their forests, if what I hear rumored be true."

"Son," she smiled a little more strongly at Bran as he climbed his crutch to stand, careful to make it appear effortless although I noted his clenched jaw. "Do not forget us. Know that you go with our love and our regard."

A loud cheer began in the back of the Hall and quickly gathered force as it moved like a wave across our clan, reaching the High Table with a roar. Bran ducked his head. When he raised his face to our family and turned to speak to the crowd, there was no disguising either the bright fierce joy in his smile or the excited sparkle that lit his mysterious blue eyes, fragmented as they were by the silver tumble of his hair.

"Thank you! Mother, Father, friends! How could I ever forget my people? You who have given me life itself! Wherever I go in this great world's realm, it will be your songs I sing, this earth I remember beneath my feet and in my heart." Bran kissed both his fists, placed them on his chest, and flung them wide in the ancient gesture of farewell.

"A toast!" Father called, raising his mead horn.

"A toast!" Iorwerth echoed, eyeing Chalan with a look that promised trouble. My brother raised his horn but waited to drink until he saw Sari, who now stood behind Maelgwyn's chair waiting to pour wine. Her posture and veiled profile were as remote and haunting as a goddess' and although she did not look at him, Iolo saluted her with his mead, drinking deep, his eyes passing from her to Maelgwyn with the trajectory of a javelin.

"A toast!" The crowd roared, the Druids themselves joining in as the white-robed priests relaxed their stately positions and began to mingle with the warriors and villagers spread throughout the Hall.

"A toast!" Grandmother's voice rang out, turning to Merlin, her rare smile flashing like a salmon in a swift-moving stream. She clapped Chalan's son, Lleu, firmly on the back and gazed into Bran's joyously triumphant eyes.

"A toast!" Blind Hawk and his son Chalan's voices rang out together as they clasped Father's forearms in the embrace of peace.

"It is a good beginning, brothers." The aging, frightening-visaged priest gripped the two younger men's arms tightly.

"My Lords, this does indeed bode well for those of our people who chose to remember the Old Ways." Uncle Merlin joined them, canting his head towards Blind Hawk.

Before Father could introduce him, Blind Hawk's horrible face lit in a smile that made his wrinkles dance like spiders fleeing across a web. "Is that you, young Emrys?"

Merlin's voice was softer than usual, almost as if he had turned shy, "It is, my Lord. Helios will be delighted that you still walk this earth's realm."

"How is the old rascal?" Blind Hawk raised one hand, exploring Merlin's face with authority, pausing as his fingers encountered the Moon Singer tattoos on Uncle's temples.

He whistled. "Helios of the Heatherlands must indeed be pleased with you. That old grey beard has never honored anyone else with what you bear. Nor is it an easy thing to carry."

"I admit there are mornings I rise and long to be rid of it!" Laughter was not far from the surface of Merlin's voice. "Yet, it has brought me here, to this place of dragons. I admit that I am eager to see what awaits us."

"Many births hold death within them, son." Blind Hawk's voice turned thoughtful. "Be careful what you conjure."

Merlin clasped the old man's hand. "I will, Lord. I promise. For now, I ask your blessing, as one hawk to another, eh?"

The Hawk laughed and embraced my tall mysterious uncle with his short, flabby-skinned arms. He looked like a duck hugging a crane—but the beauty of the old man's voice as he sang the ritual blessing made me feel ashamed of such an undignified comparison.

When the Druid's blessing was over, he put his hand upon Merlin's bowed head. "Come, Shield Brother of the Mysteries, let us drink mead and talk of nothing more important than the sand beneath the sea—or perhaps the touch of a warm woman on a cold winter's eve, eh?"

Merlin clasped Hawk's arm. The old Druid turned. "Come, son, Cadwallon, let us make merry while we can!"

Near them, watching from the dais, Uncle Maelgwyn raised his Roman wine goblet slowly, his gaze flickering from Tegid and Iorwerth to Chalan and Father then down the table to examine Chalan's son, Lleu. A small smile flashed beneath the trimmed moustaches of his face, but his soul-shuttered eyes remained as cold as winter-iced rock.

"A toast to better days, husband's brother." Mother stood and walked slowly towards Maelgwyn, crossing behind Father's High Seat, beneath the gleaming dragon shield to where Uncle sat. "A toast, to healing in this Hall." Mother raised her horn.

After a pause that stretched for many heartbeats, Maelgwyn raised his goblet in reply and clinked it politely against her horn. "To better futures, Lady". His smile made me shiver.

I got up to run to her, but before I could move, Cynan pulled me down the dais steps, jumping up and down in excitement.

"Come on, brat, let's toast!" Cynan spun me around in circles and then let go, leaving me to stagger among the overexcited hounds. More of my braids worked loose and fell around my face like loose threads of an unraveling cloth. Before I could recover enough to shove him back, the harpers began to play again.

Cadfael opened with one of my favorite songs, a tale of long-dead warriors slaughtered because the message to their Lord had gone astray, leaving them to fight outnumbered ten to one. They all died, of course, but gloriously, hacking hands and limbs from their enemies until they were too tired to lift their own swords.

I was not the only one who loved the tale and the Hall was soon filled with loud voices—warriors, Druids, and bards alike—lifting the rafters with drunken enthusiasm.

As the last chord died, voices called out for Bran. My brother limped proudly to take his place beside Cadfael and began a slow lament for lands now vanished beneath the sea. The crowd quieted to listen.

Cadfael handed Tali a small harp and together, accompanied by the many visiting bards, who had come to Dinas with their clans, they joined their harps to Bran's, dancing the scales of time as Bran began to sing in a voice that held the crashing of the waves, the terror of the deep, the last prayers of the drowning.

Listening to Bran and the harpers blend their songs together, I yawned and let my spirit soar with imaginings. I had put myself on the back of a hawk traveling east beyond the great river, when I felt Mother's cool hands remove my headdress and gather my head into her lap. There, I curled and slept.

Woven into my dreams, I heard a great commotion in the Hall.

"The Vortigern has arrived, puss," Mother whispered in my ear. "You must rise and greet him."

chapter 12

The burly southern warlord swaggered towards Father, close on the heels of Selyf, Tegid's Shield Brother. Our warriors jumped up, drunk and dangerous, to flank Father and the guest chieftains who sat with him on the dais.

Vortigern's own honor guard followed the southern King closely—their manners as foreign in our Hall as roosters set loose in a Roman bath. More like a pack of pirates than proud soldiers, they gazed contemptuously past the crowd of warriors who menaced them, looking with greed at the rich hangings on our walls and the beautifully-cast shields and swords of my ancestors.

But it was Father's priceless golden dragon shield that made them jabber like squirrels, pointing over the heads of the finely-costumed chieftains seated at the High Table.

Maelgwyn dropped his bored posturing and got eagerly to his feet. "Brother, may I present, The Vortigern, Overlord of the Silures, the Dubonni, the—"

"Enough! This man knows who I am!" Vortigern sought to stand straight, looking at us sternly out of small pig eyes. He staggered, either from tiredness or drink, and had to be steadied by a tall blonde warrior who stood close enough to be the warlord's shadow.

A Seaxon! It was the first time I had ever seen one of the Sea Wolves in person and rubbed the last of the sleep from my eyes to make sure I wasn't dreaming.

"Indeed, I do." Father's tone stopped just one shade short of rudeness. Instead of rising, he leaned forward, offering Vortigern a horn of mead—fine drink that even I could see would be wasted on the man before us.

"Be welcome to this Hall. If you come in peace," Father paused, "your stay will be one of peace."

Vortigern took the horn, tilting it back so far that his face disappeared from sight. I watched, fascinated, as the motion revealed a greasy length of beard interwoven with small braids, teeming with food crumbs and small life forms that visibly rippled as I stared.

"Be wary, Gwen." Unnoticed Merlin had left the group of Druids he had been sitting with and now stood on the dais behind Mother and me. His clasp upon my shoulder was steadying. I sat up straighter, remembering my rank. An Ordovice princess did not show her true feelings when confronted by an enemy.

And that Vortigern was an enemy I had no doubt.

The warlord threw the dregs of the horn on the rushes for the gods, belched with satisfaction, and faced us again.

"Your brother speaks highly of you." Vortigern belched again. Had the man not carried such a thick aura of danger—a sense that he was capable of any act, however bloody—I would have felt sorry for him. He made himself ridiculous: a king without pride or honor.

"I thought it best I visit your mountains to see what mettle of man you are for myself."

"And now you see." Father rose. "However, Lord Vortigern, I would wish you to postpone our formal meeting until tomorrow, when we are rested, and can bring greater wisdom and better company to the table."

Vortigern laughed, spewing saliva in all directions. "Well said, Ordovice, well said! But what of my needs now? As yon skinny-arse can attest, my men and I have moved so quickly through your Cristos-damned forests, we have not stopped to shit, let alone eat—let alone seek out the ladies, eh?"

He ran appreciative eyes over Mother and then turned to me, raking me up and down with an expression that made my stomach curdle.

Mother placed her hand tightly over mine.

Selyf—skinny-arsed as any of our warriors—approached the dais.

"Thank you, Selyf, for seeing our guests safely to Dinas." Father turned to Vortigern and the tall Seaxon who shadowed him.

A short muscular warrior detached himself from Vortigern's ragged honor guard and walked crisply to stand beside the southern king in the time-honored stance of a Shield Brother. I had no time to wonder why he was so late to appear, for Father stood, gesturing for servants to attend him.

"Sit and rest upon our benches," said Father. You will share the finest foods our kitchen can offer. When you hunger no longer, Selyf will lead you to your beds in the new guest house next to the Warriors' Hall."

Justly proud of the stone guest house that he had designed and helped to build, perhaps I was the only one who noticed Father's emphasis on its location next to our warriors. Vortigern would be watched closely.

As weary servants grumbled their way into the kitchen to serve yet another meal, Father added, "And as to the ladies, Lord Vortigern, my Hall is not a brothel. If you did not bring your own women and your men find no one willing to bed them for a trinket or for the joy of their company, you must do without."

This raised grumbles from Vortigern's men, causing Father to raise his voice in a manner that did not brook argument. "The punishment for rape is severe in my lands, Lord. A servant's honor is worth five cows, the rape of a highborn woman carries death."

The men's grumbles grew ugly, our warriors turned threatening. Maelgwyn rose quickly, throwing a look at the southerner's tardy Shield Brother, "Lord Vortigern, I have heard it said you are a master of tawlbwrdd."

The warlord's eyes turned speculative. "That is so, young Maelgwyn."

"Then perhaps I can interest you in a game?"

"The stakes?" Vortigern shrugged, winking at the tall man who stood beside him. The Seaxon's blonde plaits were not braided like ours, but hung loose upon his chest tied with rawhide strips at the ends instead of the more elegant feathers and small braids and stones with which our warriors adorned themselves.

"I've been admiring that fine ring you wear—"

"This bauble?" Vortigern wrenched it off and tossed it to his man. "And if I win?"

Maelgwyn's smile cut across his face like a dagger. "Come here, Sari."

"No!" Mother stiffened. The hand she had placed over mine tightened painfully.

Surprised from sleep, Sari uncurled from the corner of the dais where she had retreated and stood, blinking in confusion.

Iolo sprang from his seat at the warriors' table, meat dagger in hand.

Grandmother smoothly intercepted him, holding his arm in what looked like a request for aid to anyone who did not know her. "Lord Vortigern—lovely as she is, it would not be wise to bed such a one."

The warlord's eyes were already glazed in a leer, watching Sari's graceful oblivious progress down the dais. "And why not, white-hair?" he snarled.

Grandmother ignored the insult although the hillfort folk murmured and three Druids rose in outrage.

Grandmother quelled them with a wave of her hand. "She is a seer, Vortigern, the first our people have had in three generations. The priestesses of the forest claim her. Any man who touches her from this day forward will be cursed. His balls will turn black and fall to the ground like dead leaves. He will go blind. All other men's hands will be raised against him. King or commoner, he will die despised and alone. This, I, Lady Rhiannon, Sage Singer of the Ordovice, tell you. May it be on your own head if you harken not to my words."

The Vortigern's face had paled as Grandmother spoke, whether from fear at what would happen if he took Sari to his bed or because he now understood that he had just insulted one of the most powerful priestesses in the North. He who had made it his business to bring back the most ancient of old ways in a South that had all but forgotten them.

Iorwerth paled, as well. Under cover of releasing him from her grip, I saw Grandmother whisper fiercely to him. Whatever she said had the effect she wanted, for he bowed bitterly to her and took himself from the Hall without a backward glance.

Maelgwyn opened his mouth to say what we were all thinking— for if Grandmother spoke true, Maelgwyn's future manhood was in question. But, after one look at Father and Grandmother, he appeared to think better of it and seized one of the prettier servant girls instead.

After a whispered conference with her, Uncle smiled again. "All is not lost, my Lord. While it would appear wise to forgo the pleasures of the beautiful Sari..."

He scowled so ferociously at the veiled young woman that I breathed a sigh of relief when Grandmother appeared at her side and lead her away to a bench near the back of the Hall where a small group of priestesses clustered.

After a final black look, Uncle paid Sari no further attention. Instead he pulled the new servant girl to his lap and began squeezing her breasts. "This luscious peach, Alys, can be had for the winning."

Alys giggled as she looked from Maelgwyn to Vortigern. Beautiful she was, but she was also the laziest girl in the kitchen and Maeve and Kerinne had long ago despaired of keeping her away from the Warriors' Hall. Now, clearly enjoying the attention, she batted slow-witted, but lovely eyes, at Vortigern, whose own calculating expression turned gleeful. Making up his mind, the overlord bared rotting teeth in a wide grin and swaggered up the dais steps to join Maelgwyn as Uncle carefully set up the carved tawlbwrdd pieces.

Passing the girl, Vortigern brushed crumbs from the stained linen of his tunic and straddled the bench beside her, thrusting his great belly proudly above his sword belt. "A juicy sweet, indeed, Maelgwyn." He grabbed Alys' other breast. "Look to your wager."

"Ugh!" I whispered to Mother.

"Ugh, indeed. And I think it high time you were in bed, daughter. Let us take our leave."

We were not the only ones to give in to exhaustion. Now that the crisis with Vortigern appeared to have passed, villagers, fort dwellers, warriors, and servants all wearily made for their beds.

Finding beds for our many guests was a task greater than most kings usually faced. However, Father and Mother did well enough, assigning berths with an eye to fairness as well as protection. Blind Hawk, Chalan, and Lleu would bed in the guest chambers in the Hall. Druids and visiting warriors would either make their way to the Warriors' Hall or bed down in the Hall itself, or take their cloaks out beneath the late summer stars. The old guest house beside the Hall was large enough for the visiting clan chiefs, leaving the new guest house to the tender mercies of Vortigern and his band of Sea Wolves—with Selyf and Tegid's men sharing their quarters and keeping a hawk's eye on our uninvited visitors.

And Cynan, lucky Cynan, would get to sleep with Iolo and the warriors in the coveted Warriors' Hall.

Too tired even to pout, I watched Tegid leap up the dais stairs. "Has the ragamuffin lost her finery so soon, Mother?"

"Shh, she's sleeping."

"No, I'm not!" I denied crossly, although Tegid looked to have three heads.

He kissed me. I snuggled against his big-brother smell of fresh sweat and mead and laughter. The tunic he'd put on after wrestling Iolo was fresh-washed and smelled like the sun he reminded me of.

I think I kissed him back. Later I could not remember. Perhaps I only hoped I had.

chapter 13

I woke in darkness, to the smell and sight of predawn mist roiling in through the unshuttered window of my chamber, a chill reminder of the coming of autumn. Careful not to disturb snoring Hwyrch, I grabbed the first tunic I could find, hopped into my trews, and carried my boots and stockings out the door.

Reaching the small landing beside Mother's summer weaving room, I balanced against the cool stone of the arrow-slit windows, trying to put on my boots without making a sound. Outside, to the east, dark and fog held the world. Watchfires flared like comforting red stars along the guards' walkways. Through gaps in the mist I could make out the humps of mountains, floating like pillows above the fog, Yr Wyddfa towering above them all.

I reached out to the invading mist as if I were a small child again, trying to catch and hold its white tendrils in my hands. I had no more success with this than ever, but the hands I brought to my face smelled of the fog's long journey; of far away secrets and snow-covered mountain glades, of pine forests and wet whispers of joy— trembling with the promise of an exciting day.

Outside, I was still careful to be quiet. The mist was thick on the ground and the predawn silence held, but Dinas was stuffed to overflowing with strangers and I had no desire to rouse anyone before my mission could be accomplished.

A pile of stones lay near the stables. I hefted the most promising one. This time it would be Cynan who would wake with a rock to the head.

I was creeping towards the Warriors' Hall when I heard muffled voices coming from the direction of the stables. Recognizing Uncle Maelgwyn's clipped speech, I tiptoed closer. Instinct warned me not to make a sound.

The stable doors were open, unusual this early. I merged with the door shadows and slid inside, taking cover behind a bale of hay.

"You'll find Nestor grateful." Torchlight threw Maelgwyn's shadow against the back stable wall, lurking there like a hawk-nosed giant.

"Today then?" Useth slung his clumsy bulk over Father's fastest pony. His voice was as grating as ever, but it held a note I had not heard before, as if he were a village cat and had torn a rat to pieces.

"Today. An accident. Or you too will join the shadows," Uncle snapped.

Useth dug his heels cruelly into the pony's sides and rode out without speaking again.

I curled into as small a ball as possible.

What did this mean? With Maelgwyn anything was possible.

Mother. Mother would know.

Uncle took his time leaving, looking slowly around him. He neared the shadows of my hiding place and began to hum, widening his nostrils: a predator scenting a meal.

I froze, terrified of what he would do if he discovered me.

Finally he doused his torch in a trough of horse water near the stable's doorway and took one final searching look behind him, examining all the stable's nooks and crannies: ponies, stalls, tack, and hay, illuminated now in the gradual light of dawn.

I held my breath.

He left, whistling softly.

I stayed where I was, listening as night sentry, Nudd, called out a weary challenge. Useth whined a tale of being plagued with a toothache and in need of a forest wise woman.

The wooden fortress gate creaked open. In the silence that followed, the jangle of the pony's bridle and the fog-softened sound of its hooves leaving Dinas seemed louder than they should have been in the muffled misty air.

I crept out from my hiding place, noticing for the first time the sweet scent of newly-scythed hay. Finding Mother was the best course, but I dawdled, pretending to myself that I was waiting to make sure Maelgwyn was far away. The truth was that I sought comfort in the familiar stable smells, in those scents that I loved more than any of Mother's perfumes.

I took a deep breath of horse-sweat, manure, worn leather, and hay; that indefinable sense of promise that stables always gave me—of journeys yet to be made, adventures yet to be dreamed. Amidst the rustlings, snortings, and chewings of sleepy ponies, I sat quiet, trying to pretend that evil had not entered this beloved place.

Where was Tali? I got up to search his usual sleeping place. His threadbare cloak was crumbled in the straw, but there was no sign of my friend.

Uncle's voice and the things he had said to Useth slithered in my thoughts like snakes. I squared my shoulders and ran outside, heading to the Hall to find Mother. Father's Shield Brother Hwyll stood guard at Mother and Father's chamber in the Hall. "Your parents rose early and decided to walk in the grove before folk began to seek them."

An indulgent smile lifted the ugly scar that cut across Hwyll's cheek and chin, disfiguring a face that had once been as handsome as Father's.

I ran rudely away, pushed by my increasing sense of danger.

The full light of dawn now filled the courtyard and buildings of Dinas. Servants and villagers were stirring, their rustlings and morning grumbles as familiar to me as my own face. The simple, everyday sound of their voices made me even more frightened.

I raced faster, pushing through the fortress gates that a yawning Nudd was opening for the day. Midway down the hill slope of Dinas, I found my parents sitting on the rocks beside the Goddess Pool, shadowed by a copse of rowan, hazel, and oak. Bran was with them and was just passing his harp to Tali when I ran into the glade. He waved me beside him with a smile.

"Shadow, look," Tali touched the strings of Bran's harp with awe. "Bran has given me his harp, *Riversong*, to play when he goes to the lands of the Decleangli!"

"It is a fine gift, son." Father ruffled Bran's strange silver hair.

"No more than he deserves." Bran listened to the soft rippling laughter of his harp as it danced beneath Tali's hands. "Father, you know Tali's talent, can you not free him from Useth? Let him serve you in the Hall."

Father tore free a blade of grass and examined it closely before he answered. "Useth swears he cannot do without the lad."

Tali stopped playing. He held the harp steady, staring at the surface of the water. He didn't move, but he was listening so intently I could feel it.

"The man's an ass-wipe, Father. You know it. He beats Tali all the time."

"It is his right to do so. Tali is a slave. Besides—"

"Tali was not born to be a slave," Bran interrupted passionately. "You have but to listen to him, Father, to know he was born a bard. I do not care where he was born. He—"

"All right, enough!" Father raised his hands, laughing.

Mother touched Tali's bowed head with a smile. "It is said among our people that the harp picks its own master, regardless of birth. Surely, husband, we are blessed to have yet another bard at Dinas."

"I will think on it." Father threw the stem of grass away. "Would you like to play for us, young man?"

Tali ducked his head in acquiescence and began. Perhaps I was the only one who noticed the pain in his guarded green eyes. He masked it quickly, bending over the harp, letting his fingers fly with the same grace they exhibited in any task he undertook, from currying a restive pony to braiding wildflowers in my hair.

At first the music was joyous, like water falling down a mountainside and rushing back up again. But then it turned sad, entering the early morning light around us like a sudden frost that freezes budding flowers, preserving their beauty as it kills them. Music that sorrowed like a ship sailing into the horizon never to be seen again.

I was reminded of what had happened in the stables. "Mother, Father, I came to find you."

Tali stopped playing and looked at me.

"And so you have. What is it?" Mother sounded amused.

"Uncle Maelgwyn."

Father sighed. "What happened?"

I told them what I had overheard, how Useth had ridden out before dawn.

Mother placed her hand on Father's lap. "What think you?"

Father spat into the weeds growing beside the pool. "Perhaps I should send Hwyll to track this horse master of ours." He stood with a sigh and extended his hand to help Mother rise from the flat rock where she had been sitting. "What can my little brother be plotting now? His friend the Vortigern is already under our roof."

"Do you think he means to murder?" Mother asked.

Father shrugged. "Who knows the twists of his mind? I am weary to death of him. Tegid has already gone to his lady love's steading or

I would ask him to keep an eye out for him. Iolo will enjoy the task instead, I have no doubt—and Hwyll will be more than a match for fat Useth. However," he looked at Tali who still sat on the rocks, throwing pebbles moodily across the water's surface, "this causes me to think more deeply on the need for a new bard at Dinas."

Tali rose slowly. Father looked him up and down with the intensity of a king's challenge, nodding at last. "Perhaps, it is time I reviewed the running of my stables."

Tali ducked his head to hide the quick flash of his smile. "Thank you, Lord!"

Bran clasped my friend's arm, searching for his crutch with the other. "You won't be sorry, Father. Tali here can already harp better than Cadfael."

"That's not saying much." I muttered, careful to keep my voice low.

Mother heard me anyway. "Come, daughter. There is work to be done."

The morning passed in a whirl of household tasks. Our allies were making ready to return to their clan lands the following day and the Druids had already melted back into the mountains. But Chalan Grey Wolf, his father Blind Hawk, and son Lleu intended to stay on through the next fortnight, making plans for the exchange of hostages and our new fledgling alliance. Nor did Vortigern and his men seem to have any intention of stirring from the new guesthouse, although from the disgusted expression on Father's face when he passed the warlord—already deep in his cups at mid-morning—he would be encouraging them to move on at the earliest possible opportunity.

For now, we had our work cut out for us. After helping Mother gather late summer herbs to replenish her medicine pantry and dragging Andelis' heavy laundry baskets to the river, I ran back and forth from the twin springs, bringing water to Maeve's kitchen. By the time I turned to help Kerinne's friend, Nynnid, sweep the soiled rushes from the Hall, I had almost forgotten the mysterious scene I had witnessed in the stables at dawn.

In mid-afternoon a shriek rang out from the direction of the village and Nudd ran up the hill calling out, "Lord Cadwallon...Lord Cadwallon..."

He was followed by every villager that lived within the earthworks of Dinas. By the time the procession entered the Hall, the freemen and women who lived on solitary crofts beyond our ramparts, as well as most of our guests had joined in.

Merlin appeared at my shoulder. "Be strong, child," he said, his hand heavy upon me. I tried to break free, wanting to be closer to the excitement.

Father and Mother entered the Hall at the same time. Father, rushed and sweating from the courtyard, threw a comradely arm over the shoulder of the bleeding Gull warrior whom he had been sparring with. Mother ran from Maeve's kitchen, her everyday homespun spotted with barley flour and cooking ash.

Iolo loped in, cursing, from the stables as the crowd parted to make way for Deria, Tegid's forest lover. She was weeping, wailing, long fingernails gouging at her cheeks. Behind her, carrying a large bundle wrapped in a length of sacking, strode her father, old Tinthos, a woodcutter, whose strength was still a legend in the forest although he was long past his prime.

The old man gently laid the bundle in front of the banked central hearth and bowed to Father. "Lord, I bring evil tidings."

Mother ran across the Hall and knelt, tearing at the sacking.

Father was beside her in less than a heartbeat. "Rise, wife." His voice was stern, as cold as the barrow stones of the dead.

There was no holding me now. I pulled Merlin forward, pushing through the crowd until we stood next to Cynan and Bran, at Father and Mother's side.

"So be it, child." Merlin sighed, but he no longer tried to stop me.

Iolo took a dagger from his boot and cut the sacking away.

Tegid's face was so bruised I barely recognized it. A bloodless jagged cut ran the length of his face, destroying the bridge of his nose and the jaunty line of his blonde moustaches. His long blonde braids were dark, still dripping water. Somehow their darkness made the unearthly grey pallor of his bruised face that much more terrible.

This was not my brother. My laughing brother.

I fell on my knees beside him, hearing a loud, strangling sound in the distance, not realizing until I heard the sound repeated again and yet again, that the screaming came from me.

Mother knelt beside me, rocking me, her own tears wetting my head.

Screams, heart-felt and ritual, rang out as the shocked tale was passed from one to another until it reached the back of the crowd. Selyf and the rest of Tegid's warriors pushed through the crowd. When he saw his Shield Lord dead upon the hearth stones, Selyf ululated like the women, slashing his arms with a dagger. The sun had left the sky, never to return.

Only Father remained aloof. He knelt beside my brother's body, as stiffly as if he were an old man. Even as he cradled Tegid's head in his lap and began the ritual words of an ancestral sending, no tears escaped. Nor did he reach for his dagger as the warriors did. No cuts appeared on his chest and arms. He sat, as one already dead, before the body of my brother, his oldest son.

Nor did Iolo turn the dagger he had used to cut the sacking on himself. He sat beside Father, running his hands over Tegid's broken body. And, indeed, it was broken. Once the sacking had been removed, we all saw that Tegid's body had been battered mercilessly.

"Lord, I offer you my heart in sorrow." Tinthos placed his hand on Father's shoulder; rank forgotten in the face of death.

Raising his voice, the old man addressed us all. "Your son Tegid bade my daughter good day and took the fells path back to Dinas. It was midday before Deria went to the pool beneath the falls to fetch water for her mother." Tinthos placed his hands on his daughter's head as she knelt, weeping, beside Tegid's body. "She found him floating facedown in the pool. The path is treacherous, Lord, you know it well. He must have slipped on a rock and could not stop himself from plunging over."

Not Tegid, I thought fiercely. For all that Tegid was the biggest man I had ever seen, he was as light on his feet as Iolo—a combination that had made him one of the most fearsome warriors of our clan.

Father must have felt as I did, for he came back from the shadows long enough to shake his head.

"Father, look—" Iolo pulled at Tegid's bruised and swollen right hand.

I pushed out of Mother's arms and knelt beside Iolo to see better.

A sharp gasp and a babbling of whispers broke out among the grieving folk. Iolo held up Tegid's tortured hand for all to see.

The third finger of his hand was gone.

Tinthos spoke in horror. "Lord, I did not see this when I wrapped him. What does it mean?"

"Father, where is Tegid's ring?" My voice squeaked into the shocked hush around me.

Father and Iolo both turned to me. But it was only Father I saw, Father whose wise brown eyes were red with anguish.

"She's right, Tad. Tegid loved that foolish ring." Iolo gently clasped his own warm hands over Tegid's mutilated fingers.

The ring had been a simple thing, of native jet arranged around a fine stone of southern lapis. It had hurt his hand sometimes, for it was too small for him, yet he swore he'd never remove it for it had been given to him by Father after Tegid had killed his first Scotti warrior and Father had made him a part of his own honor guard.

"Foolish perhaps, but so like Tegid to hold on to such a thing. That boy knew how to love more than any of us." Father lowered his head. His shoulders shook. Silent tears ran down his face.

As if this were a signal, the ritual mourning began again.

Iolo did not wail. He ran fingers up and down Tegid's brutalized body in a manner that I thought was rude. I was about to tell him to leave Tegid alone when my living brother froze as still as Tegid. He had been exploring the contours of our dead brother's back. Now Iolo turned the body over, tore Tegid's ruined tunic open, pulled his body over again, and leaned over his back for a closer look.

"Iolo, stop!" Mother tried to pull him away.

Iolo shrugged her off, reaching for Father's hand. "Tad, look," he whispered, placing Father's hand beneath Tegid's shoulder blade, in a spot of battered flesh that would have covered Tegid's heart.

Father looked at Iolo with such great weariness that I wanted to cry out to Iolo to leave him alone. He did not resist as Iolo moved his hand over the spot he had located.

In the heartbeat it took for the furious light to dawn in Father's eyes—Merlin touched my arm. "I am with you, child. Stay close. No matter what happens."

Father rose. Iolo stood with him. They exchanged a long look. "Where is Maelgwyn?" Father whispered.

Iolo bowed his head. "I am sorry, Tad. I was coming to tell you. He slipped away from me at the Warriors' Hall. By the time I got to the stables he was gone."

"Go!" Father's voice lashed like the whip he never used on his horses. "Find him. If it takes the rest of your life, find him."

"Father." Iolo knelt at Father's feet.

Father put his hands upon Iolo's head. "May my shield—" His voice cracked. Mastering himself with an angry toss of his head, he continued the ritual words in a voice that turned the flowing chant into merciless daggers. "May my shield rise upon your arm. Ride swiftly."

He touched Iolo's flushed cheek. "Fight well. Return in triumph."

As Iolo left the Hall, Father turned to face us all, visitors and Ordovice alike. "My son, Tegid, has been murdered. By a cowardly arrow in his back. It is clear his ringed finger was taken as proof. Iolo has gone to avenge him."

In the commotion and shrieks that followed, old Tinthos threw himself on the floor at Father's feet. "Lord, I did not know."

"Of course, you did not, woodcutter." Father raised him up and gestured for his daughter, who now sat, alone, huddled and weeping, on the harper's bench. "Bring her," he whispered to Mother.

Looking like a wraith herself, Mother gripped the weeping Deira by the shoulders and held her. The tall girl collapsed, wailing, in Mother's arms. Mother held her, her own face an agonized mask of grief, then led her, stumbling, to stand with her father.

Father turned to Selyf, Tegid's friend and Shield Brother. "Have you seen Hwyll?" The warrior shook his head, the ritual cuts bleeding freely down his high cheekbones and muscled arms.

Father placed his hands on the bowed heads of the woodcutter and his sobbing daughter. "Know that your love for my son was one of the greatest joys of his life. He will live forever in your hearts as you will live with him in the Halls of Anwnn."

Father kissed them both on the cheeks. "He was blessed to have known you. May your grief water the earth of our land."

Deria clung to him.

"My heart sorrows for you, Lord." With a dignified nod, Tinthos led his daughter away. Folk parted for them and Nudd saluted with his spear as they passed through the open door of the Hall.

For a heartbeat the Hall was silent. Grandmother stepped from the hallway behind the high dais, climbed its two stairs, and stood beneath Father's great dragon shield, her hands outstretched above us. She wore the same wreath of autumn leaves and berries she had worn at last night's feasting—lifetimes ago—but her gown this day was the coarse homespun of the kitchens.

The Hall of Emrys is dark tonight._ She began the ancient chant. Mother, stood, weeping, and moved to join her.

Their two voices entwined. Others joined them in the lament.

The Hall of Emrys is dark tonight,
   Without fire, without bed.
I shall weep a while, and then be silent.

The Hall of Emrys is dark tonight,
   Without fire, without candle.
Who but the gods will keep me sane?

The Hall of Emrys is dark tonight,
   Without fire, without song,
Tears wear away my cheeks.

The Eagle of Yr Wyddfa is screaming tonight,
   Wallowing in the blood of white-skinned warriors.
The Eagle of Yr Wyddfa, I hear him tonight,
   Bloodstained is he, I dare not go near him.

The Eagle of Yr Wyddfa is screaming tonight,
   With his loud cry, greedy for the flesh of my son.
The Eagle of Yr Wyddfa, I hear him tonight,
   With his claw uplifted, greedy for the flesh of the one I love.

The song rose and fell around us, a mantle of sorrow from the time Anu first birthed the world.

"So sang the bard Llywarch in lament for his Lord." Grandmother began keening. "So sing we today in lament for our loved one, Tegid ap Cadwallen ap Cunedda Iron Hand. May his rest be of eternal sweetness. May he rise in the arms of dawn."

Mother made the sign of her White Cristos. Grandmother ignored her, but her mouth tightened as Mother bowed her head.

Nest and the village women began to wrap Tegid's body, preparing to carry him to Grandmother's bedchamber in the lonely North Tower where she and Mother would prepare his body for its journey to Anwnn. It would have been Deira's right to join them, but she had chosen not to stay.

Merlin clasped me in his arms, his lean, tautly-muscled frame and elusive forest scent a small comfort in the nightmare that surrounded me.

"It is a sorrow that he died. But remember, little one, that he is greatly mourned. It would be much worse if he had perished far from those he loved in a place unknown to his kin."

"How can you say that, Merlin! You heard what Father said! Our brother has been murdered!" Cynan burst into our embrace, burrowing against Merlin as if our Uncle offered the only shelter in the world.

Before Merlin could reply, Father's Shield Bearer burst through the weeping crowd. For the first time in his life Hwyll ignored the ancient law against bringing weapons into the feasting Hall—goading a whimpering Useth in front of him at swordpoint.

The stable master looked frantically from side to side. Seeing Father, he cried out and ran, throwing himself at Father's feet. "My Lord!"

"Get up, you sniveling pig." Hwyll's sword prodded Useth's fat backside. "Stand! Face the Lord you've wronged."

Useth ignored him, clutching at Father's boots in panic. "He lies, my Lord! He lies!"

"What is this, Shield Bearer? Why bring this groveling fool to me at such a   time?" Father kicked Useth away.

"Because," Hwyll's sword drew blood this time. The stable master moaned in terror. With a ring of metal, Hwyll sheathed his sword at last and the scarred warrior looked at Father sadly. "Cadwallon, this rat-spit is the reason your firstborn son lies dead."

Father grasped Useth by the collar of his tunic, pulling the stable master so close to his face their noses touched. Useth cried out in terror. "It's not true, Lord. He lies, I swear it."

Father threw him to the ground. Useth scrambled away, his tiny frantic eyes looking for an opening in the crowd. But wherever he looked, folk moved to block his escape.

Hwyll said nothing more. What he withdrew from his pouch said all.

It was a man's white finger, bruised and bloody, sawn off at its root. Yet for all the torture it had clearly undergone, a small gold ring with a design of jet and lapis was still visible near its bloody severed end.

In the deadly silence that followed, Hwyll spoke again. "It was in his pouch, Lord. And this creature was well on his way to the coast when I caught up with him."

"Who is your master?" Father's voice rasped.

At the look in Father's eye, Useth foolishly began keening again.

"Enough!" The blow cracked the stable master's face, knocking him to the ground. "If you speak now, you die quickly. Otherwise," Father held out his hand. Hwyll handed him his sword. "You will die in pieces—so slowly that you will call on the demons of Anwnn to take you into their mists rather than face one—"

Father cut Useth's face and continued, ignoring Useth's screams—*"more"*—another cut—*"heartbeat"*—two cuts—.

Useth's howls died to a monotonous wail. *"Alive."* Father cut off his right ear.

"Now, speak! Killer of my son. Who sent you?"

Crumbled on the floor, Useth rocked back and forth, yipping in agony like a hound. His cries took on a cadence that sounded like speech.

"Do you value your eye, stable master?" Father stood over him, Hwyll's bloody sword raised.

"M-mael-ggwyn." Useth collapsed, weeping at Father's feet.

Father's nod was expressionless. "Take him."

Hwyll bundled the stable master in front of him. The shocked crowd in the Hall followed Father outside. He stopped only once, claiming his own sword from the rack of weapons resting near the door.

Frozen in shock by the sudden bloodshed in the Hall, I did not move until Grandmother grabbed my arm, pushing me to the front of the crowd to where Father stood outside, waiting as Hwyll pulled the screaming Useth up and tied him to one of the beautifully-carved doorposts that guarded Dinas's Hall.

"Watch, child," Grandmother gripped my shoulders, "and remember what it means to be a King."

As casually as if he were squatting a horse fly, Father cut Useth's throat. Hwyll held the sagging head high by its greasy hair, waiting.

With a cry that held anguish as well as vengeance, Father raised his sword again. This time Useth's severed head rolled with an ugly thump to the ground.

"Mount it on the pole, Shield Brother. Let it stay to feed my son's soul as he journeys to Anwnn."

He passed Mother on his return to the Hall. "And this time, wife, do not think to meddle. The head stays in place. I will not have my son's memory mocked, Cristos or no Cristos. It stays."

Mother nodded, white-faced. I sensed she might even have agreed.

"Do you think Maelgwyn can be caught?" she asked, following him into the Hall.

Father's sharp laugh held a world of bitterness within it. "Fast as Iolo is, I doubt if he's a match for my little brother, who is no doubt on a ship to Eire by now."

"Eire?" Mother pushed through those few folk who still remained, stunned and frightened, in the Hall, clearing a spot on the benches. "I thought he had nothing but disgust for Nestor and his Scotti."

"Do you still believe anything that came from that serpent's mouth? Do you not remember how quickly poor Tulach disappeared, when I sent him to Eire to give my brother news of Cunedda's death?"

Mother's face grew white. She grabbed his arm. "Do you mean—"

Father stopped, hanging his head on his chest like a blown horse. "Wallon, do you mean—"

"Of course, I mean." Father collapsed against a cluttered trestle table. Turning away from her, he stared into a bowl of congealed morning porridge as if it contained the answer to Arianhod's greatest riddle.

When he finally looked up at Mother, his eyes were bleaker than I'd ever seen them. "And it was you who warned me of him. I did not want to believe the extent of his evil. I have been blinded, wife, blinded by sentiment and hope."

He pulled Mother into his arms, breathing her in like a flower. "Did you not see the dagger Maelgwyn used so proudly at last night's feast?"

"I had no time to note it, husband." Mother shook her head, her voice held just a trace of its usual comforting lilt.

"It was Scotti work, love." Father kissed the top of her hair.

Tangling one of his hands in Mother's flowing hair, Father turned and raised his eyes to the doorway where Useth's head had been mounted. With his free hand he made the ancient sign of blood vengeance.

"I did not think of it until today, when I cradled my dead son's body. But Maelgwyn has ever been one to flaunt his wealth. Ever since he was a boy, he has not been able to resist showing off his prizes like a magpie. I believe he did go first to Eire, but instead of finding it too cold and dangerous for his tastes, he made a pact with Nestor. My throne for Nestor's gold. Maelgwyn as Nestor's client king."

Mother drew Father to her, holding him close. "But why Tegid? Why not you?"

"Because Tegid was easy." Father's voice caught. He took the mead horn Mother offered and drank as if he's been traveling for many days without water. "Because I am too old and crafty to ambush without a great deal of effort. No doubt, Maelgwyn thought my death could wait until he'd picked off my sons. He did not expect to get found out so soon."

He looked at her with empty eyes.

"My son is dead, Ceri," he whispered. "My son is dead."

He put his face in his hands and wept, Mother's hands gentle on his heaving back. At last, he raised his face; death in his voice.

"Maelgwyn shall die for this. Slowly, terribly, he shall die." He gripped Mother's shoulders, his hands still wet with tears, "Mark me, woman. He dies at my hand."

Mother placed her own hands on Father's face, looked into his eyes, and nodded as if she too took a vow.

"Yes, my Lord—and, to think, had it not been for Useth's trophy-gathering, Maelgwyn would have succeeded. There would have been no reason for us to suspect that Tegid's fall had been aught else but a terrible accident."

"Except that Tegid was more graceful than a cat, Father." I said. "It would have always been suspicious that he fell on a path he knew like the tips of his fingers."

Father and Mother turned at the sound of my voice. Neither seemed pleased to see me watching them from the shadows of the empty harpers' bench.

"Where's Cynan?" Mother asked.

"Talking to that horrible new boy, Lleu, in the Warrior's Hall."

Suddenly, I felt lonelier than I'd ever been. Cynan had his warriors, Merlin had gone into the forest to comfort Tinthos and Deira, even Hwyrch had deserted me to help Nest and Grandmother prepare Tegid's body.

"I came to sit with you." I walked across the Hall to join them, willing myself not to cry.

"Come here, my heart." Mother pulled me into her lap and held me. I felt a little better, but my comfort disappeared when I saw the look in Father's eyes.

He placed his hand gently on my shoulder. "It is a sorrow that none of us could riddle out what you overheard Maelgwyn say this morning. Had we done so, perhaps your brother might still be alive."

His words echoed in the nearly deserted Hall. They went through me like a spear. "If only I hadn't been so stupid," I stood, pushing Mother away, sobbing, "Tegid would still be alive!"

Backing away from them, I tripped clumsily over the corner of a bench. Ignoring the fierce pain that lanced up my leg, I kept backing further away.

"Tegid would be alive!" I screamed.

"Gwen, no—" Mother cast a furious look at Father. "That's not what we mean."

"But Father's right. If I would have been smarter—braver—I could have stopped them from killing him!"

"Gwen!"

But I was too far gone for them to reach. Mother stood, trying to catch and hold me.

But I was no longer her baby. I fought her, kicking and sobbing. "Leave me alone!"

One of my kicks connected hard on her shin. Wincing, she dropped her arms.

Father slapped me.

I ran into the farthest corner of the Hall. He looked sorry, but stood his ground. "You have lost your senses, child. Come, sit with us."

"It's all my fault!" I screamed at him, furious at them both. "My brother is dead because I let them kill him!"

I ran out of the Hall before they could stop me, heading for the only place I could think of where I could be alone. The ruins of the South Tower.

chapter 14

I ran blindly across the courtyard, my head fixed like a charging bull, dodging by instinct the folk who still crowded the fortress.

At last I reached the ruined tower and stopped to catch my breath in its shadow. The sky had been sunny earlier, but now clouds were massing from the north and a cold wind mounted around me, thick with the anger-laden air of a coming storm.

Good. No one would come outside to find me.

Dislodged rock skittered across the courtyard. I spun around. The noise had come from the direction of an abandoned storage shed.

No one was there. I was alone, yet even from this distance I could hear the ritual mourning. My hands clenched in despair. Tegid was dead. I had let Useth kill him—I had no home anymore.

Someone grabbed my elbow.

I screamed.

"Are you Cadwallon's daughter?" The new boy, Chalan Grey Wolf's brat. Perhaps he had been the source of the noise I heard?

It did not matter, he was here and unwelcome.

"I'm sorry, I didn't mean to frighten you."

I pulled my arm away, furious. "I am not afraid!"

He laughed. I had forgotten the sharpness in his fierce grey eyes. Now he looked at me as if it was I—not he—who was the fool.

"Your pardon, M'lady," he bent on one knee, swept out both of his arms, and bowed his head so low it almost touched the ground—offering me a mocking parody of a supplicant's bow, "Why hast yonder pile of rocks not been carted away to build some crofter's wall?"

It was so unexpected; he almost succeeded in making me laugh at his mincing mock of highborn manners. Then all the pain came rushing back.

"Go away."

He dropped his joking poise and looked sad.

"Please," I added.

"As you wish. What is your name?"

"Gwenhwyfar."

"I am Lleu. I am sorry for your brother, Gwenhwyfar. It is a misery. I wish there was something I could do."

"Just go away," I said ungraciously, and pushed past him—as if I had some pressing appointment with the brooding stones that waited.

"I am at your command, fair lady. But," he paused, frowning as a stone broke loose from the upper floor and crashed noisily down the side. In the silence of the place, in the threatening, storm-filled air, the sound echoed far too long.

"This place holds unhealthy memories." He searched my eyes. "It is cursed. But you know that, don't you?"

"Please leave."

"Be careful." His bow was mocking, his words were not.

I stayed in the entrance of the tower, watching until he disappeared into the Warriors' Hall. He looked back twice, each time looking first at me, then his gaze swept up and down the crumbling tower with an air of concentration I did not like. Who was he to question why the South Tower still stood when folk feared it?

A crow cawed.

I almost called him back. Why? So that I could explain to a stranger that I wanted to be cursed?

Stones scattered on the path behind me again. I jumped and entered the ruins, goose-bumps rising on my arms. Today I would find refuge here. No matter what had happened before.

Determined, I crossed the circular floor, hopping over piles of rubble until I reached the old trap door. It stood open, the breath of the underground tunnel as dank and foul as I remembered. Peering into its depths, I shuddered, yet its darkness pulled me down, like one of Merlin's tales of the Roman river of death.

Had Cynan and I left it open? Had someone else been exploring?

With an effort, I broke free of the tunnel's dangerous pull and pushed through a pile of rubble, finding a place to lean against the rough stone wall. Its dampness leached into my tunic quickly. Cold and miserable, I closed my eyes.

You are alive, I told myself. *Alive! What do a few shivers matter when you will feel the sun again?*

I drew my legs to my chest, put my head upon my knees and wept.

Tegid, my brother, must now be in a place as black and awful as the tunnel's heart. For him there would be no sunshine.

When I could weep no more, I crawled to the tunnel's entrance and looked into its mouth again. I spat, defiant. If Tegid could exist in a place like that forever, I could stand it too. I deserved to stand it. I deserved to be alone and die.

The first thunder of the approaching storm crashed open the sky.

I made myself as small as possible.

Rain pelted past the ruined beams, drenching the rubble on the ground, revealing forgotten tile patterns of a once-beautiful mosaic floor.

I curled up even tighter; watching the mysterious designs dance beneath the murky water shadows. Holes in the stone wall facing me revealed a sky filled with the green-grey of the storm. More stones crumbled and through the newly-exposed gap, I saw the wind-swept branches of the only oak still standing near the tower.

It looked angry, this oak, no more like the gentle trees that surrounded the Goddess Pool than a pup resembles a starving wolf. Still leafed in green, its branches waved like demented men, their greenery shredded and cowering in the wind.

"Tegid, I'm sorry." My voice was a small lost thing within the belly of the storm.

I woke to the laughter of men.

The rain had stopped. Full dark had fallen beyond the crumbled stone walls.

Two torches flashed, sweeping across the tower as if they were looking for something.

I lay still, gathering strength, trying to control the chattering of my teeth and the shivers that wracked my body. As soon as I moved, my legs needled in pain. I stood up with an effort: I had been remembered and—like it or not—it was my duty to join my grieving family in the Hall. "I'm over here."

"Who's there?" The voice was startled, the accent strange. One of the torches wavered and almost fell to the floor.

I hopped on the leg that could bear my weight, rubbing the other back to life, shaking with cold. "Cynan...Mother...Is that you? I'm over here!"

Two torches lit on me at once. "Ah what have we here, my Lord?"

Too late, I recognized the slurred accent of the Sea Wolves. Vortigern's pirates.

I backed away and dropped to my knees, crouching in the stone pile, sorry now that I had cried out.

"Let us see, Glythu, for a spirit it has a most pleasing voice." The second man's voice was deeper, slurred with drink as well as strange speech. Yet it was familiar. Heavy footsteps approached me. One of the men stumbled, swore, and came on.

There was no use hiding. I stood to my full height and thrust my chin up, remembering that I was a princess of the family who ruled this fort, trying not to think of the torn condition of my clothes or the filth upon my face.

Their torches roamed up and down my body. I squinted to make out the men behind them. In the glare I could see little but that one was fat and bearded, the other tall and lean.

With a pleased grunt, the man with the deep voice handed the other his torch. "It looks as if we have found ourselves a sweet innocent, Glythu. Hold my torch, I will investigate further."

He lurched towards me, grabbed my arm, and pulled me against his body. I gagged at his stench and raised my hands to push him away. Memories tumbled through my panic. The Vortigern!

His free hand roamed beneath my tunic. I punched his chest.

He laughed, ripped my tunic in half, threw it to the floor and gathered me into his arms, gesturing to the tall man.

It was the Seaxon that I had seen bow before us in the Hall last night!

He reached me in one long stride and tore the trews from my body.

Furiously, I punched Vortigern, who held me. I spat in his face and screamed.

His friend held both torches high and laughed. "A little spitfire, your innocent."

"Not for much longer." Vortigern growled, his face looming over mine. His breath was thick with sour wine and decay. The filthy beard I had watched in disgust last night rubbed against my face. I shoved with all my strength, trying to push him away.

"I believe we have ourselves a princess, Glythu." The filthy man chucked me under the chin. Then, holding me against his belly with one hand, he reached for my woman's parts.

I wiggled as hard as I could, kicking, punching, trying to get away. He laughed. I screamed. He slapped me. I spat in his face.

He slapped me harder, hissing like a snake as his fingers reached, trying to break into my woman's fold. It hurt. *Mother, it hurt.*

I hung my head, dizzy, the pain was fire.

I had to get away. Had to fight. Had to think.

It did no good. He pinned me to him. His fingers pushed into me. The pain. *Pain.*

I spat in his face again.

Vortigern raised his hand. Before he could hit me, the other man stepped closer, "Come, girl," he leered, holding both torches in one hand.

The two flames jumped together, burning. In agony, my eyes fixed on them, dreaming the flames would dance free and set the men on fire.

"Come, girl," fat Vortigern mimicked, removing his hand from my woman's parts, clasping me to him with both hands.

I closed my eyes on the fat man's nightmare face, gaining strength to make a grab for the torch.

His tongue licked my face like a hound's. "Relax."

I leaned back suddenly, a move I had seen Iolo use at wrestling. The shift loosened Vortigern's grip for a heartbeat. I kicked as hard as I could.

He dropped me.

I ran.

"Get her, Glythu." He sounded bored.

I darted for the opening of the tower, dodging as the tall man came after me. For a heartbeat, I thought I would make it, but I skidded on rubble and went down, screaming.

Glythu scooped me up with one hand before I could scramble up and run free into the rain that had begun to pound the stones again.

I grabbed for one of the torches he carried but he held them effortlessly out of my reach, laughing, taunting me, then he threw me like a struggling cat into Vortigern's outstretched arms.

The southern lord laughed, grabbed my bottom, and squeezed hard. "Pretty spirited aren't you? Of course, I would expect fire from a princess." His voice growled as he ground his mouth into my ear. "But,

I'm afraid that no one will hear you, my dear. No one is near." He moved one of his hands to my chest and began to play with my nipple, pinching it, hurting.

I grabbed his hand, pulled one of his fingers back and bit it.

He slapped me. Much harder than he had the first time.

The pain was blackness. I hung my head, closing my eyes to stop the ringing in my head. I kept them closed. This was a dream. I knew this was a dream. When I opened my eyes again, I would wake up. The monster would be gone. They would go away when I woke up. *Mother? Hwyrch. Where was Hwyrch?*

I opened my eyes. Vortigern's eyes gleamed at me, bloodshot and smiling. I screamed as loudly as I could. I kept screaming, hitting him, kicking as hard as I could.

He put his hand over my mouth. I couldn't breathe. His small eyes glared into me. "You might as well relax, little one. If you're good, I might even give you a pretty bracelet when I'm finished." His hand kneaded my bottom.

I kicked him. He just laughed and squeezed tighter, pulling me against his great fat belly. I arched away, wiggling as hard as I could, trying to flip away.

His tall friend laughed. Loud and foul and dark as a gull without a soul. The torchlight flared high. "It appears she is not eager for that bracelet my Lord."

The fat man just laughed and gripped me tighter. "Then she shall have something else instead!" He pulled me towards him, pulling me down so that I was pushed against the thick hardness beneath the metal of his belt. He lowered me to the floor. "Quiet now, or you will feel my fist again."

He touched my woman's fold, pulling the soft parts of me apart. One of his fingers tried to push inside me again.

I bucked away from him, kicking. The filth of the floor ground into my back, smelling of rot and small dead things. I tossed my head back and forth, back and forth, screaming.

He slapped me.

I took a deep breath of air and screamed again.

"Get over here with those torches, Glythu. I want to see where my pleasure is coming from."

I grabbed his arm and tried to push him away.

He slapped me harder. Stretching my arms out to my sides, he leaned over me, bringing his eyes up to my face. "If you don't stop that, I will take my pleasure and kill you after. You will not be the first." He fingered the dagger at his belt. "Now be silent."

I swallowed a great sob and hiccupped in terror. He grunted as he felt my body grow slack and raised himself up far enough to fumble with his belt.

"Shall I hold the child down for you, my lord?" The shadow man asked.

The fat man glared down at me and nodded with satisfaction. "I believe she's learned her lesson, Glythu. Haven't you, my dear?" He pulled his trews down to his knees. I looked over his head beyond the open stone ceiling, to the place where everything disappeared in shadows that reached all the way to what was left of the ruined top of the tower.

I wondered what it felt like to die.

He was on top of me again. I couldn't breath. The hard thing pushed to move my legs apart. I clenched them back together and screamed one final time as loudly as I could. Knowing it was hopeless.

"Little bitch!" He growled and raised his fist.

A great thick mist rose from the open trap door behind us, blanketing the tower with fog so thick I could not see the nightmare men anymore.

The Vortigern swore, a long stream of curses that ended in a scream. "Glythu—help!"

He jumped off, away from me, yelping in panic.

I rolled and huddled in a corner as far away as I could get.

The mist followed me. It fell around me like a warm fur, cuddling against me, murmuring and sighing as if it wanted to speak.

Beyond my corner, the fog began to grow even thicker, swirling as if it were gathering itself together to dance. Somewhere deep in its mass, I heard a sound I had hoped never to hear again.

It was the clicking of many daggers coming fast, rising from underneath the floor. An evil wind rose from the trap door. It smelled like rotting bodies, as if an army had died and been left to fester beneath the flies and sun.

I managed to stand, not caring that I was naked, only wanting to get away. But the mist took shape around me, holding me as Mother did when I was frightened. The scent of it was like the forest mist at dawn, as if I were walking in a dew-covered apple orchard with no cause to be afraid.

Beyond the shelter of the mist's arms, I saw a yellow fog rise above the men who had attacked me. Fire flared from the fog. My dream of torches had come alive. Now it was they who scrambled, frantic to escape.

I sat up within the arms of the mist, pushing it away, needing to be free.

Within the fog two slanted sparkling eyes began to glow, as brilliant a green as the emerald stone in Merlin's favorite ring.

Vortigern's string of curses ended in a wail. He stumbled, fleeing over the stones; keening in fear, holding his head in his hands.

Look. The mist parted to show me the fog-thing rising higher, wind revolving around its head. It roared with the fury of a mountain. Flames arrowed from it, flying in a slow, remorseless dance until Glythu and the Vortigern were surrounded.

The Seaxon ran. The fire pursued him, gobbling him up like a wolf with a rabbit. He died, screaming, his body flaming at the last like meat skewered over a cooking fire.

Watching his servant die, Vortigern wailed in terror. The fire-circle tightened around him.

A tall man stepped out of the shadows of the trapdoor, raising his own hands to part the mist. He reached the spot where the fire-circle hovered. But now the fire changed form. It became a giant cloud with great green eyes and a smile filled with flames.

The man reached up to pat it, as if it was a favored hound. Wherever he touched it, red glittering scales appeared.

The fog shifted. Out of its depths emerged a great red dragon. It put its long snout in the tall man's outstretched hands and waited.

The man scratched a spot just above its flaring nostrils. "Well done, Cymry! Well done indeed!"

"Merlin!"

I started to rise.

Wait! The mist held me.

The dragon raised its head and arched its neck above the trembling Vortigern, slanting its beautiful green eyes in what looked like laughter. Then the great beast looked over at Merlin as if asking what it should do.

Vortigern screamed again. The beast arched its back, annoyed, spitting fire from its nostrils.

"Not yet, Great One." Merlin said. "Fire is too clean a death for this raper of children. Something much more fitting lies in store for this worm." He turned to the hysterical king, now babbling for mercy, his trews still around his ankles.

"Rise Vortigern, son of Vortiper, usurper King of the South. Rise and know the curse of this bright land that you have defiled." The Mage's voice took on the sing-song of a prophecy. "You will die at the hands of this child's mother-kin. Know that after death your soul shall know no peace, but shall wander—eternally—in the mists beyond Anwnn's protection. You will die a thousand times, Usurper, torn to pieces by eagles, ripped apart by horses, spat into the whirlwinds that blow beyond the edges of this world realm…Each death you die will be more painful than the one before until you run mad, pursued by all the demons of the hidden paths… And even then your soul will know no peace—"

Far beneath us came a great rumbling.

"Uncle!"

Merlin turned as if noticing me for the first time.

He whipped off his cloak and threw it in my direction, then spun to face whatever foul thing was coming through the open doorway to the tunnels.

The cloak floated through the air, as if carried by unseen hands and wrapped itself around my nakedness. The mist tried to keep me within its arms, but I knew that I too must face whatever was rushing up the tunnel.

I broke free and raced to Merlin.

A great roar shook the ruined tower, casting the few stones that remained on the roof tumbling down around us. The outer wall collapsed utterly, exposing storm-bitter sky and the same angry oak I had seen before I slept.

A cloud of black smoke swirled above the tunnel, darker than the storm. Fangs of a giant serpent took shape within, as beneath, thick giant coils slithered viper-fast from the earth.

The red dragon arched its back, spitting fire.

"Now!" Merlin shouted.

Sighting the dragon, the serpent reared up, its slanted eyes as empty as the realms of the dead. It spat a vicious narrow stream of fire.

The dragon ascended into the storm-filled sky. My own heart soared. Unfurling its wings, the red dragon hissed once. Its own fire rippled out like falling water at the rising head of the snake.

The white monster roared in pain.

Answering with a screech, Merlin's dragon cried out to the clouds.

The heavens opened and torrents of new rain pelted down.

The Mage raised his arms.

The red dragon screeched again, descending faster than an arrow, aiming its dagger-sharp talons at the writhing snake, claws extended for the kill.

With a great roar, Merlin's dragon slashed. Blood coursed down the white snake's body, immediately washed away by rain. Triumphant, the dragon gripped the snake's huge head in its mouth and flew up into the sky again, shaking the serpent as if it were a water rat.

Furiously, the snake whipped the end of its tail at its tormenter, knocking the dragon's head free. Quicker than a sword thrust, it wrapped its great coils around the dragon's muzzle, trapping its breath, imprisoning its fire.

Before the dragon could move, the snake flipped across its chest, tearing its wings. Coiling lower, with a triumphant groan, the great snake raised small wings of its own in excitement and squeezed down on the dragon's stomach as Merlin's beast fought to free itself. The snake kept coming, still flying, until it had covered almost all of the red dragon's body like a coil of rope around a post.

"Now, Cymry!" Merlin's cry was all but lost in a crash of lightning from the newborn storm. "Do not let the Lurking Wyrm destroy us!"

Suddenly, I heard groans and screams of awe and terror behind me. The people of Dinas had come rushing and were now gathered in a wretched huddle outside the ruined walls.

"Goddess be praised—you are safe!" Grandmother leapt across the stones, her face beaten by the rain, her long white hair wet vines that whipped against me. She picked me up as if I weighed no more than a basket of herbs.

I pushed her away—"Leave me alone!"

With a fast glance at the monstrous beings writhing in battle in the sky, Grandmother set me down.

"Mother, I have need of you both," Merlin shouted. "The red dragon must win or we shall all perish. Concentrate."

Grandmother straightened and glared into the sky, not bothering to shield her face from the rain.

I did so, too, as hard as I could. Weariness and terror fell away. I was left with rage—a fire of my own that burned so brightly I could hear its song. I offered it to the dragon.

Beside me, I heard Grandmother chanting. Her long arms were

raised to the sky, her face open against the rain.

"Now!" roared Merlin and threw his own arms up. A stream of fire bolted from between his hands, racing towards the imprisoned dragon.

The great snake opened its fangs in triumph. Poison dripped from its mouth. It rose above the red dragon, preparing for a final suffocating squeeze.

Merlin's fire reached its coils and danced around their length.

With a final desperate lunge, the captive dragon rocked the snake off balance. Freeing one of its talons from beneath the snake's coils, it dug its freed claw deep into the snake's body.

Surprised, weakened by Merlin's fire, the snake loosened its coils. The dragon pulled its second talon free.

Still captive, it hissed, rolling them over and over in the sky, rocking until it was able to plummet both of them to the ground. Reaching earth, the red dragon shook its great head back and forth, like a horse trying to rid itself of flies, loosening the snake's coils even further.

Steaming tendrils of dragon-fire now escaped from the dragon's mouth. Joining the flames that Merlin conjured, they set the great serpent's tail on fire.

The white snake flipped its head in fury, its fangs extended to bite. But the pain in its tail was too much. It let go of the dragon's mouth and slithered free, arching back, spitting in rage.

Triumphant, the dragon shook its head and roared. *Free!*

The snake sprang, poised to tear out the dragon's throat.

Roaring now in vengeance, the Mage's dragon dodged the lightning strike of the snake and spat fire into its eyes, biting down on the back of the white monster's head.

A peal of thunder rocked the hilltop. The weakened snake's tail lashed viciously at the dragon again. But this time, Merlin's beast dodged easily and began to rise into the air, the snake's head still clasped within its teeth.

But, as the dragon spread its wings to fly higher, it faltered, thrashing with rage. Its injured wings fluttered, helpless, no longer strong enough to support it.

The great snake dropped from the dragon's mouth, falling to the earth with nightmare slowness.

The wounded dragon roared to the skies.

In answer, another crash of thunder split the rain-storm sky and a spike of lightning danced into the dragon's mouth. It plunged to earth again, pouncing on the dying serpent that now lay, twitching in anguish, across the mud and rock of the tower.

Crowing in triumph the dragon spat fire up and down the white snake's coils.

With a cry, I collapsed, nestling against Grandmother. Her thin arms held me, cradling me against the wonders around us.

From far away I heard Merlin's dragon roar again, a fine long cry that reached beyond the mountains to the stars.

"So perish all enemies of this sacred land!" Merlin's voice shattered the storm, seeming to come from the clouds, although he stood less than a spear's throw from me.

"Though there be white wyrms aplenty that seek to invade our shores, the red dragon of our people will not be mocked. There will come a day—and it approaches soon, good folk, in which the Dragon will ride again to free our land of enemies.

"Stand watch for him, I charge you. Be worthy of his might, for he will be a warrior king unknown since the days of the ancient ones, unknown since the days when the Druids held sway in our land, and mead flowed in the bellies of heroes. A warrior king to last the life span of the land itself! Ride with him, Ordovice, he will bring back the days of glory when the goddesses and gods of old roamed the hills and valleys of Albion.

"Keep watch and ride with him, for he alone will free us!"

When I opened my eyes, the folk had gone, gathering to stand beyond the tower. Only Grandmother and Merlin remained with me. Merlin stood with his foot upon the fat King's body. It looked as if he was dead, but I saw his arm move and he stirred. Grandmother was gazing at Merlin in astonishment. I knew then that a spell had been cast. The man who had hurt me was frozen, visible only to my own kin and to me, hidden under Merlin's command until Merlin himself chose to free him.

A hand touched my shoulder. I looked into the rain-wet face of Mother. "Gwen, we have been searching for you." Her tired eyes looked over my body, at Merlin's cloak. She looked at Grandmother. "What has happened?"

Grandmother nodded at the man now struggling beneath Merlin's casually placed foot. Mother's eyes went back to me then to Vortigern again, growing wider and more horrified each time they traveled the distance between us.

"Gwen?" She placed both hands upon my shoulders and looked full into my eyes. Within our circle the rain had lessened. Behind its soft curtain, her exhausted violet eyes darkened into pits of horror.

I drew back from her and took Grandmother's hand. Grasping the wet folds of Merlin's cloak around me I curled into as small a ball as possible and closed my eyes.

I wanted only to sleep.

Muffled by the cloak, I heard their voices. "Mother, it can't be! The Vortigern is an animal, but even he would not dare!"

Grandmother stroked my hair and said nothing.

"Mother, please—"

"The grove, daughter. You know of it."

"Yes..." Mother whispered. "Of course, I know of it."

"Then do what must be done."

I raised my head from beneath Merlin's cloak, welcoming the cold touch of the rain. Mother crouched beside me. When she saw my face, she raised her hand to touch my cheek. I shivered, pushing away from her.

After a heartbeat, she rose, staring beyond us at the man who now lay spelled and frozen beneath Merlin's foot. Her bruised eyes narrowed into those of a hunter.

"I will do so."

She tore at her cloak. As it fell to the mud, her treasured Cristos Chi-Rio brooch flew across the lowering sky, a flash of gold, disappearing beneath the ruins. Had she thrown it? Had it fallen?

She turned back to Grandmother. "Bring the Goddess knife."

Not stopping to glance at the charred body of the great white snake, Mother walked through the still-raging storm. Nor did she bother to listen to the fearful, excited murmurs of our people who had gathered beyond the tower to marvel at the great wonder they had seen.

Straight-backed as an arrow, she walked through filth and mud, looking neither to the right nor the left, as if she walked on a fine-woven carpet, her eyes fixed on the hills and the forest beyond.

Above her Cymry, the red dragon, rose, shrieking in triumph, its wings made whole again. Looking up into the sky, I watched him and knew that I, too, now bore the dragon's fire.

For, I, too, had survived.

chapter 15

I woke to soft singing. The smell of an apple wood fire, costly precious wood, wafted over me.

I lay in darkness, letting the music wash over me. I never wanted to open my eyes again.

Strong hands caressed my chest; I recognized an ointment of rosemary and burdock dissolving against my skin.

Sudden pain tore into my stomach, lancing into my woman's folds. I sobbed and opened my eyes.

Thin cool fingers touched my forehead.

"Child?"

I was in a chamber filled with expensive beeswax candlelight. The blurred figure seated beside me had white flowing hair instead of the curling raven locks I wanted.

"Where is Mother?"

Grandmother removed her hand from my forehead as if I had slapped it away. "She'll be back soon."

The pain was far too great for me. I closed my eyes, breathing the heavy smells of the room—a dying swimmer desperate to reach land. Burning apple wood, meat broth, melting beeswax, and a dizzying variety of Grandmother's herbs followed me into the darkness.

The singing began again.

When I opened my eyes again it was daylight.

Dim sunlight danced through the one open window, illuminating bundled herbs, a scarred oak table, the colorful patterns of village weavings. We were in Grandmother's private hut, a dwelling she had built beyond the clustered freeman's homes of stone and wattle-and-daub, far enough away from the Hall and stables to afford her privacy.

Grandmother sat dozing in her favorite high-backed chair near the crackling hearth fire. Apple wood again, its costly logs protecting us from evil. A cauldron hung from the arm of an iron tripod, ready to be swung above the fire at a simple push.

This time I recognized more of Grandmother's herbs: the healing fog of rosemary, the nostril-flaring meadow-heal, the soft scent of valerian. Overpowering all was the hearty smell of my favorite venison and leek stew, steeped in wine.

The pain between my legs was not as sharp as when I first awakened, still, it attacked me like nettles as I tried to sit up.

"Grandmother?"

She slept on.

The room swam around me as if I had just rolled down a hill.

"Grandmother?"

She started awake this time and crossed the room to where I lay upon her own cot. "Did you dream?"

I shook my head. Then I remembered and pressed my face against the nubby sheep's wool of a blanket. "There was a cave …"

The fire crackled. Outside the window a freeman shouted for his child. Nightmare images shimmered beneath my closed eyelids, threatening to take me again. I fought the air with my fists.

"Speak, girl! It will ease you."

But I could not speak. For all I saw was fire. All I felt was fear. And pain.

I started to sob.

"Hush, now." Grandmother began to hum a melody I did not recognize but one that made me think of a soft forest glade where harmless woodland creatures—deer and rabbit, fox and squirrel— gathered to graze and play. She rocked me in her bony, muscled arms. Grandmother who was so rarely gentle, whose fierce temper pushed all but me away. "You are a princess of the Ordovice, Gwenhwyfar. Do not let him rob you of your courage."

"Where is Mother?" I asked again.

She did not answer, rising to feed the fire. Angry sparks flew up towards the roof-thatch, adding to the heavy smoke in the room. Outside a pony neighed, a man laughed. She settled beside me again. "Your mother will return soon."

I nestled against her sagging breasts and closed my eyes. Surprised by dripping water, I opened them again. Tears were spilling down her face. I touched their cool wetness in wonder, exploring the multitude of wrinkles in the caverns of her cheekbones. The black depths of her eyes were ancient beyond sorrow.

"If I could spare you, child, I would do so. For what comes on the next tide of life is naught but danger and pain."

Her face softened into a wistful smile the way it did when she touched the bark of a favored tree and did not know that I was watching,

"Yet, we must have courage. For the power of love is still great— and will not be forsaken."

Her words made little sense to me. Yet there was something I could fix on to keep the darkness at bay. "W-what will happen to the Vortigern?"

"He will die."

"And Uncle Maelgwyn?"

"Rest, Gwen." She disentangled herself from my arms and placed a weighted hand on my forehead, forcing me to lie back on the furs. "No more questions."

I clutched at her sleeve. "Grandmother, I have the right to know."

She met my eyes. I fought the heat, fought the sleep that crept upon me. My eyes watered with the effort of staring at her, but I did not drop my gaze. To look away, I knew, was to lose any hope of learning what I needed.

At last, she nodded. "Maelgwyn has disappeared—no doubt gone to join his allies in Eire. If he does show his face in Ordovice lands again, your father will destroy him. Brother or no brother."

Pain flared in my stomach. I sat up and locked my arms around my knees, forcing the agony away. Tegid lay unavenged. I must be strong, I must learn what could be done.

"As for *him*—the southern filth who attacked you—" Grandmother clasped my chin in her hands and turned my head to look at her. "His men have been told that he went hunting—and must have gotten lost."

She smiled, exposing still-white incisors. "Of course they do not believe it, for, of course, it is not true. But the women are guarding him. He is ours."

I put my head between my knees and breathed deeply. The pain was still an ocean, but I could no longer flee. So the monster king with his dagger-fingers was in the hands of the clan's women now. "What will happen when his warriors find out we have taken him?"

"Enough!" Grandmother's hand came up. "You must rest. Lie back and sleep." She pushed a curl behind my ear and pulled my beloved wolfskin from beneath the crumpled furs, arranging it carefully around my neck. I petted it with joy. She must have fetched it herself from my chamber. "Tomorrow when you rise, you can try some of that stew you smell. It is best you sleep first."

"But—"

She placed a finger on my lips. "You must let yourself be healed. Tomorrow Hwyrch and I will bathe you in rosemary water."

I tried to rise.

She pushed me firmly back into the furs and kissed me softly on my cheek. "Rest."

When I opened my eyes again, I saw Grandmother watching. "Where did Mother go?"

Grandmother winced as if a sword had cut her.

It was quiet for so long, I did not think she would answer.

"She journeys to protect you," she said at last. "Now sleep."

CHAPTER 16

Three days later I was strong enough to be moved back to my own summer chamber in the eastern tower. Grandmother disappeared from my bedside and Hwyrch took her place. A single morning of Nurse's scolding and fussing was enough to make me yearn for Grandmother's stern company, but beneath that yearning was a much greater ache, for Mother had not yet appeared at my bedside. Something in my heart broke at her continued absence, even as my body healed and I restlessly paced the length of my small room.

I leaned over the stone sill of the window seat, balancing as far out as I could without falling. This high up the builders had not had to worry about defense, so the windows of my chamber were gloriously wide instead of the dreary arrow slits we made do with at lower levels and they opened on a pleasing view of silver-touched river and mountains. Today, a rich breeze, heavy with the scents of early autumn, danced into my braids, freeing strands of my ever-rebellious hair.

I inhaled two deep breaths of sweet sun, leaf, and earth-scented air, sighed deeply, and tried again. "When can I go outside?"

"Tomorrow." Hwyrch continued to fold the winter tunics she had fetched from the clothes chest as if I had not spoken. I resorted to a sullen silence.

After several heartbeats of this treatment, my talkative nurse continued, "Things should be more settled by then. Talk of dragons and murders will have calmed and there is Tegid's funeral to prepare for."

A spasm of grief clenched my stomach. Since I had awakened in my own chamber and endured Grandmother's ritual healing bath of rosemary, I no longer tensed at every shadow but I was still afraid to close my eyes and needed Hwyrch's arms around me before I slept.

In the mist and light of day, I would sometimes pretend that Tegid was still alive, just away on one of his many adventures, attacking Scotti pirates or visiting the forest steading of his lady love.

I will avenge you, brother, I promised, then carefully stored this pain with all the others, nestled within my innermost heart.

"Shadow!" Cynan burst through the doorway, vaulting over my hound, Morag, who had been napping on the entrance stones. He flew across the room, tackling me from the window seat.

"Ass-wipe!" My heart sang. I punched him. Not giving up his advantage, Cynan grabbed my fists, pinning me to the cold stone floor. Both of us ignored Hwyrch's furious scolding, even when she left off folding tunics and tried to separate us.

Cynan found my most vulnerable tickle spot. Upside down and giggling wildly, at first all I saw above my brother was a hooded face laced with shadows and morning light.

Bright teeth flashed in a familiar smile.

"Merlin!"

One merciless twisting pinch to Cynan's abdomen and I was up and running into my uncle's open arms.

He swung me up, pretending to fly me across the chamber and out the window, paying no heed to Hwyrch's foolish flapping.

At last, Uncle gave in to her and set me down on the window seat. Removing his cloak, he kissed Hwyrch's cheek. "Enough, dear lady! See she has come to no harm—"

Nurse grunted, unappeased. "You should know better, Lord." She pushed Merlin away and returned to her folding, fixing Uncle with her fiercest eagle glare. It fell short, as usual, of its intent to terrify since Hwyrch's eyes bore more resemblance to a sparrow's, and her many chins wobbled too much to frighten even the most craven rabbit.

Cynan clambered up beside me and leaned further out the window than even I had dared, taking great gulps of the blustery wind. He turned to me, Father's dark brown eyes in his much younger freckled face lit with excitement.

"Now that you're better, Shadow, you can help Lleu and I stoke Huw's fires. Iolo says we must have enough new spears to arm ten handfuls of warriors! Look at my new burns!"

I examined the angry red patches on his forearms jealously, both of us pretending Hwyrch did not exist as we balanced precariously on the window seat.

"Lleu taught me the best way to work the bellows, if you—"

"Are you talking about that Druid brat that's taking Bran's place?" My voice snapped, sharper than I meant it to, filled with a memory of clear-seeing grey eyes and an unbidden warning about the South Tower.

"He's not so bad, once you understand his accent."

"Gwen," Merlin pushed his way between us, sitting in the small unoccupied space in the middle of the window seat, "how are you feeling?"

Snorting at this change of subject, my brother leapt up to wrestle with Morag, who had already taken advantage of our distraction to finish my breakfast before Hwyrch could stop her.

"What will happen now?" I asked.

Merlin sighed, running his fingers through his unbound raven hair. Without his prince's circlet he looked younger, although his forest-eyes were anchored with bruised purple shadows.

"Your people face great danger—the greatest since the red-cloaks came to murder the Druid priests of Mona countless generations ago."

Cynan stopped romping with Morag and joined us, sitting cross-legged on the floor at Merlin's feet.

"Forces are abroad now that have not walked this earth realm since ancient times." Merlin looked seriously at both of us.

"You must get used to dragons—and to talking salmon—and the *mendrad*, those soul destroyers that slip in and out of shadows, and feed on the newly-dead. For they are real."

Ice snaked up my spine. "What can we do?"

"See clearly, train well, stand bravely. That is all one can do. That and honor what is best in this world." Merlin kissed the top of my head, murmuring a blessing. He did the same to Cynan who squirmed.

Merlin laughed at him. "Brave warrior, you must get used to my ways. It is both blessing and curse to walk with spirits—to hear the voice of trees when you desire only to eat your supper."

Grabbing an apple from a bowl Morag had overlooked, he tossed it lightly in the air. Shimmering in the dust motes, one apple turned to two, then three, spiraling up and down, caught, then thrown in Merlin's hands.

Laughing at our expressions, he tossed one to Cynan, the second to me, and took a large bite of the third. "If anyone can steer Dinas Emrys through its coming battles, it is your Father. Cadwallon is Druid-trained as a warrior, though he still has difficulty mastering his emotions."

"It isn't Father's fault Maelgwyn is evil!" Cynan jumped up, tossing his apple core through the window.

"True," Merlin paused, visibly gathering his thoughts, "but it is best never to let love of kin blind you to their flaws—though I admit kin as flawed as Maelgwyn are blessedly rare."

"But you haven't told us what will happen now." I threw my apple core to Morag and rose from the window to take a seat on my bed. The sweet autumn wind no longer pleased me. It had turned cold and foreboding, bringing with it the scent of something terrible approaching Dinas. Tegid's murder, the attack of the southern King, even the red dragon that had saved me merely fed it.

Without taking my eyes from Merlin, my fingers searched the bed furs until they found my beloved ragged wolfskin, lying discarded on top of the bed. Big as I was, I discovered I was kneading it like a kitten seeking its mother's teat. Merlin was still talking, but I no longer heard him, my mind and heart filled with dark visions of my own. A great and powerful enemy stalked the lands of my clan. This I saw. An enemy that walked on two legs like me—but one in league with other creatures, with forces much more terrifying than human swords.

I saw no escape.

"Gwen—are you listening?" Merlin was beside me. "Shadow—come back!"

Responding to his tone of voice—a tone I'd rarely heard and always at times of importance—my spirit settled and I saw the disheveled cozy bedchamber again, felt the softness of my wolfskin, and Morag's anxious tongue on my bare legs.

Whatever he saw in my eyes must have reassured Uncle, for he merely placed a comforting hand upon my knee.

"I was saying, there are things I cannot tell you, either of you." He gestured for Cynan to leave off his restless pacing and join us on the bed.

"What do you mean, you can't tell us?" Cynan snapped. He boot-stomped to the bed and flung himself across the furs.

"You're the greatest Mage our lands have ever seen—even Grandmother says so! You can make dragons come and storms appear. Why can't you tell us what we should do next?"

Merlin stood. He, too, tossed his apple core out the window, watching it arch to the earth with a heart-deep sigh, then picked up his cloak from the chest where he had flung it and squatted on the floor beside us, letting its finely-woven black wool trail unnoticed on the stone flags of the floor.

"Because, that is not the way of magic, child. It is given to Mages to understand the powers of nature, the great forces of the universe, of the unseen realms. But the mysteries of the future reside in the human heart—and those secrets are not given to even the greatest Mage. To know such things would be to trespass on the very nature of the world—and that is something magicians should never do."

"But what about your prophesies—of how a great king will rise? That is part of the future." I asked.

Merlin ignored me, tossing Morag's marrow bone across the room. He watched with a smile as the young hound scrambled to fetch it, knocking over an empty stool in her eagerness.

When, at last, he turned to me, his smile was tinged with such sadness, I put my hand on his shoulder.

"Those prophesies you speak of come from the gods themselves, child. It is they who decide what they feel we should know—and what should be kept from us. I am but their conduit—a messenger appointed to cross strange seas."

His voice turned bitter, he studied his hands as if they had somehow betrayed him. "If I could live without their burden, I would do so in a heartbeat."

I gave him the last apple remaining in Hwyrch's dish. His smile became his own again. "Did you know the followers of the Cristos believe the first humans were told not to eat this fruit, for it would bring them too much sorrow?"

"That's silly." I loved apples.

"Perhaps," Merlin took a large bit of his own. "For some it is already too late, sorrow has already come. But you asked me a question. What will happen to Dinas? Although I cannot speak as a Mage, I can tell you as a man."

Cynan was pacing again. Now he picked up the stool Morag had knocked over and moved it closer to Merlin before he sat down. Hwyrch folded tunics behind us, her rare silence a mask for how hard she was listening.

Merlin put his palms together and raised them to his face, blowing on them; a gesture I knew meant he had given the question much thought. "You know that our folk guard Vortigern's men?" He waited for our nods before he continued. "Perhaps you do not know that these men are only a small part of the force that the Vortigern tried to bring to Dinas, for he did indeed intend to conquer your hillfort and subject the Ordovice to his rule. Somehow, he was alerted to Tegid's escort and managed to secret the largest part of his forces away. Your Father thinks they are lurking still along our southern borders.

"We know now it must have been Maelgwyn who warned him that your Father was wary of his intentions. What we do not know is where his warriors are now—and what they are planning. Or, if indeed, they yet know that Vortigern is missing."

"Is his Shield Brother still here?" I asked, remembering the squat warrior who had arrived late to the feasting. I saw his face again and, with it, I remembered the strange look he had exchanged with Maelgwyn. A look heavy with secrets that I had not thought to question at the time.

Merlin inclined his head. "A good thought, Gwen. I will find out."

"What of the Scotti, Merlin?" Cynan asked, scratching Morag's ear. "If they have given refuge to Maelgwyn, could he persuade them to invade us again?"

Merlin stood to stretch, cracking his back and knuckles as he released a pleasant groan. "It is good that you already think as rulers should. You may be right, Cynan. Although, one is never sure what goes into the thinking of the Scotti, your Father has already set a double watch along the western shore."

Uncle kissed the top of my head and nodded to Cynan. "Farewell now. I must help your father see to our defenses, for an attack from the South or West—or both—is likely. Soon."

Bowing to Hwyrch who graced him with a tight fleeting smile, he started for the door, then stopped in the middle of the room as if he had forgotten something. "Two things more I would say to you. Let this be your lesson of the day, since it would not be wise to adventure far until Vortigern's warriors are found."

His hand clasped the hilt of his sword. "The first is that what happens in the south of Albion matters to all of us—though it may not seem important now—for if Vortigern truly disappears, the rightful heirs of the southern tribes will return. They are two brothers. The older, Ambrosius, has taken shelter in our eastern kin lands across the sea. His younger brother, Uther, has been murdered by Vortigern, but not before he took a wife from the royal house of the Dumnoni and sired a young son. Of that son, Arthur—" he stopped and shrugged, "you will hear more of him at a later time."

Suddenly, he returned to my bedside and put his hand on my head. "You must rest, Gwen." His lips brushed my cheek. "For the second lesson is this, know that you are both safe—for now—at Dinas."

He bent to whisper in my ear. "Healing and vengeance are two sides of the same sword in this matter. Only remember that you are loved."

That night I woke from deep sleep to see the full moon watching me beyond the stone casement of my open window. I thought of Merlin's words— what would a sword that called for healing and vengeance look like?

I called for Hwyrch. There was no answer.

Fully awake now and curious, I rose. Hwyrch's furs lay neat and undisturbed beside me. Her cot was empty.

There came a soft rustle from the stairs.

Tiptoeing to the doorway, I was just in time to see a tall shadow, soft-footing away.

Not taking time for my boots, I grabbed my cloak, slid out of my room and followed, taking care not to slip on the clammy chill of the winding stairs.

The cloaked figure pushed open the thick oak door at the bottom of the tower, careful not to let it creak. Outside, the night-torch in front of the curved stone wall flashed on metal, making visible a broad sword in the shadow's free hand. As she glided across the courtyard the full moon's light seemed to caress her.

I followed.

I was almost sure it was Hwyrch I followed, but the eeriness of the night and all that had happened to me conspired to weaken my confidence.

And, if it was only Hwyrch, why was she carrying a sword?

Torches flared in a sudden gust of wind, causing fire shadows to dance madly against the black stones and empty spaces of the courtyard.

I was weak, exhausted by even this much effort. To go farther into the night was dangerous. Yet, even as I looked longingly up the stairs towards my bed furs, I knew I had to continue.

The hooded figure moved gracefully into the wind, halting suddenly in the shadow of the new guest hall. Positioning the sword beneath her cloak, she raised one single black-gloved hand to clutch the hood of her cloak against her face. Seeming confident that the rising wind and late hour would let her pass through Dinas unseen, she headed towards the little-used northern gate.

For one final heartbeat I hesitated. Then, avoiding the gate, the shadow slipped through a narrow gap between the wood fencing of the ramparts—a gap that I had never noticed before—and I slid through behind her.

It was well I moved quickly, for in the time it took me to push silently past the rotting wood, the shadow walked rapidly down the hill and disappeared beneath the trees that clustered on Dinas's northeastern slope, working her way towards the palisades at the foot of the hill. Trying to catch up to her, I wove between their trunks, grateful for the thick calluses on my feet and the games of hide-and-seek Cynan and I had played on this treacherous slope.

Crouched at last in the tall grass at the bottom of the hill, I watched as my quarry strode confidently towards the lone sentry who guarded the lower eastern gate. To my surprise, she passed beneath the watchtower without a challenge, not even pausing to remove her hood. The guard was one I did not recognize and he merely saluted her politely and turned to go back inside the rickety shelter of his sentry post.

Why were there not more sentries? Dinas was preparing for war.

Too late to waste time with questions. Taking a deep breath, I tiptoed past also, following the hooded figure beyond the final ramparts and into the forest.

The night breeze rose as I entered the trees, filling their leaves and branches like ocean waves crashing on the shore. It ruffled my hair as Merlin liked to, as if it sought to tease me.

The full moon silvered the trees ahead, illuminating the path in front of me.

An owl hooted. A mouse shrieked. I did not look back.

chapter 17

Soon our path became a deer track covered with pine needles. My bare feet wiggled in gratitude, sinking into their soothing softness.

There were rustlings in the undergrowth.

Small creatures. It was just small creatures. Yet they sounded bigger than rabbits or badgers.

I stopped. The noises stopped too, continuing as soon as I tiptoed forward. The thicket beside me started to shake, as if whatever was stalking me had been joined by many others.

Nervously I peered into the black night that crowded the path, looking up just in time to see the dark-cloaked woman turn onto an even smaller path, one that would take us into the heart of the forest, a place of tall and ancient trees, dense brambles, and deep forgotten pools. A secret place where the oldest magics lived.

The mysterious rustling suddenly stopped, leaving a heavy moon-filled silence that was somehow worse.

The Dark Goddess hunts tonight.

The voice came from nowhere.

I hid behind a tree.

Stop it, witless girl! You are a princess of the Ordovice—you have as much right in these woods as She.

Grandmother's voice, as clear as if she was standing beside me.

The forest seemed empty of life, its low-lying thickets black, dappled with moonlight. Trees loomed above me, gripping the sky, their late summer branches intertwined like a poorly woven roof.

The wind rose again.

I made the sign of the night goddess, set my face to the eastern sky and stepped back on the path. The full moon shone through the interlaced branches in triumph, cold as an enemy in ambush.

Thorns cut deep into my right foot. I bit my teeth against the pain and continued without a sound, threading my way up the hillside, not daring to look behind me.

Under these stars, there would be no mercy.

The cloaked shade traveled deeper and deeper into the oldest part of the forest, walking for so long that I was ready to sink to the leaves in exhaustion. Suddenly she slacked her pace, looking about in all directions.

I slid behind a rowan tree and waited.

The black hood paused and stared at the tree that hid me. The hood slipped back and a plump familiar face was illuminated beneath moon shadow.

Hwyrch. There could be no doubt.

I started to call out.

No.

Sweat ran down the middle of my back.

Hwyrch's stare released me at last. Fixing on a spot to the east, she stood on tiptoe as if looking for something, then began walking again, replacing her hood as she moved away.

I inhaled one slow breath of relief, counted a handful more, and followed.

Nurse's stride lengthened as she hurried towards whatever she had seen. If the long night's walk over treacherous ground had tired her at all, she showed no sign of it.

I tripped over a tangled root and fell upon the path, lying, my face pressed against earth and stone, too weary to move. The thickets rustled in a gust of wind, coming alive as they had done when I had first entered the forest.

Get up!

I stood. Nothing was there. No creatures, no small forest animals. I was alone.

Yet the rustling grew ever louder around me.

What was it?

Terrified, I ran after Hwyrch's cloaked shadow, tearing my feet and legs on brambles, caring for nothing but the horror of being left alone.

"Who comes to Ceridwen's Fire?" The harsh voice challenged Nurse's shadow from some hidden spot within the trees.

I jumped back just in time, taking shelter behind the branches of an aging pine.

"A Warrior of Anu." The softness of Hwyrch's Decleangli mountain speech was unmistakable. She took a single step forward and raised the sword she carried, laying it flat across her outstretched palms. "I bring the Goddess Sword."

"Good. The others await you." The sentry stepped out from beneath the trees and showed herself long enough to bow.

With a nod, Hwyrch hid the sword beneath her cloak again. Her gait relaxed into the lumbering one I recognized. She stepped past the sentry into a large clearing where a bonfire roared. A circle of women waited, dressed as Hwyrch was in hooded cloaks so black that even the full moon did nothing to reveal the features of their faces.

Alert for other guards, I circled past the sentry and hid behind the biggest tree I could find, an ancient oak that had seen more winters than I could imagine.

Many shadows milled around the grove greeting each other in soft voices. I stared in wonder. Knowing it was hopeless, I still tried to guess at the hidden faces of the women.

They began to dance.

I watched, swaying instinctively, yet my gaze was pulled to the opposite side of the fire where a tall stake stood. A large man, covered with blood, was roped to it, his head hanging in exhaustion upon his chest. His groans could be heard even above the high crackling of the great fire and the murmuring of the women as they arranged themselves into two circles, one inner and one outer as the dance became more intricate.

The man's stake lay within the eastern edge of the circle. The dance quickened, the women weaving around him. Their bare feet kicked and stomped in a pattern that grew wilder and wilder. Swirling, long robes flying, suddenly, they threw back their hoods and raised their arms, calling out as one upon the Dark Goddess: Ceridwen the Huntress. Goddess of the Night.

Huddling beneath the oak, I remembered Grandmother's tales and Hwyrch's whispered stories of the Death-Bringer and knew within my blood and bones that it was she who had walked with me this night. She who now stood guard beside me, her bloodthirsty huntress eyes trained on the dancing circle before me—and the doomed man they guarded.

Ceridwen. Who walked the night and ruled the stars...who

guarded the mysteries that swept like carrion birds through the ruined stones of deserted ghost Halls. She who haunted the bedtime tales of children.

Despite my terror at spying on what I now knew was a sacred ritual, I crept carefully closer to the staked man.

When I was close enough, I raised my eyes from the ground and stared at his face. It was him! My heart sang so loudly, I jumped back, sure it would be heard by the dancing shadows who had now linked arms and were flinging the long hair of their heads back and forth, raising their soot-blackened ritual faces to the night sky.

The Vortigern who had tried to rape me, who had beaten me and threatened to kill me, now stood, tied, as helpless and bloodied as a trussed chicken, waiting for whatever the dancing women had in store for him.

I raised my face to the sky. It took all the power I felt rising inside me not to throw back my head and howl like a wolf in triumph.

Two black-hooded figures emerged from the shadows beyond the fire. Instead of joining the dancers, they raised their voices in wails that escalated up and down, twining around each other like a braid through wild hair. The dancers stomped and roared in answer.

The shorter of the figures plucked a small drum from the ground and began to beat upon it. The women of the inner circle raised clasped hands and took two steps towards the fire, answering the rhythm. Shouting, they retreated, taking two patterned steps back. But the drumming shadow was dissatisfied. It darted in amongst them, quickening the beat, roaring a challenge as it dodged in and out among the dancers, sometimes crouching, sometimes leaping as if it were a hunter, urging on its comrades.

The drumbeats echoed in the fire-filled air, the pounding of ten handfuls of hearts, the pounding of spears, of thunder upon lost mountains.

The dance grew in frenzy. Women danced closer, ever closer to the fire. Amidst the sparks that flowered around them, they roared back at the insistent drum, howling with rage.

At last, the drummer dropped behind them, beating a heart-stopping crescendo. Her hands were blurred streaks, unrecognizable as human. Her scream rang across the glade. Then she fell silent and dropped to her knees.

The drumbeats faded slowly into the lightning-charged air and a second shadow came forward, tossed back its hood, threw back its head with a measured, ritual cry, then raised its arms in command.

Squinting against the glare of the fire, I saw Grandmother's soot-blackened face. Fierce and frightening, a dark liquid gleamed on it, glistening above the soot.

She raised her arms.

"Ceridwen's fire, Ceridwen's chosen. Ye are here to do the Dark Goddess' work. What say ye? Are ye willing?"

A sharp, raging chorus of sound answered; I cringed as if the cries were a living animal. My fingernails dug into tree bark, seeking comfort, finding none.

The women opened their circle, and moved farther apart, including the staked man in their range. The kneeling drummer rose, went to a glistening pile of knives that lay close to the high crackling fire and picked one. She threw back her hood and held it high with both hands, letting the curved blade glimmer, caught between moon, stars, and fire like a twist of jeweled sky.

The woman's gaze moved slowly around the circle, meeting the eyes of every cloaked priestess in turn. She paused when her eyes traveled close to my tree and stared at the thicket where I hid, as if she could see right through the tree's trunk and uncover me. She said nothing however and I dared to shift closer for a better look at her face.

Mother.

My blood froze.

"I believe you were told to get rest this night." Merlin's hand was on my shoulder.

I screamed before I could stop myself.

The Mage moved in front of me, making an impatient motion, as if he were swatting a fly. My scream died before it could reach the ears of the women.

"What —?"

Uncle put a finger to his mouth, his fire-lit eyes furious. "It is I who will ask questions this night. Though I have no need of them. It is clear from your actions what you have chosen to do."

"I am sorry, Uncle Merlin." I hung my head, sorry only to have been discovered, needing to be in this grove more then I could express in words. "Please don't give me away!"

Beyond us women began wailing, their voices rising in a wavering lament so loud it seemed to shake the stars.

Mother moved across the clearing and stood in front of the bleeding man. He was already near death and paid no attention as Mother passed the knife before his half-shut eyes.

"Do you really think they do not know you are here, child?" Merlin's voice softened a bit. He regarded me with pity, no trace of the respect I craved. "How else do you think you got past the guards—or through a hole in the ramparts that does not exist?"

I shivered, suddenly conscious of how cold my feet were getting. How many thorns had cut them. How much they hurt.

Women's wails rose all around us, from the watchers along the path behind me to those within the glade. Suddenly the crowd of shadows in the clearing parted, making a new circle around the stake where the King was tied. Arms linked, they began to sway.

Mother reached up to Vortigern, the knife clenched in both her hands. Even from where I hid, I could see that she was shaking as she cut the ropes that held him. Other black-cloaked women rushed to catch him, to lay him, motionless at Mother's feet. A woman stooped to pick up the drum and began to beat it again. Its cadence echoed in the night, accompanied by the sharp pops and crackles of the great fire, and the sudden sharp and yipping dog calls of the women.

Mother raised the knife. She lowered it swiftly. Twisting, slashing.

Her victim screamed once, a long unbelieving wail. The women answered with ululations of triumph.

The knife flashed up again, dripping with blood. It descended. This time the southern king's scream was weaker, fading into the wind even before the women's cries drowned it out.

The Death of a Hundred Cuts.

My gentle Cristos mother's teeth bared in a snarl. She reached down and raised blood-stained hands to her face, anointing her cheeks and forehead, tasting the doomed King's blood with her tongue.

This mother who once told me tales of butterflies.

"No," Merlin's own eyes swept the crowded fiery grove in front of us, "I would have spared you this, if I had been gifted with the power to do so. But each being walks in the shadow of their own fate and, you, my dear, are not destined to escape the doings of this night."

The women's cries rose in intensity. Despite myself, I shrugged the Mage's comforting hand away and craned my neck to see what new horror was happening.

Merlin swore beneath his breath and spoke in his most commanding voice, "As always, Gwen, you have plunged headlong into the bramble thicket, without counting the cost."

Stung by the bitter tone of his voice, I turned from the nightmare in the glade. On Uncle's night-shadowed face, the crescent tattoos between his eyebrows and at his temples blazed with green fire. His eyes were stern, judging me from the realm of the gods.

Now, I had no shelter. No friends, no allies. I moved away from Merlin and huddled beyond the trees, arms crossed to hold myself against the pain, no longer caring if I was seen.

The night, the fire, and its screams seemed to go on forever.

I felt the Mage behind me, although I had not seen or heard him move. "Forgive me, child." This time his touch on my shoulder was gentle. "Evil begets evil beneath a baleful moon this night."

His sigh was beneath the wind, heavy with sorrow and longing. "I spoke without thinking. I grow weary—and angered that an innocent must lurk in the shadows of this god-cursed bloody grove."

I huddled against the warmth of his robe and felt the forest move through me. I spoke. *"Meachith yersth, Merlin Uthuleth dea Sangorsil."*

Merlin's long fingers had tangled through my hair, as soothing as the ancient blessing he had offered me that morning—a lifetime ago. At the sound of my voice, they stopped moving.

His sharp intake of breath was the only sound I heard, although mere steps beyond us the night was filled with blood-curdling screams and women's triumphant howls. The man who had tried to rape me was being skinned alive.

"Sa, Gwenora de Yrouth. Mea salith, berea denani. It would appear you know the forest's speech. Your Grandmother will be pleased."

I turned from the grove and looked up at him.

The Mage smiled, the shadowed moon and leaping fire illuminating his face. His crescent moon tattoos began to glow again, but this time their green fire was soft.

Yet his eyes were still distant. As distant as that of the god I had once mistaken him for.

Uncle sank to the ground and I collapsed with him, curling into his lap like a small child, closing my eyes against the screams of the night.

Dreams of fire and curved swords fled across my soul. A harsh hand shook my shoulder.

I batted it away and tried to nestle back into my cloak, hearing leaves crisp beneath me as I moved. "Gwen. Wake up! The time has come!"

Confused, I blinked my eyes. Grandmother pulled me to my feet. I swayed, rubbing my eyes, trying to stand on feet made of ice.

Merlin had disappeared. Grandmother and I were alone beneath the tall tree shadows. Squinting past her kneeling body, I saw the glade fire still burning high. Nor had the cloaked women left. They still formed a circle, although they danced more slowly, the moon sinking beneath the forest behind them.

"Come!" Grandmother gripped my hand in the no-nonsense clasp she used when she was annoyed with me. I was pulled into the glade.

No one cried out in surprise.

Exhausted and frightened, I looked around the circle. Now that I was closer and they had removed their hoods, I recognized many of the freewomen and servants of the fortress, and some village women, as well. Fat, twinkling-eyed Andelis, the laundress, was clasping the hand of Nest, the midwife. Both nodded solemnly at me.

Someone shouted beyond the fire. I turned and met my mother's eyes.

Her face, hair, and body were covered with so much blood, I barely recognized her. Graceful as ever, she rose from her crouching position with the litheness of a deer.

Her hand clasped the crescent moon-shaped knife she had used to skin the headless carcass of Vortigern which now lay beside the fire, an unrecognizable grizzly mass of rippled red and white. Here and there, sharp points of bone cut through what was left of his body, pointing like nightmare fingers at the night sky.

Hwyrch darted forward. With a sharp glance at Grandmother, she took my hand and led me into the midst of the circled women. As the women made way, Hwyrch slid her hand from mine, joining it firmly with the palm of the woman beside her.

She left, rejoining Mother and Grandmother beside Vortigern's corpse.

Afraid to look behind me, wondering if this was all still a part of my dream, I stared into the fire. Grey, swirling shapes flew high above the sparking flames, a part, yet not a part of the smoke that rose in heavy clouds, thick enough to blot out the stars.

A yipping cry began again, somewhere in the circle. Echoed by the woman holding my hand, soon all the women uttered it, like wolves upon a hunting trail.

I raised my head to the smoking hot sky, snapping with sparks of fire. My throat opened. I sang with them.

Hwyrch, Mother, and Grandmother entered the circle, crouching like hunters. Grandmother straightened, swinging a dripping human head by its bloody, matted hair and the three of them danced their grisly trophy into the inner circle, raising the head to each woman as they passed, dashing perilously close to the flames in a warrior's frenzy. When they came to me, Grandmother gestured for Hwyrch. Nurse drew the great sword she had taken from the fortress and handed it, gore-covered, to Grandmother, who held it high with one hand, swinging the bloody head with her other.

Two women ran behind her and dug a small hole in the earth. Grandmother turned with a grunt and lowered the sword, hilt first into the ground. The other women braced it with earth then backed up a step.

Grandmother raised the head a final time with an ululating battle cry. I forced myself to look— the mean small eyes that had leered over me were wide open now, the terror in them frozen forever. I stepped back, drawn despite myself to the bloody horror of his face.

The echoes of Grandmother's cry still rode in waves around us. Screaming her fury again, Grandmother plunged the head upon the up-thrust sword blade in front of me and knelt, gesturing for Mother to come to her side.

Mother walked slowly towards her, backlit by the fire so that all of her that I could see at first was shadow. She carried something outstretched in her arms, much as a servant would carry a tray filled with food. She knelt beside Grandmother and held it out to me.

I walked to her, unwilling, obeying some dark thing within me. When I was close enough to touch her, I looked into Mother's eyes, trying to see beyond the blood that darkened even her beautiful lashes, trying to see some remaining trace of the mother I loved. She whose rose-water scent rose around us both as she laughed and bent over my bed telling stories that made me believe trees could sing and sheep could dance.

There was nothing of my mother left, only blooded, sorrowing eyes.

"The skin is yours," Grandmother's voice was harsh, cracked with smoke and fire, "Gwenhwyfar ferch Ceridwen Sweet Singer ferch Rhiannon, Sage-Singer of the Ordovice. Burn it as a future Queen steps out to claim her destiny!"

But it was Mother who handed me the skin of the king. Mother who arched her brows in a horrible parody of the playful, demanding songstress I knew. I hesitated. Mother dared me with her silence.

My arms rose to take the glistening, gory thing from her before I was aware they had moved.

I touched it. The skin was wet, slimy with blood, stinking of blood and fire. I could feel the dead king's terror.

I dropped it in disgust. *"No!"* I backed away.

Mother caught it before it hit the ground.

Some women gasped, but Grandmother simply nodded, gesturing into the sky. "I see. And you would leave these spirits unavenged?"

I followed her hand and saw, beyond the smoke swirling above us, those same bits of grey swirls I had noticed when I first came to the fire. As if they saw me watching, they drifted down into the fire itself, emerging one by one, crowding towards me on all sides of the severed head.

They were children, although the tallest looked to be almost full grown. Tall and lovely as a spring willow—despite the fact that I could look right through her and still see the fire. She drew shimmering yellow hair back from her face, exposing a throat which bore a deep, bleeding line across it.

I reached out to her, blinking away tears.

"Aye, Gwen," Grandmother's voice seemed to come from the clouds, "he killed them all. And she, his own daughter, Rowana. Not enough to take his pleasure from them, he silenced them forever—and enjoyed the deed as well!"

I reached out my hand to the yellow-haired spirit. She smiled sadly, covering her torn throat with one hand, reaching to touch my hair with her other. When her fingers landed, I felt a soft, chill breeze surround us both.

"No one else can see them child, save you and me. And perhaps your mother if she has finally stopped running from her birthright."

I pulled my gaze away from the spirit and looked in wonder around the circle. The black-cloaked blooded women stood frozen. Even my mother knelt, still holding the skin. Her eyes were motionless as if time itself had stopped and she, like all the other women in the grove, were spelled beneath the hands of the Goddess.

Suddenly I remembered the soft rustlings I had heard as I made my way through the forest. Reading my thoughts, Grandmother smiled grimly. "Aye, they followed you here, trusting that one of their own would help avenge them."

"What must I do?"

But I did not need to ask. I took the stinking skin from Mother's unmoving, outstretched hands, this time ignoring the gore that slid from it, drenching my hands.

"You must burn it to set them free. And by so doing, you will set yourself free as well, Gwenhwyfar ferch Ceridwen."

Trembling like a newborn colt, I watched Grandmother approach me, the blood upon her robe somehow less fearsome than the stains upon my mother's face.

"Child, there is no greater magic in this wide world's realm than that which comes when Earth's Goddess mates with the God of Sun and Sky. Life itself springs from such power."

A spirit-girl of my age tossed long hair out of her eyes and giggled, then leaned over to spit on Vortigern's bloody head. The children's ghosts surrounding us tittered. A toddler's fat cheeks puffed out with laughter.

"This vile ghost tried to take this sacred power and twist it into darkness. You fought him, little one—and survived his knife. But your spirit is chained to his and will not be free until you cast his skin into the fire. The last of him will be gone then. Only his head will stay," she spat into the dead man's eyes, "condemned to guard this grove for eternity."

Fire-wind whipped her hair and gown. "The flames will cleanse his evil and send it from your soul." She raised her arms to the sky. "Fire will free these innocents to go beyond the mist, to the Isle of Apples that they long for. There they will dance in the orchards of Arianhod and sing Epona's horses to sleep..." She paused to stroke my cheek.

I looked into her eyes, lost. "Let them go, Granddaughter. You who will be Queen one day, must learn true power now."

I turned from her and walked towards the fire, extending the horrible skin in front of me. Women stirred as I passed, rising from their haunches, stretching drugged and tired limbs. Across the fire, a tall woman I had never seen before blinked her eyes and yawned, then looked guiltily around, as if to make sure no one else had seen.

I stumbled closer to the flames.

The cloud of spirit children flew around me, while some grew feet and walked beside me. The tall girl floated to the side, a hairsbreadth in front of me, as if even in death, she wanted me to remember that she, too, was once a princess.

When the heat of the fire was strong enough to singe my face and hair, I took a steadying breath and flung the bleeding skin as far into the flames as I could.

The fire enveloped it with a hungry sigh, raising a wind that rushed across my face and lifted the children's spirits high above my head, dancing as they merged with the smoke. Some called back to me, many in languages I did not know. They were waving and I waved too, the water of tears running down my face as I watched the yellow-haired girl float far into the sky.

Just before she vanished into the depths of the pre-dawn sky, she turned and smiled down on me, her teeth gleaming softly against the smoke, her face made lovely. Lit by fire and stars, she blew me a kiss and disappeared.

My own soul yearned to follow.

Grandmother's hand gripped my shoulder from behind, "Well done, Granddaughter! Well done indeed!"

I stumbled and fell dizzily against her, aware only of the copper scent of blood.

chapter 18

There was smoke…there was fire…blood…and pain…great pain, as if my soul were being ripped from my chest.

Voices.

Mother's cool hand on my forehead. *Why was she not prepared?*

*I was not sure she was ready. I did not know if…*Grandmother's voice, a hesitant croak. *The gate was left open. Her spirit chose its path—*

She wanders now between the worlds. Thanks to you. Hwyrch. Hwyrch? A dream. Let me sleep. But a dream. *Even the most humble slave knows better than to meet the Dark Goddess without protection.*

A chant. The smell of herbs. A humming far away.

No more.

Mother's arms. Tears upon my face. *I should have been here. Should have known—I let you advise me. You who are worse than a raven covered with blood.*

Grandmother weeping. Weeping with sounds like a sword being sharpened on a whetstone. Rocking me. My face, my feet, dripping with blood.

Rocking. I danced, covered with blood, spinning with joy.

No!

Come, daughter.

I run to Mother. She gathers me in her arms, against her favorite embroidered linen gown. I close my eyes, then wake, for she is laughing. A knife drips blood above me.

"Give me your heart," she whispers.

I run, screaming.

No!

Voices.

She needs to find her own way home. Leave us. Please. Hwyrch. At her breast I hear the songs of the Decleangli mountains.

Sleep.

Covered with blood.

Sleep.

A drum beats...chanting...the *estethra* come...

The tunnels of the South Tower open...

"Gwen, you must try to wake." Hwyrch shook me, gentle but insistent. "The Scotti are coming! Dinas is under attack! You have slept three sunsets away!"

I closed my eyes tighter, pushing her away. Images of bleeding knives...women's hair filled with fire...a full moon's mouth full of fangs ...I burrowed into the furs, seeking safety.

She cursed, shaking me until my teeth rattled, pulling me up to stand. "No more time to let your wits wander or you'll be lost forever!" Dizzy, I collapsed against her, my toes leagues away from the world.

She poured water over my head. I sputtered, opened my eyes. Her own were bloodshot with worry. "Good, you're with us again!" she snapped, bundling me out of the small guest chamber into the chaos of the Hall. "The Scotti will be on us before midday. We must join your mother."

I fought to free myself from her grasp, so weak I only staggered. "Not Mother!"

She slapped me. The shock of it was enough to force my spirit into my body, locking my dark visions and the blood smells that surrounded me behind a door—a door that threatened to open at the slightest push.

"You must come, child."

I followed, too dizzy to protest, dimly aware that it had been Hwyrch's arms that had cradled me, her mountain lullabies that had followed me into the abyss.

We entered a Hall in which all sense of order had disappeared. Kitchen slaves shoved past us in panic, ignoring Maeve's furious commands to slow down. Women fled, clutching their children's hands. A lost toddler stood near the ashes of the central fire, screaming his lungs out as freemen and women dodged past him.

"Enough!" Father's Shield Brother Hwyll stormed through the open doorway. "You call yourselves Ordovice! Frightened mice, the lot of you! Stand, I say!" He caught a fleeing servant by the neck of his tunic and shook him like a rat. "Stand!

"But—" a horse-faced woman shouted, "the Lady Rhiannon said—"

"The Lady Rhiannon said you were to pack what was needful and bring food and drink to the caves." Grandmother took two great strides into the Hall, her gaze withering everyone she passed. "You were not told to behave like crazed fools. The Scotti are almost upon us. They will slaughter you like pigeons if you do not follow me now!"

Without another word, she turned on her heel and left the Hall.

"Kerinne, get these ninnies into some kind of order." Maeve bustled forward, with a polite nod to Hwyll. "Your pardon, warrior. We'll see to the women."

Hwyll spared her a brief nod before disappearing into the courtyard, his stern eyes lightening as Maeve waddled through the throng, cuffing slaves and freeborn alike, comforting children, and overseeing the swift packing of bannock and smoked venison.

Hwyrch knelt to scoop barley cakes into a sack. I broke free; still weak as a newborn calf. "I'm not going into the caves!"

I dodged into the confusion of the courtyard. Chieftains bellowed orders, warriors cursed, all of them overridden by the frantic neighing of ponies and the ringing clash of spears and swords. Manure and mud, excitement and fear were everywhere, fierce as ancient gods.

I ran through it all, clutching my side in pain, one desperate thought in mind. *Father.*

As if my thoughts had conjured him, Cadwallon Long Brow stormed across the courtyard, Iorwerth at his side. My brother loped away to the Warriors' Hall where his men swore at prisoners who cursed back in the Southern tongue—Vortigern's men. Good! No doubt Maelgwyn's would be there too, now that he also had disappeared.

I staggered, falling against the side of a storage shed. "Father!"

"Stay!" Father commanded. Grabbing my elbow so fiercely I cried out, he steered me to the eaves of old Huw's smithy.

Before either of us could speak, Maelgwyn's former slave, Sari, darted across the courtyard like a small bird. She looked furtively behind her, made a mysterious sign on her forehead, and stealthily entered the blacksmith's doorway, ignored by the crowd of warriors as they jostled and shouted for the arrows and lances that Father's Shield Brother Hwyll was tossing from the entrance of the forge.

Snarling at me to be still, Father called her.

Startled, Sari looked around, the soft veil she wore wafting above her nose as she turned to face him. Measuring Father with her strange black eyes, the girl grabbed a handful of arrows from the neat stack at Hwyll's feet and ran to him before the grizzled warrior could stop her.

She bowed deeply to us, clutching the stolen arrows like a precious child.

Hwyll shoved her roughly aside. "My Lord, I am—"

Father waved him away. "I will take care of this."

Turning to Sari's bowed head, he spoke in a surprisingly gentle tone, "You know the song of arrows?"

She raised her face and met his eyes. Our language must still have been a mystery to her, but she clearly understood his intent, for she mimed inserting an arrow in a bow. The soft linen of her veil was thin enough for me to catch the sudden whiteness of teeth as she smiled.

Father hailed a passing warrior. "Your bow, Rhys."

The young man was well-muscled, but short, his bow made to match his height. As he hesitated, Father grabbed the weapon from him and tossed it to Sari.

The girl caught and hefted it with ease, murmuring as she examined it. With a quick glance at Father, she notched an arrow and bent the bow back, sighting a target with the relaxed stance of an expert archer.

The arrow flew over the heads of the crowd, piercing a tunic left to dry on the branches of an old oak near the Hall, a goodly distance away. People screamed and scattered, thinking, no doubt, that the Scotti were already attacking.

Father showed his teeth in a warrior's approval and nodded at her, "Again!"

This time she aimed at a rat scurrying in panic from the stables. Her arrow caught the creature in its side with such force that its body was flung into the air. A village woman screamed and dragged her curious son away before he could touch it.

"You are indeed full of surprises, young woman."

Sari looked puzzled. Father returned the bow to Rhys and sank to his haunches beside her. "Go to Hwyll. You may have all the bows and arrows you need!"

A lovely light dawned in her eyes as the girl received the meaning of Father's speech.

"Hwyll!"

Father's busy Shield Brother's brawny arms were filled with newly-sharpened spears. He turned, trying to mask his irritation at yet another interruption. "Aye, Lord?"

"See that our newest warrior is outfitted with a bow and arrows to suit her. She is to be welcomed as an ally!" he added when Hwyll rolled his eyes and two nearby warriors groaned.

Sari dropped to her knees at Father's feet.

"T-thank yew..." she said, her voice like soft music in the wind. Then she placed her hands around her neck and lowered the neck of the shawl she wore pinned around her homespun servant's gown, exposing the ridged scars of a slave collar. "N-no more!"

Her hands danced in the air, miming a fierce sword thrust. With a second bow that included me and a gentle touch of her fingers on my cheek, the mysterious foreign girl skipped lightly to Huw's smithy, as if she were no older than Cynan.

Heartbeats after she disappeared into the smithy, I heard warriors shout their approval—Sari must have given them a demonstration. I almost smiled, despite the fury of my father's face as he now turned to me.

"What possesses you to run about like a wild thing in the midst of battle-ready warriors?" Any temptation to smile disappeared immediately. Father's bloodshot eyes pinned me to the outside wall of the smithy as effectively as rope or spear.

"This is no game, girl! We could all be dead by sunset!"

I gripped his arm and met his eyes, willing him to understand. "Hwyrch is trying to force me into the caves!"

"Of course—"

"No, Father! I will not go!" No use to speak of my terror at the thought of being in the dark again. "I want to fight with you and Iolo!"

"There you are!" Hwyrch skidded up beside us, red-faced and gasping, her giant frame quivering with exertion. "She ran from me—as always, Lord!" She grabbed my arm and twisted, ignoring my cry of pain. "This time, you must tell her to obey!"

Father looked from Hwyrch to me, paying no mind to the chaos of shouts and action around us. Whatever he saw in my eyes caused him to lift my chin in his hand and kiss my forehead. "Take her to the top of Cunedda's Tower, Hwyrch. You will be safe there."

"But, my Lord—"

Father cut short Nurse's protests with a wave of his hand. Dropping down to a squat beside me, he continued speaking to her, "You know the hidden passage?"

"Yes, but—"

"Then use it, if all is lost." His face was on level with mine, his eyes searching my own, "This day will bring vengeance or death, daughter. If you would be a warrior then mind your orders as all good warriors do. Hwyrch is your Commander, obey her—or you will answer to me."

"Thank you, Father." I swayed with exhaustion, then mastered myself and touched his summer-bronzed cheek, letting my fingers stroke the stiff length of his moustache. "May Lugh guide your spears this day."

He nodded gravely at my blessing, as if I were a blooded warrior, and turned to Hwyrch. "I will send word to Ceri that our daughter bides with you, safe in Cunedda's Keep."

Without another word to me, he strode away, heading for the inner gate of the ramparts. Scores of warriors and villagers accosted him. In a matter of heartbeats, he calmed them with orders and tasks, joining Hwyll and Iolo as they assembled their men beside the gates.

"Well it looks like you've gotten your way again, girl! Hurry!" Seeing me sway, Hwyrch swore and scooped me up as if I were a small child, racing through the panicked crowd.

We were almost at the North Tower when I heard her.

"Gwen! Thank Cristos you are well!" Mother stood in the shadows of the new guest hall, one hand over her heart as she labored to catch her breath. "Come! Take refuge with Cynan and me."

She closed the distance between us and put her hand on my head in a gesture she had offered more times than I could count. "It would ease my spirit if you were beside me. Although," she hesitated, tilting her head at Hwyrch who stood quiet, her ordinarily mobile face expressionless, "I know well your nurse is a match for any boatload of Scotti, I still wish us to take shelter together."

Almost, I leapt free from Hwyrch's arms and let Mother lead me away. Almost, I breathed her attar of roses—a scent she carried even now—and let it comfort me as it always had. Instead I hid my face, watching her from the corner of my eyes.

Mother had always been the radiant sun upon my world, shining like a goddess on the many paths that I explored. Always gentle, always safe despite whatever blood or fire or magic threatened to overwhelm us.

But she had covered herself with blood in the Dark Goddess' grove. She had turned to wield the same blood-drinking knife that already held Father and Grandmother's soul. Seasons later, I would come to understand, but now all I saw was that the blood upon her hands could easily have been my own—for she had done nothing to protect me. It had been Merlin who saved me from Vortigern. Hwyrch who had sung me home from other realms.

I met her exhausted violet eyes and saw her lashes coated with blood again, her elegant hands still holding the knife that had sent a king to Anwnn, screaming in agony.

"Don't touch me!" I spat, huddling against Hwyrch, my fists clenched in fury.

"Don't speak to your mother like that!" Hwyrch ordered, yet she cradled my head against her breasts.

Mother looked sad, not angry. "I had hoped—" she began.

"You are nothing but a murderer!"

Hwyrch bundled me away. "I am sorry, lady," she called over her shoulder.

I held tightly to my rage as we approached the tower. It was a comfort in the strange cold place that had opened in my heart. "Hwyrch, put me down," I whispered as we entered the dank stone shelter. "I promise, I won't try to run."

She snorted, her foot on the first step of the spiraling stairs.

"Please, I'm sick."

An irritated sigh. She dropped me, none too gently, on the steps and passed me a flask of water.

I pushed it away, holding my stomach in pain. Nurse crouched beside me then, her hand on my forehead, both of us ignoring the tumult in the courtyard behind us.

I gripped the front of her gown. Fevered, swallowing vomit, I began to cry, the words pouring out before I could stop them. "Why did I have to go into the forest?"

She stared at me, assessing. Whatever she saw caused her to hunker down farther and gather me to her. "You did not have to. Your spirit chose its path, Gwen. Another girl would have slept the night through. But by burning the part of that bastard that you did, you set all the souls he murdered free."

"But why did *I* have to do it?"

"It was to heal you as well, child. But you were not given time to prepare." A cloud passed over the sun, plunging the entire stairs into darkness.

With a sigh that indicated she had come to a decision, Hwyrch squeezed my hand. "Your Grandmother is a great priestess, but she suffers from a blindness of the soul, from a deep wound that has never healed though it was inflicted long ago. It causes her to rage, to seek vengeance without remembering the dangers of invoking the Dark One."

She took a slow breath and met my eyes. "It is why she let you carry a blooded sacrifice without teaching you how to cleanse yourself after the fire went out."

I closed my eyes against memory, trying to let Hwyrch's scent of milk, sweat, and rosemary overwhelm all else.

"You have asked often enough why your Mother and Grandmother tear the Hall apart with their battles. It is not mine to speak of, Gwenhwyfar, but I will grant you this: the same blindness that ails your Grandmother has been thrown across your Mother's eyes as well, twisting the bright spark within her, causing her to act from fear instead of the kindness she believes in."

This time I accepted the water Hwyrch offered. I did not understand all that she spoke of, but, at least, she was speaking of what I most wanted to know. "Then you have heard of the *estethra*?"

She shook her head, annoyed. "The *estethra* is a part of the story, yes."

Seeing my face, she added, "But only a part—and not mine to tell."

She rose briskly then, as if she already regretted speaking.

"What is mine to give," she continued, forcing me to rise, steadying me as I faltered, "is a ritual to help you cleanse yourself of the dark things you have seen and done."

We stood together on the first of the tower's many stairs; she as solid as the mountains she was born to, and I as wobbly as a suckling lamb.

"You will remember the tales I told you of the Goddess Ceridwen's cauldron that gives dead warriors life again?"

I nodded, sinking back to the stones. Nurse stared at the northern ramparts beyond us as if the arrow-slit window gave out on a landscape visible only to her.

"It is a tale that hides truth of a different nature. For in this world's realm, Ceridwen's cauldron is filled with living water from a lake or stream. Bath in it, cleanse yourself, and ask the Dark Lady's protection;

her permission to enter her realm and escape with your soul intact. Wash yourself a second time and ask Bright Anu to forgive you. Then pour water back from the cauldron into the lake or stream, thus asking the Dark Lady to send deserving warriors you have slain to their ancestral halls with honor."

She extended her hand and raised me up, helping me slowly up the stairs. "Are you strong enough to walk?" At my nod, she pushed me up the next stair, careful to stand behind me.

Her next words floated with the dust motes that swirled up and down the curving stairs. "Perhaps your Grandmother sought to honor the Goddess by giving your mother her name: Ceridwen. But the Dark One will not be contained within ramparts of stone or sides of wattle. She is as free as the black wind that comes from the sea—to kill or guide as she desires."

The air of the stairwell was suddenly charged, as if the stones were listening. I watched Hwyrch's words rise up like living things—tendrils of the curse that haunted us.

"Enough!" She swatted my rump. "Since you have forced us to seek refuge beneath the sky instead of within the earth, we must make the best of it. Move!"

I led her slowly up the stairs, mulling the answers she had given, barely strong enough to put one foot above the other.

We passed the landing of Grandfather's room, empty now, save for its ghosts. I saw again the old king's fierce eagle eye and dipped my head to his spirit.

Reaching the topmost landing, we pushed through an ancient oak door. Rusted hinges squealed like startled rats. Instead of a room covered with gloomy dust, filled with broken furniture, the chamber awaiting us was illuminated by a large open window, clean and comfortably furnished with a bed, stools, a small table, and a Roman-styled couch along the length of the inner wall—where a cloaked man sat waiting.

Hwyrch growled a warning. Thrusting me behind her, she advanced into the circular chamber, looking to the right and left. She spied a staff leaning against the hearth and grabbed it, turning on the intruder with a snarl.

"Nurse! I will not harm you!" The man flung back his hood and stood.

Merlin!

"Mage, must you frighten an old woman to death!" The staff

crashed from Hwyrch's hands "What are you doing here?"

Merlin walked to the small table without answering and waved his fingers above a tarnished silver bowl at the table's center. Apples appeared, so many they overflowed the bowl and tumbled to the stone floor with soft thuds of welcome. A swift sword-slash of his arm conjured cold venison and a basket of bannocks so hot they steamed.

"There is much I would tell you and our time is short." Merlin poured us water from a jug he created with a twist of his hand and sat down to eat with us.

I reached greedily for a bannock.

"Take care." Hwyrch snatched it from my hand, saying to Uncle, "She's had naught but broth and gruel for three days. I'd not see her sicken from overeating."

Merlin knelt by my side, searching my eyes, but speaking to Hwyrch. "Her body has been weakened, but the sickness is within her soul—and that's a healing that must be sought in chambers other than this.

"Do you want to become stronger?" he asked me.

When I nodded, he cut a small piece of venison, murmuring a blessing as he gave it to me. I chewed, my head dipping towards the table in exhaustion.

"Come, both of you." Merlin towed me across the room. "Look at the mountains with me." The wind from the open window blew his long black hair behind him, exposing the Moon Singer tattoo marks on his temples, accentuating his harsh cheekbones and hawk-shaped nose. "Come," he repeated to Hwyrch.

Hwyrch groaned but obediently raised her bulk from the tiny stool. "What is it, lord?" The note of challenge in her voice was sharp enough that I glanced at her in surprise. Perhaps she too wearied of this new god-haunted realm where magic and bloodshed went hand in hand, whose gates were now open and refused to close.

"No slight of hand, no demons of Anwnn, I assure you. Simply this." We joined him at the window. Behind us, I knew frightened folk scurried and cursed to be ready for the Scotti. But the high wind caught at my heart as surely as it tossed my hair. I looked past Merlin's finger and beheld the solemn beauty of the mountains, their flanks dancing purple, green, and grey beneath moody flashes of sunlight, their peaks still dotted with last sunturn's snow.

"This is all that matters," Merlin's voice was low. He turned to

Hwyrch with a smile, "Don't you think so?"

Nurse was not in the mood to be played with. "Aye, they're lovely now—from here. But if you'd ever had to spend a winter in them, you'd think different."

Uncle laughed. "There is that. You do well to have Hwyrch as your protector, Gwen. She could teach sense even to Druids."

Hwyrch was not to be distracted. "Why are you here, Lord Emrys?"

He did not take his eyes from the mountains. "The battle to come will be more cruel than most, for it is driven by Maelgwyn's hatred and, as you both have cause to know, the blood-thirst of kin is this world realm's greatest curse."

"But what of Vortigern?" I asked, standing beside him, letting the wind whip my hair loose from its braids. The blessing he had given me was working; I felt as if I'd arisen from a deep night's sleep. I longed to snuggle against him as I had done so often in the past. But the new coldness in my heart forbade me to act like such a child.

"The Vortigern and his greed have been but a pawn for Maelgwyn to play with, and pawns are easily disposed of." Merlin's hands turned white, clenching the stones of the window's sill. He turned to me, the rising wind beating against us both.

"Yet, you were right to notice Vortigern's Shield Bearer, Gwen. He was not taken captive and confined in the Warrior's Hall with the rest of the Southerners. It is likely he escaped to fetch the rest of Vortigern's forces. And if they advance on Dinas from the south as the Scotti attack from the west—your family will be fighting two forces instead of one."

"Maelgwyn's doing no doubt." Nurse grumbled, fetching an apple from the still-overflowing bowl and beginning to peel it with her small belt-dagger.

"Aye, you have it, Hwyrch." Merlin crossed the floor to take the apple Nurse offered. "Maelgwyn's lust for power and his jealousy of your father, Gwen, have brought him to the brink of madness."

He sank to the couch, fingering the sword at his belt. "I believe Maelgwyn struck secret bargains with Vortigern as well as the western Scotti, and this is why Vortigern started north. Maelgwyn must have agreed to help him overthrow your father—no doubt in exchange for the kingship of Dinas."

Merlin combed his fingers through his wind-tossed hair then lowered them to the golden prince's torc that winked regally around his neck in the dim light of the chamber. He gestured me closer.

I obeyed. He wove his hands into the air, creating a serpent from the sun-flecked dust motes that floated before us. The serpent's fangs parted a handspan from my face. On an ordinary morning, I would have clapped in appreciation. Today, I did not flinch.

"The power of kingship can become as twisted as an adder's coils in the wrong hands." Eyeing my stony expression, Merlin flicked his wrist, causing the serpent to vanish. "For a bitter man like Maelgwyn, it must have seemed better to become a client king of Vortigern—or even Nestor of the Scotti—than to live in the shadow of the brother who has bested him all his life."

"But what can be done?" I walked back to the window, preferring the wind-tossed mountains to any more displays of magic.

"I have come to ask your help." Merlin looked from Hwyrch to me. "Soon I will descend those stairs to help my sister's husband fight in the coming battle. And since we face great odds, and since I fight in battle not as a Mage but as a warrior whose only power is that which spear or sword or arrow will give to any man, I too may perish before sunset. As could your father, Gwen, and Iolo."

I glared at him. Must he dwell on what I already carried in my heart?

"So I seek a boon of you, Gwenhwyfar ferch Ceridwen. If I die today, I ask you to forgive those who love you. Even if they have acted in ways that you do not yet understand."

He joined me at the window and caught a green leaf from the air, changing it to the orange of autumn. "Love, my dear, is a bitter goddess, one that insists on loyalty, often at the price of your soul."

I stomped away.

He followed me across the room and spun me to face him. "For your own soul's sake, do so. If we live to see the sunrise, I would advise you to leave Dinas for a season and seek the Healer's Village. Perhaps the forest priestesses can rid you of the poison you now carry in your heart."

The thought of living with the forest healers in their simple huts behind the mists of this world, leagues from everything and everyone I knew, added kindling to the rage-fire that burned inside me. How dare he! "You are speaking in riddles, Uncle," I said in my coldest voice. "It is my father who will decide when I will leave Dinas and where I will go."

Merlin looked amused. Furious, I pulled away. "You have no right to advise me!"

The Mage's eyes turned to green ice. "Be silent!"

So rare was Merlin's anger that my own rage crumbled, tumbling away inside the new cold place within me. "I-I'm sorry."

I wept then, lost; clutching my arms to my chest, holding myself, for neither he nor Hwyrch made a move to comfort me.

At last, Uncle's fingers were on my shoulder. "It is well, child. Your tears are a sign of healing. Now," he gestured for Hwyrch to join us, "there is more I would say to you."

"If I survive this day's battle, I must go South," Merlin raised a hand as I opened my mouth to argue. "There is a boy there whose need of me is even greater than your own, for he is the son of the rightful heir to Vortigern's usurped throne. I have spoken of him before. His lord father Uther died this summer at Vortigern's hand and the boy, Arthur, is now hidden away from the warlords who seek his death. He has no kin—as you do—to protect him."...

Tears welled up again. Furious at my weakness, and at the pit that opened within me at the thought of Merlin leaving, I willed my voice to sound as strong as I could make it. "W-when will you come back?"

The Mage drew me to him. Beneath the folds of his cloak, I felt the hard leather of his armor. "Not for many sunturns, I'm afraid."

Quietly, desperately, I wept against his chest.

"*Slanathra, Gwenhwyfara.*" He took hold of my clenched fists and stood, gently disengaging me.

I swayed. He placed his hands upon my head and murmured a blessing in the ancient forest tongue.

"I must go," he said. He squeezed Hwyrch's shoulder. "Do you know the hidden stairs?"

Hwyrch snorted like an irritated pony. "Her father asked me the same. Do you think me a ninny? Of course I know them!"

"Good." Before Merlin could say another word, Nurse surprised me by giving him one of her bone-crushing hugs.

Merlin looked startled, then returned her embrace, murmuring a blessing over her grey head. He pulled away then and kissed her brow, softly, as if he honored a goddess. "Stay safe, both of you."

With a wave in my direction, he pushed aside a faded bedside hanging and leaned on two stones set in the center of the ledge behind it. They swung open with a screech of long disused stone, revealing a rectangle of pitch blackness.

A fog of damp trapped air filled the room. "If danger threatens, this passage will see you outside, near the middens. Hide there or escape outside the northern gate if you can."

Merlin disappeared into the blackness.

I pushed past Hwyrch in time to see a fold of Uncle's cloak vanish around a turning of the narrow stone stairs. Despite my fear of dark hidden places, there was something sweet and mysterious in the sight. "It's like an entrance to the lands of the Tylwyth Teg!"

Hwyrch rolled her eyes. "Hardly, just to the same muddy courtyard you cross a score of times a day."

Still, she put her large calloused hands upon my shoulder. "Rest, girl. And pray to the Goddess that—Tylwyth Teg or not—we will have no need to use those stairs this day."

She let the hanging fall, hiding our escape, and lay back on the couch to rest. I paced the chamber like a trapped hound. Renewed by Merlin's spell, my body was no longer exhausted, but my heart and soul were frantic. Battle was close but my mind could only circle one foolish, childish question that had nothing to do with warfare: *"Why hadn't Mother protected me?"*

And my mind gave its answer: *She has killed for you. Is that not enough?*

The cold place inside me grew colder. No, it was not enough. It was worse than nothing.

I curled up on the window seat and closed my eyes.

I must have slept for Hwyrch was shaking me. "The battle has begun!"

I jumped up to see, but there was no window facing the inner courtyard, although I could hear the battle raging. Screams...blood... fire...I could see it in my heart. All those I loved were facing death on the ramparts below.

I broke free from Hwyrch and put a foot upon the hidden stairs. The fear and pain and torment of all that I had seen and done since Tegid's murder swirled up to greet me within its damp trapped air.

"Stop!" She dragged me back, carrying me, struggling and screaming defiance, to the open window. "You will wait here as your father told you!"

I kicked her.

She slapped me hard enough to snap my head back.

I swallowed in shock, fighting blackness and pain, and stared at her.

Nurse's mild-brown eyes narrowed with fury. "This time you will obey, if I have to kill you myself!"

ChAPTER 19

Hwyrch's nails dug into my arm, drawing blood. She had never truly hurt me before, despite all the causes I had given her.

"Stop it!" I screamed. My fists and kicks pounded uselessly at her determined bulk.

"You will listen this time! You will...you will..." Suddenly within her ranting, I heard the whisper of something I could not name.

I pushed hard, broke free and ran, crouching in a corner. Only then, watching her approach me, did I understand what I had heard. Sorrow. And loss, great loss.

Hwyrch's bleak eyes traveled up and down my body—a body she had known and nursed for all its eight sunturns.

"I love you, child. I would not have your death laid to my charge."

Then, at last, I understood. So engrossed had I been in my own pain, I had forgotten how Hwyrch had come to us, why she had first taken up watch at my bedside.

"Your own children died in battle," I whispered.

She snorted. "Hardly battle. 'Twas murder, pure and simple."

My nostrils curled at the choking smell of fire. The screaming outside grew louder. "H-Hwyrch?"

She stood grimly in the doorway, looking down the stairs. "If anyone—*anyone*—comes up these stairs, hide behind the hanging, and climb down those fairy stairs of yours as quickly as you can. Run as fast as you can to the caves."

Someone pounded on the tower door far below. Hwyrch swore. "Why I ever let you come here is beyond me. You'd be safe now if you weren't so spoiled!"

The pounding grew louder, followed by cursing in two different languages. I ran to her, burying my head in her lap, "I'm sorry."

Hwyrch's usual lap-scent of rosemary was overwhelmed by acrid sweat.

The door below us crashed open. "Go," she whispered, hugging me close, "behind the hanging."

Shouts echoed up the stairwell. Weapons and armor clanged against the stones. Men were running, pushing, laughing with excitement.

"Hwyrch?" My hand was on the weaving. "Come with me."

Nurse shook her head. Picking up the staff with which she'd almost brained Merlin, she took up a position, hiding behind the door.

I didn't move. The men were coming faster now. Her eyes swept over me, frantic. "Go, child. May the Goddess be with you."

A Scotti curse outside the door. Still I hesitated.

"Now!" Hwyrch screamed. I ducked behind the hanging and entered a realm of utter blackness.

Behind me, I heard a shout, a thud, fierce cursing in Hwyrch's mountain tongue, the melody of lost mountains quickly drowned beneath harsh laughter and the rasp of iron. A shriek of agony, a final thud. Silence.

Scotti curses cut the heavy silence answered by the guttural barking syllables of the Sea Wolves. Vortigern's Seaxon? And Maelgwyn's Scotti allies.

Boots thudded into soft flesh. Men tore across the room. I clutched the back of the hanging, kneading it in terror.

Go! Hwyrch's voice, as clear as if she was still beside me.

I took one step forward into the blackness. The floor gave way beneath me.

I tripped, spreading my arms out to stop myself and touched cold clammy rock on both sides. Beneath me, the blackness admitted no light at all, yet I cautiously set one foot in front of the other, and the stone steps curved up to meet me, cradling me in giant hands.

Shouting grew frenzied behind me. Invaders ripped the chamber apart seeking gold that was not there, plunder that had never existed.

They had killed Hwyrch for nothing.

I fell to the stairs. *Let them kill me as well.*

A feathered touch on my shoulder. *Get up, child! Quickly!*

Nurse's spirit illuminated the blackness of the secret stairs. She put a finger to her lips and—with the same stern glance she'd given me when

I'd torn yet another tunic—she glided, leading the way down the stairs; stairs that now glistened with luminescence, as if they were indeed an entrance to the fairy realm.

All too soon the door to the courtyard was in front of me. Hwyrch floated beside it, already growing less substantial, thin enough that I could make out splinters in the door behind her. A sad smile lifted the grim contours of her other-world face. A soft touch on my head, the whisper of a kiss on my cheek and she was gone.

The door's heavy, mold-covered handle gave way as soon as I touched it, opening on a nightmare.

Vortigern's Seaxon Sea Wolves had indeed joined Maelgwyn's Scotti to plunder Dinas—and they had already breached the walls. All around me lay the dead and dying, many lacking limbs or heads, bloody eyes staring up at a sky rapidly filling with crows.

I had emerged near the middens close to the little-used northern gate, just as Merlin had said. But before I could scramble to a hiding place a shrieking crowd of women and children pelted towards me from the direction of the stables, a band of hooting Scotti close on their heels.

The hidden caves that sheltered those too young or old to fight had been discovered! I turned, blindly, seeking help—and saw Iorwerth's warrior band rush furiously across the courtyard trying to intercept the Scotti before they could reach the women and the babes they carried.

And I remembered. A soft summer morning. Tali complaining that Maelgwyn's men were exploring the shed that hid the secret caves, asking question after question.

Maelgwyn's spies. And women and children would die because of them.

Wolf-snarling, Iolo jumped effortlessly over the crumpled body of old Cadwgan, the best storyteller in the village, and came on, brandishing his blood-drenched sword.

"Stand! Protect the children!" Mother's voice pierced the din of battle.

The frightened women began to obey her, making a circle with the youngest and oldest behind them, pulling out meat daggers, breaking off tree limbs to use as clubs. They faced the Scotti without flinching, my diminutive Mother in the forefront, tossing a dagger from hand to hand as she crouched, daring the enemy warriors to come closer.

Before the Scotti could advance on the women, Iolo's band reached them, slamming into their flanks, swords and spears flashing so fast I could not distinguish single thrusts, only a whirling dance of iron. Distracted from what must have seemed an easy prize—for many of our women were very beautiful and most of the highborn ladies wore valuable jeweled rings and gold-worked brooches—the invading pirates defended themselves with fury.

But they were no match for Iolo or his men. My brother fought like one possessed, as if all the demons that had ever stalked him now rode his battle arms. His bloodshot eyes spat fire; he leaped, pivoted, thrust, and killed, again and again, always twisting out of reach before an enemy sword could find him, oblivious of the blood that covered him or the wounds he had already taken. Like a hero of old, my brother fought and Tegid's Shield Brother, Selyf, joined him. Together they cut through the Scotti warrior band like summer sun through mountain mist, until at last the Scotti scattered, regrouping beyond the stables, where the bulk of the battle was being waged.

"Are you all right, Mother?" Iolo swept her a half-mocking bow.

"You do your father honor, son!" Mother wiped her face with one grimy slender hand. Iolo blew her a kiss and gestured his men forward to follow the pirates.

"Ladies, we will take shelter in the Hall." Mother led her rag-tag group of survivors away, somehow managing to look as dignified as a battle commander on parade, instead of an exhausted blood-covered queen.

She did not see me where I crouched, huddling behind a broken cart near the stinking middens.

Seeing that the battle raged elsewhere, I began to rise. "Stay down, you little fool!" Merlin tackled me. An arrow slammed into the wood of my hiding place, a hairsbreadth from where my head had been.

"Uncle!" I sobbed against his bloody leather breastplate.

"I must go, child." He hugged me. "Your father is holding his own, despite the numbers arrayed against him. And even now Chalan Grey Wolf of the Decleangli is returning to help."

Even coarsened by battle, Merlin's voice held the ring of prophecy. "But the tide has already been turned by the courage of your own kin. And Grey Wolf is an Eater of the Dead—a chancy friend at best."

He pushed me in the direction of the narrow northern gate. "Once you've reached the forest, find the east-facing deer trail. Follow it until you come to the old bear's cave."

Seeing my face, he misunderstood. "Do not worry. You will be safe now. Look and remember—" he gestured towards the fighting in contempt, "that those whose only motive is greed die quickly when faced with courage. They panic easily and forget what little battle plan they had. No matter the numbers, girl. This is most often the way of it, if good men do not lose their heads."

He looked more closely at my face. "Ah, but battle strategy is not what you want to hear of right now, is it? Where is Hwyrch?"

I shook my head. He drew me close again. I took deep breaths of the sickening copper-scented blood on his armor, let the cloying stickiness of it mat my hair, seeing Hwyrch's blood pour out unheeded on the cold stones of a deserted tower chamber.

"I am sorry, Gwenhwyfar." Despite the shrieks of the dying, the hissing of arrows, the baying of battle hounds, he began a mountain lament for the dead, a keening song that Hwyrch herself had taught me. I joined him, our voices soft. Twining together, they reached into the sky. When the death song was over, he brushed the bloody hair from my face.

"She loved you well, Gwenhwyfar ferch Ceridwen and died to protect you. Live on with the courage that was in her heart."

"Well, isn't this sweet?" Maelgwyn rounded the shadows of the tower, coming closer as I staggered to my feet.

Merlin was already on his feet, sword drawn. "It would seem things have not gone as you hoped, my lord. The gods apparently still dislike you."

He tilted his sword in a rude salute, crouching to await Maelgwyn's rush.

"Brother!"

Maelgwyn spun, bloody sword in hand.

"Caused enough trouble for one day, haven't you?"

"Not quite, 'Wallon." Growling obscenities, Maelgwyn ran at Father instead of Merlin, slashing at Father's right side.

Looking bored, Father jumped agilely to the left without touching his own sword, Maelgwyn's swing missing him entirely. Then Father crouched. But instead of countering, he waited as Maelgwyn rebalanced and came at him again. Again and again, Maelgwyn swung. Father dodged, parried, and jumped, sometimes giving ground, sometimes feinting, never attacking.

"Fight, you bastard!"

Father laughed. "When I find a foe who deserves it, I will!"

Losing all restraint, Maelgwyn swore and charged Father like a red-eyed bull. This time, Father met Maelgwyn's blade with his own. The screech of metal on metal echoed across the embattled hilltop, a hilltop that now grew eerily silent, broken only by the cawing of scavengers and the desperate cries of the wounded or grieving.

"It is over," Merlin whispered. "Cadwallon has won."

Oblivious to all but each other, Father and Maelgwyn stayed, eyes and swords locked, for several heartbeats. "You will die for this, you know." Father said.

"I doubt it. You do not even have the courage to swing a blade."

Father pushed away. "It is not I who chose this path. Remember that."

With a flurry of moves, Father cut under Maelgwyn's guard, then above it. Shocked by this sudden change in tactics, Maelgwyn gave ground. Father continued hammering at him, moving so aggressively, he opened his guard. Maelgwyn recovered, thrusting savagely. It was what Father had waited for, for he jumped back as Maelgwyn overbalanced and brought his own blade across his brother's face, scoring a deep cut across Maelgwyn's nose and cheek.

Roaring with rage, blood pouring across his face, Maelgwyn rushed Father again.

Contemptuous now, Father parried his thrusts with ferocious grace. Dropping to his haunches, he cut below Maelgwyn's body armor, slashing Maelgwyn's unprotected thigh.

Breathing heavily, eyeing Father with fury and dawning fear, Uncle rushed in again, half-blinded by the blood on his face. Stumbling, he aimed wildly at Father's legs, trying for a hamstring.

"Will you never learn?" Father parried Maelgwyn's blade. Knocking it up, away from his own body, Father slashed at Maelgwyn's face again, this time blooding the unmarked cheek.

"Not so handsome now, are we little brother?"

Jeers broke out. I looked up to see our warriors gathering, many leaning on each other, exhausted, bleeding, limping, but alive, gloriously alive.

Chalan, the Decleangli Lord, jeered the loudest as he and his men joined the watchers, having just marched through the eastern gate in a belated attempt to help us. Late as they were, our warriors were delighted to welcome them, clapping them on the back, making way for them to witness Father's final battle with Maelgwyn. Despite all the odds—the gods had been with us! We had won!

"Welcome back to my hearth, Lord Chalan," Father shouted, holding Maelgwyn at sword point, his eyes steady as death as he glared at his brother.

"Let no more blood be spilled tonight. Almost no more blood," he added.

With a twist of his blade, he sliced Maelgwyn's wrist. Uncle's sword clattered to the earth. Maelgwyn himself seemed past caring. He swayed, but remained standing, refusing to meet Father's eyes.

"Take him, Iolo," Father called, sheathing his own sword and clapping an injured warrior on the back as he wove through the crowd. Avoiding the scattered corpses, Father headed for the Hall.

"Guard him well. But do no further harm to him. He will answer for his crimes tomorrow."

Iolo obeyed, forcing his own prisoner forward at sword point. Iolo's tall Scotti captive walked proudly, still menacing despite his bound hands for he wore a great bearskin cloak and a helmet topped with a human skull that made him appear even taller than Merlin.

It could only be Nestor Lack Tongue, Gormach's brother, the Scotti chieftain who had conspired with Maelgwyn to invade us. His cold blue eyes swept over Maelgwyn and Father with no more feeling than a snake might have for the mouse it plans to devour. It did not seem to matter to him that he was a captive. He surveyed us all as if he owned us.

Warriors cheered and pounded their gore-covered spears against the bloody earth of Dinas as Iolo turned Nestor over to Father's Shield Bearer and bound Maelgwyn's arms behind his back with a vicious wrench that forced a grunt of pain from my dazed uncle's lips.

Hesow, a big-bellied chieftain of the Gulls, swaggered over to the newly-arrived Chalan. "Looks like we've done the fighting for you, Grey Wolf!"

It was a fool's speech, and, watching the Decleangli Lord from across the bloodied mud, I saw Chalan's fox-clever eyes turn cold. His hand went to his sword hilt. Metal rasped as he drew it out of its scabbard.

Hesow jumped back in surprise.

Slowly, deliberately, Chalan replaced the sword. "I will forgive you this time. Never again." He took a heartbeat to examine Hesow's face as if to memorize the fat chieftain's features.

Not noticing this by-play, Father stopped on his way to the Hall, shouting brisk commands. "Hwyll, gather your men and care for the dead. Lord Merlin, help the Lady Rhiannon with the wounded. The rest of you—" Father turned to include all those gathered in the courtyard. Raising his arms in victory, he roared, "Come join me in consuming what little remains of our mead!"

With answering shouts, most of the warriors and many of the freemen followed, leaving the men and women Father had commanded and those who still mourned to gather the dead and to care for the wounded.

Merlin's hand was on my shoulder, his slender fingers squeezing gently in a familiar gesture of comfort. But comfort was beyond me now.

"You are leaving?"

"At sunrise." He ran a finger down my cheek, flicking a falling tear away.

I shook my head and moved away from him, watching Grandmother's healers carry the wounded into the new Guest Hall. Near the middens a young woman knelt in the mud beside the body of a freeman, tearing at her face and hair, keening at the sky.

"Do not mourn for Hwyrch, Shadow. She died a hero and has gone to join her children and her man in the golden star-lands of Anu's beloved."

Merlin stooped to pick up a rock, examining it in the way he had of making small things matter.

"I am sure your parents will give you leave to visit the forest healers."

Putting the rock in the small pouch he carried at his belt, he begged a rag from a passing healer and began to clean his sword. Meeting my eyes at last, he squatted in the dirt beside me.

"Shadow, you have endured far too much for a child whose only notion of cruelty before Lughnasa was being banished to your chamber for putting worms in your tutor's porridge."

Like a secret cave filled with snow and exposed to sunlight, the ice in my heart cracked open as he held me. I wailed like a baby half my age.

Merlin stroked my hair, murmuring nonsense until I quieted enough for him to continue. "The women of the healer's village have lived there for a thousand sunturns, long before the red cloaks came, long before even the great rock circles were raised to please the gods. They will know the path to help you heal. Even if all they can offer is rest."

I buried my head against his leather battle dress. *Hwyrch*. Had I not been a selfish fool she would still be alive.

"Enough, Gwen! *Slanathra.* I have told you Hwyrch has gone to be with those she loves. She is no doubt already scrubbing the faces of her own children and insisting her husband eat more venison then eight men can consume."

Despite myself, I began to giggle.

"Now, rise, my dear—look around you. It is time to leave Dinas, is it not?"

Obediently, I gazed at the familiar courtyard, at the great stone towers, the damaged but still proud Halls, at haphazard huts, at stables filled with my beloved horses, at all the nooks and crannies and secrets of the only home I had ever known. Grandmother's healers were at work restoring order, but it was a sad, weak thing. Death, fire, and smoke still held sway. With Merlin leaving, Cynan, Father, and Iolo were all that remained of the family I had loved. All the others I once trusted had been killed or changed into people I no longer wanted to know.

"I will go to the forest, Uncle." I stood as tall as I could, tossing hair from my eyes. "Will you speak to Father and Mother before you leave?"

Merlin inclined his head and reached down to tussle the hair I had just rearranged.

"It is a good decision, Gwenhwyfar. I will speak for you."

I did not answer. I could not speak, even had I chosen to.

Sari skidded to a halt beside us. She took off her veil and I saw her face for the first time: tanned and lovely, blood-stained and filthy.

She waved her bow proudly, bowing with a little dip of her head when she saw Merlin. "I kill s-six." She held up five fingers.

Merlin met my eyes. I couldn't help but answer his smile, though it broke my heart to do so.

chapter 20

That night, still in shock, I bedded down with Cynan in the Hall. There, amidst snoring warriors and our favorite hounds, we talked deep into the remnants of the night, keeping our separate terrors at bay by sharing them with each other.

Cynan told me of the death-filled heartbeats when the Scotti pirates had discovered their hiding place in the caves beneath the storage shed. I was silent—still hoping to keep Nurse's death a nightmare from which I could awake—until he spoke of how Mother's courage had rallied the women and allowed the children to flee across the courtyard.

"Where was Grandmother?" I asked.

"Standing with Maeve and the warriors on the ramparts, shooting arrows and overturning caldrons of boiling water on the heads of Maelgwyn's Scotti!"

Cynan's voice regained some of its usual color, although his eyes were bloodshot and his freckled cheeks were pale with exhaustion. "I wish I could have helped them—but you know how hard it is to sneak away from Mother!"

"You will be fighting soon enough." I turned my face into the flank of my hound Morag, suddenly too weary to talk.

Cynan lay down too, putting a comradely hand upon my shoulder.

I lay quiet, listening to his breath grow deeper. When his snores began, I gently removed his hand and sat up, gazing into the embers of the fire near the harper's bench. The embers told me many stories, but they could no longer give me peace.

I would never feel Hwyrch's arms around me again.

I must have slept despite myself, for the next thing I knew, Cynan was shaking me. "Maeve said I could have these, but only if I shared with you. Here," he pushed something under my nose, "before I change my mind."

The aroma of honey cakes was too powerful to be ignored; still in a dream-fog, I crammed their savory, still-hot sweetness into my mouth as if I had not eaten for days.

After the first bite, memory returned. I pushed them away.

Cynan slapped my back. "Father's coming!" he said. "I heard him tell Hwyll to fetch Uncle Maelgwyn."

I opened my eyes wider and jumped to my feet. Crowds of freemen and warriors were assembling around the central hearth, pushing to get a good vantage point. The mood was grim. Not even Andelis the laundress or Nest the midwife had a smile for me.

The Hall doors were flung open, revealing a rare sunny morning with no trace of the usual mist. Dawn had come and gone, taking Merlin with it. He had not even said good-bye.

Maelgwyn was shoved into the Hall. His costly chain-mail armor had been taken from him and he appeared before us dressed only in a torn and bloody tunic. Haughty as ever, Uncle quickly recovered his balance and shrugged off the guards who tried to force him forward. More king than captive—despite the filth on his face and body and the heavy chains that weighed him down—his eyes roamed the Hall, lighting first on one man then another, his obsidian-eyes shadowed with contempt.

He stared at me for many heartbeats, as if we were the only people in the room, his expression growing more and more venomous. I met his gaze unflinching, as coldly as I could, even though I was frightened. What had I done to merit this special hatred?

"Murderer!" Glaina, the village's finest weaver screamed and rushed out of the crowd, a dagger in her hands.

"Patience, woman." Hwyll gripped her arm before she could stab my uncle. "Justice will be served this day."

Father rose from his High Seat. The crowd's hush was heavy and complete. "Maelgwyn ap Cunedda Iron Hand. Brother. I call your actions treason. The life of this good woman's husband and countless other warriors rests at your feet. Your honor lies in the filth of the middens. What say you?"

Maelgwyn spat into the rushes at Father's feet and said nothing.

Father let the silence stretch for a long time. Watching the shadows that filled his eyes, I too remembered Tegid…Hwyrch…all the good men and women who had died because of Uncle.

"Does your tongue betray you, brother?"

Maelgwyn tossed a slender warrior braid back from his face. His teeth flashed in a predator's smile.

"I merely choose not to waste my wisdom."

"Then let your wisdom be wasted until your carcass feeds the wolves." Father stood, outstretching his right arm in judgment, exposing his dragon tattoo.

"For your honey-poisoned tongue has brought war and death to our people." Father's dragon seemed to writhe in a shaft of early morning sunlight. "It has flooded our ancestor's earth with blood. It has murdered my first-born son. All these are acts of base cowardice. Never once have you come forth to challenge me in honor—before the eyes of the gods and of our people."

The Hall was absolutely still. Not even the hounds paced.

"Hear my words, Brother. Hear them, Ordovice. Because this man's tongue and this man's right hand have brought nothing but misery and destruction since he first drew breath, given life by the same mother who bore me," Father paused, the king's stone face upon him, "I command that this man's tongue be cut out and that his right hand be severed from his arm that he may never raise it against my people again."

Glaina the weaver's voice rang out in the bitter silence of the Hall. "Will you not slay him, Lord?"

"I prefer to let the gods dispose of him." Father turned back to Maelgwyn.

From my vantage point near the dais I saw Uncle's arrogant mask crumble. He was staring wildly at Father, who continued to speak calmly over the rising shouts and tumult of the people.

"After this sentence is carried out, we shall place my brother in a coracle. And cast him out to sea. Give him an oar and let the gods decide if he reaches his allies in Eire or perishes beneath the Sea Lord's wave daughters."

At a nod from Father, Hwyll stepped down from the dais where he had been standing in his rightful place beside Father's High Seat. The Shield Bearer's scarred face was set as coldly as Father's, yet I, who had known him since I took my first toddling steps, saw a glimmer of satisfaction in his winter-lake eyes.

Maelgwyn's guards roughly turned Uncle's sagging body and

followed Hwyll from the Hall. As they reached the entrance and could see the courtyard where the Shield Bearer waited, hand resting grimly on his sword, Maelgwyn's paralysis broke at last.

"You cannot mean it, brother!" He struggled with the guards, trying to break free.

Father said nothing. He had taken his seat again and stared into the far distance of the Hall, at things none of us could see. He did not look at Uncle who began to wail as the guards dragged him outside.

The folk of Dinas followed, eager to see Maelgwyn destroyed.

I ran to the entrance of the Hall in time to see my uncle shake off his guards and stumble, chains dragging, back to the Hall. "Kill me, you bastard! Let me die a man!"

The guards pulled him down before he could enter the Hall and threw him to the earth at Hwyll's feet.

"You will die the death you deserve—dog!" Father's Shield Bearer spat on Maelgwyn where he sprawled, face down in the filth of the courtyard.

"Kin-slayer! Coward!" He kicked him, then nodded grimly at the guards. "Stand him up!"

I sank to a bench near Father's dais and closed my eyes, dimly aware of a triumphant shout from the crowd. My belly heaved, for I knew the meaning of the shouting. Maelgwyn's hand had been cut off. Now Father's warriors would drag my uncle to Huw's smithy where, amidst the fire and bellows that had brought me entire afternoons of pleasure, Uncle's tongue would be torn out by the people he had wronged.

I put my head on the rough oak plank of the table and sobbed.

A hand touched my head.

"Go away!"

It began to stroke my hair. An unfamiliar hand.

"I wish I could give him a clean death."

I raised my head. It was Lleu, Chalan's son, the Druid brat, the fosterling who was taking my beloved Bran's place.

"Leave." From the corner of my eye, I saw Father rise and walk slowly from Hall, walking towards the quarters he shared with Mother, with no trace of his usual grace.

Shouts followed by ululations came from the direction of the smithy.

"I spend a great portion of my time wishing things were other than they are," the Druid brat continued as if I had not spoken. "Your uncle

Merlin may have some wisdom to offer me, but I have yet to find a reason why we must maim and murder each other from sunrise to sunset. No other creature seems to have such needs."

"Are you saying my father is wrong?" I sat up, the sickness in my soul replaced by anger. How dare he judge our King?

"No. I am saying he is making things worse by not killing Maelgwyn outright. This," he gestured in the direction of the jeering crowd, "is not a day to be forgotten. Its darkness will linger, its cruelty will grow."

His newly-deepened voice cracked. Had it not been for that, he sounded like Merlin, for his speech had taken on the sing-song quality of the Mage's other-world seeings. As it was, I was reminded he was only two sunturns older than Cynan—and a safe target for my rage.

"How dare you pretend to understand! Maelgwyn killed my brother."

Lleu tilted my chin, just as Merlin always had, so I was forced to meet his eyes. I tried to shake free, but found myself staring at him instead. Eleven sunturns had given his ocean-grey eyes a depth that made me think of hidden caverns beneath the sea. They were melancholy, shifting from dark to light, shadowed until he chose to bring their secrets to the surface.

This was what he offered, even as I roughly pushed his hand away.

"How can you know this? How dare you!" But my voice was softer than I meant it to be.

"I just do." He shifted away from me not breaking eye contact. "I get feelings a lot of the time. And they're almost always right."

I refused to be the first one to look away. Fortunately, I was tall enough that I was almost at eye level with Lleu. I dug into my soul, resisting his pull, much as if I was digging my toes into sand so as not to get swept out with the tide.

"You are very sure of yourself, aren't you?"

A smile lit up his solemn, too-old face. It was like a star falling, arching across the night sky. There, but gone so quickly it might have been imagined. Still it warmed me and my belly unclenched.

"No, I'm not actually," he said. "It's my mother's people I get the feelings from. I have nothing to do with it really."

"Who are your mother's people?"

"The Lake Dwellers."

My stomach clenched again. I made the sign of protection, shifting as far from him as possible without seeming cowardly. The Lake People were the fiercest Old Ones of all, famous for their spellcraft and hatred of humans.

"You have heard of them, I see." This time his smile lingered, teasing.

I tossed my head and glared at him.

"They are not evil," he continued, "no matter what you've heard. Only shy," his smile widened. "And very powerful."

Hwyll roared into the Hall closely followed by an angry crowd of villagers and fort-dwellers. I sprang up, careful to put distance between myself and Chalan's son as if I was guilty of some wrongdoing I did not understand.

"Where is the King?"

I pointed to his chambers.

Without a word, the Shield Bearer strode past me, knocking loudly at Father's door. "The sentence is completed, my Lord."

Father trailed Hwyll into the Hall, retaking his High Seat with a heavy sigh. Still, he composed his features as he gazed from face to face, nodding from time to time, to acknowledge those who grieved a loved one.

"Iorwerth, come forward."

My oldest surviving brother shouldered his way gracefully through the throng, bowing formally to Father.

"Kill the prisoners." Ignoring the gasps and the rising cheer that greeted his order, Father handed Iolo his own sword.

"All but one of the Southerners. Tell that one to return to the lands of the Roman-lovers and tell him to take this message with him. Let it be known throughout the realm that we in the North are not baubles to be traded in a marketplace. We will not be invaded or bartered for gold within our own lands."

Father motioned for his mead horn. Taking a long draught, he looked again around the Hall, this time lighting on the faces of his allies, lingering on Chalan's fox-narrow features, coming to rest on Grandmother, meeting her grim elated smile with one of his own.

"As for the Scotti, kill them all."

Bitter cheers rang out. "Burn their bodies in a pyre for the gods. Send a healer to my brother to staunch his wounds. Let Maelgwyn Silver-Tongue see his friends, the Scotti, burn. Tomorrow, we will travel to the western shore and gather at the Roman fort to watch my traitor-doomed brother's coracle set sail for the realms of the horizon."

Suddenly, as if he knew I needed him, Cynan stood beside me, grabbing for my hand and holding it as tightly as if we were lost in the haunted tunnels again. Lleu stood behind us. I felt his hand reach out to steady me, then hesitate and withdraw before he touched me. I straightened my back and moved away from him, clenching my brother's hand.

The warriors left to carry out Father's commands, closely followed by the folk of Dinas. The Hall was nearly empty before I could bring myself to look at Father. He slumped against the white wolfskin of his High Seat as if he had drunk too much mead.

Shadows hid Father's dragon tattoo from my sight. Never again would it glow for me as it had ever since I was a babe in his arms.

"Come." Cynan led me out of the Hall, pointing as we passed the doorpost, still stained with Useth's blood. "They'll put Nestor the Scotti chief's head up there now." He tried to sound gleeful, but sounded bone-weary instead.

No more words were needed between us as we walked to the Goddess' grove. I took a seat on my favorite rock overlooking the still waters of the pool. Here, in the company of untold memories of the family I had lost, I wept, my vision filled with ghosts. Mother and Father were dead to me. The tortures they'd inflicted, the deaths they'd ordered …all of it consumed me. They were as bloodstained as the Dark One, the Raven's Goddess, feasting on the new and rotting dead.

I wept for Hwyrch…for Merlin, who had abandoned me.

Cynan's own eyes were bloodshot, but dry. "We must go back." But he made no move to leave, awkwardly patting me on the back as if I were a hound that needed reassurance.

But it was not Cynan who finally reached my spirit, forcing me to stand again, and reluctantly turn my face to Dinas. It was not Merlin or Hwyrch whose scoldings were behind me now, buried with my childhood beside this sweet and hidden pool. It was the unbidden memory of Chalan's tall, ocean-eyed son and the sudden flash of a smile across his ordinarily guarded face that helped me rise, toss back my hair, and begin to walk up Dinas' blood-soaked hill to face the fate that awaited me in the Hall of my ancestors.

chapter 21

The next morning, Maelgwyn was marched to the sea in chains, placed in a coracle, and laughingly given an oar. Yet, despite our people's curses, his boat did not sink. Instead it sailed peacefully into the horizon towards Eire—the land of his Scotti allies.

Although we knew in our hearts that Maelgwyn faced almost certain doom on the western sea, folk longed to see his death with their own eyes and raged that he had not been killed outright. That night the Hall of Dinas was filled with angry murmurings, my brother Iolo loudest of all, challenging Father's decision not to mount Maelgwyn's head on a pole beside Nestor's.

But Father listened not at all, contenting himself with wishing me good-bye.

Merlin, true to his word, had spoken with my parents and Grandmother about letting me stay in the healers' village.

"Are you sure, Gwen?" Father asked for what must have been the tenth handful of times. I could stand it no longer and answered with a quick polite hug, a distant nod to Mother, and escaped to huddle with Cynan and Tali in Tali's new quarters near the kitchens, for Father had honored his promise to Bran and let Tali apprentice as a bard.

Over a stolen pitcher of mead, we pledged eternal friendship and, despite my frozen heart, I promised my brother and our best friend to teach them every spell I would learn in the seasons I would be gone.

The next morning Cynan and Tali came with me into the forest. We followed Nest who would be my guide to the healers' village and Sari who would be presented to the Mountain Druids at their river sanctuary near Modron's pool, two leagues before my own destination was reached.

There she would be trained in the ways of the Goddess-blessed, the far-seers who had served the land since the days of my earliest ancestors.

If the girl had any fear of what awaited her, she showed no sign of it. She skipped beyond us, a tiny smile dancing across her delicate features, visible now for she had stopped wearing her veil. Seeing me, Sari's smile widened, she eagerly turned this way and that, trying to see everything at once. Joining Nest, she began pointing first to a tree, then to a bird, then to a flower asking their names, repeating them over and over to herself.

For our part, Cynan, Tali, and I spoke not at all, our hearts too full for words, letting the forest and the memories it held for us speak for us instead.

The dawn mist had lifted, exposing rocks and rushing water as we reached the river's bend. Cynan stopped walking.

"Wait, Shadow." He leaned against a boulder, eyeing Nest, ready for a fight, for this was as close to the healers' village as he and Tali were allowed to come.

After one irritated sigh, the midwife watched us without complaint, giving us time for our farewells, keeping a sharp eye on Sari who was wandering up the trail, exclaiming over the roots of an ancient rowan tree.

"I'll miss you," mumbled Tali. Refusing to meet my eyes, he picked up a fallen branch and whacked at the bramble thicket encroaching on the narrow forest track.

"Liar, you'll be far too busy to care!" I punched Tali in the shoulder. Instead of fighting back, he hugged me. I hid my eyes against the weave of his short cloak, hugging back fiercely.

"Good-bye, brat," my brother whispered. I reached for him, then let him go and took two steps towards the river, pretending its loud foaming crash over rocks was more interesting than my brother's face. I dared not meet his eyes. I would not cry. My throat hurt, my eyes burned. I would not cry.

"Good-bye," I said and turned away from them, almost running into the forest before they could see the treacherous tears spill out over my warrior-cold eyes.

"Wait, Gwen." Nest commanded, huffing after me.

I let Sari and Nest pass, their voices rising and falling in a conversation that mingled with the rushing waters of the river.

I did not look behind me for a long time, clutching a river rock like a weapon in my hand. When I finally did look back, the forest trail was empty. Cynan and Tali were gone.

PART II

NORTHERN WALES: 468-474 CE

chapter 22

It would be six sunturns before I saw my home of Dinas again. Sunturns in which much of my grieving was healed and I learned the most ancient secrets of our land: the songs of stones, the speech of autumn winds, the language of rivers. Sunturns in which I learned to love a way of living far removed from the blood lust and majesty of human halls.

The mists of the healers' village parted easily for me that first morning and Nest left me quickly before the mist could take her as well. Inside the village I was welcomed and cosseted: given a hut to live in, friends to run with, plentiful food to eat. Accompan-ied by my village friend, Eleri, and a white wolf named Chinon, I followed the healers' headwoman Arias as she ranged the forests, mountains, and valleys of the healers' realm, invisible to us at Dinas. There I was taught to understand the whispers of the ancients, those beings who had withdrawn from our world long before the standing stones were raised.

Yet for all that I absorbed of humility and kindness, I was restless for the human world that was my birthright.

It was more than simple yearning. Part of me sensed that Merlin had been wrong. The healers did their best, but guilt and rage were still imbedded in my spirit like woad dye on a weaving, forcing me to seek answers in the fortress I was reared in—not within the gentle whispers of the village, no matter how much I might wish it.

Thus, six sunturns later, when the summons to return home arrived, I was relieved.

That final morning, Arias, the headwoman, led me to the passage that separated us from the earth realms. For the last time, we walked through the garden of the healers and I bid farewell to the neatly planted rows of every flower, fruit, vegetable, and herb the world offered.

"We will remember you, Gwenhwyfar." I glanced down at Arias, the tiny dimple-cheeked woman who had become as dear to me as my own breath. "But you must leave us."

My heart caught as a rainbow of iridescent butterflies darted past me, flying across a horizon filled with all the plants and trees of Earth.

"Can I truly never return, Lady?"

The healer shielded her eyes as if she too tracked the butterflies' flight.

"Your place is in the world, child. Though you carry the forest inside you."

She patted my cheek and took my hand with a wink, gesturing into the tree-swept horizon. "It is in your blood, this magic, and we have helped awaken it. May it serve you well."

She chuckled, reaching up to ruffle my hair. "And worry not about your courses. The Goddess works in her own good time."

I ducked my head, refusing to smile. At fourteen sunturns, I was taller than most full grown women. Yet my breasts had only begun to swell and the thatch of hair on my women's parts was as sparse as sorrow at a wedding. Nor had my moontide bleeding begun—a source of secret shame.

I sighed, taking her hand. "I will miss you."

She drew her belt dagger and cut a lock of her hair, handing it to me. "And I you, Gwenhwyfar, daughter of Ceridwen, granddaughter of Rhiannon Sage Singer. Braid this with whatever treasures you hold dear. Thus will my spirit always watch over you."

I placed her hair in my belt pouch and walked with her to the misted barrier of the hidden village. Left alone, I began to pace, filled with nervousness and foreboding at my return to Dinas.

Chinon, the white wolf, joined me, his presence as calming as ever. We stood, waiting until I saw Nest approach the foot of the hill. With a final nudge of my hand, Chinon whuffed and was gone.

"I've come," I called to the midwife, working my way down the slope of the misted hilltop.

Whatever note she heard in my voice, Nest guided us home in silence. A very small part of me remembered and missed her chatter, wishing for anything to keep the confusion of my feelings at bay.

Yet I was grateful to have time to remember an unfamiliar forest that had once been as well-known to me as my own body. To recognize an alder tree whose branches were scarred by lightning. To catch sight of a newborn fawn hidden behind the boulder Cynan and I had once made into an enemy fortress.

Strangely, I could barely remember the faces of my own family and was half-terrified to see them again.

Yet when the familiar towers of Dinas came into view, my heart sprang into my throat. I ran ahead of Nest, pelting up the hill as if I was a little girl again. The healers' village, Arias, Eleri, the women I had loved there, all the lessons I had learned fell away, tucked into my spirit like the folds of a long ago, still-beloved dream, never to be forgotten but no longer the very air I breathed.

I ran past bossy old Gwern, the sentry, without stopping, then skidded into the Great Hall as nervous as if I had been gone for twelve sunturns instead of six. Would Cynan remember me? Tali? My face heated at the thought of the Druid brat, Lleu. What of Father, Grandmother? Mother? And there I stopped, for despite all the seasons of healing, all the wisdom of the Old Ones I carried, the thought of Mother still sent ice into my blood.

chapter 23

As for the rest I need not have worried. From the first shouted, *"Shadow!"* Cynan shared my heart again. There were times that spring when Tali, Cynan, and I grew silent, when our changing bodies caught like bramble snags in the fabric of our childhood closeness. But always one or the other of us would recover quickly and run, whooping, down the great hill of Dinas or gallop our shaggy ponies across the river's meadow, screaming taunts as we had always done.

That Tali was quieter, preoccupied with his harp, and that Cynan's new bed in the Warrior's Hall had invested him with a boy-man's swagger, I barely noticed. For my part, I tried to hold onto the serenity I had learned in the healers' village—a serenity I was hard put to remember in the tension-ridden atmosphere of Dinas.

Even though both the Scotti and the South had remained silent after Father's war, we watched our borders tirelessly. So many warriors now manned the pirate-watch camp on our coast that their women joined them and a round-hutted family village was built in the shadows of the deserted red-cloak's fort of Segontium.

It was there that Lleu had spent the winter, learning a warrior's craft from my brother Iolo. They returned the fortnight after I had come back to Dinas.

My heart thudded like a witless girl's as they entered the open doorway of the spring-scented Hall, Iolo's wary eyes gleaming as he clapped Lleu on the back.

In the six sunturns since I'd seen him, Iolo had grown into a handsome whipcord of a man. His alert eyes danced across the Hall, alighting on me. With a wolf howl and one graceful lunge, he was beside me.

"What ho, beautiful sister, you have seen fit to return from the gods, have you?"

"Stop it!" I beat at him. Forgetting all trace of dignity, I was a little girl in my big brother's arms again.

"Welcome back, sister," he whispered into my hair so none but I could hear. "Look, you Decleangli pup, what the winter winds vomited back—"

I punched Iolo in the chest and turned at last to Lleu who had come up silently and stood, watching our antics with the bittersweet smile I remembered all too well.

At seventeen sunturns, he was everything I remembered and more. Tall enough to top me by a handspan, his training as a warrior had given him the muscled chest and arms that no doubt made the silly girls of Dinas chase after him like puppies. He clasped my arm in his. His sad smile turned into a mischievous grin, and I forced myself to meet his mysterious grey eyes with cool politeness, masking the surge of heat that rampaged within me.

"Lady Gwenhwyfar." He took my hand and sketched a kiss across my fingers.

"Foster brother. Welcome back." I said in my most regal tone, careful to extract my hand before the tingle his lips had caused could reach my face and turn it red. Instead, the flush spread throughout my body, lingering in my women's parts like an unsettling storm cloud in a tranquil sky.

He looked at me and grinned again. "It's good to see you, too."

Arrogant brat! I bit my lip and nodded curtly. "If you'll excuse me," I made my escape, as if I had urgent business elsewhere, although no one had called me. I did not care about the new woad tattoos Lleu carried on the temples of his face. Nor about the single warrior braid that fell across his chest like an eager whip—no matter how much more handsome and dangerous it made him. The Druid brat was now a man. These new warrior marks were proof that his father, Chalan, had allowed him to be initiated by the men of our clan as well as his own Decleangli.

I escaped the Hall and set off to the Goddess' grove. Restlessly, I paced beneath my favorite oak and watched the willow fronds dance along the night shadows of the sacred pool. The full moon began its graceful flight across a star-ridden sky, and still I paced, tossed between anger and desire, seeking the words I had learned in the healers' village.

Words to calm me, to take the flush from my body, the confusion from my spirit.

That I sought them without success was, perhaps, a trick of the Goddess. For, she was, indeed, watching and escape from her would not be as simple as had been my retreat from my parents' Hall.

Rising at last, I heard a silver sigh among the grasses. I threw a stone into the pool, knowing full well she was laughing at me.

chapter 24

"But why must I continue to learn Latin? The red-cloaks have been defeated. And we hated them to begin with." I had lain in wait for Father on his way to the stables, trying to catch him in a good mood.

I saw his eyes begin to narrow with impatience and threw up my final argument. "Cynan doesn't have to take lessons anymore."

"*Cynan* doesn't have to study because he spent all the sunturns you were gone swearing and sweating over the same studies that you are now too lazy to undertake. Isn't Decus to your liking?"

Father caught the hunting spear Hwyll threw and stopped before the stable door, making it clear he had more important things to do than argue with me.

All around us men mounted their ponies and called out to each other in jesting high spirits, heading out on the hunt. The new stable master, Rathoq, brought Father's favorite hunting pony to his side.

"Well?"

In truth my new tutor, Decus, was more than satisfactory. Although no one could take the place of Merlin, Decus was from an island far away upon the southern sea and told wonderful stories of bloody battles, crafty kings, and wooden horses. His good-natured hound-like face and his yellowed gap-toothed smile were becoming increasingly dear to me as we conjugated boring verbs and munched on Maeve's honey cakes.

"He is a good teacher, Father." I kicked at a clod of horse dung, refusing to raise my eyes. "But I am wasting time learning the language of dead people."

Father jumped on his pony. "We will not discuss this again. Whatever you think of Latin, it remains the language of south Albion and the folk across the Narrow Sea. You will one day be a queen, daughter. It is time you behaved like one—and stop whining like a child."

Fury lanced through me. I clenched my fists and gritted my teeth, watching Father's warrior-proud back and the tail of his spotted black pony disappear through the gates of Dinas.

My argument about Latin had begun as a playful protest, like so many I had once had with Father which ended as he picked me up, laughing, and spun me over his head, convulsed with giggles, while Mother or Hwyrch looked on in disapproval—knowing I had gotten my way yet again.

Now I stood in the muddy courtyard like a Roman statue, letting the bustling life of Dinas ebb and flow around me, deaf to the cheerful conversations and the horseplay of warriors; my rage turning to bitter ashes in my stomach as I realized the truth.

Father had changed greatly in the six sunturns since I'd seen him. His once lustrous brown hair was threaded with silver and his proud limed moustaches were as white as Yr Wyddfra's snows. Worse, his wise king-eyes were often empty of feeling, as if his spirit had gone seeking answers to questions he did not know how to ask. He laughed less, and refilled his mead horn more frequently.

But I was still his daughter, the little girl who had always made him laugh, who could wheedle him into her way of thinking as easily as beeswax perfumed Mother's chamber.

Now I had lost him, as well.

Fists clenched beneath the folds of the long linen gown Mother now forced me to wear, I spun on my heels and stormed into the kitchens, carefully composing my face before I greeted Cook Maeve, set to give me a lesson in caring for the precious spices she and Mother hoarded like gold in a locked chest. More life-saving knowledge for a queen. I would not let Father hurt me again. Just as I maintained a careful distance with Mother, I would not let Father come near my heart again.

Three days passed and I held to my resolve, aware that Father watched me from the corner of his brooding eyes. Visitors came and went, and I paid them little attention, serving the guest mead as Mother and Grandmother had taught me, slipping among the trestle tables and up and down the dais as graceful as a forest doe, barely aware of what I did.

Twice Father started to speak to me, only to close his mouth again. Both times I looked at him with as cool a grace as I could manage, glad of the chain-mail I had placed around my heart, remembering the brutal face he had turned on his own brother; holding fast to it so I would not weaken and fall into the wolf-trap of a child's love.

The third morning, on a day that the spring rains had grudgingly stopped and hesitant sunlight was fighting the clouds, Father sought me out. He found me dutifully weaving beside Mother and her women in Mother's new summer weaving room in the West Tower.

Instead of leaving, Father sat on a stool and watched in silence as I worked, feeling myself as out of place as a fox in a bed chamber. I did not disappoint him—or perhaps I did—for I threaded the loom without speaking and, as was my habit since I had returned to Dinas, let the women's conversations flow around me as if they spoke another tongue, making polite and queenly comments only when necessary.

"Come with me, Shadow."

I looked up in surprise at his use of my old nickname.

"I have something to show you."

Without a word, I left Mother's chamber, following Father down the winding stairs of the tower, across the muddy courtyard and into the stables, refusing to allow my curiosity to show.

"She's waiting for you, Lord." Rathoq, the stable master, stepped aside.

Father lit a torch and led me deep within the stable's darkness, where only weak sunlight penetrated. It was where we put new or skittish horses so they would not be disturbed by the busy comings and goings at the front of the stable.

He held the torch high, illuminating a sleek red-brown body and large liquid eyes. I caught my breath. The beautiful mare pranced towards us curiously, arching her graceful neck like a queen.

"The traders you gave mead to yesterday brought her from beyond the southern sea. She is yours, daughter."

"Mine?" My throat closed. I sounded more mouse than girl.

"Yours," Father said, handing me one of the dried apples he always carried, saving them throughout the winter to treat his beloved horses.

He patted the elegant mare's flank, not looking at me.

I stood still at the door to her stall, star-struck, as if I was meeting a goddess. Indeed, Epona herself could not have been more beautiful. Shyly, I held up the apple. The magical creature approached me. Nodding regally, she greeted me with a nuzzle, breathing softly into my palm before snatching the apple.

Dancer, I whispered. Shivering with delight, I explored the sides of her face to find the places she most liked attended to.

"Like her?" Father's eyes were on me now. It was a long time since I'd seen his smile unshadowed by care or bitterness.

All my hurt and anger fell away. I threw my arms around his neck, something I had not done since I was a little girl. Now, however, I was tall enough to do so without stretching.

"*Like her*! She's magic! Thank you, Father! Thank you!"

He spun me in a circle; I was too tall to pick up anymore.

"Ever since I knew you would be returning to us, I have had traders scouring the ports for just such a mare. She is three sunturns old," he said proudly. "Bred by Sari's people, the same desert lords that once supplied the red-cloaks' cavalry."

I watched as he petted her. Within a heartbeat his well-respected horse wisdom led him to a spot behind her ears. Dancer snorted in contentment.

"Thank you." I hugged him harder than I ever had. "She is the most beautiful horse I've ever seen."

"Gwen—" Father held me against him, kissing the top of my head in the way I remembered from long ago.

I pulled back to look at him. He ran warrior-calloused fingers up and down a curling strand of my hair, pushing it behind my ear. Then he took my face in his hands. I said nothing, only stared at him, honoring whatever he was trying to tell me with silence. A spasm of anguish arrowed across his eyes, followed by an entire world of feelings, tumbling across his expression as quickly as acrobats across a dusty courtyard.

Frightened by his intensity, I understood that to look away would be to refuse my father's soul.

"It's all right." I whispered.

He hugged me. I felt him convulse inside my arms, terrified to feel the moisture of his tears run into my hair. "Gwen, I—"

"It's all right," I said again. "We are still alive. You have kept us alive. That is all that matters now," I murmured fiercely—and knew for the first time this was true.

At length, he quieted and watched as I petted Dancer.

"Can I ride her?" I asked, wanting more than anything to return to a world where my father was once again the lord of all that I saw around me.

"I was wondering when you'd ask!" He helped me gentle the mare, saying nothing as I cut slits in my gown to make riding possible. I leapt upon her back for the first time, barely able to breathe for excitement, and Father walked us as far as the courtyard.

Dancer moved like liquid fire beneath me, I had never felt such pure soaring joy before.

"Take her down to the river meadow. Let her get used to you before you take her up the high tracks." I looked down at him in surprise. Why speak to me as if I had never sat a pony before?

A small smile flirted with his features and disappeared. "I am overcautious these days, my wild one. Forgive me." He bowed and took my hand in his. This time the smile stayed long enough to linger in his eyes. "It is time, dear daughter, that I return to the ruling of men."

He signaled for two warriors to accompany me.

I leaned over to kiss him, then set my face to Dinas' gate, too excited to look back to see if he was watching. For I knew, in my heart, Father stood there, alone.

My first afternoon with Dancer passed all too quickly. We galloped back to Dinas and I rubbed her down, whispering sweet secret words against her flanks, kissing her on her soft nose when she wuffled at me in answer. My spirit was overflowing, as if I had flown to the top of Yr Wyddfra and danced with the gods.

At last, I patted the mare's neck, gave her some fodder, and bid her a reluctant good-bye, then pelted across the courtyard, late as always for my Latin lesson with Decus.

I collided with Mother in the entrance to the Hall.

She stumbled, starting to laugh.

"Gwen! What fire do you flee?"

I drew up short, responding in the cool tone I adopted on the rare occasions she spoke with me about anything more important than lessons.

"I am sorry, Mother."

The light that had appeared in her bruised violet eyes died immediately.

"It is of no consequence, daughter," she said politely. "Only remember that a queen does not run like an escaping slave through the Hall where she is expected to rule."

I fought the impulse to roll my eyes. To give Mother even that much power would be dangerous to the wall of distance and formality I had built between us.

I bowed my head and continued past her, ignoring the hand she placed on my bare wrist and the sudden memory it brought to me.

I was a small child again, curled in her lap, giggling madly as she tickled my stomach, blowing on it with her mouth. "Who does Shadow love?"... tickle..."Who does Shadow—" ...tickle, tickle..."love?"...

"Mommy!" I gasped, breathless, "Shadow loves Mommy!" She blew on my stomach again. "Who?" She laughed, her long black curls tangled in my fists, her eyes as warm as the hearth fire that snapped in front of us.

Before I could escape, Mother's small fingers moved hesitantly up my arm. Nothing that the healers had taught me prepared me for the physical pain that seized me. No matter how much I tried to forgive her, I had only to look at her and other, more recent, images appeared.

This new Mother stood before me, blood covering her face, knife clutched in both hands, the gore of what had once been a man sliding down her arms, dripping in nightmare rivers from her hands.

Her hand fell away when I did not stop and I sensed her tiny figure leave the Hall, trailing a subtle cloud of rose attar and the soft scent of sunlight behind.

Decus was waiting for me on his usual bench. It had become our habit to meet mid-afternoons in the almost empty Hall where we were in easy reach of Maeve's kitchen.

He cut a hunk of cheese from the wheel Maeve had saved for him and gave it to me. We started to work our tedious way through the speeches of Cicero.

"Shadow!" Cynan skidded into the Hall and jumped on the trestle beside us.

Food, scrolls, and wax tablets flew into the air. "Merlin's back!"

I reached the doorway before Cynan could say another word, running as fast as I could. Neither of us bothered to say good-bye to my good-natured tutor, who no doubt took the opportunity to finish off what was left of our meal.

Tali joined us in the courtyard and we ran through the eastern gate, tumbling, jumping, running down the hill, laughing like a pack of fools, ignoring the sudden spat of rain that drenched us.

Merlin had reached the second ramparts overlooking the ditch at the bottom of the hill. He dismounted hurriedly as he saw us coming—

most likely to protect his horse from our onslaught.

We gave him no time to speak, merely crashed into him, shouting. It was surely a test of his wizardry that he did not fall down.

When at last we calmed enough to let him speak, the rain had stopped and a watery spring sun illuminated the world. Merlin gathered us to him in a hug. I stepped back a pace, remembering how abruptly we had parted so many seasons ago. He seemed not to notice, for, laughing as if we were hound puppies, he intoned a blessing so grand it seemed to dance in the air, strengthening the sun itself.

"It is well—very well—to see you sprouts!" We began to walk with him up the hill. I led his horse, a dappled grey with mysterious black eyes.

"I am weary now," he cuffed Cynan's cheek, "and will need to speak to the old folk of Dinas first. But, perhaps, after a night's sleep, I will be ready to go adventuring with you again. Are you free to join me tomorrow?"

Were we free? Ha, let anyone try to stop us! My brother and Tali hared up the slope and I turned to look at my beloved uncle, forgetting to be angry at him for deserting us, searching anxiously for signs that the seasons had changed him.

His hair still fell as thick as ever, though he had not bothered to wear his prince's circlet and I imagined I saw a few more strands of grey than I remembered. His body was still as lanky and as fit as a young warrior's. But I saw new lines across his forehead and an indefinable sense of sadness in the other-world green of his eyes.

He met my scrutiny with one of his own.

"Aye, Gwen, we've both changed a bit."

Grinning, he showed a newly-chipped tooth that made his smile resemble Iorwerth's. "You, my dear, are growing into a rare beauty."

"Come on!" Cynan called. He and Tali stood, panting at the summit of the hill where the gate of the final ramparts shadowed their bodies like the hand of a giant.

I let go of Merlin's hands and drew my arms across my chest, fighting a sudden chill.

"Come on!" Tali echoed, his long limbs and hair flying like a whirlwind as they raced down to meet us again.

"Have you forgiven me yet, Shadow?" Merlin whispered.

I kissed his cheek in answer. Shaking off my foreboding, I ran to join the others, the rain-wet tall grass clinging to my calves as I hiked up the gown I had already ruined riding Dancer.

We laughed and clapped each other's shoulders, dancing in wild exuberant circles, as if we had never known sorrow or loss. The sun was shining again—and Merlin had come home!

chapter 25

The next morning we assembled by the eastern gate, sleepy-eyed but excited, punching each other to stay awake. Tali brought a sack of provisions from Maeve's kitchen and Cynan wasted no time in raiding it.

"Shall we go?" Merlin strode from Father's guest house, fastening his cloak with the new brooch Mother had given him at last night's feast.

Cynan closed Tali's kitchen sack, grabbing four bannocks for himself, and we ran, slip-sliding down the fog-covered hill with dramatic jumps and laughter.

I paused to walk with Merlin. Mother's gifted brooch shone bright gold in the morning mist. Mother and her jewels—she was worse than a magpie! I bit my lip, remembering a long ago Lughnasa night when she had adorned me with the treasured hair ornaments of my ancestors, of how we gazed and laughed at our reflections in her handheld bronze mirror as she prepared me like a sacrificial queen for the raven-cursed feast that followed.

"It is good to have you back, Uncle," I said formally.

"I have missed you, Shadow." He picked up a long stem of grass and turned it over, smiling in a manner that reminded me of Arias the healer. "The fates are not often so kind as to let me choose my own road across Albion."

"How is he—that southern boy you watch over?" I asked, fighting down my jealousy.

He threw the grass stalk away and watched Cynan and Tali shove and push each other, as giddy as small boys on the forest path ahead.

"Sometimes I wish—" he shook himself as if coming awake and placed his hand on mine, "I could romp like a child. I never did, you know. Always at the call of one master or another."

His smile melted my heart. "Though they taught me well, I suppose. Enough to save Albion for a handful of seasons."

I said nothing, suddenly shy. I kept my hand in his until the trail narrowed and he gestured me to go ahead.

"He is well, the boy you ask of, fit and fierce—always asking questions. Much like you, my dear."

I snuggled against him, all my childish resentment at his comings and goings forgotten. He was here again, that was all that mattered.

All around us the forest was waking up in muddy spring delirium. A finch flew down and perched on a rowan branch, trilling as if overjoyed to see us. I ran to join Cynan and Tali. Turning back to wave at Merlin, I saw an expression on his face that frightened me. He was watching us with his usual mixture of love and amusement, but then his eyes darkened. He held up a hand in an ancient warding gesture, as if all the violets of spring had been crushed and he was too late to stop their destruction.

"Merlin?" Six sunturns with the healers had given me enough skill to recognize a true seeing. I was no longer a little girl to be protected. I needed to know what he had sensed.

Before he could answer, someone came up behind us, swiftly, moving with the grace of a tracker.

"Lord Merlin, Lady Gwenhwyfar." Lleu smiled at his own formality, yet his expression remained tense. "May I come with you?"

The Mage hesitated, then nodded. "It is well, child of the Lake Dwellers—son of Chalan though you be. You will enjoy this day's lesson."

We had reached a clearing and Cynan and Tali joined us just in time to hear Merlin. "A lesson, Uncle? What will it be today?" Cynan vaulted up on a fallen tree and straddled it. "Will we learn to call a raven—or how to stay warm in a blizzard?" He grabbed my arm and pulled me down to sit with him. "Or will you teach us where to look for poisons so that I can practice on my sister?"

I hit him and we wrestled until Merlin raised his arm.

As always when the Mage claimed our attention with so much as a raised eyebrow, we stopped our wildness and listened.

"The day I trust you fools with poisons will be the day the gods will send me to Anwnn with an escort of slavering hounds—and rightly so!" Uncle regarded Cynan and me with the stern teacher's eye that used to make us giggle. "However, I do believe you may be ready for a chance to experience life as other creatures know it. Today," Uncle paused dramatically, letting us wait as he settled on a ragged stump, "you will take the first steps towards shape-shifting. Today, an animal will choose you and you will follow it—"

Before Uncle could continue, we began to shout and interrupt each other like a flock of crows. Shape-shifting was one of the highest magics. That Merlin thought we were ready for it was high praise indeed.

"Which animal will come, Merlin?" I imagined myself a bear...a wolf...a mountain cat...

Merlin sighed, reading my thoughts as easily as ever. "An animal does not need to be dangerous to teach wisdom, child."

Cynan rolled his eyes. "With your personality, I think a badger might be fitting."

I shoved him. Tali started to chuckle. Lleu stood apart from us, eyeing Merlin carefully.

The Mage's voice cut across our horseplay, as serious as I had ever heard him. "For you, Gwen, I had in mind a squirrel."

"A squirrel?" I did not bother to keep the insult from my voice.

Cynan swallowed his laughter, although one look at Tali set him off again. "A wise choice, Mage!"

"And for you, Cynan, I think a mouse might suit."

"A mouse!"

"Yes, brother dear, a little mousie."

"Gwen!" Merlin's voice was so stern, I jumped up from the log where I had been wrestling with Cynan. "It is time you both learned to honor reality. There is great magic in small things, you know," he added more softly, "gentle ordinary creatures are often the greatest souls. Watch—"

A squirrel leapt joyfully down from a branch of the oak tree behind us, climbing up and down Merlin's outstretched arm. Resting at last on his palm, it looked up into Uncle's eyes, twittering as if it had things to tell him.

Merlin listened with the politely inclined head he used when he was listening to something of grave importance.

The boys gathered closer, listening to the silly creature as if they were entranced. The air grew still around us. I stifled a yawn and tried not to shuffle my feet, longing to go down the trail and discover something new.

At last the talkative squirrel paused as if waiting for an answer.

Merlin nodded. Without looking at me, he commanded, "Raise your arm, Gwen."

The small creature hesitated, then, as I grudgingly obeyed, he jumped from Merlin, across my forearm, pausing at the curve of my elbow. It raised a paw against its white chest, staring up at me as I looked into its hopeful black eyes.

What did it want of me? And what could it possibly give me that was useful?

"Look deeper, girl." Merlin's voice turned guttural, as deep as a hound's growl. Have you forgotten the healers' teachings already?"

I obeyed. The creature began to chatter at me, its voice pitched high in excitement. It babbled in strange syllables as if the world held so many wonders, they had to tumble out all at once.

I giggled. Encouraged, the squirrel seemed to grin. Flicking its bushy tail across my forearm, it reared up as if to say something of a private nature to me.

Interested despite myself, I leaned closer. But it jumped down and ran away, glancing back over its shoulder before it disappeared into the thorny brambles beneath the trees that lined the clearing.

Now it was Merlin who chuckled. "Runala would like you to follow him, Gwen."

Runala?

As if to punctuate Merlin's words, the squirrel emerged from the wet bracken a good spear's throw from where we sat. It looked at me, chattering in a bossy manner that sounded a great deal like Grandmother when she was annoyed.

"Go, Gwen. We will catch you up at the small falls." Cynan was trying not to laugh out loud.

I turned in dismay to Merlin. "Yes, go, Gwen. Runala will not lead you astray."

Knowing better then to argue, I bunched my short cloak around me and trod reluctantly into the mud and bracken, grateful now that I had donned my thickest leather boots.

The world off the path was wet and damp, covered with ferns when it was not miserable with thickets, misted like a world of the ancients. The squirrel broke cover and ran up and down a tree trunk presumably in delight that I was silly enough to follow it. Still, I felt myself smile. The foolish being reminded me of Selyf's youngest, a toddler given to sudden shrieks and mad dashes across the Hall in pursuit of me.

I followed more willingly and found myself in a clearing where the squirrel and its family scampered up and down the trees as if they were my own kin and friends playing tag on the hills of Dinas.

I must have dozed for when I awoke, the squirrels were gone and a vision of the healer Arias shimmered in front of me. Shivering at the suddenness of it, I was slow to note the alarm in the cozy headwoman's eyes. *Danger comes, child. Seek the truth your Grandmother has hidden.*

A branch snapped. Nervously, I turned around, feeling the weight of the forest watching me. No longer playful. No longer friendly.

Though I heard nothing, the back of my neck grew cold. Something stalked me, a menace I had not felt in a long time, not since I had left Dinas as a child.

I ran from the clearing: plunging through trees, falling, snagged by brambles and my own panicked fear.

Stumbling, frantic, I came upon the path again and, stood, panting like a winded pony, angry at myself. I had to think. To stay calm. I could no longer run from unseen danger like a terrified child—I was almost a woman grown. I must face whatever hunted me with courage.

More than my life might depend on it.

Glancing uneasily at the trees—for that last thought had not been my own—I felt a lightening in the atmosphere. A final rustling of leaves and whatever menaced me was gone.

Shafts of sunlight broke through the misted canopy. Birds began to gossip again. I grabbed a stout oak branch to use as a walking stick—so shaken were my legs—and made my way to one of the safest places I knew.

I spent the rest of the day in a spot that I had loved as a little girl: a grassy knoll beneath an aging willow whose spring-light branches swept the surface of a deep and restful pool. Here, finally, I was able to calm myself and return to our meeting place without alarming the others, for I knew that the warning had been meant for me alone.

Rising, I determined to push fears and forebodings aside, yet my heart remained wary and I longed more than anything to return to the innocence of the morning and the rampaging of squirrels.

When I got to the small falls, only Lleu was waiting.

"They've gone to Fychan's steading for a hot bowl of stew and left me here to freeze, waiting for you." Lleu stretched and ambled down from the high rock where he had been sitting.

"Was it worth it, following a squirrel?" His grin was mischievous, but I heard the interest beneath it.

"Yes, it was." I answered shortly, deciding then and there to push the truth of my day aside. "What animal claimed you?"

"A wolf," he grinned.

I stepped back a pace to see if he was joking, but Lleu's expression was level. He shrugged as I stared at him.

I nodded as if his news meant nothing. "Let's join the others. I'm starving!"

I started down the path to where a hot meal waited, pretending not to care that he had been chosen by an animal I coveted.

"I have food. Cynan and I shared out Tali's sack before we parted. Stay and talk with me awhile."

Still filled with the eeriness of the day, I hesitantly joined him on the rocks beneath the falls. The coldness Lleu complained of seeped into me, but, as I listened to the cascading falls, fierce with spring snowmelt, I forgot where I was. Hearing only the water's song, suddenly, I was able to escape my forebodings: I forgot to be hungry, forgot to be cold, imagining I was a mermaid diving deep beneath the power of the falling river.

"Up, lazy one!" Unnoticed by me, Lleu had left the rocks and cleared a space at the edge of the forest where he crouched, blowing on a tiny flint-sparked fire. When he saw he had my attention, he gestured beneath the trees.

Reluctant to let my little girl imaginings go, I sighed and got up to gather pine cones and the driest branches I could find and sank on my haunches beside him. If he sensed the strangeness of my dream-spelled mood, Lleu gave no sign.

I held out my hands to the growing fire and bit into the salt-dried salmon he handed me. As the taste of river-tanged meat filled my mouth, all my new shyness returned.

We ate the meal in silence, absorbed in our own thoughts.

Lleu offered me his water skin. "I was afraid, at first, to be a wolf. It brought me too close to my father's realm for comfort."

I drank, thinking of my beloved Chinon, then watched as Lleu emptied the water skin, staring in fascination at the way the muscles of his throat contracted. He had removed his hunting cloak and the warrior-strong muscles of his arms and chest were revealed beneath the looseness of his tunic.

A slow smile dawned on his face as he lowered the skin and saw my eyes on him. I looked away quickly, furious at the heat I felt rising in my face.

"Your father still haunts you?" I asked, breaking the sudden intensity between us.

"I despise him. Although it is his right to demand my return next summer, I do not wish to go."

"Really?" I tore my eyes from the waterfall and looked back at him again, remembering the conversation we had shared in the black days before I left Dinas for the healers' village. It was enough to take my mind off the beauty of his body for I remembered that he, like me, had sorrowed in his childhood.

"I thought he was an unusual man, but clever."

"Clever, he is. Never doubt it. But, don't ever mistake his charm for kindness. Beneath it, he is a bastard."

He handed me the last piece of bannock. I took it greedily. "It sounds as if you are well away from him."

Lleu's eyes softened as he watched me gobble the bannock down. "Let's not talk of my father on such a beautiful afternoon."

"Agreed, but do you think my brother, Bran, will be safe at his court?"

He did not reassure me as quickly as I wished. Instead he skipped a stone across the pool beside us, beyond the waterfall's reach. He watched it skim three times across the water before he answered. "I hope so."

It was not the river's breeze that made me shiver.

"Don't worry, Gwen. Bran knows well how to take care of himself." He reached out to pull a lock of hair behind my ear.

No man but Father or Merlin had ever touched me like that. I fought the urge to pull away, just as I fought the urge to lean against his shoulder. I did neither. Desperate to mask my confusion, I looked across the waterfall's pool pretending to be fascinated by the drifting branches of a willow.

"Now tell me," Lleu continued, "what do you think it will be like to be a squirrel?"

I laughed and pushed him away. "I'll race you to Fychan's hut."

I got up before he could argue to stay. Got up while my treacherous legs would still support me.

"Coward," he laughed, but followed my lead, careful to put out our small fire before he leapt over the rocks and raced past me. We ran, neck and neck, taking foolish chances with the rocks and tree roots that infested the trail.

We reached a meadow wide enough for us to run beside each other and arrived at Fychan's steading, gasping for breath.

Our eyes met before we pushed through the deerskin flap of Fychan's wattle-and-daub hut.

"Coward." Lleu said again. He circled me with his arms and kissed me.

Before I could resist, his tongue was on mine. We clung together, long enough to share the heat rising from our bodies, then he let me go, pushing me inside the hut ahead of him.

"You're beautiful," he whispered and then he was beside me, laughing with Cynan and Tali as Merlin and Fychan rose to greet us.

I took my place beside the fire and gripped the hot bowl of mutton stew Fychan offered. Blowing on my hands to keep them from burning, I crouched on my haunches beside my brother and friends and listened to the conversations swelling up and around me.

Somehow I managed to answer most of the questions asked of me, as if my body were not in an uproar, as if my eyes were not yearning to follow every move the Druid brat made, as if my entire spirit was not tilting with the wind.

chapter 26

By the time we found our way back to Dinas the setting sun had reddened the sky over the ramparts and folk were already gathering in the Hall. I ran ahead of my companions, anxious to have a short time alone to puzzle out the raging whirlpool of feelings this strange magic of a day had set loose within me.

What did I know of Lleu really? What gave him the right to think he could do such a thing? And why, most of all, did I still feel heat when I thought of him? Not just heat, but an awareness that what he thought mattered to me: that his eyes, his face, his body were mysteries I wanted to solve.

Casting about for a distraction, I saw Grandmother standing, tall as ever, her long fingers resting on the carved fox's face on the pillar beside her. Her hand dipped casually to fondle the sculpted vine leaves that surrounded it, listening as Sari spoke to her. Watching the play of Grandmother's fingers upon the leaves, I followed their pattern as they circled around the pillar, masking and revealing mysterious shapes of animals, humans, and gods. Worlds within worlds. Shivering, I turned away from the carvings and looked at Sari.

Six sunturns free from Maelgwyn's clutches and set loose for the coming summer from the rigorous training of a seer, the former slave girl glowed with beauty. Since joining the seers, she had gone back to wearing the veils she had once discarded and now, with the bottom of her face covered with soft swaths of flowing cloth, she was as rare as mist rising from a far-off rainbow.

Turning from her conversation with Grandmother, Sari's eyes searched the Hall, resting on my brother Iorwerth as he laughed his way through the crowd. Her eyes followed him as he jumped the dais and flung himself to the bench beside Father's empty Seat.

Restless as ever, Iolo's own gaze swept the Hall. When he saw Sari, a slow smile spread across his face.

The seer dropped her eyes immediately, but not before I—newcome to such awareness—saw them darken in acknowledgement. The girl placed one small hand on Grandmother's arm and, with a slight bow, slipped away, heading towards the lower table where she joined Nest and the village women, already well along in their feasting.

Grandmother watched her go and glanced sideways at Iolo who now sat, sipping ale, gossiping with a visiting trader who stood behind him on the dais. Grandmother smiled, but it was a grim smile and I wondered at it. Why would she care where Iolo's eyes rested?

Familiar fingers ruffled my hair. "We will meet beside the harper's fire after you have consumed your usual great quantities of meat and bannock."

Merlin was smiling, but I stiffened, not in the mood to be teased about my appetite.

"Runala tells me he looks forward to your shapeshifting. Indeed, he feels, if he did not know better, you were born to be a squirrel."

I snorted and darted away before Uncle could tease me further, only to run headlong into Mother, almost knocking her against a trestle board.

"I'm sorry," I said stiffly, looking beyond her to the villagers' table where Cynan and Tali had already sprawled, regaling a group of cow-eyed girls with boastful stories.

"Gwen, I'm sorry too," Mother's voice caught. She coughed, looking as if she wanted badly to say something.

Whatever it was could wait. In this at least, I knew where I stood. I was taller than she was now, and made sure my shoulders were as straight as possible.

"It's all right, Mother. It was my fault." I bowed as if I were a courtier and ran to join Cynan, Lleu, and Tali who were now tearing into venison and rabbit stew as if they'd been starving for half a moontide.

"Save some for me, you great hog!" I shoved Cynan away from the honey cakes.

Cynan shoved me back and turned to the pretty girl beside him, passing her a platter heaped with his favorite chicken parts.

"My lady, would you care for some fowl?" he questioned, in a cuttingly accurate mimic of the insufferable eastern cousin we had had to tolerate for a fortnight earlier this spring.

The girl, a lamb-wit named Mera, giggled far more than the jest deserved. Emboldened, my brother bowed to her, his head coming suspiciously close to the plump breasts that pushed out of her low-cut gown like apples on display.

She lowered her lashes demurely. I tried not to gag.

Lleu slid down beside me. Would he not leave me alone?

"Are you all right?"

"Fine," I snapped.

He eyed me with care but said nothing more, turning instead to Tali. "Will you be playing tonight?"

"I think so." Tali smiled shyly, as if, after all this time, he was still not able to believe his good fortune. "Iolo has requested the *Lament of Hew for his Wife*"

At the mention of that well-loved ballad about a pompous ass and his unfaithful wife, I leaned forward. "Will you be playing anything else?"

Tali raised an eyebrow. "Do you have something in mind?"

"Do you know *The Lover's Question?*" I asked, refusing to look at Lleu, sensing rather than seeing his sudden interest in our conversation. It was an old sad song I had requested, with a melody I cherished in which a young girl asks her lover if he will remain true to her.

Under cover of throwing a bannock to Cynan, Lleu whispered, "Not sure of me yet, are you?"

Arrogant pig-headed rooster. I pretended I hadn't heard him.

Whether or not Tali had seen our byplay, he sketched a bow at me. "Anything for you, sweet lady."

Cynan and Lleu groaned. Mera, sensing that no one was paying attention to her, gave a pretty pout and asked Cynan to pour her some ale. He obeyed too quickly, spilling some of the horn in her lap, kissing her cheek, then her lips, in apology.

A burst of shouting from the warrior's table drowned out all other conversation. Instinct turned me to the High Table, in time to see Merlin put down the piece of chicken he'd been gnawing and turn hooded green eyes towards the door.

"Sing for us now, Tali!" Lleu called.

Before Tali could answer, a hound rose, growling. At his signal, all the other dogs stopped pacing and rose as one. A blast of chill air fluttered the torches. The entrance doors flew open, crashing against the stone walls with a dull thud that silenced the smoke-filled Hall.

Father strode in, flanked by sentries. Hwyll and a small band of his favored warriors fanned out around him, guarding something in their midst.

"Lord, this is indeed a welcome surprise. We did not expect you until the half-moon." Mother paced quickly down the Hall to greet him.

Father bent his head to kiss her. For a heartbeat, watching them, it was as if time ran backwards and they were the parents I had once adored.

Stepping away from her with a smile, Father addressed us all. "Nor would I have come—dear as you are to me, wife—had we not come across two most unexpected visitors."

Father's warriors stood aside, revealing a tall woman covered with more jewels than Mother wore on even the grandest occasion. The stranger gazed at us like a captured mountain cat, her feral golden-brown eyes alert, biding time until she could unsheathe her claws and attack.

Bejeweled as she was, her hair hung wet and bedraggled, falling loose over the shoulders of a borrowed warrior's cloak.

A girl stepped out from the folds of the woman's cloak, like some changeling from a harper's tale.

I jumped up on the table to see better.

The girl—for the wet black ropes of hair falling past her knees left no doubt that the strange creature was female—looked about our Hall like a princess from another world. Her deep golden eyes were more subdued than the woman's, but filled with strange lights, as if whoever possessed them was capable of anything.

Father looked from one to the other. "We found them, bobbing like Roman corks, in the deep seas beyond the Druid's isle of Mona."

"Had your man not saved us, Lady, my daughter and I would have drowned." The woman swayed with exhaustion, but forced herself to stand erect, meeting Mother's eyes. Her husky voice cracked. "You will find us grateful."

Paying no mind to the conversation, the girl continued to examine our Hall. Perhaps a sunturn or two older than I, clothed in ragged homespun, she nevertheless was poised as regally as her mother. Her gaze lingered on Father's prized oak pillars, noting the carved plant and animal faces, blessed with Druidic runes. Her strange cold eyes narrowed in dismissal and—although I was standing at the far end of the Hall at a commoner's table—her gaze then fell on me. Her harshly beautiful face registered surprise, then contempt, as if she was too fine a creature to bother with someone so lowly as me. Still, she stared and kept staring.

I tossed the curling strands of hair from my eyes, arched my brows in a fine imitation of Grandmother at her haughtiest, and glared back at her.

Merlin's thoughts swept through the air, speaking in my mind as if there was no distance between us at all.

"Sit, Gwen. Observe before you challenge. Do not call attention to yourself."

I shrugged him off with my mind and met the strange girl's gaze for another heartbeat before I took my seat again. She had a much slighter build then the woman. I was a good two handsbreadths taller; a fact that gave me some small satisfaction.

The girl's eyes traveled down the High Table, then came back to where I was sitting. Her eyes grazed over Cynan, pausing, then stopped to stare at Lleu. I rose again.

Merlin's hand appeared to be reaching for a bannock. Instead I felt it clasp down on my wrist—two spear lengths away.

"Control yourself!" he snarled, his voice unheard by all but me.

"You are welcome in this Hall." Mother said the ritual words with more curiosity then warmth. She was interrupted by Grandmother who came up behind her with the speed of a hawk bearing down on its prey.

"Ula, is it not?" Grandmother eyed the older stranger as if she had just seen maggots crawling from a stewpot.

The woman studied Grandmother's face. "So it would seem." Her voice lightened in what sounded like amusement.

"If you know this stranger, speak, Lady Rhiannon." Father looked from one to the other, trying to riddle it out. "For she has not yet offered her name, though we pulled her and the child from the straits of Mona."

"Aye, I know the bitch, Cadwallon. Better you had cast her back in the ocean while you still had the chance."

I ignored the gasps around me and walked closer to the dais to hear better, Tali, Lleu, Cynan, and Mera edged up close behind me.

Father raised his arm for silence. "Lady, whoever she is, she merits the courtesy given a guest in my Hall."

"Not this one, Cadwallon. Allow her to breathe our air at your peril." Grandmother stalked out of the Hall, followed quickly by Sari.

I started to follow them, curious to find out what Grandmother knew. Again, Merlin's hand yanked me back.

Pretending to stub my toe on something in the rushes, I sat down on a bench, sending an angry thought Merlin's way. "*Why—*"

"Be quiet and listen." I rubbed my arm where his invisible fingers had grabbed it, amazed how much it hurt.

Looking at my tormentor on the dais, I saw that Merlin's own face was pale, the Moon Singer tattoos on his cheekbones stood out like black feathers against snow.

The woman turned to Father and let the warrior's cloak slide from her shoulders, revealing a finely-woven linen overdress that clung, still-wet, to her slender body. "I am indeed called Ula. I did not speak when you rescued me for I was afraid."

"Afraid?" Father handed his own travel-stained cloak to a body servant and took his seat on the dais.

"The folk of Mona's isle still worship the Old Ones, as you know. They had cast me into the water covered with these jewels as a sacrifice to Dylan and his Wave Daughters."

The whispering in the Hall stopped. A hound beside the hearth growled a warning at another. Ula shrugged. "Two fisher-folk died in the last full moon's storm. They blamed me for it and sought to appease the God."

"And the child?"

"She is my daughter, Eithne. When she saw me thrown from the fisher's boat, she broke free of the folk watching from the shore, and threw herself into the sea. To save me or to die with me, I know not."

The girl had been staring at the floor rushes, now her strange hawk-golden eyes swept up to stare at her mother's face. The woman kissed her hair, her tense expression softening as the girl clutched for her hand.

Ula addressed Mother. "You will find us grateful," she said again. "I and my kinfolk."

"And who are your kinfolk, Lady Ula?" Father asked.

Mother gestured to a servant to bring meat.

The woman flung her head back, brushing drying grey-black hair from her face.

The long jewels she wore in her ears caught the torchlight and gleamed in sudden fire.

"My brother was Long Tooth of the Eastern Scotti, Lady." She smiled into the shocked hush.

Mother drew back as if bitten. Father rose. All around us folk were standing in rapidly dawning rage.

"You speak of one whose head adorned a pole outside this Hall, Lady." Father gestured the guards away.

I glanced at Mother. She had recovered and was sitting more calmly. If she remembered what she had done with Long Tooth's head she gave no sign.

"You speak of one who killed my kinsmen—who made widows of many in this Hall."

"This I know," Ula bowed her head, then met Father's eyes, her back as rigid as a queen's. "And I say again, you will find gratitude among my kinfolk. No matter what has been before."

"How came you to Mona?" Father sat down, his hands clasped tightly on the wolfskin covered arms of his High Seat. "And do not seek to riddle me, Lady. I begin to see why the fisher-folk choose you of all others to cast into the sea."

Ula harsh face cracked into a fleeting angry smile. I saw traces of once-great beauty. "I was cast out from my people. I and my child."

"Why?"

"The truth of Eithne's birth was discovered. As ruler of the Sunfacing Scotti in my brother Long Tooth's stead, I was to mate only with kings. My girl's true birth was hidden. She was given into the care of others so that I could become Queen."

"And how did your deception become known?"

She shrugged. "An enemy furnished proof that Eithne was my true daughter and I was banished from my homeland. Forced to flee in a coracle by moonlight. I who by rights should have been given a dragon-prowed king's ship manned by warriors."

Father ignored this bit of arrogance. Breaking off a bit of bannock, he leaned forward. "And the true father of this child?" His voice had grown very soft, still easy to hear in the listening silence of the Hall.

The woman shrugged a second time. "I cannot see that it matters, Lord."

"Oh, but it does, Lady."

"Why so?" She looked sincerely puzzled.

"I warn you, do not play with me." Father gestured to Hwyll, who wasted no time in walking towards Ula and her daughter, bringing two additional warriors with him.

Ula's feral eyes narrowed. "It has naught to do with you, Cadwallon. They said Eithne's father was a demon."

Ula stroked her daughter's hair as if to comfort her. A woman seated near me gasped aloud. There were rustlings up and down the benches, but the girl's hawk eyes only slit upwards in amusement.

"Aye, but you know better, Lady." Father's smile was slow, filled with menace. There were currents here I had no knowledge of although I felt them as an animal senses an oncoming storm.

Ula lowered her eyes. "Aye, that I do, my lord." Her right fist closed over a dagger that wasn't there.

Father nodded, satisfied. Rising, he gestured for Merlin to attend him. "We will say no more of this matter. You and your *daughter*, are welcome in this Hall until your kinfolk can come for you beneath a flag of treaty."

Father raised his hand as Ula opened her mouth to argue. "Or, if indeed you speak the truth—that you are a fugitive in exile from your native lands—you may stay until other arrangements have been made for your safe journey beyond the borders of Ordovice lands."

Ula sank back on the bench, and leaned her head against the wall, closing her eyes, as if defeated.

Father did not bother to look in her direction again, though he motioned Merlin closer. "Enough of this! It has been a long journey for my warriors. Tali, come forward please!"

With a smile at me, Tali rose and strummed the opening cords of the *Lament of Huw for his Wife* followed quickly with *The Lover's Question.*

But, by now, I was too preoccupied with the appearance of the strangers and the fierce undercurrents I had sensed around them to pay attention to Tali's fervent rendering of *The Lover's Question*. Nor did I note the way he looked at me as he plucked the final chord.

Folk relaxed a bit, but most still whispered in excitement or worry. The war with Maelgwyn and the Scotti was only six sunturns behind us, not nearly long enough for the scars of a mountain people to heal. There were still many who mourned kin lost in the battle of Dinas.

Standing behind the King's Seat, Merlin bent his head. Father spoke softly into his ear.

I watched the two strangers as they spied upon the Hall. Eithne's eyes lingered on Lleu. He shared a horn of mead with me, seeming oblivious of the intensity of her predatory stare.

And I remembered: myself, as a child of five summers, swimming with my brothers on the coast. We had been laughing, diving under and then jumping over the waves, dunking each other when we wanted to wrestle.

Cynan had thrown me into a wave trough. I surfaced, laughing. But as I turned to face the sea, all I saw was a great high wave coming towards me at terrifying speed. Cynan was closer to shore and screamed for Iolo.

The wave crashed over me. I couldn't breathe. I tumbled beneath it, sand filling my open mouth. It pushed me, choking, to the bottom and pulled me with it out to sea.

Iorwerth swam after me and pulled me back to shore. But I took no more joy in waves. I had become terrified of the ocean.

Now, as I watched the strangers, I knew them to be as deadly evil as that wave. And I wished with all my heart that Father had not saved them from drowning.

chapter 27

At dawn the next morning, Merlin left at Father's request, to investigate the truth of Ula's story.

Before he left, he came to wake me in my old summer room, the chamber I had once shared with Hwyrch in the eastern tower. Never a graceful riser, I grumbled as he shook my shoulder.

Merlin's eyes were weary and stern above the shadows of the rush light he carried. "Rise quickly, I must leave and I want to spend some time with you."

Rubbing sleep from my eyes, I sat up, threw an old gown over my sleeping shift and followed him outside the tower into the thick morning mist.

He waited to speak until we were midway across the meadow that separated our earthworks from the forest. Tall wet grass brushed against my shins. I shivered, and not just with cold, for it was a time of ghosts. Past dark, yet not yet light. Mist covered the world like a winding shroud, muffling sound as well as sight.

"I must be gone from you for a time, Shadow. This business of the Scotti witch woman will take but a moontide, perhaps a bit more. But after that, I must journey south again and stay there for two sunturns or more."

I found myself reaching for his hand. A hollowness opened inside me. When I could speak it was but two words, "Why now?"

Merlin sighed and squeezed my hand gently. "There is a great power rising in the South, child. It rests yet only in the heart of that young southern boy you so resent—Arthur is not much older then you."

I could feel him looking down at me, sensed the care behind his words. But I kept my eyes on the pine needles and rocks beneath my feet, watching the tendrils of mist that all but hid them.

He crouched down beside me. "Gwen, look at me."

I raised my face, willing him not to see the tears. I was far too old for them. "But you just got back, Merlin! Who is this Arthur that he demands so much of your time?"

"Ah, hush, sweet one." He gathered me to him.

Old as I was, I began to cry like a little girl, the familiar wood-smoke scent of his tunic making it all worse.

"Would you have our land be conquered by villains and pirates like your Uncle and the Vortigern?"

I shook my head, burrowing deeper against the soft wool of his traveling clothes. "Then I must go to see that this boy is given the training in the Old Ways he will need when the time comes."

"But what about me? And Cynan? And Tali? And Lleu?" As upset as I was, a tingle ran through me as I spoke Lleu's name. "We haven't even shape-shifted yet!"

He laughed. "We will do so when I come back from Eire. That I promise! It will take but a moontide or two for me to discover the truth of Ula's tale. Much as I would care to, Shadow, I cannot linger," he sighed, petting my hair as if it was a pony's mane. "I must go South again within a fortnight of my return to you"

He kissed the top of my head and lifted my chin. "There is one thing I would ask of you, child. I have asked it before and will again."

He paused and remained silent until I reluctantly met his eyes. "Try to understand your mother. No one has ever died of embroidering, you know."

"Then I will be the first!" If he, a Mage, did not know that the problems between Mother and I went far deeper then arguments about chores, I would not tell him. My tears had stopped, but another different sorrow rose, one that had plagued me ever since I had left the healers' village.

"Merlin, who will help me practice the forest magics when you are gone?"

He looked a bit surprised. "Surely, you have not forgotten your Grandmother?"

"But, she is so busy..." Perhaps I did not need to add that Grandmother's bitterness made me shy from her now, after the sweetness of Arias the healer.

"She has much to teach you still." As ever Merlin seemed to read my thoughts. "Your Grandmother is more than she seems. But for now," he shrugged, "simply remember what we have learned together, what the healers have shared, and what you have learned for yourself. Practice Gwen, and grow...Before you know it, I will be back to see what you have accomplished."

"But—"

"And then, of course, there is always Lleu.".

"Lleu! What do you mean?" I was horrified to feel blood rush to my face and knew Merlin must see my blush.

"So it is like that already, eh?"

I ducked my head, infuriated and embarrassed.

Merlin laughed, a rich rippling sound that dipped and soared through the mist. "I am glad for you, child. Lleu possesses both wisdom and talent. He is of the Old Ones in ways that neither of you yet understand."

I snorted and took a step away from him into the trees beyond the path. Searching beneath the mist for something to distract us both, I found a rotting acorn amid the bracken that had survived both the rooting pigs of autumn and a winter filled with snow. I held it up and tossed it over my shoulder.

Merlin caught it in midair and turned it over in his palm with a delighted smile— as if I had handed him a King's jewel. "Do you remember the first thing I ever taught you about magic, Gwen?"

I thought back over the many conversations we had shared along this very forest path and further—in mountain meadows, on lake shores, in the Great Hall itself. I remembered the time we had gone to meet the Arch-Druid on the sacred isle of Mona. Yet I knew, it was none of these that Merlin referred to. "Do you mean the time you showed me the apple?"

He grinned at that. It was a smile I rarely saw from him, a smile that made the lines of care and power carved into his face disappear. Tall as I was, he picked me up and tossed me into the air as if I were a feather. When he set me down again, he squatted beside me in the clammy morning mist. I giggled and began to trace the crescent moon marks on his cheekbones, as I had done when I had first met him long ago. They marked him as the Mage he was and, as always, he preferred to hide them beneath the long free fall of his hair.

"That's it, Shadow." He gave me back the acorn. "Now remember what I told you and look at this tiny scrap of the forest...Tell me what you see."

I remembered what he had said about the apple. It had been many seasons ago, in the first days after he had come to live with us at Dinas. He and I had been exploring an abandoned orchard and had gotten caught in a late summer rainstorm.

Ignoring the weather, Merlin picked an apple from the sodden ground and began to twirl the fruit like a juggler.

I was wet, soaked, and miserable. Eight sunturns old: a cranky little girl.

"Can we go home now?" I had asked.

He tossed the apple to me. I caught it by reflex. Angry, I started to throw it away.

"Wait!" he commanded. "Look at what is in your hand."

Grudgingly, I obeyed. Beneath the shiny red-gold surface, a small doorway appeared and opened. I screamed and dropped the fruit.

"Pick it up!" Merlin's voice was distant, yet as hard as iron. It was a voice I later come to know well, a voice of power that he used when his patience with me was exhausted.

I squinted my eyes into the pouring rain that slammed and puddled against the ground beneath the trees. I found the apple I had dropped and held it up for his approval.

He gestured impatiently. "Look again."

The doorway was still there, still open. Shielding the apple from the rain with a corner of my cloak I saw the door had opened on a forest filled with tiny apple trees. Some were winter bare, some covered with spring blossoms, others ripe with red-gold fruit. A delicious scent of blossoms mingling with sweet autumn cider rose around me. Oblivious now to the rain, I bent over the fruit, hearing the strange, gurgling music of another world.

Speechless, I regarded Merlin.

He took time to rearrange his own drenched cloak before he nodded. "You see, Gwen, true magic comes from seeing what is really there. All things natural to this world's realm contain the seeds of beauty. If you honor them they will hear and help you—if they choose to do so."

Remembering now, I smiled. Gazing at the surface of the winter-softened acorn, I let my fingers play along the smooth cold surface, until they reached the bumpy ring that banded it. As my fingers touched the band, the acorn sprang open, as if it was a locked chest and I had turned the key. Inside, stood an oak tree, so tiny I could barely make out its branches, yet behind it was another and another. Music rose like a sweet wave from far away, parting the mist so that I could see Merlin clearly.

He was smiling at me. "You see, Shadow, great things are usually contained in the most ordinary of places. Never forget this. It is the heart of all magic."

"That is why you had me follow the squirrel, isn't it?"

Merlin held out his hand. I gave him back the acorn. He passed a hand over it, murmuring words in a language that sounded like the forest tongue but was somehow different, as if a bard were singing into the wind without a harp.

"Small things do not always like to give up their secrets, child." He handed the acorn back to me. "You will one day be a queen. Never be so proud that you forget this."

I put the acorn in my belt pouch and hugged him. "Must you go?"

"You know better than to ask," he said, ruffling my hair in the same way he always had. "The mission your father has given me is of great importance to us all. The Scotti woman and her offspring have power to affect the coming storm. It is best we know as much as we can of them"

"You'll be back for the midsummer festival?"

"If all goes well in Eire, I will be back. Didn't I say I would come? Your midsummer revels should never be missed." Despite the lightness of his words, Merlin's face had become as distant as the unseen lands he traveled. A magician prince again, no longer the playful uncle I adored.

His face was pale, his eyes grim and exhausted.

"I will miss you terribly."

He kissed my hair. "It shall pass, child. And when I return from the South, I expect you to have applied the lessons I have tried so hard to drum into that thick skull of yours."

"I will try, Uncle."

Too sad and near to tears to stand beside him without breaking down like an undignified baby again, I walked farther down the trail. The mist had all but gone, revealing a world taking its first breath of spring. Early sun cut across the path like a sword, illuminating the snowdrops and tiny violets that bloomed, shy as fairies, beneath the great forest oaks. Near the trail, high stream waters tumbled over rocks, the cascading rhythm pierced by the trilling of forest larks.

The air itself was so full of promise, I wanted to take great gulps of it—to eat it like a honey cake. Yet all my heart had room for was the thought that Merlin was leaving—and after one short midsummer visit, I would not see him until I was a woman grown.

I wished the world back to winter.

After Merlin's leave-taking, I dressed in my old trews, ignoring the pile of new gowns that sat, smug as well-fed cats, in my clothes chest.

I was chewing moodily on a bit of hardened cheese in the Hall when Mother appeared, the Scotti girl's hand held firmly in her own.

"Gwen, this is Eithne—a guest in our Hall." This last Mother added as she saw my already-glum expression grow darker.

I nodded at the girl. I had hoped to avoid her, but Mother would make that impossible. "Since the pack of you plan to help drive the sheep up to their summer pastures, perhaps you could take Eithne along?"

"She'd no doubt find it boring." I rose, stretched, and began to turn away.

Eithne glared at me, her slanted eyes narrowing with contempt.

"Nevertheless, Gwen, it might help her pass the time to be with others her own age." Mother's voice had taken on the sweet tones of a threat.

"Come on then," I sighed, turning to the witch girl. "Morgant will be waiting for us."

Eithne tossed her head and preceded me through the door of the Hall.

"You'll have to change your clothes," I called after her.

She paused in the doorway not bothering to turn around.

"You can't ride through the mountains in a gown like that," I continued. Clearly, the girl had spent her life indoors, not lifting a finger unless it was to brush crumbs from her newest silk overdress.

As if to answer my thoughts, Eithne smoothed her hands along the rich linen of her embroidered overskirt and looked me up and down. "And just where would I find trews as filthy as your own? Perhaps a slave might lend some to me?"

I almost flew at her and stopped myself just in time, knowing that it was precisely what she wanted and would only make things worse. "I see they do not believe in teaching manners in the Halls of the Scotti. Of course, I shouldn't be surprised. Pirates have little use for such things."

I sauntered past her, sidestepping her kick. "My brother may be able to find clothes to suit you, highness. Although you are a bit broader in the stomach, still—"

She lunged at me. I jumped back, laughing.

"I wouldn't go on your filthy sheep run for all the treasure in the Mountain King's Hall!" she screamed.

I shrugged and went outside, leaving her, shrieking, behind me.

"Gwen, aren't you coming?" Lleu ran across the courtyard, already filthy. "Morgant won't wait much longer."

Clearly, he had been working with Father's new horses, one of his greatest loves. Now, he paused in front of me, pushing sweat and hair from his face, leaving a smear of thick muck on his cheekbones, where it blended with his new-made warrior tattoos.

I smiled at him, suddenly happy. It was hard muddy work to drive the sheep up to their summer pastures in the mountains, but the ride through the spring-dappled mountains would be worth it.

"I'm ready! Just let me get Dancer." I had already skipped into the stables when I heard Eithne's voice behind me.

"Oh, Lleu! Do you think you could find me a pony? Lady Ceridwen has asked me to come with you." No longer shrieking, her voice had become as warm as honey as she spoke to Lleu.

I kicked a hay bundle, cursing.

At the sight of Dancer, happily chewing her morning oats, my heart lightened. In the few days since Father had given her to me, I had fallen ever deeper in love with the beautiful young mare. She could run faster than the wind itself across the meadows where I raced her, showing much greater spirit then my beloved old pony, Shadlock, would ever dream of.

"Good morning, princess." Dancer nosed my tunic in welcome, searching for the dried apple slices I carried. I pulled them out and she dipped her head, nosing gracefully at my open palm, letting me stroke the dark red brown of her flank.

We joined Cynan and Lleu in the courtyard and rode out to the winter pen to help Morgant organize the shepherds' supplies.

Then we waited. And waited.

By the time Eithne was outfitted with suitable clothing and given provisions for our stay in the mountains, Morgant, the head shepherd was fit to burst. His normal ill-temper notched up to fury at the delay and he turned from us all, giving curt instructions to his sons and the men who had come to help.

My brother, Lleu, and I took our places in back of the line, ready to work our way. The ride back would be easy, but the ride up to the summer pastures was always a challenge. Even though the worst of the spring mud had dried, the mountain trails were still close to impassable and we would be responsible for catching any sheep that tried to stray.

At last, we were ready. Grandmother passed the journeying cup to Morgant whose polite sip did little to mask his irritation at Eithne's delay. With an abrupt shout and wave, he started us off.

I grinned at Cynan, my heart rising at the thought of full days away from the everyday chores of Dinas. Cynan kicked his pony to ride beside me, clasping my hand as we waved grandly to the guards on the palisades.

Despite Morgant's grumpiness, the rest of us were in good spirits, grateful for the weak sunshine that danced hesitantly on the newly-budded branches of the forest trees. But whatever ill god had possessed Mother to invite Eithne, I knew not, for as soon as we left Dinas, she kicked her borrowed pony brutally and galloped ahead of us, sulking, clearly as dim about sheep as they were about themselves.

She was, however, not so dim about Lleu.

Midway up the mountain track, we came to a plateau where we could rest. Eithne wandered over to join us where Lleu, Cynan, and I sprawled, happily munching cold venison, looking up at the pine-covered mountains that enclosed us. I saw her coming and turned away, pretending she didn't exist.

"I wonder if it's true that Epona still visits these hills?" Lleu asked.

"I'm sure she does." I took a large bite of venison and chewed it thoughtfully, "She is the goddess of horses after all. These secret valleys would be the best place in the world to raise her herds."

Eithne found a large rock beside us. After eyeing it with annoyance, she rubbed the loose earth and small pebbles from its surface with a corner of her borrowed cloak and sat down. "I doubt that Epona would bother with your mountains, Gwenhwyfar. She would be much more likely to go where the pasture was finer—where horses grow a bit larger then hounds. In Lleu's kingdom, for example."

She reached her hand out for Cynan's water flask. My brother finished drinking and handed it to her reluctantly.

"Our ponies might be small, but they can cover terrain that would kill one of those lumbering giants you speak of." I willed myself to stay calm.

She shrugged. "Lleu, tell me of your family. How came you to be here—among these Ordovice." In Eithne's mouth, *Ordovice* came out sounding like a wasting disease.

I flicked an imaginary insect from my tunic, remembering to take deep breaths as Arias had taught me.

Politely inclining his head, Lleu answered her. Cynan rose to join the shepherds, bored with a story he already knew. I stayed, watching Eithne's golden eyes darken as Lleu spun his tale of the alliance between my family and the Druids of his Wolf Clan.

"How exciting it must have been for you to be raised by your grandfather's Druids!" Eithne sighed and leaned nearer to him. "Don't you ever get bored in this backwater land?"

I snorted. But Lleu answered her in a serious voice. "No, not at all. There is much to see and do here."

He paused. I felt his eyes on my back and turned to look at him. "Much to learn."

Eithne saw us and was quiet for a heartbeat. Then she smiled at us both. "Oh, I suppose—if you like slogging through mud and filth and ice and snow…"

Her eyes were on me, she seemed to have forgotten Lleu. She continued in a voice like droning bees. "If you like eating half-cooked meat in a Hall that smells of smoke and shit…listening to the same boring harp sagas every night while you pick lice out of your hair—there would be much to learn at Dinas Emrys."

She smiled sweetly at me.

I rushed at her, all my good intentions forgotten.

Still smiling, triumphantly now, Eithne crouched into a battle stance, reaching for the knife she carried in her boot. "Come on then, little princess of the dung-heap!"

I had nothing but my food dagger, but I drew it. We circled each other.

I locked eyes with her, remembering that much from Iolo's knife-fighting techniques. Frantically, I searched my brain, trying to remember what else I should do.

"Stop!" Lleu yelled and jumped between us.

Eithne grabbed the chance, ducked under his arm and came at me. Stepping back I stumbled. She was on top of me, smashing my hand until I let go of my knife. Kicking up, I grabbed her knife hand with my free hand and twisted as hard as I could. She was stronger then she looked. Holding onto her knife, she increased the pressure until the blade was so close to my face I saw only a blur.

Panicking, I bucked off the ground as hard as I could and howled like a wolf—the battle cry Cynan and I used in play battles. She drew back at the noise—just a little—but enough for me to knee her and roll free.

I jumped up, spitting in rage. She was already up, lunging at me. But this time, her knife arm was held back by a red-faced Morgant. "Stop it, you little bitch, or I'll throw you off the mountain!"

Eithne was too far gone in rage to heed him. Long hair streaming free from the jeweled net she wore to contain it, she spat like a cat and tried again to go for me.

Morgant twisted her arm back, cursing. With a final shriek she dropped her knife and stood panting, both arms now pinned behind her, glaring at me.

Cynan rushed to my side.

Morgant roared at the crowd that had gathered. "Back to work, all of you! We've got a long way to go before nightfall!" The shepherds dispersed leaving me to stand with Cynan.

Lleu stood in Morgant's shadow, watching me. More then once his eyes flickered to Eithne, who now stood breathing calmly, arms still pinned by the shepherd.

"Are you all right, Gwen?" Morgant asked in a voice not quite as gruff as usual.

I nodded. He turned to Eithne. "I've a mind to tie you up for the rest of the day."

"Don't." Lleu jumped down from the rock he'd been standing on. "She won't do it again. Will you?"

Red-faced, Eithne was cursing Morgant to a nightmare afterlife. When she heard Lleu's appeal, she grew silent, eyeing him up and down. At last she nodded.

"You are sure about this, princeling?" Like many folk at Dinas, Morgant had taken to Lleu and treated him as if he really was part of our family. The oldest of us, Lleu had the right to make the decision. But it did not sit well with Morgant—and it did not sit well with me.

What was Lleu doing? How could he defend her? She almost killed me!

Morgant looked the foreign girl over and spat into the tall grass a hairsbreadth from her feet, "The youngster vouches for you. Just see that you get no more ideas. I'll be watching." He gave the pinned hands a none-too-gentle shake and loosed her. "And next time—guest or not—I'll see you taken prisoner."

Eithne tossed her head and walked towards Lleu, without so much as a glance at the shepherd or me.

She looked up at Lleu's face then lowered her eyes. "Thank you."

He colored. "Just behave yourself." He pushed past her and joined Cynan and me as we helped pack up the supplies.

At a nod from Morgant, the shepherd's oldest son helped Eithne mount. Without a word, he directed her to follow him past the complaining sheep, to the back of our line. As she passed me, already mounted on Dancer, Eithne's eyes turned murderous. I met her glare with a snarl of my own and we moved out to climb the steepest part of the pass.

The happiness of my day was shattered. Why had Lleu stood up for a girl who tried to kill me?

My heart sinking, I watched as Lleu kneed his horse ahead of us. Once the most treacherous stretch of trail was behind us, he began talking to Morgant as if sheep were the most important thing in the world.

I tried not to look at Eithne, tried to pretend that I was too important to be bothered with such a murderous little witch. But I found myself glancing back at her more and more frequently as the afternoon shadows lengthened. And every time I did, I saw her golden eyes gleam as they watched Lleu's back.

chapter 28

Beneath the soft golden blues of twilight, we drove the bleating sheep around the final bend of the mountain trail where the sweet high meadow lay. The young shepherds yipped with excitement, racing their tired ponies towards the stone bothies that would serve as their summer homes.

Morgant pushed through the high-spirited crowd as we set up camp for the night, distributing bannocks and nutbreads Maeve and the village women had baked. Rubbing his hands and grunting his thanks when Cynan passed him a water skin, the grizzled shepherd crouched beside us at the cooking fires, promising to broach the mead casks after supper. Cheers rang out. Tired as we were, we were all young and strong drink was always welcome.

Taking comfort in the warmth of the fire and the horseplay of my friends, I still yearned for time alone and escaped to bring water from a nearby stream.

Instead of returning right away, I stopped to rest, putting the two heavy water buckets down to flex my aching hands. The sky was now as dark as a mourner's gown. The god-star had appeared in the north, bright enough to silhouette the mountain peaks that ringed us.

I spun in a circle, craning my neck to see as far as I could, forgetting the pain in my hands and the sorrow and confusion of the day as more and more white stars appeared, forming a ceiling of the gods.

Long ago, Mother had said it was good luck to wish on stars, many of whom were maidens like me, living among the sky clans.

I choose my star carefully. It shone high above the god-star, almost on the roof of the sky, apart from the nearest cluster. I thought it might be a young girl like me, wanting to live alone in her own small Hall, a spear's throw from her kin.

What did I wish for? To wish Merlin back would not be right. From the jumbled, hurtful day, one face stood clear. Lleu. Lleu and the way he had looked at the angry witch girl. Not just pity or anger had crossed his face—there had been something more.... and I wished the Scotti girl away, beyond the sea, taking her arrogant mother with her to trouble us no further.

As I wished, I saw Eithne's face clearly. She was, I knew, very beautiful. Her long black hair and golden eyes made her look older than sixteen sunturns. She looked a woman grown, with the high breasts and ripe hips to prove it. I had seen the way the shepherds looked at her. They were suspicious of her power, for I saw them make the ancient warding signs if her gaze fell upon them. But they made the signs secretly, as if to spare her feelings. And when she looked away, they watched her as they would have watched a glorious sunrise.

Thus I made my wish from fear: *Let her leave us.*

An owl hooted. I jumped. Cynan came out from the shadows of a small tree grove near the stream.

"Was that you pretending to be an owl?"

He flapped his arms and danced around me in circles, hooting like a madman. "Aren't you impressed? Hwyll is teaching us animal calls as part of our warrior's training."

At another time, I would have asked him to teach me how to make such sounds. Tonight, I only asked help carrying the water.

"Are you all right, brat?" He peered at my face, shadowed beneath the light of the half-moon. "You look mazed—more then usual, I mean."

He skipped away before I could hit him.

"I'm fine. Just thinking."

"She bothers you a lot, doesn't she?"

"She tried to kill me, Cynan. And she would have if she could have gotten away with it."

He put his arm around my shoulder. I leaned against him, a bit shy. This was not the way we usually behaved together.

"Teach me to fight, Cynan. Really fight," I whispered. "It is not fair that women are not trained alongside their brothers."

"Grandmother says it was not always so." He took his arm from my shoulder and picked up the bucket. "Last moontide, she came to the Warriors' Hall to teach us how to care for wounds. After she was finished, she addressed us all—boys and men—to remind us that, before the red-cloaks came, Ordovice women trained for battle and fought and died beside their men."

"I wish I could have lived then." I straightened my back, no longer feeling the weight of the water pail. "But, I'm alive now, and I want to learn *now*!"

We were coming up on the camp. Men bustled around us, laying down pallets for the night, checking the bleating sheep that had been herded into a natural pen shaped by rock at the southern end of the meadow.

Cynan stopped walking and looked at me. "Then you shall, sister. I will see to it if Father won't." Beyond the shadows of his face, the fires burned high and welcoming. In the distance I heard Morgant's voice, organizing the first watch.

I hugged him, sloshing water on us both.

"Thank you."

He patted me awkwardly. "Brat that you are, Shadow, I don't want to see you killed. The next time that little bitch tries something—trip her up and slit her throat."

I looked up at Cynan's face. The hurt and confusion I had been carrying since the fight fell away. "Trust me, brother, I look forward to it."

I could not sleep. Camp noise died around me until all was quiet save for the occasional soft cries of sheep and nearby rustlings in the grass as small animals made their journeys through the night. Still I tossed atop my deerskin pallet.

I looked up at the stars, willing them to speak to me. At last, I gave up, wrapped my cloak around me, and left the circle of the camp. At the northern end of the meadow lay a circle of tall stones. Smaller then other circles of their kind, the rocks of this gathering were so old that any clan marks of their coming had long been covered by the earth. Some leaned as if they had drunk too much mead, others slanted towards each other as if whispering. I walked into the center of them and found a seat upon the flat altar stone. In the depths of the night mist it seemed to be the only thing that anchored the other stones to the earth.

Here, far from human fires, the only light came from the half-moon and its attendant stars and from the mist itself.

"Grandmothers..." I whispered.

A shadow detached itself from the tallest stone. Lleu.

He sat beside me on the altar stone. "It is beautiful here, isn't it?"

I said nothing, furious that he invaded my night.

The silence between us continued, taking on a bitter quality, not like the silences that we had shared in the past. We both knew how to turn our attention inwards and sit quietly together. But this was not a friendly silence.

He threw a pebble into the mist, his voice edged with anger. "When will you come to understand that I am your friend? I do not hate you."

The pebble landed somewhere beyond the stones without a sound. "How could you defend her? She tried to kill me!"

"Gwen, do you still not understand? A being that walks in shadows—as she does—should not be granted any more attention than is necessary. Eithne lives to stir up trouble. She feeds on fear. To have made her prisoner would have given her far more power than you. Surely, you do not want that!"

I did not speak.

"Gwen," he touched my shoulder, "look at me."

Reluctantly, I raised my eyes. Beneath the half-light of the setting moon and stars, his face was shadowed, watching me. "Do you really believe I would ever seek to harm you?"

I looked at him for long enough to feel the damp rock chill of the stone seep through the weave of my cloak. Still I searched his face.

"All right," I answered, softly. "I believe you."

"You are cold," he smiled.

I rested my head on his shoulder and closed my eyes, hearing the early birds begin to call hesitantly to each other. Lleu rubbed my arm to warm it and gathered me closer to him. "We are destined for each other, you know."

I shook my head. "Your father seeks a higher bride prize then the daughter of a northern wilderness chief. I heard Father tell Mother that Chalan wants to wed you to the daughter of the Silurian king." It had been only a moontide ago, right after I first returned to Dinas, when I passed through the Hall and overheard Father speaking.

A moontide ago, yet if I closed my eyes, I could still remember the smooth weave of the wall hanging that I touched, listening to Mother's polite answer, neither of them caring much beyond their sovereign interest in the network of allies and marriage alliances that spun eternally from Dinas.

Alliances and allies. Now, my fingers dug deeply again, so deeply into the weave of my cloak, they tore its strands apart. I felt the cold stone beneath me, trying not to weep.

"Father does not control my fate, much as he would like to."

I looked at him, puzzled. The sky had begun to lighten in the soft breath of dawn. The smile he offered was grim, almost sad. "You forget, I am the grandson of the most powerful Druid to walk these mountains since before the red-cloaks came. And my mother, as I once told you, is of the Lake Dwellers."

"Tell me about her."

He took one of my hands and chaffed the coldness from it with both of his own. "Father was returning from a hunt and a spring storm separated him from his companions. He made camp alone near the Pass of the Flying Swans and saw her bathing in the moonlight in the waters of Lake Bala singing with her sisters on stones close to the shore.

"When he called to her, she was afraid and disappeared beneath the waters. Yet he could not forget her and went to his father—my grandfather Blind Hawk—and asked him for help.

"Grandfather agreed and told my father to return to the lake, that all would be as he wanted; for my father was his only son and Blind Hawk denied him nothing." Lleu squeezed my hand so hard, I winced. "Father returned to the lake and waited.

"Blind Hawk cast a spell upon the lake waters and my mother rose from the depths. She huddled, shivering and naked, on the rocks, crying to rejoin her sisters beneath the surface. Yet every time she tried to dive to join them, an invisible wall would rise around her and she could not move."

Lleu dropped my hand and made fists of his own which he held quietly against the thighs of his homespun trews.

"Father rowed his coracle to where she sat, imprisoned on the rocks. He carried her to the boat and rowed with her to the shore.

"He raped my mother on the gravel of the shoreline. Three times he had her as small lake waves ebbed and flowed about them and when, at last, he'd had his fill of her, he rose and presented her with his finest golden arm band, worked with amethysts and amber, and left her alone, weeping, beside the lake."

Pale dawn light suffused the world around us. Morning mist

entered the stones with the determination of an army, so dense it cut us off from everything but each other. Lleu stopped speaking, listening to another world, just beyond the ken of understanding. Yet I knew before he spoke it, what the end would be and I drew closer to him, one of my hands reaching out to cover his own.

"Ten moontides later, my father received a strange messenger. It was the darkest part of winter, yet the man wore but a sealskin cloak and low spring boots, despite the deep drifts of the passes, which were closed to all but the most foolish traveler.

"He bowed to my father and laid Chalan's own golden arm band on the rushes of the floor beneath the king's High Seat. 'My lady bids me tell you of a son born during the first storms of winter. If you would raise him as a Prince of your clan, you must claim him when the snowdrops return to the valley of the Dying Swans. If you can win him from her father, you may raise him as your own.' "

"You were that baby, weren't you?" Forgetting in my excitement, the sorrow in Lleu's voice, my hand tightened on his.

Lleu blinked as if he had awakened. He turned to me in surprise. "Yes, I was. I had the tale from my mother, herself, when I was allowed to visit her as a child during snowmelt." He shook my hands away and stood to stretch.

"But what did your father have to do to win you back from the Lake Dwellers?"

He shook his head. "That is a tale for another time, Gwenhyfar. Now," he planted a playful kiss on the top of my head, "I must ask you not to share what I have told you. Not even with Cynan. The story is for you alone."

"But—"

"Promise!" His hands dug painfully into my arms.

"Of course, I will not speak of it, what do you take me for?"

"Now that question has far too many answers, some of which may not please you at all—"

I threw a tuft of grass at him and soon we were wrestling on the grass, much as I always did with Cynan. This felt altogether different and when he pinned my arms to my sides, I struggled to get free.

"I'll let you up in a heartbeat, but remember, I too can be as stubborn as one of these great rocks." He leaned close, his smile as fierce as a pirate's, kissing my cheeks, my nose, my mouth.

I closed my lips against him and tried to break away—although I did not try very hard and soon found my arms lifting, holding him close against my breasts as heat raced within me. His lips sought mine again. This time I met him, opening my lips beneath his tongue. When we could speak again, he whispered hoarsely in my ear. "In this we are as one. And I tell you, my father knows nothing of my destiny. Nor—if I speak with honor—do I."

He kissed me hard and deep. "Yet I know you are as much a part of me as the wind upon the sea."

My body arched, melting against his. He pulled up, supporting himself on his arms and kissed my nose. "I have seen but seventeen sunturns and you barely fourteen, but I know that in the days to come, I will have no other by my side." He freed a raven's feather from his warrior's braid and handed it to me "Take this as my pledge to you." He kissed my cheek and then my mouth.

"This I swear by the Goddess and the God." His mouth on mine was hard, yet cool, softening as it touched my lips. He jumped up. I was free.

I sat up, watching him disappear into the mist, going back into the world of human campfires and old jests, of wet sheepskins hung up to dry on low-hanging branches.

Wrapping my dew-drenched cloak around me, I huddled in the tall grass beside the stones and drew my knees close to my chest, twirling the raven's feather over and over in my hands, thoughts and feelings ripping through me like a lightning storm at sunset; giddy with his kisses and the strange feel of his body cresting mine.

It had been six sunturns since I had felt the wine-sodden, heavy crush of Vortigern upon me and, despite the peace of the healers' village, the night terrors had not fully ceased. Yet I had felt no fear, no rage, when Lleu kissed me, only a sense that a door had opened in my world. Where it led, I knew not, only that I would walk inside, no matter what awaited me.

chapter 29

When I was a little girl, anytime the world confused me, I lost myself in action. Sometimes I hit my brother, sometimes I ran madly down the hill of Dinas, pin-wheeling my arms as if I was a bird in flight. Sometimes I sought the stables and went riding. That is what I decided to do now.

Returning to my sleeping furs only long enough to hang them up to dry and change into dry trews and warm boots, I sought the corner of the meadow where I had last seen Dancer. She came at my whistle and nuzzled me in greeting. Delighted with her, I pulled out the dried oats I had taken from my pack.

She chewed noisily. I leaned my head against the smooth muscles of her neck, drawing strength from the sweet horse smell of her. "You've never had to bother with boys, have you?" A sympathetic nicker. "But I don't suppose stallions are much fun either, are they?" She dipped her head as if in answer and lowered her head to graze again, letting a steaming pile of manure loose from her backside. I giggled.

"Ready?" I grabbed hold of her mane and leapt up on her back, marveling as always at the new view of the world she gave me. Kneeing her forward, I felt the response in her flanks, shifting eagerly beneath me for Dancer loved to run as much as I.

"Twice around the valley, shall we?" She whinnied, gaining speed without my urging, beginning to canter, then to run.

I knew the path, knew that the track around the meadow was well-worn and flat. No dangerous surprises, no sudden tree roots, bogs, or ground holes existed to slow us down. Despite the mist, we galloped, my tension and confusion about Lleu falling farther and farther behind with every drum of Dancer's hooves upon the wet ground.

Yet I could not outrun myself nor the passion and wonder he wakened within me.

Dancer leapt over a rock. My heart soared, airborne, the power of my feelings flying joyously into the mist. We hit the ground and dreary recognition came—no matter what Lleu and I promised each other beneath the stars, our parents would force us along the paths they demanded.

We completed the first pass around the valley, and were edging into the wide turn that would take us through the horse pasture and out again, when I heard a sharp crack in front of us. Peering into the dense wet of the surrounding mist, I saw nothing. The sound came again, sharper this time. Dancer slid on the slippery grass and reared up in alarm. I struggled to right myself. My body began to slide; I tried one final grab at Dancer's mane—and my hands closed on empty air. With a cry, I let go and rolled off the horse, turning a somersault in midair. Landing flat on my back, the wind knocked from me, I rolled quickly away from Dancer's crashing hooves.

A rabbit ran in front of me. A girl shouted. "Did you hurt yourself?"

I sat up, furious. It was Eithne, appearing in the mist like a brightly-colored butterfly. Dressed in plaid trews of red, blue, and green, a rich crimson tunic, wearing so many golden arm bands that she clanged like a warrior going into battle.

The witch girl stopped in front of me and began to laugh. "So this is the vaunted horse-craft of the powerful Ordovice! A princess who loses her seat to a bunny?"

Before I could obey my instinct—which was to rise and strangle her—I remembered Lleu's words. Knowing he was right, that Eithne gained power only if others gave it to her, I got to my feet calmly, ignoring her.

Dancer, now on all fours, looked embarrassed. She walked cautiously to where I stood and bent her head, nosing my neck in apology. I mounted without a word, hiding my grunt at the pain in my rump behind a cough.

Dancer arched her neck beneath my reassuring hand, only then did I speak. "The ruling family of our clan is taught manners in our Hall. Do you plan to stay long enough to learn some?"

Eithne stooped to pick up a small stone. "I would rather be cast back into the freezing sea then stay longer then I must in your stinking robber's Hall." Idly, she threw the stone over Dancer's head. The horse's ears flickered. At my whisper she quieted.

"Then perhaps I could arrange another swim for you, Princess." I whistled under my breath to Dancer and we moved slowly into the mist.

Small pebbles hit my back. Dancer neighed in alarm.

"Go," I whispered, leaning across her flank, my face buried in the warmth of her neck. "Let the bitch see how fast you are!"

Dancer snorted and jumped forward, rushing the mist so quickly I almost slid again. But this time I caught hold of her mane and laughed wildly as the world raced past us. Far behind, I heard a shout, "Beware me, Gwenhwyfar. Do not think us finished!"

I risked my balance enough to turn and offer her a gesture my older brothers had taught me. But even her vivid clothes were already lost in the mist, so fleet were Dancer's hooves.

Chapter 30

The next morning the mist finally lifted enough for us to start down the mountain paths without fear of riding off a sudden turning in the trail and crashing to our deaths on the rocks below. Tightening the girth on his saddle, Cynan exchanged a glance with me, heavy with anger. Had it not been for Eithne's presence we would have stayed camped in the meadow with the herders for many more days. Racing horses, gathering high mountain herbs for the healers and seasonings for the cooks of Dinas, we would have spent long windswept nights cuddled beneath our furs beside the sheepherders' fires drinking unwatered mead and listening to old Rodric's stories until the stars themselves grew tired, blissfully free of all interference. This was what we had always done on this springtime journey to the mountains.

Now, because of the unwelcome pirate's brat and her quickness with a knife, we were returning home to dreary tutors and mind-numbing chores days earlier then we should have.

My brother and I rode side by side, bringing up the rear of the procession, reluctant to leave the freedom of the high meadow until the last possible heartbeat. The summer herders, already settled in their bothies, came out to wave us on, calling out messages for their kinfolk at Dinas. I grinned as a tumbling lamb ran across the meadow, trying to catch up to a mother who seemed far more interested in sweet grass than in her offspring.

Smiling, my eyes met Lleu's, as he slung himself into the saddle of black Meriel, the horse Father had gifted him with when Lleu had accepted the warrior marks of our clan.

The Druid brat's eyes deepened; his smile widening as he saw that I had attached his raven feather to one of my small braids. Shy, still confused at the powerful feelings that rose whenever I looked at him, my own smile disappeared. I turned away from him, pretending to study the snow-crusted summit of Yr Wyddfa.

When I looked again, Lleu had already ridden past me on the flat meadow trail. The stiffening of his back made me feel ashamed of my shyness, a shyness that felt more like fear if I spoke truly.

He nodded to Eithne where she rode, sullen, in the center of the herders, surrounded by Morgant's many sons. Was Lleu lingering beside her? I tried not to stare as he spoke to her, letting my breath out when he passed her too, watching with a silly-girl pang as he cantered down the trail, towards Morgant, so far in front of me that I could barely see the wild brown curls of his hair.

I kneed Dancer forward. The pirate brat was waiting for me. "So, Gwenhwyfar. It would seem that your suitor has grown bored with you already. Or perhaps he chooses to ride with those who know how to handle their horses."

My hands whitened on Dancer's reins, careful not to jerk the horse. *Say nothing.*

Not so my brother, "I see you've not yet broken free of your keepers, baby witch."

Eithne stiffened.

Cynan wasn't finished. "Don't think your deeds on this journey will disappear as easily as the sheep we just left. You have violated your guest right and your mother will stand forfeit for it."

Eithne looked Cynan up and down, her pouting lips thinning. "A bit old to be tattling to Daddy, aren't you?"

Cynan bowed his head. "True, but I will not have to. Believe me, Eithne, all here will be only too eager to tell of your actions. It is not often that we have such rude children in our midst."

"You smell of shit, little boy. I wonder if it belongs to the sheep—or do your clouts need to be changed?" Eithne removed a sapling whip she must have made herself as none within Father's Hall would dare mistreat their horses and snapped it over her pony's head.

Her poor lazy borrowed mare, startled and plunged forward, forced to gallop until Eithne, followed by her unwilling escort, drew up beside Lleu and Morgant at the head of the column. She disappeared with them down the first turning of the trail.

Cynan shook his head in disgust. "Let's hope we're rid of her soon.

Meanwhile, your battle lessons start tomorrow."

Once on the mountain trail, we rode much more carefully. Even without the sheep herds, we still had pack mules and our own horses and ponies to contend with. It was still early when we reached a small plateau above the most treacherous part of the track where Morgant called a halt so we could be rested for the descent.

"Coming?" Already off his pony, Cynan slung his food pack over his shoulder, heading for the boulder where we always rested when we stopped here.

I lingered over the knots on my saddle pack, hoping Lleu would stop to speak with me when he saw I was alone. But he was busy talking to Eithne, his bard-like fingers moving in the air as they did whenever he was speaking of something important.

I bit down on my lip in frustration and jerked Dancer's straps hard enough to make her snort.

Feeling a fool, I chewed hard bannock with Cynan, watching him draw pictures of horses and sheep with a stick in the wet ground beneath our rock. Usually I loved to watch my brother as he magicked what seemed to be living, breathing creatures out of a few lines dug in dirt. But today even watching him shape a rearing stallion did not move me. Pride kept me from glancing too often at the spot in the grass where Lleu had spread his cloak for Eithne to share.

"Hey brat, what ails you?"

I tossed hair out of my eyes, angry at myself for being miserable. Who was Lleu after all, but a fosterling, a selfish boy who would leave us one day? A boy who would say—or do—anything beneath the stars and then forget it in the morning.

I stood up. "Race you to the ponies."

Cynan threw his drawing stick in an arc that soared across the boulder and over the edge of the mountain. "Never get tired of losing, do you?" His grin was warm, easily reaching his eyes.

Longstanding love filled my heart. Who could ask for a better brother than Cynan—brat though he was? Solid, teasing, as welcome as hearth-fire on a rainy day. Here was someone to trust—not some stranger with grey eyes that changed with every passing cloud.

"Try me!"

We ran. I almost won.

The hardest part of the trail came next. There was a longer, wider track that was safer, but on our way up the mountain, we had discovered it buried beneath a late winter landslide.

Now rain began to fall and we needed to get home before mud made the already dangerous mountain path impossible to travel.

Mist began to rise again. I dismounted and led Dancer along the narrowing track. On our left was a rock wall, broken by shallow caves, and occasional trees stubborn enough to have rooted in the tiny bits of soil the rocks allowed. To the right was a sheer drop, a breathtaking, dizzy view of the tops of pine trees and rock scree in the valley far below.

"Gwen?" I jumped and Dancer startled behind me. Talking softly to soothe her, I peered into the mist and saw Lleu come forward from the shelter of a large overhang, leading his horse by the reins.

"We waited for you," added a much less welcome voice. I glared into Eithne's eyes.

"You needn't have bothered."

Lleu put his hand on her shoulder, pushing her gently forward. She gripped his hand possessively; however it was me she spoke to. "I would like to apologize, Gwenhwyfar," she mumbled, looking at the mist, the ground, the cliff face, anywhere but at me. "I have treated you poorly."

I looked in surprise at Lleu, who shrugged. "I thought it time we all got along."

"Well, whoever's idea this is, can we *move*, for Anu's sake! It would be nice to get home before Samhain." Cynan was not usually this nervous and I looked at him carefully. His eyes betrayed nothing but irritation.

"I'm glad to see that you are in your usual good spirits, Princeling." But Eithne obeyed, leading her pony in front of me. I made way, still surprised and mistrustful. Lleu fell in line behind Dancer, leaving Cynan to bring up the rear and we cautiously resumed walking on the steeply descending trail.

Until now, the journey had been filled with good-natured jests and stories tossed back and forth along the line like leather balls thrown into the air. Cynan and I had joined in with all the dirty songs we had learned from Iolo's warrior band. Now, however, as we negotiated the treacherous slope, the men grew silent. The only sounds to be heard were the dripping of the rain and the jangling of saddle packs, the neighs of ponies and a slew of cursing.

"Look out!" cried Eithne.

Despite everything I had ever been taught about mountain travel, I recoiled. Dancer neighed and reared up behind me. Frantically holding on to the reins, trying to calm her as she plunged, I saw in the mud beneath her hooves a small red snake wiggling across the path. It darted into a low crevice in the rocks, but Dancer's panic grew worse.

Lleu backed away from her, giving me as much room as he could to maneuver.

"Sshh, Ssh, girl. Be still, be still!" Dancer landed a second time on all fours, blowing air out of her nostrils in terrified snorts, her alert, kind eyes widening in panic. "There. It's all right. Just a snake." Her eyes fixed on me and she took a shuddering breath. In great relief I stroked the twitching muscles of her neck, murmuring endearments.

"Gwen! Be careful!" Eithne screamed. She ran at us, flailing her arms.

Dancer reared again. This time, her back hooves slid in the trampled mud and disappeared over the side of the gorge.

"No!" I lost my own footing, but braced myself against a rock, trying to pull her back with the reins. But more mud gave way and she slide backward. For a heartbeat, she clung to the shelf of the trail, scrambling with her front legs to regain the safety of earth beneath her, but she was too far overbalanced.

Lleu's knife flashed, cutting the reins that held me to her. The rain whipped down in a sudden squall, Dancer's wide dark eyes fixed on me for the last time, pleading with me to bring her back.

"No!" I broke free of Lleu's arms, too late. A blur of chestnut, a final terrified whinny and she was gone.

I lay flat in the mud, trying to see where she had fallen. Through gaps in the mist, I saw her body tumble in a sickening dance, end over end, until it broke on a narrow rock far below us. Her graceful neck shattered, Dancer lay in a rapidly growing pool of dark blood.

I crouched to hurl myself from the cliff and join her, but Cynan pushed past Lleu and pulled me back from the edge, holding me as I shrieked and pounded him with my fists.

"Let me go!"

Cynan held on tighter. Morgant joined us, working his way up the narrow track. "I am sorry, Gwenhwyfar." He put a calloused hand on my heaving shoulder and patted me roughly.

"I know you put great stock in the little mare. She was a good horse, Princess," the sheepherder added. "Even now she will be dancing across Epona's everlasting fields."

The thought of Dancer there, in the other-realms only made me cry harder.

"What made her startle?" Morgant asked the others gathered on the path.

Black fury descended. "She did!" I tore loose from Cynan and ran at Eithne. She stood beside the rock wall of the path, wet and sodden like the rest of us, but with a smirk of triumph that vanished as soon as I leapt on her.

"You killed her, you bitch!" My hands pressed into the soft tissue of her throat. She gagged and clawed at me. I bore down harder. "A snake that color doesn't live in these mountains! You called it—and when that didn't work you screamed to make her shy again! You're going to Anwnn to join her, bitch!"

"Gwen!" Lleu and Morgant grabbed me, almost toppling over the cliff in their efforts to control me. But, at the last, it was Lleu who knelt beside me, loosening my grip on Eithne's neck, pinning her with his arm as she tried to attack.

"If you accuse her, you must do so with honor, not like a clanless savage in the middle of the wilderness. She is a highborn guest," he continued, as she struggled against him, rubbing the red marks on her neck.

His expression as he looked at her was one I'd never seen on his face before; it contained anger and something else: a fascination that made me want to scream at him in rage.

With a sudden cry, Eithne broke free, reaching for the knife at her belt. Lleu removed it from its sheath before she even touched the hilt and passed the blade over her eyes.

"Don't even think to try that again." Tossing the knife to Morgant, he pulled me beside him.

I spat in her face.

"Gwen!" Fresh clouds burst open above us. Rain slanting into his face, Lleu grabbed me by my shoulders and spun me behind him, bruising my shoulder against the hard rock face.

Eithne growled and would have charged me, but Morgant bound her hands in front of her with a short measure of rope.

"Stop it!" Lleu shook me. Wild with rage and grief, I spat at him too. Rain washed the spittle away in a heartbeat, but Lleu's eyes narrowed. "You now prove yourself no better then she. Charges must be brought. And I warn you, spellcraft is not easy to prove."

"She killed my horse, Lleu. Cynan, you saw what happened! Tell him!"

My brother stepped forward and clasped my arm, having watched the madness overtake us in silence. "I saw, Shadow. And I will speak of it, don't worry. But what we know and what we saw are two separate markings on a trail."

"That's right, Gwenhwyfar." Eithne's voice was thick with satisfaction. "You will but make a fool of yourself. All know you had trouble controlling your horse —"

"Liar!" I broke free of Cynan's clasp, but Lleu gripped my arm before I could reach her.

"Am I? Really?" She smiled. "Think, Gwen."

I cast my mind back. Suddenly I remembered sounds coming out of the mist to bother Dancer that morning. Remembered a brightly-clad Scotti brat, running a rabbit across our path. Remembered and felt the truth fall into place like an old key opening a rusty lock. The morning had been but a test. Her apology but a trick to get close to me.

"Now, of course," Eithne's smile widened, "we are all sorry for the loss of your horse, but you can't blame me for the poor thing's fall. I had nothing to do with it. I was only trying to help you calm it down, after all."

"By screaming?"

This time, it was Morgant who took my arm. "Princess Gwenhwyfar, this gets us nowhere. We must ride on if we hope to reach Dinas by nightfall. Accounts will be settled there." He eyed Eithne grimly. "Lady, you ride with me."

She looked him up and down, her golden eyes gloating, imperious, despite her tied hands. "I will not forget this, sheepherder."

Morgant gave the dry chuckle that was the greatest sign of amusement he ever offered. "Nor will I, *Lady*. Now be kind enough to accompany me to the head of the line. I want no further losses."

Eithne cast a final glance at Lleu, but if she expected him to intervene for her again, she was mistaken. He nodded at her and she was led away by one of Morgant's herders. Yet he watched until her form disappeared in the rain and mist that cloaked the trail.

With a sob, I leaned against him. Cynan joined us and I cried in both their arms. I saw Dancer's broken body every time I closed my eyes. Dead. She was dead. Like Hwyrch. Like Tegid. Dead.

I started to moan like an old woman. Dimly, I was aware of Lleu's comforting murmurs, my brother's sorrowful humming.

I saw Dancer as she'd been that morning, neck arched proudly, sniffing keenly into the wind. Now she was gone forever, taking with her the joy of dew-meadowed mornings, the fierce song of the wind as it whistled past us as we rode. Gone. Lost, beyond recall.

A deep pit opened up inside me.

I clutched at the drenched, wet clothes of my brother and Lleu and knew that no other horse would ever take Dancer's place. And no cold revenge would bring her back. Eithne had succeeded.

"Come, Gwen. I know you mourn her, but we must ride on." Cynan whispered, patting my back.

"Give me but a heartbeat more." I plucked some tiny wildflowers from a rock cleft—the only flowers I could see—and threw them over the edge where Dancer's body lay.

Food for crows now, I thought swallowing back a miserable, bitter sob. "*Slanihara, nheoresa,* Dancer. Go with Epona, I will look for you in the clouds. Forever...I will look for you..." I blew a kiss into the gathering darkness and turned back to Cynan and Lleu.

"Let's go home."

chapter 31

The rain grew worse as we moved miserably down the mountainside. I huddled deep within my sheepskin cloak, not caring, watching the slanting downpour of the rain with eyes that saw and yet saw nothing.

Cynan pulled me up to ride behind him when we reached the bottom of the mountain trail. Lleu paused before he mounted, staring back at me, rain pouring over the contours of his face. Although I met his eyes, I could not forget his hand upon the witch-girl's shoulder. Thus it was my brother's hand I reached for, my brother's back I leaned against, taking a small comfort in his familiar smell of wet sheepskin and clean earth.

Guards at the lower watch towers hailed our sorry group. Shouting bad jokes about the many uses of sheep, they waved us up the muddy hill track. No one, not even Morgant, answered nor traded the usual insults and so the sentries fell silent again, staring morosely into the merciless rain.

Once into the stables, I slid off Cynan's horse. Ignoring the stiffness of my legs, I ran across the courtyard, hoping to find Father in the Hall.

He was there. Mother sat across from him at one of the lower tables, intent on a game of tawlbwrdd. Mother's hand hesitated first over one piece, then another. Father's eyes heated in triumph.

Before I could run to them, Ula entered from the corridor behind the dais. "Cadwallon, that servant you foisted on me is a disgrace! The girl should be whipped!" Father turned reluctantly away from the gameboard and stared at her. "I'll see to it if you don't!" Ula balled her fists into the fabric of her skirts and disappeared into the shadows of the corridor.

"No Lady, you will not!" Father stayed in his seat but his voice roared through the Hall. "Servants are not beaten here, unless I give consent. I care not what customs you follow elsewhere!"

Ula returned to the Hall, her arms still fisted at her sides, ready to do battle.

"Need I remind you, Lady, that you remain here as a guest, only as long as it pleases me? I could as easily cast you and your child out into the rain or throw you into the dungeons beneath my Keep and let the rats play with your hair, as to honor you with a place at my board."

"You will live to regret these insults, *Lord*."

"Father—"

He and Mother looked at me in surprise. Ula grit her teeth.

"My horse has been killed. I seek justice."

"Your horse?" Mother started to rise. Father put his hand on her arm. She looked up at him and sat again.

Father mounted the stairs to the King's Seat on the dais and motioned me closer. "Approach and speak the tale."

At these ritual words, a knot unbound within me. I bowed before my father as if I were any other freewoman and the story spilled out of me. It was only as I described Dancer's slide from the mountain trail that I felt my lower lip begin to tremble and bit down hard against the choking rush of tears.

When it was over, I bowed again into the silence and stepped back to take a seat on a bench.

"And what say you, Cynan ap Cadwallon, Lleu ap Chalan, Morgant of the Herders?"

So intent had I been on telling the tale, I had not heard them come in behind me.

"It is as she said, Lord." My brother answered.

"It is as she said." Lleu echoed.

Father turned to Morgant. "I was not close enough to see for myself, Lord, but I've no doubt of your daughter's honesty. Not after what happened on the journey up to the sheep pasture."

Father raised his eyebrow. I had forgotten the knife fight with Eithne. At Father's command, Morgant stepped closer to the dais and told Father what had happened the day before Dancer was lost to me.

Father heard him out. Even from as far away as I stood, I could see his eyes growing colder and colder in fury as the tale unfolded. At its end, he asked, in the soft deadly voice we knew to dread, "And where is the young lady now?"

Morgant strode to the doorway. Gathered under the eaves of the Hall were two of his sons, one of whom held the rope binding Eithne's hands together. They approached Father's dais, Eithne walking straight as a fire-hardened spear between them.

"How dare you tie my daughter's hands!" Ula flung herself against the shepherds, beating them with her fists.

Morgant pushed her aside, none too gently.

"I will have your head for that, peasant!" She spat in Morgant's face.

Morgant wiped his face calmly with the filthy sleeve of his tunic and turned to Father with a gratified sigh. "You see how it is with them, my Lord. Her daughter is a hellcat as well."

Father wiped his hand across his face, clearly stifling a smile. "Still, Chief Herder, these are highborn guests—if what they claim is true. We cannot tie their hands— as yet. Loose the girl."

"But, Lord—"

Father shook his head.

Mumbling beneath his breath, Morgant cut the rope that bound Eithne's hands in front of her.

"Come forward, child."

Instead of approaching Father, Eithne ran to Ula.

"I said, come here, girl!" When Father spoke like that, even Eithne dared not argue. Turning her back on Ula, she flung her head high, and minced to the dais.

Father's gaze on her was like the depths of winter. His eyes followed the wet length of her long black hair. At last he spoke. "Do you have aught to say in answer to this charge, Eithne ferch Ula?"

Eithne shook her head. "I will not trouble to dignify your daughter's lies, *Lord*."

"Then you will kneel and hear my judgment." A guard came forward and pushed Eithne to her knees. "Come forward, all."

Everyone but Ula gathered closer to the dais as the ritual words rang out. Mother's hand touched down upon my shoulder.

I let it stay.

"For the death of Dancer, horse of the High King's daughter, Gwenhwyfar ferch Ceridwyn, I can find no blame to lay upon this child's head—"

"But, Father! She—"

"Silence!"

Mother's hand tightened.

"For the attack upon my daughter's person, I fine Eithne ferch Ula of the Sunfacing Scotti, thirty head of cattle." Father outstretched his arm as uproar broke out. "For raising a hand against a member of her host's family, I fine Eithne ferch Ula twenty head more."

"This is an outrage, Cadwallon! Eithne did no wrong. Gwenhwyfar began the fight. My child did but seek to end it!"

"That's a lie! Father!" I broke free from Mother's hand and pushed through the small group beneath the dais.

"Hush, Gwen. I have heard the tale and judged the forfeit." Father turned to Ula and smiled, grimly. "Since the ladies had no cattle swimming with them when we pulled them from the sea, I will take five measures of gold in place of breeding heifers and bulls."

"You are mad!" Ula tried to leave the Hall, but two sentries blocked the door.

"Bring her to me."

Ula was dragged the length of the Hall, kicking and swearing to gods I had not heard of. She was thrown down on the floor beside us. Father continued as if there had been no interruption. "Since your daughter wears but one small ring, I will have the remainder of the measure due Gwenhwyfar from that treasure hoard you wear upon your own limbs, Lady."

"Never!"

"Then you will see how the hospitality of my dungeons appeals to you—and to your child. It was she, after all, who brought this upon you."

"My kin will have your head for this, Cadwallon! You will be boiled in oil, your flesh torn apart by horses—"

"My eyes gouged out, my manly parts severed...yes, yes, so I've been warned." Father gave a yawn. "Do you offer them willingly—or do my guards take them from you?"

Furious, Ula pulled two thick golden bands laden with amethyst and amber and a green stone I had not seen before from her arm. Father sat motionless. With a curse, she wrenched a sparkling necklace of delicately patterned birds from her neck. Father raised an eyebrow and motioned for his warriors to advance. She snarled and unfastened the intricately worked golden girdle from her waist, letting it slide to the floor in a whispering cascade.

"Now. Your daughter's ring." Father extended his hand towards

Eithne.

"No!" The girl backed away. It was the first time I had ever seen true fear in her eyes. "It was my father's. You cannot take it! It is all that I have of him."

"Then perhaps its loss will teach you what happens when you overreach yourself."

"No!" Eithne spun around, but was brought back by a guard.

"Cast your ring upon the pile, child."

"Cadwallon! You go too far!" Ula clasped her daughter's hand. "You know well what you do to her. Such cruelty should be beneath even you!"

"Enlighten us, Lady. Why do you think me cruel?" Father clasped the carved arms of his throne. His eyes grew avid.

Ula flushed. Her bitter golden-brown eyes narrowed, a cat prepared to spring. Suddenly, she shouted—a mad woman's shout— raising her long arms in a parody of Father.

"Give the bastard your ring, dear. We will take our vengeance soon, within the next turning of the seasons. By the time the leaves wither on this god-cursed hilltop, these fools will be no more."

Sobbing, Eithne obeyed her mother. Twisting the gold ring from her finger, she threw it angrily upon the pile of jeweled gold beneath the dais.

It was only then that I recognized it, for Eithne had swaddled it with yarn to fit her small finger. It was the carved Scotti ring Uncle Maelgwyn had worn at the feast of Lughnasa, six sunturns ago.

I recoiled.

"Father—I do not want this!"

Eithne spat in my face. "Take it, weakling. Soon you will be under my knife again –and this time you will die!"

Chapter 32

The next morning, I woke; a nightmare of thoughts still whirling within me. So Eithne was my cousin. Uncle Maelgwyn's child. Was he still alive?

I was halfway to the stables before I remembered: Dancer was gone. I crumbled miserably beside a storage shed and wept until I was exhausted. There would be no warm-muzzled greeting this day. No magical ride across the meadow.

Having no appetite for food or people, I left the fortress, running in the direction of the village, hoping to visit Nest, the only person I could think of that I would like to see this morning. Ever since the stout midwife escorted me back from the healers' village, we had begun an unlikely friendship and now shared a special bond. Her bracing no-nonsense advice put me in mind of Hwyrch at times, but she possessed the soul of one dedicated to bringing life into the world and I needed her soft capable arms to hold me now, to tell me that death would not always conquer those I loved.

I slowed to a walk on the path to the village.

Grandmother met me before I could enter the turning that led to Nest's cottage. "The bitch is gone. Her whelp went with her." Her voice cracked. She gripped my shoulders and dug her nails deep into my flesh.

A crowd had gathered behind her. A woman screamed. Another sank to the ground and broke into sobs.

I smelled something terrible. A ghost slide across my spine.

I pushed away from Grandmother, into the crowd.

Morgant lay in a pool of blood, already attracting flies. His intestines had been ripped from his body, spread out on top of his chest in what looked to be some horrible pattern.

His right hand was missing.

My empty stomach roiled, bile rushed up, filling my mouth. Flies gathered around the bloody open pits of his eye sockets.

Someone had gouged them out.

I vomited.

Grandmother's hand slid firmly across my forehead as I spewed, anchoring me in the world.

Wordless, she handed me the rough linen cloth she used to wrap the herbs she gathered.

I wiped my mouth and stared into her face. The villager's cries wove in and out of my awareness. I tried to stand, but stumbled to my knees. Again I tried. This time I made it to my feet and stood, swaying beside her.

Grandmother's eyes refused to meet mine; instead they flickered above my head, glaring into the forest as if challenging something I could not see.

She spat on the ground beside us. "The bitch is gone." she repeated, gesturing at Morgant's ruined body. "And her whelp with her. This is her parting message. The forfeit she felt she was owed." She took the blanket a villager held out and covered Morgant's body. "This is dark magic, Gwen. The worst I have seen since before you were born."

I shook my head, still swaying, grabbing onto a tree to steady myself.

Grandmother took my hand. "Come child, it is time you learn the whole story. You have long been curious about the *estethra*. They are part of this tale as well. As are the shadows behind your Mother's eyes—shadows you know nothing of—as busy as you are casting her out of your heart."

I tried to pull away from her.

She did not let go, merely began to walk into the forest, dragging me with her, as if I were a sheep.

"Stop!" I cried in fury.

She turned back to me, her arrogant black eyes dangerous, her lip curled in a snarl as malevolent as a wolf's. "Do not think what you want matters now, Granddaughter! You do not yet know what those two are. I tell you, they have risen from the darkest pit of Anwnn. And they have marked you as their prey."

Chapter 33

The way to Ruag's hut was even longer than I remembered, in spite of Grandmother's shortcut up the mountains. Staggering behind her up the steep deer track, my rage faded, leaving ice in its wake. No more death, the forest whispered. I climbed stubbornly, my heart growing even colder as rain began to fall. Mist made the rocky trail almost invisible, causing Grandmother's lanky form to appear and then vanish, leaving me alone in this god-haunted realm.

At last we reached the tumbling babble of Ruthan's brook and the old healer's hut beyond. Grandmother reached for my hand, as if I would suddenly take it into my head to disappear.

We stepped over the half-submerged stones of the threshold. I broke away from her and stood, braced against what was left of the eastern-facing wall, the crumbling wattle-and-daub beneath my fingers a welcome reminder that I still inhabited the earth.

Above us, the rain slowed to a sullen drizzle, the sky grey as sheep's wool beyond the collapsed thatch of the roof.

"Sit." Grandmother started a fire in the tiny hearth. She now spread what was left of a once finely-woven blanket on the ground beside it.

I obeyed, taking those few steps as slowly as I could, watching the collection of rotting roof bracken, straw, and heather at my feet as if it would come alive at any heartbeat.

"Look at me."

I raised my gaze reluctantly. Grandmother's eyes were bloodshot, her face ravaged. But suddenly the firelight cast new shadows and I saw a young woman of great beauty, her long black hair a mass of tumbling curls and Druid braids. "I brought you here—to the home of my dearest friend—because I cannot speak of these things anywhere else. My tongue cleaves inside my mouth and sorrow freezes my thoughts." Grandmother shrugged ruefully, her familiar mannerisms strange and sad within this new body. Fascinated, I watched the play of fire and rain mist dance between us.

The past swooped close; an eagle upon a rabbit. The powers I'd gained in the healers' village were no match for the terror I felt as I sensed what was to come.

"Ula is more dangerous than you or your mother and father understand." Frantic not to hear her, I watched as this old-new Grandmother dug through Ruag's wood pile, managing to find dry branches near the bottom. "She will stalk you just as her mother Satienda, once stalked my children."

"*Your* children!" My absorption in the woodpile ended. Despite myself I was pulled back to the fire, to Grandmother, to the nightmare I did not want to hear.

"Yes, my children. It is true, they are no longer spoken of. A solemn vow was taken, a spell cast upon our people, to forget, claiming a plague took their lives. Only your mother escaped. And Merlin." Grandmother's new unwrinkled face smiled in a soft and unfamiliar way. She stared into the fire. "I should have known the power had to go somewhere."

"But—"

"It was a long time ago. I was a giddy young girl, easily persuaded to love a man because his arms and thighs were as muscled as a mountain cat's." She smiled, far away from me, inside a tongue of fire that sparked high above the ruined hearth "Ah, but he was a prince...summer-sky eyes and a smile that rode into my heart like a Roman stallion."

Knowing now it was useless to fight, my heart entered the fire with her. Flames spilled into my heart. I saw with her eyes.

"His name was Edern."

Grandmother's love leapt within the fire: a stalwart laughing man, his hair and moustaches the color of autumn leaves bronzed with twilight.

"Handsome," she mused, "and brave. So brave. The first one into battle, the last one to leave. My parents liked him not. But after all, what do parents matter?" She favored me with a wry wink and cast another branch on the fire.

I drew closer to her, telling myself it was merely to stay warm.

"We had many sunturns of joy...many nights of moon-filled love... six children." If she heard my gasp, she paid no attention. "Six. Your mother, Ceridwen, the youngest...Sixteen sunturns we had before Getherax came."

Now I saw a Druid recognizable by his braids but his robes were torn and tattered, his face and body twisted. The fire danced higher. I looked again, more closely, and saw the same man. This time he was clothed in soft white linen, his robe bordered with stars and sun; his body tall, his darkly handsome face radiant with majesty.

"Aye, girl. He was a trickster, a shapeshifter of great power. All my husband's charm was no match for his enchantment."

I saw this Druid, Getherax, take Grandmother's husband's hand. They sat together on the King's dais as my young Grandmother looked on, her black eyes cold as flint beneath a hidden sun.

Grandmother placed her hand on my brow and invited me inside her. I forced myself to bear the trance again; the cold fear where there had once been joy, the breath held waiting for the arrow to fly, the sword to dance.

"There was nothing at first to make me suspect that Getherax was anything but what he pretended to be—a visiting hermit from the Druid's Isle of Mona come to our mountains to seek his own visions of what the future held for our people. Many came to our clan lands in those days, for the red-cloaks were gone and the Druids no longer needed to dwell in forgotten caves.

"I, too, thought him kindly in the beginning. But as summer bowed to the winds of autumn and Getherax stayed on, talking late into the night with my husband, a dark thing began to rise within my beloved. He began to neglect his people. He no longer rode with the warriors, no longer judged the complaints of the villagers, no longer came to my bed..." Grandmother paused, twisting her hands in a young woman's sorrowing gesture, a thing I had never seen from her before. "Then Satienda came."

A woman, tall and eagle-eyed, appeared beside Ruag's hearth. She was beautiful in the way a raven is when it glides across a winter sky, stark and wonder-filled, exalting in a realm of death. She joined Getherax and together they walked beside my grandfather, King Edern, deep within the forests of the Ordovice.

"My husband began to rave. He slept now with the warriors in the Hall, his head snoring amidst overturned horns of mead and trenchers of untouched meat on the oak boards of the king's dais, his men afraid to wake him for fear of his terrible rage. Rage that had never existed until the arrival of Getherax and Satienda.

"But I heard him. Afraid to sleep myself, seeking comfort in the past, I roamed the night and found myself beside him. There, beneath the guttering light of dying lamps, in a Hall filled with faithful sleeping warriors, he raved of blood and curses, the Old Ways. For, Getherax demanded we return to the dark ways of blood sacrifice, ways the Druids of Mona and the mountains had long held wrong, save in the most desperate of times."

The new wood I added made our fire roar, its flame tendrils reaching beyond the hearth as if to summon us closer. I wrapped my cloak tightly around me, seeing within the fire's shadows a Hall filled with danger, danger that stalked like an invisible wolf past unsuspecting herdsmen.

"As the dark days of Samhain approached, I took my children to the mountain steading of Yr Gwion where my parents lived—having renounced the world of men for a forest life of prayer and simple pleasures. There, I sought to rest my spirit, to seek solace in my own mother's arms," Grandmother ruffled my hair, without taking her own gaze from the fire.

"And to plan a way to wrest my husband free from those western demons who possessed him, who had come to all but rule our clan, while I, Queen of the Mountain Ordovice, was powerless to stop them."

"Rest is what I found there." Grandmother smiled and I saw a forest clearing in front of me. Late autumn frost rimed the tall grasses and a thin sheet of ice decorated the small pool at its center. Yet, despite the leafless oaks and rowans, eternal holly bloomed amidst a snug circle of rounded huts. Smoke escaped in welcome from simple hearths.

An old man laughed, leaning on a walking stick, watching a brood of children play. The youngest girl jumped madly up and down on the ice-scum of a puddle until it finally cracked, then launched herself in triumph at the others, her new leather boots fresh-coated with mud.

"Aye, Ceridwen was always the wildest of them—ever urging her older sisters to commit the most foolish of acts."

As I stared, astonished, at this bright blackbird of a child racing towards her older brothers and sisters with a laugh as radiant as dew upon a mountain meadow, I sensed my mother's adult sorrowing face behind me, so real that I twisted to see if she had joined us. But my eyes met only shadows and mist. Beyond the circle of our fire what little light existed outside Ruag's hut was growing weaker.

I turned back to the joyous scene just in time to see my child-mother collide with her sister—a sister with hair so light and fine, it looked to be silver beneath the autumn sun. Bran's hair. Laughing, they ran to a nearby stream where they joined another older girl and three older boys, the oldest of whom was as tall as my brother Iorwerth and looked to be almost a man. The old man who watched them followed more slowly, leaning heavily on his blackthorn walking stick, carved in the old way with ancient runes.

"My father. My children. Ceridwen, you know." Grandmother reached for my hand and turned to face me, the first time she had done so since the fire had been kindled. "The silver-haired girl was named Rhiannon, my oldest daughter. Her sister was Derwena. The boys, Arofan...Brychan..." the names fell like stones through the fire-mist that surrounded us, "and Meden. Our eldest. He bears the look of Bran, does he not?" She paused, not seeing me. "Yet he is much like Iorwerth in manner." She added softly to the fire, as if he, in truth, stood beside her.

I watched the children play—these unknown uncles and aunts. Grandmother's voice wove through me, dancing like sun sparkles on the stream where they romped; pushing, laughing, and shoving.

"We were happy there for a season. But my husband called us back for the midwinter ceremonies. All but your mother went, for she had grown attached to her southern cousins—my sister's Dumnoni kin—who also visited our parents in their sanctuary. Ceri became fast friends with my sister's child, a girl of her own age." The fire-shadows danced higher, shifting, and I saw my child-mother, eagerly guiding her small pony behind a train of others, giggling with another girl riding beside her. Ceridwyn turned once, farewelling her family with a bright-smiled wave. "I thought it would do her no harm to be with them for a sunturn..." Grandmother's hand dropped mine, she held herself, rocking slightly as she nodded towards the fire. "Even then, your mother hungered for the South...

"The rest of my children and I made ready to accompany my husband's messenger, but the man grew impatient. 'Lady, let us hurry! A storm approaches.'

"With his words, a heaviness of spirit descended on me, such as I had not felt since we arrived at my parents' steading. My mind was in tumult, for I had not been able to design a plan to free my husband from the influence of the dark ones. And, fool that I was, I saw no recourse but to return."

Grandmother's voice deepened. No longer a silver thread across the fire-visions, it stumbled, grew silent; bringing chaotic images of wind-blown trees, of spiraling snow through mountain passes, of women weeping, their keening voices cresting within the howl of the storm.

"My steps were slow," Grandmother's voice began again, faltered, then gained strength. "My hands grasped the reins of my pony tightly, fighting the urge in my heart to go back, to leave Dinas and all its dark secrets forever, to order my children back to the rushing waters and simple pleasures of Yr Gwion. Where they would be safe.

"Safe from what, I did not know nor seek to question. Only the most ancient part of me was desperate not to follow my husband's shifty-eyed messenger." Grandmother's old-young face aged before my eyes. Wrinkles scored her cheeks and forehead, making deep paths on both sides of her mouth as she pressed her fist against her lips, a little girl's gesture.

Helpless, frightened, I watched my harsh Grandmother rock like a terrified child. "Foolishness, I told myself. You are getting to be as mad as your husband. You can do more for your children and your people by returning to face those evil Druids who threaten the peace of your realm.

"But the first morning we set out, I fell from my horse, twisting my ankle. I, who had ridden before I could walk. I, who, like you, could never stay far from the stables; I fell from my horse—on a path so smooth an infant could ride it.

"My ankle began to swell. I grew dizzy. We were close to a healer's hut and the messenger halted there, ordering three of my husband's guards to stay with me until I was recovered enough to travel. I argued. He insisted I stay.

"Queens, I reminded him, do not take orders from messengers. He glared at me then. 'It is your husband, I obey, Lady. He would have my head if I let you risk this journey as you are.'

"Despite the pain in my leg, I limped away from the fussing healer. Ignoring the warriors who moved quickly to surround me, I waved farewell to my high-spirited children, watching until they disappeared around a bend in the forest track, gossiping like songbirds as they rode. Only then, my heart torn with frustration and fear, did I allow myself to be escorted inside.

"That night, the blizzard struck.

"I could not sleep for terror. At daybreak when the snow stopped falling, I roused the guards, insisting that we try to make it to Dinas before another storm closed the passes. But my guards stood firm and the healer, scuttling beneath them with downcast eyes, agreed. I was not to attempt the journey until I was fully healed.

"A fortnight later, I was finally permitted to mount my horse again. Through waist-high snows, I urged my escort on, riding, half-mad with foreboding. All around us the world was silent, save for the dripping of snowmelt and the cawing of ravens perched on naked winter branches, watching as we passed.

"When at last we reached the first gates of Dinas, I rode ahead, calling out for my children, not caring how I must sound to folk who knew me as their Queen. But the village beneath the fortress was silent. It was early morning, yet no sentries were at their posts; the inner gates lay open to the winds. I rushed up the hill, kneeing my pony through the unmarked snow until we gained the inner palisades. The fortress was deserted. No smoke, no signs of life, save for three ravens perched upon the roof of the Hall. They watched me, brooding, as silent as the realms of Anwnn from whence they traveled.

"Inside, the Hall reeked of warrior stench, of vomit, sour wine, and rotting meat. It too was deserted, save for my husband, sprawled in drunken sleep upon the dais. I called for servants. No one answered.

"I ran outside. Leaning against the ramparts, I looked down the hill, searching for any movement at all. My escort had disappeared. Unbelievably, I was alone.

"I searched the back rooms of the Hall, the kitchens, the freeman's huts. No one. Until, at last, I found a young girl, a servant, cowering in a storage shed.

"What happened here, child? Where are the children of the High King of Dinas?"

The girl gazed up at me—a fledgling before a hawk. "I—I—"

"Out with it!" I shook her.

"They have been s-sacrificed—" she stammered.

"You lie!" I slapped her, frantic. But my soul leapt, for it knew the truth.

She rubbed the reddened spot on her cheek. As if its sting released her spirit, she began to babble. "All the others have gone away. S-satienda and Geth-getherax called down the dark gods on any who offended them."

I sank to the dirt floor beside her. "Speak."

She gulped like a fish seeking water, her eyes blind to me, staring into the air as if she beheld a demon. "It was Midwinter's Eve. Getherax and Satienda led us to the Old One's hill. We were all silent—afraid. Your husband, the Lord King, walked with us, Lady." The girl clasped her bare arms around long, starved legs. "His presence kept us strong even though he too was silent and stumbled as if he had drunk too much mead."

I saw through Grandmother's eyes as she clasped and unclasped her hands, wanting to shake the girl senseless. Instead my young Grandmother sat, still as a snow-covered forest, biting into her own lip so hard that a ribbon of blood welled up and dripped down her chin.

"The night was bitter," the girl continued. "Mountain winds whipped down from the passes, snow not far behind. We knew not what to expect. I walked alone—you might remember, Lady, my mother died during the rains?"

I was inside my Grandmother fully now, seeing the girl. Hearing her tale, as if my own life depended it.

I sensed the girl's fear, but cared not, for Grandmother's own terror overwhelmed my senses.

The girl looked into Grandmother's eyes, hoping for compassion. Whatever she saw there made her shiver and turn away.

"I had no cloak," she continued in a whisper. "I had found an old blanket and wrapped it around my shoulders, as if I was still a little girl playing at being a queen, but the wind cut into it like a hunter's knife.

"At last, we reached the top of the hill and entered the Old One's stone circle. A group of Druids we had never seen stepped out of the shadows. Each carried a torch, each stood in front of one of the stones, facing the altar carved in the center.

"We were waiting for something; within our bones and hearts, we knew we waited for something terrible. The Lord King fell to his knees and began to weep. Old Morwena ran to comfort him, petting his head as if he were a babe.

"Then five priests entered the circle from the north. A great murmur arose from the people, rising into a wail loud enough to be heard above the wind, for the priests guarded your children, Lady. Those five who had returned from the mountains."

Grandmother reached out for my hand. Heartsick, miserable, I felt her calloused fingers grip mine. She pulled me against her, crushing my body against the damp wool of her tunic. *"Look,"* she hissed, gesturing towards the fire on Ruag's hearth.

I clenched the earth beneath my fingers, willing my soul to stay. Not to travel back to that long ago midwinter. But it was too late. Grandmother threw a handful of herbs into the fire. Tongues of flame rose like small dragons and I caught the scent of all-see, the truth-tellers' herb.

Now I saw two visions. The first watched the shivering servant girl continue her tale to my Grandmother. But the second joined her on the Old One's hilltop, standing with her as the priests brought Grandmother's children to the altar where Satienda and Getherax waited.

"Getherax cut the bonds that held the arms of your oldest son," the girl spoke as we watched Getherax raise the young man's arms, linking it with his own.

"The Old Ones have spoken," the tall priest shouted, snow swirling across his face. "Folk of the Ordovice, your cattle are dying. Your king has gone mad. For you have forgotten the ways of your ancestors." Getherax looked at Grandmother's groveling husband as if he beheld a rat in a storage pit. "You no longer sacrifice to the Dark One and he has come to claim your own lives in revenge."

Beneath the priests' wind-tossed torches, folk threw themselves on the frozen ground, shrieking in terror.

"I looked in your son's glazed eyes, Lady," said the girl, "and the truth blew through me like an east wind through the mountains. It was not the Dark God who hunted us. It was Getherax. Getherax who had spelled your husband. Getherax and Satienda his wife." The girl gripped Grandmother's arm, her eyes wild. "I did nothing, Lady. Forgive me. Getherax raised his knife and cut your son's throat before our eyes."

Grandmother's arms were still around me. *"Look,"* she whispered, her voice the croak of nightmares. This time I refused and closed my eyes, hearing only the girl's voice, a faint track of comfort.

"There were screams. But Getherax raised his hands. He chanted and Satienda's voice joined his, spiraling into the sky. No one moved, Lady. The wind stopped, the snow ceased. The priests' torches burned straight as beacon fires." The girl hung her head, weeping. "I tried to break free. But I couldn't even open my mouth. Your son's body fell to the ground. Satienda stretched it out before the altar; then she turned to us and smiled. It was then I knew—the Dark One hunted us after all and he had sent his warriors to seek us."

I closed my eyes. My stomach clenched. Bile rose to my throat. Helpless, angry, frightened, I heard the young girl's voice again. But I did not open my eyes, preferring the soft darkness inside me. Yet, I saw her clear, a slight and ragged moth hovering between the worlds, caught beside Grandmother's raging fire.

"Four priests brought your two younger sons forward and tied them to the altar. Each fell in their turn beneath Satienda's knife." The girl stopped speaking. Grandmother's vision-voice snarled at her to continue. I forced my eyes open.

The girl's pale face hesitated, gauging Grandmother's rage. At last, her voice began again. "When only your daughters were left alive, the spell we were under lifted enough for us to move and speak." Beside me, old Morwena cried "*Stop!*"

"Getherax signaled to a white-robed priest who emerged from the shadows of a north-facing stone. He pushed through the shouting crowd, and cut her throat. The old woman slumped against me as she fell—I tried to catch her, Lady, but..." The girl ceased speaking and began to rock herself, humming, her hunger-thin arms reaching out to clasp an invisible weight.

Grandmother caressed the dagger at her belt. "What next?"

The girl's voice was now as soft as a captive wisp of smoke. "Satienda pushed your two daughters in front of her, 'These two will share a different fate. Take them to the tunnels.' She turned back to the priests who stood behind the altar. 'Tie them. Let the Great Wyrm feed on the King's daughters' flesh.'

"We could not move, Lady. You must believe me—" the girl's voice rose in a wail. "We could not move!"

My long-ago Grandmother took the dagger from her belt. *"Where were they taken?"*

Beside Ruag's fire, the Grandmother I knew turned to me at last, her red-rimmed eyes lost. "I held the knife beneath her nose. Cut her throat only a little. Held back my own madness by the most slender of threads."

Grandmother shook her head, looking back into the fire. "That fool girl only stared at me, Gwen. 'T-the South Tower entrance,' she said. 'Y-you will not kill me, Lady?'

Her eyes scrambled back and forth from me, her half-mad Queen, to the knife I held and she began to blubber, "*I would have stopped them if I could.* We all would have fought—there was a spell, you know. A spell. Afterwards, everybody fled. I know not where…"

"You stayed. Why?" Now Grandmother's eyes bored into mine, as if it were all happening again. As if I was the servant girl, not her granddaughter at all. Her voice was a ragged echo of the commanding priestess cadence I had known since I was a baby. "Foolish child, why had she not run with the others? But when I asked she only shook her head, not knowing.

"And where is Getherax? Satienda?' I asked. I spoke gently then," Grandmother explained to me. "As if to my own daughters—to comfort them after a bad dream."

"G-gone, Lady. To haunt the North. I saw them leave with their priests the morning after the sacrifices. They crossed the meadow, following the boar path to the mountains…You will not hurt me, Lady?"

Grandmother spoke to the fire. "Her smile was so fleeting—it made her seem like a very little girl, a girl who had once wrapped herself in a blanket and played at being Queen.

"Sleep now," I said and kissed the top of her head. I brushed my hands across her eyes, until she closed them. "Then I cut her throat."

I wrapped my arms around my legs and curled myself into a small ball, moving as far away from Grandmother as I could go in the confines of the ruined hut.

She sat, unmoving, lost in memory. The horror of it would not let me leave. Much as I longed to run, screaming, into the forest, this was my Grandmother; the woman who had nursed me back to the living lands, who had let me find a place with the healers: the fierce loving priestess who had offered me my first scent of magic. Was I really surprised she had innocent blood on her hands? She who had helped Mother rip Vortigern's skin from his back? She whose own children had been murdered by fiends?

The night mist parted. Trembling, I raised my head to the stars. Above us danced the great sky bear, Arturos, looking down on the Ordovician mountains as he had since the night my ancestors first came to our clan lands. Tonight, he seemed to dance closer to the earth than I'd ever seen him. Arturos, bearer of power and songs. Bringer of hope.

There was a rustling close by. I reached for my dagger, but it was only a small doe, nosing her way past Ruag's threshold. The creature paused, her great eyes wet pools of light beside the fire. She watched Grandmother, then headed to me, her head dipping as she picked her way gracefully over the rotting bracken on the ground.

I held out my hand. She nuzzled it, then sank to the earth, curling against my side, her flanks heaving gently as she breathed. "Ruag," I whispered, patting her long neck. She huffed, put her head in my lap, and closed her eyes.

Comforted by the dead healer's spirit, I found strength to turn to Grandmother again, gradually making sense of her words.

She left the girl's body unburied. "I replaced the dagger, still bloody in its sheath at my belt and walked across the deserted courtyard to the Hall." Grandmother spoke in the same dead, distant voice that had frightened me before. "Mad as I was, with innocent blood on my hands, the winter wind blew scrapes of rags and leather swirling past me, making Dinas seem as if it had lost its moorings in this world's realm and been emptied for a hundred sunturns instead of merely a handful of days.

"A broken shutter slammed again and again, louder than a war drum. I entered the Hall.

"My husband lay, still sunk in drunken slumber on the dais. It took little effort to raise his head and cut his throat. His body collapsed against the mead-soaked trestle board that had once held our wedding feast.

"I left the Hall and entered the South Tower without looking back and fought to open the rusted trap door leading into the tunnels. When it gave at last, its groan rang out across the courtyard as if it were a tortured soul begging the gods for easy death.

"I climbed down narrow rotting stairs and followed the dark path into the tunnels. I brought no torch for I expected to die beside the bodies of my daughters, trusting my senses to lead me to them.

"I may have journeyed for days—or perhaps it was merely the length of a short winter's afternoon—but at last I saw a glowing fire and stumbled towards it.

"My two daughters sat in a pool of light lodged within the damp, weeping stones although no earthly fire existed. They had been shackled, but now their iron chains lay severed beside them. The two girls held each other, huddled like pups, seven and nine sunturns, as close companions as you and Cynan." Grandmother's grief-shattered face turned to me, etched against the fire. The doe burrowed against my hip, her ears flickering as she slept.

"I sank down beside them, calling their names, tears wetting my face for the first time since I entered the ramparts of Dinas.

"Their faces looked up at me—I could not stop from shrieking." Grandmother gestured into the fire, where the horror lived on.

I saw. Saw and gripped the doe's soft back to keep from screaming myself.

"For their eyes—their eyes were the bright yellow of great cats at night. They watched me in silence, Granddaughter. And as they watched, their pupils shrank to needle-pricks of black. The oldest, Rhiannon, slowly reached out her hand to me. But it was no longer a hand. Her nails were claws, her fingers tapered, longer than a grown woman's.

"'Mother...' Her speech was not human anymore. It was a gasp of breath stolen from the foul air of the tunnels, a dance of light that crackled across the distance between us, entering my heart. 'We must go from this place,' she told me. Her little sister, Derwena, stretched her claws out and gave me a yearning, fang-toothed smile.

"'Stay!' I begged, my own thoughts racing across the spear's length between us.

She shook her head. 'Impossible. Know we are safe. Know you are loved. Know you are watched by us. Always. Always. Always.' Her thought-words ran up and down the black tunnel. The light faded. Rhiannon rose, took her little sister's hand, and vanished into the darkness.

"Derwena turned back once before she disappeared behind her older sister. 'We waited for you, Mama.' She gifted me with another smile—so like the ones she used to offer every morning she was mine. But now her teeth were wild and could have rended me to pieces.

"Then they were gone," Grandmother whispered. I reached for her hand across the expanse that separated us. The doe woke, shook herself, and rose, leading the way to Grandmother's side. When I was again seated beside Grandmother, I took her hand and felt the familiar calluses upon it. I saw the ancient face I knew again, no longer ravaged by pain nor shadowed by its own long ago beauty.

"The *estethra*?" I asked.

"The *estethra*," she answered. Herself again, although her eyes were still bloodshot with weeping and her face furrowed with wrinkles that carved much deeper than they had at yesterday's dawn.

Grandmother patted the doe's flank as briskly as if she were a hound, sparing the creature a smile before she looked at me again. "This, Gwenhwyfar, is why I fear Ula and her thrice-cursed child Eithne. For when Satienda left my kingdom, she was pregnant with Getherax's child. When, at last, I sought the help of the Arch-Druid of Mona we tracked my children's murderers. But, deep in the northern forests, Satienda had already borne her child and given her to one of her followers to raise in hatred on an island far to the North."

"How did you find them?" Although Grandmother was speaking in her normal tones again, her voice still carried echoes too far away for my comfort, for I heard those same echoes in my own words and felt them still swirling around us, whispering beside the hearth and into the ruin-framed night sky. I handed her the water skin and waited. She drank deeply. The doe huffed, scrambled to its feet, and fled into the night as if it had heard something approach.

I went outside to search, but there was nothing.

After my return, Grandmother sat silent for so long, I opened my mouth to repeat my question. Before I could speak, she wiped her mouth, looked at me as if she was surprised to see me, and continued in her usual brisk tone: a cadence that, for once, I welcomed.

"I watched my daughters disappear and instead of killing myself, I vowed vengeance. Alone, I made my way through blizzard snows and rowed a fisher's boat across winter waters until, at last, I reached the Arch-Druid of the sacred isle of Mona. He was, indeed, well acquainted with Getherax and Satienda, for they had been busy for many sunturns encouraging the malcontents on his island to join them in their practices of dark magic and blood sacrifice.

"In the spring, we gathered a force of warriors and priests and tracked the murderers to the northern forests of Alba. Getherax and Satienda were killed, but not before Satienda's daughter was hidden from our swords. This much I learned from the old Alban midwife who delivered the witch of her child."

Grandmother coughed. Her voice deepened and she clutched her belt dagger as if she would wield it again at the least cause. "We captured the midwife, cackling on the battlefield, robbing the dead of their jewels. At first she only spat curses at me, but after her arms were grabbed by our warriors and my knife was at her throat, she begged for her misbegotten life in exchange for the tale she told. It didn't save her."

Grandmother rose, stretching, the joints of her arms popping. Grimly she nodded, as if acknowledging her younger self, and sank down beside me again. "Knowing we would find and kill her, Satienda had given her newborn babe to one of her priests, making him promise to rear it with his kin in the northern islands.

"It was a tale I tried not to believe, though the Druids assured me, the dead midwife had spoken true. Now, at last, I must honor their word."

"Why now, Grandmother?" I asked, though my heart knew. Bracing myself, I sank against the earth, breathing its rotting leaf mold in exhaustion.

"Satienda's child was named Ula. And if I had any doubt of that witch's identity, her brown-gold hawk eyes are a Roman mirror of her mother's. Ula is Satienda's child—and our family's curse."

I heard a quickly stifled cry. A branch collapsed outside our ruined shelter.

Grandmother and I both whirled in the direction of the sound, hands placed on our dagger hilts.

Mother stepped across the stones of the threshold.

"Ceri?" Grandmother's stern voice trembled.

"Mother?" Mother asked hesitantly.

"Come here, girl. You are frozen." Grandmother's voice had recovered some of its gruffness, yet I saw a clenched muscle jump beneath the skin of her temple. She turned her back on us, adding wood to an already-blazing fire.

Mother sat beside me and placed her hand upon my knee. I did not pull away, although I trembled like a fawn beneath her fingers.

"Why didn't you tell me?" Mother leaned towards Grandmother, her hand freezing in the air, a hairsbreadth away from Grandmother's back. "Why after all these sunturns didn't you tell me the truth?"

"You heard, then?" Grandmother's body stiffened as if she could feel Mother's phantom hand upon her.

"I heard."

There was silence for a long time in our shelter. Long enough for me to translate the night caws of a raven as he scolded his mate, long enough for me to learn the song of the trees as the deep night's wind blew through their high branches, long enough for tears to run, unchecked and silent, down Mother's face, making miniature rivers through the forest dirt upon her cheeks.

"Why isn't this tale told? It should be known the length and breadth of our lands!" Mother rose, paced, clasped her fists in fury, spun to face Grandmother. "You lied to me! There was no fever that killed my brothers, my sisters, my father!"

Grandmother threw another branch into the fire, watching as flames reveled around it. Placing her hands at her sides, she moved her lips in a whisper. Then she turned, wearily, meeting Mother's eyes.

"After the Druids killed Satienda and Getherax, it was decided that it would be best to forget the evil that befell my family, for such memory could serve no purpose, could only increase the Ordovice's burden of sorrow. Our people swore a pact that, now that vengeance had been satisfied, Satienda and Getherax would never be spoken of again.

"But we were fools. For evil cannot thus be forgotten. It haunts the edges of truth, destroying those so blinded—until Anwnn itself is crowded with innocents.

"But in our arrogance—and shame that the dark ones had been allowed to wander free—a spell of forgetfulness was woven by the Druids of Mona; woven of the tall meadow grasses maidens weave for bridal crowns, of the sea that salts a child's dreams, of the ferns that line a baby's bed, of the flowers that whisper the larks' call at dawn… An otherworld promise, woven and given on this world's loom. Easily given, for folk seek to forget horror if they can."

Grandmother gestured for the water skin, took a long swallow, and looked deep into her daughter's eyes. Her voice took on the ferocity of a battle champion. "Given to all but me. For I needed to remember. I could not lose my children again."

Hesitantly, Grandmother took Mother's hand. "And *remember*, I have. For all these sunturns." She ruffled Mother's hair, as if she were again a child.

Mother smiled at her. An open smile. The smile of a young girl coming home after a long journey.

"It's a good thing, too." Grandmother cleared her throat and spat angrily into the fire. "Otherwise Ula would have deceived our people again as her mother did before her."

Mother raised her hand from my knee, looked into my eyes. A question.

The rage I had felt for so long melted, as ice will beneath a pale, stubborn sun. I let her put her arms around me again. Beneath the forest sweat and grime, Mother's ever-present scent of rose attar struck me like a dagger wound. Sunturns of memories, of comfort, swept my spirit, stronger than the anger I had nurtured for so many seasons. The horror of Grandmother's tale now exposed my fury at her for what it was: an unjust need to throw spears at a loving target because I was no longer a child. Because she, whom I had once adored, had been unable to protect me.

I clung to her, now, and wept the tears of a little girl.

Grandmother joined us, sitting on the loam of Ruag's earth floor. We three clasped hands, weeping and laughing, like warriors after a great battle. At last, we broke apart again.

Still laughing with relief and comfort, I reached up to capture a tendril of early mist as it drifted past us. Birds sang to honor the rising sun. Night no longer shadowed Ruag's dwelling.

"Spell or no spell," Mother's voice was soft, muffled within the rising mist, "there is a memory of that time. It is why the South Tower is haunted, why a silence falls when you least expect it. Doubt it not, Mother. My brothers and my sisters are remembered in every clasp of a new mother's hand. Their story is told in the trilling of a dove, in the last dance of the sun at twilight."

Grandmother snorted. "Whatever fancies seize you, Ceri, we three must be ready to meet this same evil again. Ula and Eithne will return as surely as snow tumbles from Yr Wyddfra. You, especially, must prepare, Gwenhwyfar."

"This time she will not be alone." Mother rose. I allowed her hand to slip from mine, the new tenderness I felt for her still raw.

We made our way slowly back to Dinas, our spirits dancing with each other as they had never done before. Whatever waited, we would meet it proudly, I thought, as one or the other of us paused to exclaim over one foolish thing or another. Here lurked a hidden nest of heather, there a fox's den. As Dinas grew closer, we stopped more often; all of us reluctant to emerge from the forest and our newfound bond.

Then Mother drew apart from us, casting wary glances into the mist and shadows of the forest.

"*Estethra?*" I whispered, shivering in wonder. How long had they been watching us? I turned back to call, but she had already disappeared within the mist. My breath caught in my throat.

"Leave her, child. They have come to see your mother alone."

"But—" I could not explain my panic. If I left Mother now, she would be lost to me forever.

"Hsst, girl!" said Grandmother, reading my thoughts. "Your mother has waited a lifetime for this morning. Leave her. She'll be back to fuss at you by nightfall."

A softening woke within me; a sudden breeze carried an unfamiliar voice. *We will be with you always. Always.*

Heartened, I ran after Grandmother. I had almost caught up to her when cramping in my stomach made me pause, then laugh out loud. My women's blood had come at last! Joyously, I made a hurried pad of mosses and ran again, laughing, the drying blood upon my thighs worthy of a warrior's song.

"Hurry!" Grandmother called: her impatience as soothing as healer's balm to me.

Yet, as the familiar timbers of Dinas appeared, floating above the mist, the horrors I had lived through and Grandmother's dreadful tale stopped me, as surely as if I had stepped on a viper.

Safety waited behind Dinas' ramparts now, yet evil had overtaken my home more than once and I could sense it again, stalking me. Innocent tendrils of mist dripped poison, the air grew heavy with menace, ancient trees hid death, not promise as they had only heartbeats ago. *Blood,* sang the forest. Small animals whimpered. Whatever hunted now was powerful. Stronger than the *estethra,* stronger than I had ever felt it before.

"Your mother is safe, Gwen—no matter what you sense." Grandmother's voice came, disembodied through the mist. "Now hurry! We have a lot of work to do."

Knowing the kind of work she meant had naught to do with weaving or griddle cakes, I tossed my head and set my feet on the path home, sparing one defiant glance back at whatever watched beneath the trees. No matter what Grandmother said, I wondered if any of us would ever be safe again.

Yet—as Merlin had been at such pains to teach me—it was not safety that mattered most. It was love and honor that made the fire worth the song.

I followed Grandmother up the hillside of Dinas, my heart filled with gratitude and a longing to see Father and Iolo stride across the courtyard or even to wrestle with Cynan again.

I pushed thoughts of Lleu's ocean eyes and the wry twist of his smile firmly away. For that was the fire that I longed for most of all. And, I knew, its heat would change me forever.

The Island

Mica takes the cold broth I am sipping and sets it to warm upon the hearthstones.

It is silent in our cottage now. Silent for many heartbeats, despite the angry winter wind that invades the peace of our sanctuary, slamming at shutters, frightening the goat to bleating in its stall beside the door.

I do not know I am weeping until Mica places small work-roughened hands upon my shoulders, shaking me with alarm when I do not stop.

"Lady, you will grow ill again!"

How can I tell her what I did not know until now? That when evil first invades a steading—be it an Ordovice fortress or a shepherd's cottage—there can be no escape, it is a wasting disease that kills slowly, rotting all it touches—even those too fine and proud to feel its tendrils until too late.

Nor can its presence be denied, as it was at Dinas and yet again in Arthur's fortress of Camlann. It must be fought with every bit of force and wisdom and spellcraft one can find. No treaty, no alliance, can be made with darkness—or all within the Hall will die.

"Lady, you will crush it!" Mica reaches for Lleu's feather, the raven feather I have held throughout the long night of this telling. Forgotten, it now lies twisted in my hands as I weep for ghosts long-lost beneath a waterfall.

I free it, spinning it like a child's top in my swollen old woman fingers. Perhaps it is my tears that cause its deep sheen to catch the firelight and flash its inner secrets in the glow, for a raven's feather holds the rainbow, if one looks closely at its heart.

It is the one gift I have never lost.

Magic…power…passion. Kingdoms and dreams, dragons, lovers, riches, children—the spoils of an empire crowded into a warlord's tent. All lost.

A feather remains.

For it is Lleu, my heart remembers. He is the earth beneath my feet when all else has been scattered by the dragons of war, ground beneath the heel of a conqueror.

"Lady?" The little one is worried. She is still here, not yet destroyed.

"Do not fret, child." I rise to smoor the fire. "It is the love you must remember of this tale. Let me speak it straight—no matter the evil that finds you,"

I sit beside her again, crouching beside her stool, for Mica's eyes are growing heavy with nightmares once more. "It is love that saves you from madness." I stroke her hair, murmuring a northern lullaby. She leans against my hip and I rock her; her weight still unfamiliar, my body yearning for another's sleepy child curves.

I chide myself for not remembering. If Mica does not have me to fret about, she is lost, wandering about in her own family's burnt steading.

She raises her head, her dark eyes sheened with unshed tears. "I am sorry about your Grandmother's family, Lady." She holds my hand and weeps for me. Far easier to sorrow for my ancient horror than to relive the blackness of her own.

It is a long time before her sobs fade. Our darkened hut is a heavy black bowl, a weary cave warded by unseen stars, lit only by the soft glow of the smoored hearth. Mica quiets; her body slumps, trusting, against my flanks.

"Would you like to hear what happens next?" I rise, joints creaking like old promises.

"Now?" She sits up, eyes shining, ready to stay beside me all night.

"Ah, child—" My laughter rises like a rusted sword in a rotting scabbard. Unsheathed now, it shrills, drowning out the storm. Too loud, too long, it rises, until I weep again.

Mica's tiny face pinches, her eyes shadow.

I would sooner face the mists of Anwnn than bring more sorrow to this child's heart. Grinding my teeth into my lip, as if mastering an unruly stallion; I welcome my body's pain. "I cannot speak another word tonight. Tomorrow."

I reach over to pat her knee. She touches my knarled fingers with her own, gently, as if afraid that I will disappear if she clasps too tightly.

I force myself to smile. Despite what Mica has seen and lost, she is still heartbreakingly easy to comfort. "Tomorrow—after your chores are done—this old bag of royal bones will continue the tale of how Merlin helped me fight the witches, of how my brother Iorwerth fell in love with a seer he was forbidden to wed—"

"Of the *estethra*? Of your brothers? Of Lleu?" Her voice drops. "And the dragon?"

The fire is banked. I rise to claim my pallet, hurrying her along. "Yes, Mica, you will hear it all—of my brothers and Lleu. Of how Lord Arthur came to unite this sorry land with blood and magic and dreams."

I kiss her head. She smiles as shyly as Tali once did. This, then, is something I can still offer—the strength to reassure a child that there is more to life than darkness.

"But tonight, we sleep."

I tousle her hair, so like my Brea's. So like my little girl's.

I will not weep. I cannot weep.

So many dead, little Mica. So many dead. Yet you and I are still alive.

Tomorrow will be time enough to weep.

And Mica shall have her tomorrow.

Author's Note

Dragon's Harp is a work of historical fantasy set in a time and place we know very little about. Although this does give an author a heady sense of freedom, I have tried to temper this giddiness with research into early Wales and Welsh mythology. *Then*, after painstakingly building as historically accurate a foundation as possible, I cut loose and indulge my love of dragons and talking trees!

The notes that follow reflect this mixed-bag approach. They are a combination of suggested resources for readers like me, who want to know what is "real" and what isn't, in addition to general tidbits of information based on questions I am usually asked at parties when the music stops and it's too early to go into dinner.

Amidst the countless books and web resources available about the Arthurian legend, Geoffrey Ashe's *The Discovery of King Arthur* remains one of my personal favorites. Additionally, his *Landscape of King Arthur*—complete with Simon McBride's gorgeous photographs—has inspired me for almost thirty years. For anyone who yearns for the sense of mystery and magic evoked by famous Arthurian settings like Tintagel and Glastonbury, grab a copy of this wonderful book wherever you can. Mr. Ashe is not shy about sharing his opinions and you may or may not share them, but his passion for the Arthurian legend is one I deeply respect—and share.

The hillfort of Dinas Emrys which I use for Gwenhwyfar's fictional childhood is a real place near the lovely town of Beddgelert in northern Wales. It has also given me one of my favorite answers to the oft-asked question: "Where do your characters come from? "

This is always a tough one to answer and I hesitate to speak the somewhat-close-to-rude-and-politically-incorrect truth: "Well, the gold-plated bitch in Chapter 4 is loosely based on my ex-mother-in-law..." Instead I can honestly offer a kinder example that began on an afternoon I spent perusing Mr. Ashe's book and noticed his description of the excavation of Dinas Emrys. Intrigued by Mr. Ashe's description, I researched the site more thoroughly and uncovered descriptions of caves and tunnels beneath the early fortress, including what looked like the remains of an ancient pool. There was also "evidence" of Christian inhabitants in the fifth century. Curious about what exactly this evidence was, I discovered it referred to a "Chi Rio"—a Christian fish symbol on a piece of broken pottery.

Something about this image remained with me, possessing me in that mysterious way that writers recognize as "creativity in action" and civilians just put down to being batty. Who could this person have been? What was she like (And it was a "she"—I just knew it!)? Where was she born? Who did she love? What mattered to her the most? Etc., etc. And that's how Ceridwen , Gwenhwyfar's mother, was born.

For the historians among us, Gwenhwyfar's grandfather, Cunedda, may well have existed (even if Ceridwen didn't—and I *really* wish she had!). There does seem to have been an early Welsh king by that name whose family moved from present-day Scotland to take over lordship of a slice of northern Wales. One theory has it that he was enticed there by the Romans at the end of their ascendency in Britain to protect the northern coast from Irish (then referred to as "Scotti") raiders. Maelgwyn's name likewise appears in what few historical records we have of the time. His kinship with Cunedda—and his unfortunate personality—are my own inventions, however.

My portrayal of Vortigern is also somewhat less than flattering, however I do not have much sympathy to spare for him. Early history is pretty clear that this king not only did exist, but most probably did invite the Saxons into Britain in an effort to shore up his power—an act similar to welcoming a known kleptomaniac into your home and then wondering where your diamond earrings are. In *Harp* I have also gone with the theory that "Vortigern" could have been a dynastic title as well as a personal name. Hence, he is sometimes referred to as "The Vortigern", as if there was more than one of him (God/Goddess forbid!)

On a more positive note, Merlin also appears in several accounts of the time period and the long-standing tradition linking him to Wales is borne out by both folk tales and place names.

Readers curious about the history of early Wales will enjoy Wendy Davies' *Wales in the Early Middle Ages* as well as John Davies' excellent and panoramic overview, *A History of Wales.* I also found Michael Senior's *North Wales in the Making* both helpful and thought-provoking.

For readers wanting to know more about the ancient roots of Celtic culture, clearly a powerful force in Gwen's time, and in our own, as well, Barry Cunliffe's *The Ancient Celts* offers a great summary of the history, migrations, art, and culture of Gwen's mysterious forebears. Anne Ross's work is not to be missed either. Her *Pagan Celtic Europe* is a classic and her fascinating analysis of a probable sacrificial victim, *The Life and Death of a Druid Prince* reads like a detective mystery.

As I touched on in my preface, we are fortunate to have some very early Welsh eulogies and poetry (often one and the same) preserved for us, even though most of them are, sadly, only fragments. I did excerpt two in *Dragon's Harp*: "Cunedda's Death Song" and the women's chant for Tegid are both traditional laments. However, I did edit them a bit and, on behalf of Tegid, took the liberty of moving the original location of the "Hall of Cynddylan" to Dinas Emrys, renaming the "Eagle of Eli" to the "Eagle of Yr Wyddfa". In this I was responding to the power of the laments themselves. Mourning for a beloved son who dies violently is, tragically, an international human experience. It felt only right that the eloquence of this ancient grief be given voice again. I apologize if I have offended its unknown author—somehow I believe he would have understood and, hopefully, approved.

Ifor Williams' *The Beginning of Welsh Poetry* is a wonderful resource for those interested in exploring this subject further. Additionally, Rachel Bromwich's fascinating *Triads of the Island of Britain: Trioedd Ynys Prydein* is equal parts history, literature, and mythic sourcebook, including lots of intriguing bits about Welsh Arthurian names and their origins.

It was while paging through Bromwich's *Triads,* that I discovered one of the earliest written forms of Gwen's name in Welsh is "Guenhuiuar", meaning "white fairy". How lovely—and how tempted I was to use that spelling! Perhaps when the story continues...

I mentioned in my preface that I have taken a few minor liberties with Welsh geography and culture. I do apologize, especially to my Welsh readers. For those of you familiar with the geography and mythology of northern Wales, you will probably recognize that I "fudged" a bit with the landscape around Dinas Emrys and its proximity to the sea. I did this for the dramatic purposes. I also wish to acknowledge my decision to rename the Welsh sun god "Lleu" by his Irish counterpart's name, "Lugh" and the corresponding harvest festival's name, "Lughnasa", (instead of the Welsh "Gwl Awst"). I do hope that, as most of you have read the book by now, you will be placated somewhat by Lleu's alternative role as Gwenhwyfar's main squeeze at this point in her life.

Which brings me to Welsh language and its pronunciation: As readers will notice, I limited my own page to characters within *Harp* itself, however, for anyone interested in more information about this fascinating language, I suggest three websites: http://www.omniglot. com/writing/welsh.htm, http://www.Gwybodiadur.co.uk and http:// www.namenerds.com/welsh . My northern Welsh friends also point out that northern Welsh is pronounced differently than southern Welsh, a distinction I am unfortunately unable to comment on, since I can barely muddle my way through Gwenhwyfar's name. As already noted in my acknowledgements, two gifted women who don't muddle their Welsh at all are artist and scholar Jen Delyth at http://www.kelticdesigns.com and author and teacher Mara Freeman at http://chalicecentre.net. Both their books and websites have Welsh language resources and pronunciation assistance.

I will be offering more suggested resources on my website http:// www.rachaelpruitt.com, but before I close up shop, I would be remiss if I did not touch on three subjects that inevitably come up whenever Celtic legends and King Arthur are mentioned. They are goddesses, druids, and dragons.

Celtic and Welsh goddesses often have gorgeous names and a multitude of attributes and variations on name-spellings. In *Dragon's Harp* I have referred to Anu as the primary Welsh mother goddess and the complex goddess of creativity and rebirth, Ceridwen, appears here in her "dark" aspect—as the taker as well as creator of life.

It is good to remember that it was Celtic culture which birthed the Arthurian legends, at least a millennium before they were tweaked and morphed and finally scribed into written form by medieval Churchmen and Norman-French troubadours looking to charm their way beneath the skirts of pretty serving maids. It was Celtic culture that gave the world strong and mysterious female archetypes such as the Lady of the Lake and the much maligned Morgana la Faye.

Not only was traditional Celtic culture imbued with powerful Goddesses as well as Gods, but real-life Celtic women had a tendency to bash heads every bit as quickly and effectively as their menfolk (as the Romans learned to their sorrow when they made the mistake of underestimating a young queen known to history as Boudicca).

To put the legend in perspective, Arthur Pendragon, the Once and Future King, and Merlin the greatest Mage of all time come directly from Celtic culture. Lancelot, although charming, was a later addition and not a native Briton, migrating across the Channel from France (where his countrymen were already figuring out the subtle sophistication of illicit romance.).

This is the Celtic culture that "my" Gwenhwyfar is born into. It is a culture existing on the brink of survival, yet with a love and understanding of nature similar to that demonstrated by most indigenous peoples who have not forgotten their dependence upon the natural world. It is a culture in which women were honored much more highly than they were in the Norman cultures that took over the shaping of the Arthurian legend during the Middle Ages.

Anyone who has read *Dragon's Harp* knows I do not mean to overly-romanticize Celtic culture or women's place within it. But the fact remains that early Wales, Ireland, and other Celtic countries gave women freedoms—legal and social—that they did not find in other lands. More on this subject and on the Goddesses who watched over the Arthurian landscape in its early stages can be found in books such as *Women in Celtic Myth* by Moyra Caldecott and *Celtic Goddesses* by Miranda Green. Additionally, the prolific Caitlin Matthews and her husband, John Matthews, have spent their lifetimes studying and writing about the goddesses of the Celts, the women and men of the Arthurian cycle, and the relevance of Celtic spiritual beliefs to today's world. Googling their names will bring up enough titles on these subject to keep even speed-readers busy for years!

If you are more interested in the straightforward "storytelling" aspect of Celtic mythology, you will enjoy my two favorite young adult books: *Tales from the Mabinogion* by Gwen Thomas and Kevin Crossley-Holland and *The Names Upon the Harp* by Marie Heaney (wife of poet Seamus Heaney).

The Mabinogion is a fascinating collection of old Welsh tales. Thomas and Crossley-Holland have created a particularly accessible version of these engrossing stories, wonderfully illustrated by Margaret Jones. There's murder, betrayal, romance, thwarted love, magic, gentle giants, underworld kingdoms, tricksters, and war—and that's only the first page! *Names Upon the Harp*, is every bit as exciting and romantic; a beautifully written and illustrated volume of Irish mythic tales. P.J. Lynch's artwork makes this book a special treasure; her illustrations are so evocative as to be spell-casting.

For those of you who still prefer grown-up books, Sioned Davies' new adult translation of *The Mabinogion* is excellent. One of my personal favorite fantasy series is the gifted Evangeline Walton's *Mabinogion Tetrology*, a novelized four book series retelling of the Mabinogion, including *Prince of Anwnn, Children of Llyr, The Birds of Rhiannon,* and *The Island of the Mighty*. Ms. Walton, now deceased, was rediscovered in the 70s and won Mythopoetic Awards for her wonderful books. Written in the '30s and '40s, parts of them are dated, but no more than Tolkien or Lewis. Walton's prose is lyrical, her characters wonderful, and her sensitivity to an epic time and place is brilliant. She is also the only novelist to have attempted turning the Mabinogion into a work of modern fantasy. She has been a writing heroine of mine since I discovered her in the 70s and entered the brave new world of epic fantasy largely due to her example.

Now to the Druids—those much maligned, eternally fascinating, white-robed magicians of forest mist and island stars. So many scholarly tomes have been created to describe them, analyze them, revile them, or glorify them, beginning from the day they evidently shocked the toga off Julius Caesar after he supposedly witnessed one of their human sacrifices. In one of the ultimate examples of the pot calling the kettle black, Caesar documented his disgust at such practices just before returning to Rome in time to be assassinated by his professional colleagues and mentees on the floor of the most respected building in the city. One wonders if they bothered to read *his* entrails for auguries, as it was claimed the Druids did their victims!

So many books have been written about this fascinating priesthood, I am almost hesitant to pick one or two. Probably the most readable and researched treatments I know of are Peter Berresford Ellis' book *The Druids* and Miranda Green's *The World of the Druids*. Both of these well written—and generally accurate—books are occasionally slammed for not being scholarly enough. In reality, this means that both of these books are sufficiently well-written enough to ensure that you won't doze off while reading the first paragraph. They also include extensive bibliographies—ensuring that should you *want* to find a scholarly tome to put you to sleep as proof that you're really reading documented history—you need seek no further!

Ellis makes a point of criticizing New Age interpretations of Druid rituals—but, from what I've read about the history of the Druids, this is all part of the fun and has been from the days when frumpy Victorian gentlemen wore bed sheets and ivy garlands and paraded around Stonehenge muttering suspiciously Masonic-sounding chants to a rained-out sunrise.

What is clear is that nobody truly knows what the Druids did, thought, or believed, beyond the most superficial aspects of their behavior that were observed and written about by their sworn enemies—the Romans. And the Druids wanted it that way! They were a mystery priesthood after all, and, although some educated guesses and unbiased observations can be made, we have only oral tradition and the archeological record to go on. Did they—or their most ancient ancestors—build Stonehenge? Did they practice human sacrifice (probably)? What was their role in the larger culture? Were they truly the teachers, guides, politicians, mathematicians, priests, oracles, poets, astronomers, and wisdom-keepers they were made out to be? Did they, indeed, understand the use of magic? Did they practice it? Could they raise a mist to blind their foes? Harness the power of the land? Heal the dying?

Who were they really, in other words! I have also long been fascinated by an obvious contradiction about the Druids—and I'm sure I'm not the only one to ponder it. If the Druids were as sophisticated as they appear in many ancient writings (and from the scientifically-miraculous stone temples they left behind), why would they stoop to something as silly but cruel as torturing a prisoner to death so they could read the future in his death throes?

There are no easy answers to these questions. We still know very little about this charismatic priesthood. And, yes, there are modern Druids today. Not to worry, they are normal, kind, and gracious people. The largest and, potentially, the most "user-friendly" organization of Druids today is OBOD (initials stand for Organization of Bards, Ovates, and Druids, reflecting the three levels of Druidic tradition). They can be reached at http://www.druidry.com . Their website is a great place to start if anyone is interested in Druidry today and just how this is defined by its practitioners. Penny Billington's book, *The Path of Druidry: Walking the Ancient Green Way* (available on their website) is also a wonderful resource for interested readers.

For those interested in following Ceridwen's path and learning more about Celtic Christianity, the wonderful poet, Sister Fionntulach whose work graces the opening page of *Dragon's Harp*, belongs to the Céile Dé Order. With roots in the early Christian mysticism of the Culdees, this gracious contemplative order's website is at http://www. ceilede.co.uk .

Although I remain convinced we know little of what and how the ancient Druids really functioned, of all the resources I explored to research this subject, I find my intuition most engaged by the work of my fellow novelists. In particular, Pauline Gedge's *Eagle and the Raven*, Morgan Llewellyn's *Horse Goddess* and *Druids*, Donna Gillespie's *Lightbearer*, Jules Watson's *The White Mare Trilogy*, and the novels of Manda Scott are incredibly powerful and, I suspect, intuitively true in regards to how Druids functioned within their own cultures. All these novels take place among Celtic peoples before or during the Roman invasions. All feature Druids and Druid priestesses as main characters— and each book in different ways still sends shivers down my spine when I think of the scenes the authors created and the worlds their characters inhabit. All these writers do a brilliant job of world-building. My advice is to visit their books, if you—like I— remain fascinated by Druids and are not convinced that the answers to their mystery lie solely in works of non-fiction. Instead, instinct tells me, we will learn more about them in culturally-astute novels that organically recreate the world the Druids once inhabited. It is a form of alchemy—one Merlin and Rhiannon would have appreciated!

Last, certainly, never least, we turn to dragons. I am often asked about dragons. They certainly come into play in Celtic and Arthurian legends and are welcomed within the pages of *The Dragon's Harp* as well. Like their Oriental counterparts, Welsh and Celtic dragons (including Merlin's friend, Cymry) are usually protective beneficent beings— elemental guardians of the land and those who serve it. They bless those they choose to initiate with both challenges and abundance.

It was the Normans and the Medieval Church who first popularized the "dragon as evil" motif, sending holy warriors like St. George to destroy the awe-inspiring beasties for the good of the status quo. By contrast, earlier Welsh and Arthurian traditions honored their strength and majesty enough to make them iconic symbols of pride. The red dragon remains on the Welsh flag to this day.

There is a well-known dragon legend that takes place at the Welsh hillfort of Dinas Emrys, where I have set most of *Dragon's Harp*. This is not coincidence. I initially chose this location because of its beauty—and this legend. Yet it wasn't until I began to write that I realized just how pivotal this dragon's story was to become in my version of the tale.

The traditional story goes something like this: Vortigern, the tyrant king, was trying to build a fortress on top of the hill, but it kept collapsing. His Druids advise Vortigern that he must find and sacrifice a boy who has no father, place his corpse beneath the foundation stones, and let his blood stabilize the building. After looking high and low for such a child, a strange youth named Merlin is found. The tattle-tale villagers mumble to Vortigern's warriors that Merlin has no human father and was probably sired by a spirit. Off poor Merlin goes to be slaughtered, despite his mother's pleas.

Yet when the boy stands in front of Vortigern, he cleverly points out that the Druids are wrong. Intrigued, Vortigern orders his court to an underground pit deep within the hillside, where Merlin shows them a great underground pool—two giant eggs lie half concealed within it. To the amazement of the court, the eggs begin to shake, then crack open to reveal two dragons, one red, one white. Without a second's delay, the dragons begin a battle to the death.

The red dragon is triumphant, the white dragon dies in agony, and Merlin seizes the moment to prophesy. He address the entire court, telling them that the white dragon symbolizes the invading Saxons (whom Vortigern was allied with) and the red dragon's win means that the Saxons will lose. They and their client king Vortigern will be defeated by a great champion named Arthur. Merlin's prophecy comes true, Vortigern dies soon after his prophecy was made—and a legend is born.

This dynamic story captivated me from the first time I heard it. It is my honor to present it in *Dragon's Harp*, although in a rather altered form! What I was not initially conscious of when I wrote the scenes of my own version, however, is how protective this red dragon turns out to be towards children in both versions, saving first Merlin, then Gwenhwyfar in my retelling!

I would like to think that somewhere, "Cymry" is watching and approves...

—End—

αutҍοκ Bιοgκαpҍγ

Rachael Pruitt is a writer, storyteller, and teacher with a lifelong fascination for Celtic mythology and the Arthurian legend. Her Arthurian poetry has been published in *Paradox* magazine (2008 and 2009) and her article "To Dream a Dragon" appeared in the award-winning 2011 writing anthology, *Many Genres, One Craft*. She has also published nonfiction articles detailing, "Myths for Our Time"©, a personal mythology process she developed while an Artist in Residence in the Pacific Northwest. *The Dragon's Harp* is her first novel, and the first in a projected series of five books following the life of Gwenhwyfar, King Arthur's famous Queen.

She can be reached at http://www.rachaelpruitt.com

Twitter:
http://twitter.com/EraOfDragons

Facebook:
https://www.facebook.com/
GwenhwyfarEraofDragonsSeriesbyRachaelPruitt

The wonderful team who helped with this book

Jo Jayson: cover artist "Guinevere—The Queen" ©2012
Prints of Jo's gorgeous painting on the cover of *Dragon's Harp* are available. Visit her website at http://www.jojayson.com

Tara Fort: editor
http://www.memoircreations.com
A very gifted and efficient editor.

Signe Nichols: formatter and hand-holder
http://www.firebirdmediamanagement.com
For anyone new to the eBook & POD publishing world—Signe is not only a fantastic formatter, but she takes the angst out of the entire process!

Marilyn Hager Adelman: book designer
http://www.purplefishmedia.com
One of the best book designers I've ever worked with! Thanks again, Marilyn.